THE PERILOUS ORDER:

Warriors of the Round Table

A. A. Attanasio

Hodder & Stoughton

Copyright © 1999 by A. A. Attanasio

First published in Great Britain in 1999 by Hodder and Stoughton
A division of Hodder Headline PLC

The right of A. A. Attanasio to be identified as the Author of
the Work has been asserted by him in accordance with the Copyright,
Designs and Patents Act 1988.

10 9 8 7 6 5 4 3 2 1

British Library Cataloguing in Publication Data
A cip catalogue record for this title is available
from the British Library

ISBN 0 340 69629 X

Typeset by Palimpsest Book Production Limited,
Polmont, Stirlingshire
Printed and bound in Great Britain by
Mackays of Chatham PLC, Chatham, Kent

Hodder and Stoughton
A division of Hodder Headline PLC
338 Euston Road
London NW1 3BH

THE PERILOUS ORDER:

Warriors of the Round Table

For my beautiful warriors –
Alexis and Zoë

Forsaken by our dreams, naked but for our stories, with only the stars for food, the four directions for shelter, and the spirit of all that we love our only companion, we live as warriors of a perilous order, champions of kindness, who battle for virtue in the ruthless war of survival.

CONTENTS

What Has Gone Before

The Dragon and the Unicorn began this series with the story of King Arthor's parents, Uther Pendragon and Ygrane, queen of the Celts. By the end of the fifth century AD, Britain, the furthermost frontier of the Roman Empire, had become almost wholly isolated from the few centers of commerce that remained in Europe. The collapse of Rome in AD 410 left Britain without a central government, and the island quickly fragmented into scores of miniature kingdoms ruled by local warlords. With the magical assistance of Merlin, a demon given human form and converted to Christianity by Saint Optima, Ygrane allied her Celtic chieftains with the British army of Uther Pendragon. They united the many rivalrous domains of Britain and repelled the ferocious invaders from the foreign lands surrounding the island kingdom. Their fateful alliance endured only briefly, however, for the arrangement of love and war brokered by Merlin required the blood sacrifice of the king, as prescribed by ancient law. In return for Uther Pendragon's soul, the Celtic gods released their most fierce warrior, Cuchulain, to be born again through Ygrane as Uther's son, Aquila Regalis Thor – Arthor.

Arthor followed fifteen-year-old Arthor on his journey from White Thorn, where he grew up in the hills of Cymru, to the third five-year festival at Camelot, the city-fortress whose construction Merlin supervised. Arthor, believing himself a rape-child sired by a Saxon invader on an anonymous peasant woman, allowed Kyner, a Christian chieftain, to train him as a warrior of unalloyed ferocity. Arthor lived with the certainty that his destiny was death, for his enemies in battle and ultimately for himself in defense of his masters. Rankling at the subservient position fate had imposed upon him, he planned to avoid Camelot and further servitude by seeking a new and personal destiny for himself. But the intervention of Merlin diverted the youth into the hollow hills – the magical domain of the Daoine Síd, the Celtic gods. There, Arthor learned humility and largeness of heart and proved himself worthy of returning to Camelot and drawing the sword-in-the-stone, Excalibur, emblem and agency of his true destiny as high king of Britain.

The Perilous Order concerns King Arthor's first year as monarch. Though in his inmost heart he had always believed himself worthy of greatness, the authority of high king of Britain is a far more demanding reckoning than he had ever imagined. Trained to give himself entire to the horror of war, to defend against the ferocity of invading Wolf Warriors, the young king must yet learn to rule a kingdom at hazard using more than mere force. With Merlin's help, he draws to himself the capable men and women who will, for a time, by courage, moral strength, and magic establish a perilous order, a fragile league of pagan and Christian defenders, whose glory will forestall the bedarkening of the age and resurrect the derelict hope of Britain.

Characters

Aidan – clan chief, master of the Spiral Castle, the natural fastness in the highlands of Caledonia.

Annwn – the Other World, Celtic realm of the supernatural, used in this series oftentimes to identify the radiant beings who emerged with the fiery origins of Creation: cf. *Fire Lords*.

Arthor – Aquila Regalis Thor, Royal Eagle of Thor, son of Uther Pendragon, deceased high king of Britain, and Ygrane, queen of the Celts.

Azael – demon; former cohort of Lailoken.

Bedevere – one-armed steward to King Arthor.

Bors Bona – British warlord and commander of the Parisi.

Cei – son of Kyner; step-brother of Arthor.

Cruithni – king of the Picts.

Cupetianus – spokesman for the fisherfolk of Neptune's Toes.

Dagonet – dwarf vagabond and gleeman of King Arthor's court.

Daoine Síd – the pale people, the elves and faeries relegated to dwell underground in the hollow hills since their overthrow by the Fauni and the north gods.

Dwellers in the House of Fog – demons; once radiant, these masculine beings despair of finding their way back to the source of infinite energy from which they entered the cold and dark of spacetime with the Big Bang; they doffed the burning light of their prior forms, trying to adapt to the frigid,

3

near-lightless vacuum where they find themselves; they rail against Creation and do all in their power to disassemble the conglomerates of matter, believing all structure, especially organic life, a mockery of their luminous lives before their miserable exile.

Eufrasia – daughter of Aidan.

Fauni – the gods of the Greeks and Romans.

Fire Lords – angels; the radiant masculine beings expelled from the compact dimensions of Creation's origin at the Big Bang; they cherish the hope of returning whence they have come and, cleaving to the burning scraps of their fiery origin, have devoted themselves to furthering the assemblages of matter to attain greater awareness, including fostering the knowledge of science by mortals.

Foederatus – an alliance of the north tribes, the Angles, Frisians, Jutes, Picts, Saxons, and Scotii, determined to conquer Britain.

Furor, the – the one-eyed chieftain among the gods of the north tribes, possessed of the trance power to see the future; he devoted himself to fending off the terrible destiny of Apocalypse that he believed the Fire Lords inspired in humanity by teaching mortals the secrets of writing and of numbers, the globe-threatening dangers of science.

Gareth – youngest son of Morgeu and Lot.

Gawain – eldest son of Morgeu and Lot.

God – the mysterious and singular female being Who emerged with the energies of Creation at the Big Bang and Who was followed from that hyperdimensional reality of infinite energy by numerous masculine beings enamored of Her – demons and angels.

Gorthyn – self-proclaimed king of the Belgae; commander of that realm's brigands.

Guthlac – fierce wayfarer of the Picts, leader of a warband that infiltrated the Spiral Castle.

Hjuki – Lawspeaker for King Wesc.

Keeper of the Dusk Apples – goddess of the north tribes responsible for collecting the rare golden fruit used to make the ritual wine that the gods imbibe; mistress of the Furor.

Kyner – Christian Celt and chieftain of the clans of Cymru; father of Cei and stepfather of Arthor.

Lailoken – the demon who, in the guise of an incubus, attempted to seduce Saint Optima, a devout Christian nun; he was taken into her womb and birthed as an old man who aged backward; endowed with the supernatural powers of a demon in mortal form, he learned love from his mother and became converted to Christianity.

Lord Monkey – familiar of Dagonet.

Lot – Celtic chieftain of the northern clans of Britain; husband of Morgeu the Fey; father of Gawain and Gareth.

Marcus – Christian warlord and duke of the Dumnonii.

Merlin – the mortal name of the demon Lailoken.

Mordred – incest-child born of Arthor and Morgeu.

Morgeu – daughter of Ygrane, queen of the Celts, and Gorlois, duke of the Dumnonii killed in battle on the fields of Londinium; her sobriquet, the Fey, the Doomed, came to her from the Picts during her time of self-exile in Caledonia, where she practiced black magic; half-sister of Arthor, she seduced him by enchantment in an attempt to exact revenge on Merlin, whom she held responsible for her father's death; wife of Lot and mother by him of Gawain and Gareth.

Nynyve – the Lady of the Lake, the youngest of the Nine Queens; once mortal queens, made supernatural residents of Avalon by the Fire Lords, they represent the ninety thousand years of human history ruled over by queens.

Platorius – count and Christian commander of the Atrebates.

Rex Mundi – Lord of the World; the magical assemblage amalgamated by Merlin to include himself, the demon Azael, a Fire Lord, Dagonet, and Lord Monkey.

Selwa – seductive assassin of the Syrax family; niece of Severus Syrax.

Severus Syrax – *magister militum* of Londinium, trade factor in Britain of the Syrax family, an international mercantile conglomerate.

Skuld – of the three Wyrd Sisters, the Norns, the youngest and possessed of the ability to scry the future.

Someone Knows the Truth – the elk-headed god of the Daoine Síd, master of the hollow hills and the Happy Woods, where the souls of the Celtic dead bide their time before reincarnating upon Middle Earth in forms human and otherwise.

Terpillius – vampyre procured by blood magic and induced into the service of Morgeu the Fey.

Urd – the Wyrd Sister crone of the Norns endowed with the power to reveal the past.

Urien – Celtic chieftain of the Durotriges.

Verthandi – of the Norns, the loveliest Wyrd Sister, gifted with penetrating vision of all that is.

Wesc – king of the Saxons, leader of the Foederatus, ambitious for peace and enthralled with the writing of sacred poetry, resident of Britain in the province of the Cantii.

Wolf Warriors – elite Saxon fighting forces devoted to the Furor and dedicated to dying in battle for the glory of their god.

Yggdrasil – the World Tree, the Storm Tree, the Cosmic Tree, the magnetic field of the planet; its upper branches, reaching far above the atmosphere, serve as home for the dominant gods; its trunk penetrates Middle Earth, the planetary surface where mortals dwell; and its roots coil deep into the molten interior of the globe, where the world-vast Dragon, a chthonic magnetic sentience, slumbers.

Ygrane – former queen of the Celts, mother of Morgeu (by Gorlois) and Arthor (by Uther Pendragon), abbess of Tintagel Abbey and Mother Superior of the Holy Order of the Graal.

SUMMER:

A Spiral Castle in the Dolorous Wood

Arthor Draws the Sword

The sword came away so easily from the stone that Arthor could only stand there startled, with the gold hilt in his trembling hand and the silver blade flashing with sunlight. Immediately, he tried to return it to the black rock in whose cleft it had stood undisturbed and immovable for so long. But the rock would not hold the blade anymore. The sword slid from his grip and would have clattered across the anvil-shaped stone and fallen to the ground had he not quickly seized it again.

The hilt of gold felt preternaturally shaped to his palm and fingers, and the blade swung lightly through the air, a natural extension of his arm. From farther down the hill, on the slopes of Mons Caliburnus, a small crowd uttered cries and shouts to see the sword drawn so readily from the stone. They were the swordsmiths and their patrons, the merchants and warriors who had come to Camelot for the third of the five-year festivals to commemorate the setting of this sword in the stone by the wizard Merlin.

Only moments before, Arthor had attempted to purchase a sword from them for his brother Cei, who had damaged his weapon on the dangerous trek from White Thorn, their home in Cymru. The swordsmiths had mocked him, a ragged servant with no coin and nothing of worth to barter. He had shuffled uphill dejectedly, kicking at the hawkweed and dandelions in the yellow clover. He would not even have tried his hand at the sword – except that he had remembered seeing this marvelous weapon once before.

Just days ago, on his journey to Camelot, Arthor had been diverted into the hollow hills, the realm of the pale people of Celtic lore known as the Daoine Síd. Those Celtic gods were more real than mere lore – he knew that now – but that knowing sorely troubled his Christian mind. In the hollow hills, he had seen marvels that rocked the very foundations of his faith: Faerïes had deceived him and vampyrical lamia had nearly torn him to pieces; Bright Night, prince of the elves, had conversed with him; and, worst of all, he had confronted the vehement god that the north tribes called the Furor and had stared terrified into his one mad eye. The Furor would have slain him on the spot but for Merlin, who at the last moment appeared to wield this wonderful sword and fend off the rageful god. Thus, Arthor had escaped with his life intact – and with his wits nearly shattered.

This was that sword, he realized as the sundering truth staggered him and he leaned back against the black stone. *Was it a dream?* he queried his frightened soul. *Is – this – a dream?*

The loud voices now clamoring from below assured him he was awake. And the sunlight smashing off the clear blade hurt his eyes and branded his brain with the precise shape of the sword that he remembered from his trespass of the underworld. *How can this be?*

From below, the swordsmiths and warriors came running, yelling at him, 'Boy! Boy! Put that sword down!'

He moved quickly to obey. But, again, the stone would not receive the sword. He turned and lifted the blade in a hapless shrug to show that he had tried and failed.

Merlin and Arthor

The scowling crowd edged closer, then stopped their shouting all at once. Arthor thought for an instant that the beauty of the sword had silenced them. Suddenly, a dark voice opened from behind him, and he jumped and nearly dropped the blade.

'The sword is drawn!'

Merlin rose from the cliffside of Mons Caliburnus as if hoisted by invisible wings. His midnight-blue robes furled in the river breeze, and his wide-brimmed hat, its conical top bent askew, cast a dark shadow over his long face.

'The sword is drawn! Bend your knees before your king!'

'But he is a boy!' one of the warriors shouted, even as most in the small crowd genuflected reflexively before the imposing presence of the wizard.

'This is no mere boy.' Merlin stode to Arthor's side and placed his long arm across the lad's shoulders. Garbed in a hempen sack-shirt, with his short hair stiff as a hedgehog's and his pale rosy-cheeked face slack-jawed with awe, Arthor indeed appeared a callow youth. 'This young man is Aquila Regalis Thor – high king of all Britain. Kneel before him or be banished!'

The command in Merlin's vibrant voice brought everyone to their knees. Arthor, startled speechless, turned to look at the wizard. This close, he could see the subtle crimson stitching of astrological sigils and alchemic devices in the blue fabric. And within the shadow cast by the wide-brimmed hat, he beheld a strong, aged profile, pale and pocked as if carved from stone.

'Say nothing,' the wizard whispered to him. 'Hold the sword high and march downhill to your palfrey. Slowly. Remember – you are king. Carry yourself with regal bearing.'

Arthor complied, though his heart stammered in his chest and his mind blurred with questions and doubts. All eyes trained on him stared in wonder and befuddlement. None dared speak, except for one swordsmith's apprentice, a boy no older than the king himself, who cried out meekly, 'Long live King Arthor!'

The sound of his name married to the title *king* cramped his heart tighter in his chest, nearly squeezing all his breath out of him with astonishment. And if he could have, he would have blessed that smith's apprentice for not mocking him.

Merlin led the way down the hillside to Arthor's palfrey that still held the youth's dented shield on its saddle peg. The warped image of the Blessed Virgin gazed tristfully at Arthor as he marched stiffly forward, sword held high. The sight of the Holy Mother reminded the youthful warrior of the many battles he had fought for his stepfather, Kyner, chieftain of the Christian Celts, and he lowered the dazzling sword.

'What manner of ruse is this?' Arthor asked and moved to hand the weapon to the wizard.

'This is no ruse, Arthor,' Merlin replied as he took the horse by the bridle and led the gray charger around a bend of mulberry trees and lime shrubs. 'You have drawn the sword Excalibur from the stone. As of this moment, you are the rightful king of all Britain.'

'*I?*' Arthor shook his head. 'Hardly so. I am but Lord Kyner's servant. I'm a half-breed – a rape-child, sired by a Saxon plunderer on some nameless peasant woman of Cymru.'

Merlin leveled his cold, silver eyes on the trembling lad and said quietly, 'No, Arthor. You are no half-breed, no offspring of violent rape. You are the one and only child of Uther Pendragon and Ygrane, queen of the Celts.'

Camelot

Above the verdant gorge of the River Amnis, on a high plateau, the city-fortress of Camelot stood unfinished, surrounded by fields of stonecutters' blocks. The incomplete curtain walls, ramparts, and skeletal towers overlooked slopes of carnival tents and colorful pavilions, as the third of the five-year festivals blustered noisily. Jugglers and musicians entertained the throngs of Roman Britons and Celts who had gathered on the wide, emerald champaigns to celebrate their union against the tribes of pagan invaders.

A swift rider charged across the playing fields, where contestants tested their skills at archery, javelin throwing, and swordsmanship. Yells of protest assailed the rider until the crowd heard what he was shouting: 'The sword is drawn! Excalibur is drawn from the stone!'

Then, the pipers, fiddlers and acrobatic tumblers fell still and silent, and excited murmurs ran through the revelers among the feast tables and colorful gaming tents. All activity – the pig runs, tugs-of-war, round dances, target shoots and equestrian races – came to a sudden halt. Under the proud spires and tiers of scaffolded parapets and half-built vallations, a hushed excitement rippled through the festive throngs.

'Is it true?' Severus Syrax asked as the rider slid from his steed and bowed before the pavilion of commanders, whose tent walls displayed both Christian symbols and ornately knotted Celtic emblems. The swarthy *magister militum* from the great city of Londinium was the first to burst forth from the pavilion at the cries of the rider. His Persian features, outlined by precise lines of dark beard and elegantly coiffed black curls, shook with surprise. 'Who drew the sword?'

'A boy, my lord *magister*,' the rider huffed. 'A boy with a lengthy name – Aquila Regalis Thor . . .'

'Arthor!' Kyner shouted with amazement. The large Celtic chieftain, wearing a white tunic emblazoned with a scarlet cross, emerged from the pavilion and loomed behind the viperous Severus Syrax. The Celt's arctic blue eyes grew wider as he saw that the messenger spoke earnestly, and the warrior's gruff hand rose to his mouth and covered his ponderous mustache as if holding back a startled cry. 'My son – Arthor?'

Severus Syrax shoved aside the panting rider and pointed with a beringed finger across the summer pastures to where the lanky, dark-robed figure of Merlin approached, leading a palfrey by its bridle. And upon its back – young Arthor, sword upraised.

'Holy Mother of God!' Kyner cried out as if stabbed. 'It *is* Arthor!'

Obeisance and Defiance

Merlin led the mounted swordsman past the silently watching wagonloads of revelers and across the grassy tournament grounds, where combatants stood stunned at the sight of the uncouth lad holding Excalibur high in both hands. They moved slowly as if in a royal procession, and only the stern presence of the wizard kept the wide crowds from hooting derision at the youth in his hempen sackcloth.

'This is your king!' Merlin announced loudly when they had attained the range before the citadel's main gate. They stopped before the grand pavilion of yellow tent canvas and purple pennants where the warlords and chieftains stood arrayed in mute astonishment. 'This is he who drew Excalibur from the stone. On your knees before your lord – the high king of Britain – the one son of Uther Pendragon and Ygrane, queen of the Celts – Aquila Regalis Thor!'

Merlin's mighty voice rolled across the countryside and boomed in echoes from the empty fortress behind him. Immediately, the throng fell to their knees. Only the warlords and chieftains gathered before the grand pavilion remained standing until Merlin glared at them and Kyner dropped hesitantly to one knee.

'Get up, you fool!' Severus Syrax cajoled. 'Can't you see this is a wizard's trick? It's just your boy, Arthor.'

Kyner did not budge. Suddenly, a thousand innocent details ignored over the past fifteen years fell together for him into the prodigious realization that this boy, whom he had assumed was a cast-off, a churlish offspring of a pagan and a peasant, was indeed noble-born. Even Kyner's true son, Cei, the thick-jawed bully who had berated his stepbrother over the years, admonishing the half-breed to keep his place among the servants, understood at once that Merlin spoke the truth, for he had fallen to his knees before all others.

Urien, the bare-chested, salt-blond Celt of the Coast, spoke strongly: 'If this manchild is in truth the son of our former queen, Ygrane, I will swear to him my lifelong allegiance. But I will hear the truth of this from the mouth of the woman who was my queen – and not from a wizard.'

Old Lot of the North, bare-shouldered in the Celtic tradition, his great mustache fluttering with his harsh breathing, stood behind Urien and said nothing. His redhaired witch-wife Morgeu the Fey was nowhere to be seen.

'And I speak for the British warlords,' Severus Syrax piped up again. 'It will take more than a wizard to elevate this boy to the throne. Even if he is the son of Pendragon and Ygrane, he is but a child! Are we so desperate as to entrust ourselves to a child?'

Stout and with a neckless head like a block of masonry, Bors Bona beat a fist against his leather cuirass and shouted, 'We want a man of deeds for our high king!'

Marcus Dumnonii, the blond commander of the West, said nothing, but when the others turned to depart, he followed. Within moments of Merlin's introduction of King Arthor, the fields had begun to empty as the chieftains and warlords gathered their people and headed to their homes in the diverse corners of the troubled island kingdom.

Kyner and Cei

Kyner and Cei approached the king mounted on his palfrey and knelt before him, heads bowed. 'My Lord!' the gruff chieftain's voice cracked with hurt. 'Can you forgive us for having treated you as a servant all your life?'

'Father!' Arthor moved to dismount, and Merlin dissuaded him with a reproving look. The boy ignored the wizard and leaped from the horse. 'Get up, father. You need never bow to me.'

Kyner refused to stir and kept his face lowered to the ground. 'I bend my knee before my king. Will you forgive me?'

'There is nothing to forgive, father.'

'I am not your father—' Kyner spoke in a small voice. 'Uther Pendragon sired you. I merely sheltered you – a servant in my household. I am ashamed I had no more charity for you than that.'

'Ashamed?' Arthor handed Excalibur to Merlin, who accepted it reluctantly and took the boy's elbow with the sword. Arthor twisted free and approached the kneeling chieftain. 'You taught me the teachings of our Lord. You obliged me to learn to read and write both Latin and Greek. You took me with you on all your diplomatic missions to Gaul and showed me the royal courts of the wide world. And, despite my surliness, despite my ingratitude, you gave me an honored place at your side on the field of battle. You treated me as well as you treated your own firstborn, Cei.'

Cei moaned. 'My lord – have mercy on me!'

'Cei – you are my brother!'

Cei's large body shivered. 'Do not mock me, my lord.'

'Mock you?' Arthor knelt before them. 'You two alone of all the warlords and chieftains accept me as king. By this, you have shown me that you are truly my father and my brother. For however long I may reign, I will never consider you less.'

Merlin put one hand under Arthor's shoulder and physically lifted him to his feet. 'You are king. You bow to no one but God.'

'Then stand – father, brother,' Arthor said and pulled himself free of Merlin with an annoyed look. 'Stand before me that I may see your faces again.'

Kyner and Cei obeyed. Tears filmed the chieftain's arctic-wolf eyes as they gazed proudly from under his jutting browbone. Cei's broad, thick, and beardless face looked pale and frightened.

'You must help me,' Arthor told them, looking urgently from one to the other. 'I did not expect this – this great responsibility. I – I don't know what to do! Please, help me. You know me best of all men. If I am truly a king, as Merlin says I am, then you are the king's best men. Please, do not leave me alone with this fate. You must help me to fulfill now the mission that God has set before me.'

Merlin's Counsel

Merlin took Arthor by the elbow and led him away from the Celtic chieftain and his son, saying, 'I need to speak with the king in private.'

Arthor strove to twist his arm free, but the wizard's grip could not be broken. 'Whatever you have to say to me, Merlin, say before these good men, my father and brother.'

'In *private*, my lord.' The stern look in Merlin's deep-set eyes brooked no protest.

Arthor shrugged apologetically to Kyner and Cei and allowed Merlin to lead him past the mammoth pylons of the open gateway to the crowded interior of Camelot. Past a clutter of benches and stools, the wizard brought the young man to the central court. The enormous chamber was filled with the canvas awnings and thatched canopies of masons' work sheds.

'From here, you will rule your kingdom,' Merlin said, gesturing grandly with Excalibur at the soaring architecture. '*If* you can unite Britain.' He suddenly noticed the sword in his hand and passed it to the lad. 'Here, take this. It's yours – and you'll need it.'

Arthor accepted the sword with both hands. In the mirror-blue flat of the blade, he saw his blond face too young for whiskers, the hackles of his badger hair sticking out in unruly spikes. '*I* am king?' He looked to Merlin with this question sincerely held in his amber eyes. 'Why?'

'You are the son, the only child, of Uther Pendragon and Ygrane, when she was queen of the Celts.' Merlin removed his hat and revealed a horrid visage – a long, sallow skull and eyes of shattered glass in bonepits deep as dragon sockets. 'I hid you at White Thorn with Kyner so that you would be safe from your enemies – especially your half-sister, Morgeu the Fey, who would have killed you.'

Arthor's stomach winced at the mention of the enchantress Morgeu. 'She came to me ...' His voice sounded far away to him.

'Yes, I know.' Merlin took the boy's shoulders in his spidery hands and sat him down on a carpenter's bench. 'She has told me.'

'She seduced me, Merlin.' The boy's already pale face had drained to corpse-white. 'I did not know ... I thought she was someone else ... I ... I coupled with her in the night ... it was dark ...'

'Listen to me, my lord.' Merlin bent close and his haggard face filled Arthor's sight. 'What you did, you did unknowingly. Yet the deed is done. Morgeu the Fey carries your child.'

'No!' The sword would have fallen from Arthor's grasp had not Merlin caught it and pressed it back into the boy's hands.

'Be strong, my king. Be strong!' Merlin felt tempted to use

his magic on the youth, but he knew that would not avail for long. 'This is the pain that goes with the truth of your destiny as high king of Britain. The salvation of our people comes at a price.'

'Why?' Tears brimmed in Arthor's eyes. 'Why has she done this? Does she not realize that she has damned us both to hell?'

'Oh, she realizes that perfectly well, my lord.' Merlin held the boy's quavering stare with an icy gaze. 'And now you must understand, young king, that whosoever would serve heaven must first conquer hell.'

King Arthor's Retinue

Proceeding at a stately pace, two elephants, garishly painted and outlandishly feathered, marched down the cobbled road, leaving in their wake a motley procession of horn-blowers, drummers, tumblers, jugglers, clowns, jesters, fire-eaters and sword-swallowers. The noisy parade approached Camelot along the old Roman highway that led from the Amnis, where they had disembarked a gilded barge decorated with gorgon heads and tinsel-scaled serpents. As they passed through the river hamlet of Cold Kitchen flying their fairy-winged kites and rainbow windsocks, they encountered the cortege of Severus Syrax as he departed for Londinium. The revelers swept up his followers in their jubilant march and carried them all back to Camelot.

That had been Merlin's plan when he had first sent notice to the courts of war-torn Gaul that Britain would crown a monarch this summer. He had invited all accomplished court performers who wished the protection of the new king to assemble at Camelot and display their prowess. The spectacle of the trumpeting elephants and the performers garbed in flagrant silks and sequins amused even the battle-hardened troops of Bors Bona, and the warlord signaled for his army to return to the camp-grounds of Camelot.

Severus Syrax himself sat astonished atop his black Arabian stallion. Fabulously vulgar and antic as the procession appeared at first – with bears dancing at the roadside and jugglers tossing hatchets and torches – he recognized the glory that flowed past him toward Camelot – and toward the king. These were denizens of the eternal carnival, the celebration of power that had once belonged to Rome and that now gave themselves freely to the boy-king. Syrax dared not turn his back on this gala. The best hope of discrediting Arthor lay with these merrymakers, whose edge of insanity might well cut through the illusion of nobility Merlin strove to weave about the child he had chosen as monarch.

Begrudgingly, Severus Syrax pulled his steed around and signed for his followers to return to the camp-grounds.

Even the denizens of Cold Kitchen, who had become inured to the coming and going of noble personages at Camelot during the fifteen years of its continuing construction, stood beside the highway marveling at the accomplished stilt-walkers and serpent charmers whose every limb crawled with vipers. The hamlet quickly emptied as its residents followed the parade of merrymakers to the playing fields of Camelot.

Merlin stood with Arthor atop a wooden scaffold on the colossal stone wall overlooking the broad campestral where the two parading elephants had come to a halt and had knelt before him. The boy gaped at the colorful throng of entertainers who bowed in silent respect before their new lord.

'What manner of amusement is this, Merlin?' Arthor asked through a look of widening wonder, taking in the harlequin crowd of mummers, buffoons, contortionists, rope-dancers, and gleemen among a boisterous slew of trained dogs, bears, and bright-plumed birds.

Merlin feigned surprise at the lad's query, 'Why, my lord, this is your retinue – a pageantry worthy of a king.'

Jokers, Ribalds, Vagabonds

King Arthor, with Merlin standing at his side, sat on a ponderous throne of cedarwood set upon a platform beneath a purple awning. Shaded from the afternoon sun that basked the range before the citadel's main gate, he reviewed the entertainers who had traveled from Gaul to serve at his court. He wore a crimson mantle trimmed with ermine that Merlin had provided and, atop his scalp of bristly brown hair, a chaplet of laurel leaves fashioned from gold. Held loosely in one hand and resting across his chest, the sword Excalibur enhanced his regal appearance, though to all who beheld him, despite his regalia, the king appeared for what he was – a coarse youth of fifteen summers.

After passing before the king, the painted and feathered elephants, the dancing bears, the troupe of wise dogs, and the numerous skilled performers moved on to the playing fields, where they caroused in the milling crowds with the other celebrants and the Celtic and British soldiers. Already, torches had been lit and kindling gathered for the grand bonfires that would provide illumination for a night-long festival. Cooking pits smoked from under the curtain wall, and feast tables piled high with racks of roasted meats, baskets of bread, platters of vegetables and amphorae of fruit wine rested upon kegs of mead.

Merlin was proud to see that each of the warlords and chieftains who had threatened to depart had lingered. Their pennants and banners flurried in a balmy breeze above their campsites, and music and laughter seethed beneath clouds of summer castles.

Last of the entourage to present themselves to the king were the jokers and ribalds and, hidden in their midst, the vagabonds of no trade or skill. Merlin was quick to identify the vagrants and signaled for Kyner's men, who served as the king's guard, to intercept them. Each was given a loaf of bread and a bladder of wine and placed in a wagon that carried them back to the barge that waited on the banks of the Amnis.

None of the vagabonds protested except for one dwarf, an imp with red curls and a black-furred, silver-faced monkey on his humped shoulders. He ran between the legs of the soldiers who attempted to seize him and darted onto the platform where Arthor sat. Merlin reached for his staff, intent on swatting the little man and his beast away from the king.

'Do not thtrike me,' the dwarf warned through a lisp, wagging a stubby finger, 'or I will do what our Lord admonitheth and turn the other cheek!' He spun about and presented his backside to the wizard.

With a guffaw, Arthor stayed Merlin's hand. 'What is your name, dwarf?'

'My lord!' Merlin objected harshly. 'This is a crackbrain, not worthy of your regal presence. Have him removed.'

The dwarf jumped about and replied at once, 'I am Dagonet. Thith ith Lord Monkey. And you are obviouthly a king who would be a boy! How dwoll! You're lucky we're here to thtraighten you out.'

Bedevere

King Arthor liked the look of Dagonet. The dwarf had a large, beardless face splattered with freckles, the visage of a boy. His ready smile and candid blue eyes allowed for no guile, and the king summoned him to his side. 'Tell me, Dagonet, how came you into the company of Lord Monkey?'

'I needed a worthy mathter . . .'

Merlin would hear no more. He glowered at the dwarf, took his stave, and left the platform. Arthor was pleased to be left alone with someone he enjoyed talking to, and he offered no objection to the wizard's departure.

Among the arrivals from Gaul, Merlin had spied a one-armed man impeccably dressed in brown cord breeks, red leather riding boots, and a saffron *crys*, a short-sleeved tunic, with one sleeve pinned to the shoulder by an eagle's talon cast in black silver. At his hip, he wore a *gladius*, the short, razor-sharp sword favored by the old Romans. His bearing and the rub-marks on the side of his balding head caused from wearing a helmet told the wizard that this man had lost his right arm not by accident but in battle.

Merlin observed the stranger long enough to see that he ate and drank moderately, responded appreciatively to the talented pipers and fiddlers, avoided raucous fools, and keenly watched all that transpired about him. As soon as the man noticed he was being followed, Merlin approached him. Ever cautious, the one-armed soldier turned so that his back was protected by a heap of unhewn mason's blocks and bowed with curt deference. 'My lord Merlin.'

'I notice you are an unattached soldier.' The wizard leaned on his staff and tilted his head so that the stranger could see clearly the demon traits of his aspect — and if the soldier felt fear at this aspect, he did not show it. 'Why have you come to Camelot?'

'To serve the new king,' he answered at once in a crisp voice of lucid Latin. 'I am Bedevere of the fallen kingdom of the Odovacar. I have in my riding bag letters of introduction from my former masters — our holy father, Pope Gelasius, his servant, Theodoric, king of the Ostrogoths, and Theodoric's brother-in-law, Clovis, the Merovingian king.'

'You have served three great leaders, Bedevere,' Merlin said, allowing suspicion to taint his voice. 'Were you not capable of fidelity to one?'

Not a hint of offense disturbed Bedevere's placid countenance. 'I am faithful to the need of those I serve. I gave my right arm defending our holy father against the Huns and served him till death parted us and my ancestral kingdom of Odovacar fell to the Vandals. Then I took up the cause of the Salian Franks, whose warband consists wholly of free peasants with no nobility and no cavalry. I served their brave leaders, Theodoric and Clovis, until they had avenged all I had lost to the pagans. Now they are secure in their alliance with the Burgundians in Aquitaine, and my services to them had become more diplomatic than martial. I have come here to the frontier of Christianity to offer my sword to a king who faces certain doom, for it is my destiny before God to champion the hopeless.'

The King's Gala

Through the night, the festivities at Camelot continued undiminished. Song, dance, and laughter filled the flame-lit slopes and fields of the fortress plateau, and the tall, serrate battlements of the unfinished citadel blazed with torches and lanterns. King Arthor himself came down from his platform at the insistence of his new friend, the dwarf Dagonet, and danced from one campsite to the next, mingling freely among both Celts and Britons, and showing favor to all.

'Look at him,' Severus Syrax groused from under his pavilion, where he sipped wine with the British warlords Marcus Dumnonii and Bors Bona. 'He's giddy. A giddy boy. Is that our king? Bah!'

'It is good a king can laugh as well as fight,' Marcus Dumnonii offered. 'Arthor has proven himself on the field against the invaders. Kyner used to call him his Iron Hammer.'

'Does he strike harder than you or Bors Bona?' Severus Syrax plucked unhappily at the tines of his black beard. 'I say not. He is king only because he is Merlin's puppet. And we all know the wizard is an unholy demon.'

'True, Syrax, I am a demon.' Merlin's voice coughed like the wind, and all three warlords leaped to their feet, goblets clattering, wine splashing. The guards posted around the commanders' pavilion spun about, startled that the tall wizard could have passed them unseen.

'Merlin!' Syrax shouted irately, wiping wine from his silken blouse.

'You call me a demon, Syrax, and I am here to answer for that.' Merlin's silver eyes shone like pieces of the moon. 'It's true. I was wholly a demon once, an incubus that forced myself upon my dear mother, Saint Optima. But she did not spurn me for the loathsome creature I was. No. She loved me as Our Lord taught us to love all of God's creation – even our enemies. And so I am redeemed by her love and given this human form to serve the Prince of Peace and to protect the meek from the mighty. That also is Arthor's charge, and that is why I serve him.'

As he spoke, memories smoked and burned slowly in his mind, smoldering with time – so that time itself pulsed like hot coals, dark with the heat of passions that had possessed him when he was Lailoken, a demon inflamed with hatred for all life. Like every demon who had been flung through the cold void with the angels when heaven spilled its light into darkness at the moment of creation, he had raged. He had destroyed worlds, ravaged every attempt of the angels to create a sanctuary for life in this dark universe. He had hated the angels, who called themselves Fire Lords. He had believed then, as the other demons believed, that the Fire Lords were insane to sanction life in a cosmos of vacuum, where the light of origin dimmed toward nothingness. And he would have continued raging against all life had he not learned love from the woman he once tried to rape – Optima, the saint whose womb had received his demon energy and who, with the help of the angels, had woven him his mortal body of uncertain age . . .

Time jarred once more into its natural rhythm as Syrax hissed: 'Why are you sneaking about like an assassin?'

'Sneaking?' Merlin's smile revealed jagged teeth orange as embers, and he gestured with his staff to the bustling dancers and acrobats hurtling through the summer night. 'I walked directly here to speak for our king.'

'Your king, wizard,' Severus Syrax snapped. 'Not ours.'

'I understand that you have an alliance with the Foederatus, Syrax.' Merlin spoke in a cold voice, referring to the pagan confederacy of Jutish, Pictish, Anglish and Saxon armies who controlled the lowlands east and south of Londinium. 'So perhaps Arthor is not *your* king. Perhaps you would rather pay obeisance to King Wesc, commander of the Foederatus.'

'I have a trade agreement with the Foederatus,' Syrax replied haughtily. 'But I am a Christian. I would never bend my knee to a pagan.'

'Good. You will have your chance to bend your knee to your Christian king, then.' Merlin passed a slow gaze among the three warlords. 'I understand your reluctance to accept Arthor as your king, for he is young. And though he has been tried in battle, his leadership remains untested. So, I say this to you three British lords as I will say again to your Celtic counterparts: Arthor's leadership will be tested, and he will not be found wanting.'

'So you say, Merlin.' Severus Syrax glanced at the others for support and saw that they watched the wizard with awestruck solemnity, and he held his tongue.

'In the coming days,' Merlin continued, 'our king leaves for the north to secure the most vulnerable border of our kingdom, the territory between the Antonine and Hadrian walls. After establishing his authority there, he will tour his entire domain and seek pledges from every warlord and chieftain in the land. Those who swear allegiance to him will earn a place in his court. And those who do not—' Merlin's eyes narrowed. 'They will be destroyed.'

King Arthor's Hangover

The music and laughter continued into the morning, but the bright sunshine that lanced through the ranks of Irish yews on the eastern slopes hurt King Arthor's eyes and inspired a throbbing headache. He retreated into the citadel, seeking a dark alcove among the workers' trestles and dangling loops of hempen cables. Sword in hand, he curled into a damp corner and pressed the cool blade against his aching brow.

Nausea swept through him in waves, and he chewed the ermine fringe of his mantle in physical anguish. 'Too much wine,' he moaned to himself. 'Never, never again . . .'

Dizzy images of Merlin's scowling visage spun before him, silently admonishing him for his foolish excess and then loudly warning him that he must prove his worthiness to be king. 'You can not rule unless you first serve! Seek the pledges of your warlords and chieftains by serving their needs. Tour your kingdom – but not as a drunk! Use this first year wisely or stand aside.'

The wizard's challenge whirled in him, echoing dimmer, then louder. Out of that vortex rose the figure of a tall woman with muscular shoulders, flame-wild hair, and small, tight, black eyes in a moon face. 'Morgeu the Fey!' he gasped and shook his head until the vision of the big-boned enchantress smeared into the shadows.

'Ho! My lord!' Dagonet the dwarf called from among the

crowded workbenches. 'Where have you gone? You are twithe my thize and mutht dwink twithe what I have dwunk!'

Lord Monkey swung out of the dark on a cable and leaped squawking onto Arthor's shoulder. With a fanged grin, the beast thrust a rind of ripe cheese under the young king's nose.

Arthor swatted the monkey away, and it bounded into the dark with an angry shriek. 'Leave me alone,' the king groaned.

'Ah, but I have here a bladder of muthty Iberian vintage with a peppery afterbite that will pinth your thinutheth!' The dwarf strode from under a mason's scaffold with a wobbly pig's bladder in his hand. 'Come, dwink! Today you are king! Tomorrow – God help uth, tomorrow ith already upon uth! And you're thtill king! Dwink!'

Arthor waved him away. 'Leave me, Dagonet. I am sick.'

'Thick? Not at all!' The dwarf swaggered closer. 'You are king!' He unstoppered the bladder and wafted it under the king's pallid face. 'Drink, thire, and give Lord Bacchuth example of how a king revelth!'

The dwarf's leering face and the acrid stink of soured wine disgusted Arthor, and he waved his sword threateningly. 'Be gone, dwarf, or I swear . . .'

'Thwear by our Thavior'th toenailth if you mutht!' Sloshing wine, Dagonet backed off. 'I thee clearly now, thire – Lord Bacchuth' reign ith thafe from the callow liketh of you. I pway for all of uth that you hold your thepter more firmly than your wine. Lord Monkey and I depart. We will wetun anon, when your head ith no longer too big for your cwown.'

Arthor groaned. He had never before imbibed so much wine or danced so strenuously. He had been vehement in his carousing, as if enough wine and merriment could counter the abiding shame and oppressive doubts that squatted in his heart. *Incest!* The word ached in him, too ugly to voice aloud and more painful than his besotted headache. *I have engendered an incest-child! And I dare believe I could be king? The dwarf is right. No crown belongs on my head.*

He groped for his gold chaplet, found it missing, and

groaned for the justice of that. A wave of nausea swelled in him, and he gnashed his teeth, trying to suppress the gorge rising in his throat. With a gurgled cry, he vomited.

The King's Steward

Twisted with nausea, King Arthor lay in his vomit. His head pulsed with pain, and his heart clopped desultorily in his chest, heavy with despair.

'Get up.' A sharp voice struck him like a slap. 'We deserve better for our king.'

Arthor felt a strong, gruff hand under his shoulder, lifting him from the stench of his spew. When he rolled about, he gazed up at a refined face, a visage with a high, balding brow, long, thin nose with disdainfully arched nostrils, and a narrow, hard mouth, almost lipless, above a dim, beardless chin. 'Who – who are you?'

'I am the king's steward. Bedevere.' He produced a black knuckle of dessicated woodmeat. 'Chew this. It's Saint Martin's Wort. It will settle your stomach and clear your head.'

Before Arthor could object, Bedevere pushed the wort into the boy's mouth, and it was then Arthor noticed that the man had no right arm.

'Yes, a Hun has taken one of my arms.' Bedevere sat Arthor upright and with a wet cloth began to clean the youth's face. 'Now I must work twice as hard at everything. And my efforts return twice the satisfaction.'

'Leave me, Bedevere.'

'Be quiet and chew. Chew vigorously. The wort needs a good grinding. It's old. I carried it from the Holy Land some years ago and am happy to say I've had no need of it – till now.'

'You've seen the birthplace of Our Lord?' Arthor mumbled through the bitter taste of the wort.

'And the birthplaces of Zoroaster at Nineveh and Gautama Siddhartha, the one called the Awakened, in the foothills of the world's tallest mountains.' Bedevere removed the king's sword from his hands. 'I served our holy father Pope Gelasius as envoy to the courts of Persia, Jerusalem, Alexandria, and the principalities of the Indus.'

The wort had begun to work, and Arthor felt well enough to sit up straighter, his back against the soothing coolness of the stone wall. He saw that Bedevere had with him a bucket of water bobbing with cut limes. A bundle of fresh garments sat beside it with the chaplet of gold laurel leaves atop it. 'Why are you here?' he asked as the one-armed steward began to undress him. 'Why are you in far-flung Britain, you who have seen the wonders of the world? Why are you with me, here in this remote land?'

'You need me.' With an expert twist and snap of his one arm, Bedevere carefully folded the king's soiled mantle.

'How could you know that?'

'In truth, I did not – until I saw you playing the fool among your subjects. A king with no dignity is no king at all.' With a rough swipe of a wet rag, the steward cleaned Arthor's mouth and chin. 'My former masters secured their realms not only by force but with nobility. I helped until their reigns were stable. But I am sworn to serve our Lord and Savior, and I go where our faith is most challenged.' He wrung out the washrag, dipped it in the lime water, and cleansed the king's hairless chest. 'This frontier is where I belong now. And from what I've seen of you this past night, I am convinced you need me. Am I wrong?'

'Leave me, Bedevere.' Arthor spat out the chewed wort with a scowl of disgust. 'I am no king worthy of any attention but God's wrath.'

Bedevere smiled thinly. 'You torment yourself because of an indiscretion that you committed before you knew you were king.'

Arthor stayed the steward's hand. 'You know about Morgeu?'

'No. But I know something of the heart's hungers.' Bedevere freed his hand and continued bathing the king. 'Put your past firmly behind you, young king. The hope of our people depends on what you do now.'

'You know not of what you speak.' Arthor glared. 'I have fathered a child by incest!'

Bedevere shrugged and used a bristle-brush to comb Arthor's

unruly hair. 'That is a terrible deed. But you did not commit it knowingly.'

'How do you know?'

'I know men.' Bedevere unfolded a fresh white chemise fretted with purple trim. 'You are young and so you are passionate. But your hands are strong and callused with the marks of one who has wielded a sword. Yet you bear no scars. You are not a clumsy or desperate fighter but a purposeful one. Such a man does not risk his life for the Lord and then defy his God by committing incest.'

Arthor stopped Bedevere from draping the chemise over his head. 'What is this delicate blouse? I'll wear a tunic.'

'You look enough like a brute.' Bedevere pulled at Arthor's short-cropped bristles. 'Your hair is too short. A king must command brutes but must not appear a brute.'

'I'm not yet a king in my heart.'

'I know.' Bedevere squinted at him. 'You were Lord Kyner's iron hammer. He trained you to kill for him – and to die for him. But now you are his king. You are not a hammer anymore, Arthor, but a wielder of hammers. You must dress so that others see you for the master that God has made you.'

Arthor allowed Bedevere to drape the chemise over his head. 'Do you think I am worthy to be king – a man who has fathered a child on his half-sister?'

'God alone can make such a judgement.' He helped Arthor to his feet and placed the gold chaplet upon the lad's head. 'God surely believes you are worthy, for you *are* king. Whether you will remain worthy in His eyes now depends entirely on you.'

Mother Mary, I have ever prayed that I be for you the Son you lost. I have asked you to give me the strength to defend Him now that He has left us alone in the devil's world. I have petitioned you for the might to fight for Him until He returns. But I never imagined – oh, Mother Mary, I never ever imagined I would truly be king. Is this God's blessing – or a curse? I have not the spirit to be chieftain, let alone high king. You must pray for me, Mother Mary. You must pray that God grant me the grace to match the power he has placed in my hands.

Arthor and Morgeu

In the sanguinary darkness of a cedar grove, a tall, broad-shouldered woman in regal scarlet raiment stood, hands clasped over her womb. Her crinkled red hair flared about a moon-pale and round face whose small black eyes gazed with dreamy malevolence. 'Come to me now, my brother. I would speak with you.'

King Arthor dismissed Bedevere, feeling he needed to be alone with his thoughts. Sword in hand, he exited Camelot through a servants' corridor and emerged into bright daylight under a curtain wall that overpeered the mountain cleft of the River Amnis. The citadel separated him from the emerald downs where the revelers still sang and danced, and no one saw him climb the rut-warped path that loggers used to bring timber to the construction site. Even Merlin, absorbed in keeping peace between the rival Celts and Britons, was unaware that his ward had suddenly departed the festival grounds.

Morgeu found the king as he strolled with aching head and heavy heart among the giant cedars that the Romans had planted on these ridges three centuries earlier. 'Brother – at last we meet again.'

Arthor startled alert and lifted his sword toward the scarlet figure that approached from out of the huge forest.

'Put that sword down, child,' Morgeu spoke with a voice of command that Arthor's muscles obeyed before his mind could respond. 'Or do you hope to cancel your sin of incest with the greater sin of murder?'

'Morgeu!' Arthor lowered Excalibur and staggered back a pace.

'Close your mouth before a bird flies into it.' A scornful smirk curled the corners of her long mouth. 'I've summoned you here to make peace between us.'

'Summoned me?' Eyes narrowed, Arthor's hand tightened on the hilt of his sword. 'Peace? You – you deceived me! You made me believe you were another when you stirred my affections.'

'I stirred far more than your affections, Arthor. What a child

30

you are! And you would be king.' Morgeu laughed coldly. 'Yes, I beckoned you here. Why are you so surprised? Don't you know that your sister is an enchantress? I could call forth from this wood a ferocious bear to unravel your bowels from your belly if I chose. But I do not, for I have brought you here to make peace. Yes, peace.' She folded her hands over her abdomen. 'After all, you *are* the father of this child in my womb.'

Deep lines creased his smooth brow. 'In the name of all that is holy, why have you done this monstrous thing?'

Another laugh glittered from her. 'I did not do it alone, brother. Your seed made it possible.'

'Given unwillingly.'

'Oh, you seemed most willing that night in the grass under the stars.' She lifted her round face as if in happy recollection. 'It was all so very lovely – and passionate.'

'I thought you were someone else.'

Her smile slipped from her face. 'Appearances are not always what they seem. A valuable first lesson for a king.' She stepped closer, the dark bits of her eyes fixed firmly on him. 'Know this, my brother. I will do all in my power to sustain you as monarch – until our child reaches maturity. Then, you will stand aside for our son and he will rule. That is the peace I offer.'

'Arthor!' Merlin's voice boomed among the great trees.

Arthor faced about to look for the wizard, and when he turned back, Morgeu the Fey was gone.

Merlin Steals a Soul

Midnight-blue robes flapping, long staff striking the earth, Merlin came striding through the gilded shadows of the giant cedars. 'Arthor! Get back to Camelot – now!'

'Merlin—' Arthor hurried to the wizard's side. 'Morgeu summoned me here! She . . .'

'Be silent!' Merlin's angry stare seemed to glow within the shade of his wide-brimmed hat. 'I have sensed the enchantress. That is why I am here. Now go. Return to Camelot at once – and do not for the life of you look back.'

Arthor obeyed and jogged downhill, past the behemoth trees, to the logging road that returned to the fortress. Not only did he not glance back, he began to pray for forgiveness of his shameful sin and the hope that God would recall the soul his misdirected passion had set in Morgeu's womb.

That, too, was Merlin's intent. But the wizard did not pray. Instead, he raised his staff, a splinter from the World Tree given him by the pale people of the hollow hills years before. Intoning a demon chant, he called the soul of Arthor's child to him.

A shriek from beyond the wall of cedars located Morgeu in her helpless flight from the wizard. Moments later, flying among the trees and the pillars of sunlight, the soul came, a tiny sun, smaller than a firefly, and trailing a shimmering comet tail of bees. The firepoint alighted upon the tip of Merlin's staff, and the bees hummed in a vibrant halo about it.

'Lailoken!' Morgeu screamed Merlin's demon name – but to no avail. The wizard had no fear of her and had only been waiting for this opportunity to abort the abomination she carried. A grim, tight smile bent his lips but no humor showed in his long, silver eyes as he marched down the slope of giants in the company of bees.

Morgeu staggered from her hiding place in a root cove clutching her belly. She dared not run. She dared not extend her enchanting spells. All her strength was required to hold what was left of her child, the small twist of mortal clay now almost lifeless in her womb. She lay down on the spongy forest floor curled about her pain, teeth gnashing, sweatdrops glinting on her squeezed face.

Merlin slowed his descent. He did not want Morgeu to miscarry immediately. If she did, he would lose a precious opportunity to control her. He would not drown this soul or fling it free into the sky until he had gotten from Morgeu all the cooperation he could wring from her with this tiny lifespark.

Down the hillside, he watched Arthor loping, sword in hand. The dwarf Dagonet and his monkey appeared as wee figures under the massive fortress wall, waving for the king to join them and return to the festivities. Merlin swung his staff in a wide arc and pointed it at the ribald and his beast.

The soul shot out of the forest and down the grassy slopes followed by a droning stream of bees. The next moment, the monkey leaped from Dagonet's shoulder with a violated shriek as the mote of soulfire struck its silver-furred face between its large, liquid eyes and disappeared into its skull. Bees swarmed angrily, hungry for the sweetness of the soul they could no longer find, and the dwarf swept the monkey into his arms and fled howling toward the pastures of celebrants.

Mother Mary, I am ashamed to kneel here before you – I who have commited incest with my sister. I knew not that lust would deliver me to Morgeu – but I knew lust. I gave myself to my carnal hunger. I gave myself, and I was taken by an enchantress who serves the devil. Yet, I know – I know your Son wants me to forgive her. That is what He died to teach us. But how can I forgive myself?

Festival's End
The elephants ate the mounds of uncooked vegetables in the provision tents; then, foraging for more food, trampled the garden crofts that had served the construction workers. The cooks and bakers, whom Merlin had conscripted from Cold Kitchen to prepare the feasts for the festival, returned to the hamlet in protest. Since the last kegs of mead had already been drained and only a few amphorae of wine remained, Merlin decided to call a halt to the celebrations several days earlier than planned. Besides, the warlords and chieftains were eager to return to their realms and announce Arthor's claim as high king.

Arthor himself had disappeared among the numerous unfinished chambers of Camelot. Stunned by his confrontation with Morgeu, he possessed little faith in himself as king. All his life, he had believed he was despicable, a child born of violence and pain. Now, he knew – his whole prior existence was a lie. He was indeed born of noble parentage. And yet . . .

The eye of a tempest watched him intently from his depths.

With calm certainty, he knew God's vengeance would rain doom upon him for his heinous sin. The fact that he was the parent of an unholy child left him numb and nearly mindless with shock. *A terrible storm is coming,* he despaired. *A terrible storm . . . unless . . . unless this tempest calm I feel is not the watchful eye of God – but His absence!*

From a garret window where a trowel and chisel waited on the sill for the craftsman's return, he gazed out at the great gulfs of blue above the blunt mountains. Was there indeed a paternal God in heaven, as he had learned at Kyner's knee? Or was the universe a battlefield of gods as he himself had witnessed in the hollow hills? What of his beloved Mary, Mother of God? What of the Savior who promised salvation from this fallen world? Was all that as much a lie as his past? And the truth, was it as hideous as the fact of his firstborn snug now in the belly of his mad sister?

'There you are, thire!' Dagonet waddled angrily into the sawdust-strewn garret. 'That damnable wizard hath thtolen Lord Monkey from me! I won't thtand for it! I am taking my mathter back and leaving your thervith at oneth!'

'Dwarf, be gone!' Arthor pounded his fist against the stone jamb of the window. 'I need to be alone.'

'And I need my mathter!' Dagonet protested. 'I need Lord Monkey! Command Merlin to return him to me at oneth!'

Arthor turned from the window and glowered at the dwarf.

'Are tearth in your eyeth?' With a squinted stare, Dagonet tilted his head. 'You are crying, thire! Why? On thith your firtht gloriouth day ath king, how can you weep?'

'I'm not crying.'

'Ah! Of courth not. Kingth don't cry.' Dagonet jumped backward off his feet and sprang into a handstand. He walked around on his hands till he faced the king upside down. 'I wath looking awry at the world. Now I thee! You are laughing. Tearth of laughter! Wah-ha-ha-ha-ha! You are king! At your command, tearth become laughth, life becometh death! You are the law!'

34

'Yes.' Arthor straightened. 'I *am* the law.' He put a tentative hand to the gold chaplet on his head. 'If someone has done wrong, I can punish them. I can make known the crime. I can confess the sin to all and be free of it!' A stern expression aged his youthful face. 'Come, Dagonet. Let us go take back what is ours.'

The King's Authority

'Bring me Arthor,' Merlin demanded of Bedevere. The old man handed a cherry to the monkey perched on his shoulder under the wide brim of his hat, and beast and wizard stared expectantly at the steward.

Bedevere sat on a carpenter's stool in the open courtyard of the fortress, whittling a horse from a block of wood he had secured in a vise. At the approach of the wizard, he stood. 'My lord Merlin, the king should not be disturbed. He requires time alone.'

Merlin plucked the lithe figurine from the vise and turned it nimbly in his long fingers, nodding appreciatively. 'You've a good eye, Bedevere. No doubt you have assessed the needs of our liege most accurately, but matters of state are not as patient as this block of wood. Summon him at once.' The monkey spat out the cherry stone as if to emphasize this command.

'My lord, he has had no time to himself since fate has placed this great burden on him,' Bedevere protested. 'For all his battle experience, he is but a boy. Give him some time to . . .'

'Thank you, Bedevere,' Arthor announced as he strode down a stone stairway along the rampart wall, sword in hand and Dagonet hopping after him. 'I've had enough time to gather my wits.' He ducked under a block-and-tackle and went directly to the wizard. 'Return the monkey to Dagonet.'

'Sire, I have reason to hold this beast close,' Merlin began to explain, but the king's frown stopped him.

'Am I your sovereign master or not?' Arthor demanded. 'Obey me, Merlin, or end this ridiculous pretense.'

'Yeth,' the dwarf intoned imperiously. 'Obey your king and return my mathter to me!'

'This is no pretense, my lord.' With a nod, Merlin sent the monkey leaping from his shoulder to the dwarf's. 'But you must learn to trust me. Worthy reason informs all that I do.'

'I trust you well enough, Merlin.' Arthor placed a kindly hand on the wizard's forearm and felt the bony steel of it. 'You saved my life in the hollow hills – and I have no doubt that by your hand I have become king. Yet, if I am true and rightful king, then my word is law. Is that not so?'

'To be used judiciously, sire. Judiciously.' Merlin motioned to the tall, open portal of the courtyard. 'The festival is ended. You must review the lords and their company as they depart.'

'Lord Monkey ith not thound!' Dagonet cried. 'What thortheree have you worked upon my mathter, evil wizard?'

'The beast is startled yet by the bee attack of this morn,' Merlin lied. In fact, the soul of Morgeu's child that he had installed in the beast gazed forlornly from its dark eyes. 'Silence your complaints, dwarf, and leave us to attend these pressing matters of state.'

Farewell, Camelot

Cool as the carved visage of an ivory chess piece, King Arthor sat on his cedar throne. To either side of his purple-canopied reviewing stand, an elephant stood festooned in feathery sprays and chains of flowers. This tableau impressed the gathered troops, both Celtic and British, and they arrayed themselves in military parade on the fairgrounds before the citadel.

'One year!' Merlin shouted to the massive gathering. 'One year to this day, your king will sit here again before you! If by then he has not won the pledges that are denied him this day, he will step down.' The wizard looked to the king and stepped aside.

Arthor spoke from where he sat, his voice big with determination. 'I am a Christian king. I will obey the teachings of our Savior. And so, I will rule by serving. In the seasons of the year before us, I will tour the dominions of my kingdom. I will seek from you the pledges of fealty that I need to serve as your king. One year from this day, I will sit here again, even as

Merlin says. You have my word that unless I receive the pledges of every warlord and chieftain, I will stand aside.'

Arthor intended to announce to the assembly the fact of Morgeu's deceitful seduction and the unholy issue that she carried, and his grim purpose lent him a foreboding aspect that made him appear older than his years. Merlin read his determination accurately and from behind the throne cast a quieting spell so that the lad fell silent after giving his promise to serve and sat nearly immobilized.

Disdainful of the young monarch's vow to serve, Severus Syrax openly defied the new king by leading his soldiers and entourage away from the reviewing stand. He rode with his turbaned head averted from the throne, not even bothering to have his horn-blowers sound a parting tantara or the standard-bearers dip the flag of Londinium as they parted the range.

The small giant, Bors Bona, marched his huge warhorse directly before the reviewing stand, Medusa-masked helmet in hand. His boar's visage with its stubbly gray hair, sloped brow and squat nose nodded once to the king, but he also did not dip his banner or sound a salute. His armored legions marched solemnly past and did not even glance at the boy-king, their display of the warlord's strength meant to intimidate, not honor.

Next came Marcus Dumnonii, blond and broad of shoulder as a Saxon. He turned his white charger to face the king and raised with one arm the chi-rho banner of the Christian battle hordes, demonstrating for the sake of the pagan Celts that this monarch shared the faith of the British. Yet, he did not dip the flag or command his scores of horsemen and foot soldiers in chain mail and bronze helmets to turn and salute.

Urien, his long salt-blond hair tied up in a topknot as if ready for war, drove before the king in a battle chariot braced with shields that displayed intricate Celtic knot-symbols. Disdainful of the Christians, he refused even to glance at the king, though his bare-chested warriors with their swords and shields strapped to their backs gawked openly at the boy on the throne. Their families stood up in the trundling wagons to point and laugh at the child monarch glaring back helplessly at them.

Then Lot, the old chief of the North Isles, approached the reviewing stand with his two young sons, Gawain and Gareth, garbed in Celtic battle attire. They wore gold torcs about their throats and sword-belts of red leather securing their *braccae*, trousers of crushed leather. 'King Arthor, the warlords of your own faith have shown you no respect,' the aged chieftain declared. 'My brother-in-arms, Lord Urien, also offers you no countenance, because you worship the nailed god. But I will put such enmity aside – if you will receive me and my sons in private audience.'

Lot's Warning

Merlin's enchantment held King Arthor nearly motionless in his throne, until the wizard bent close and whispered in his ear, 'What you say and do now before this chieftain of the old order will cast the die of your new order. Heed me, Arthor. I saved you from the Furor's wrath in the hollow hills. Now trust your fate to me again. If you are to survive as king, if you love our Savior and His hope for this island kingdom, breathe not a word to this elder warrior of your adultery with his wife.'

The wizard lifted his spell, and Arthor rose slowly from the throne as though freed from ponderous chains. 'Lord Lot—' He blinked at the archaic figure before him, attired in buckskin leggings and boots, his chest bare but for the slanting sword strap that secured his weapon to his muscular back. The fair, long-haired boys dressed as warriors stood alertly at his side, their child faces anxious to see how their father would be received by this unlikely monarch.

Behind them, Lot's clan pressed close, warriors, women, and children eager to hear every word spoken to their lord by this boy-king of foreign faith. And beyond them, Kyner and Cei and their wagons of Christian Celts – the only family he had ever known – patiently awaited their turn to honor their native son.

'Lord Lot—' Arthor repeated more firmly, 'husband of

my sister, we should speak as brothers, no matter our differences.'

Merlin sighed audibly with relief and received Excalibur with both hands from the king. 'Remember,' he pitched a whisper for Arthor's ears alone, 'not a word. Not a word or all is lost.'

Arthor nodded grimly to the wizard, then leaped off the platform to Lot's side. Lot's clan gasped with admiration at the young king's gracious gesture. Arthor offered his right arm, and the Celtic chieftain seized it and pulled the youth close to him. 'Come away from the demon Lailoken and speak with us in private.'

They walked with arms locked through the gaping crowd of Celts toward the mammoth pylon gates of Camelot, Gareth and Gawain following. When they were out of earshot of the assembly, Lot said, 'I have heard that you were cruel from boyhood, a horrible son, a fierce bear of a boy. These past three years you brought that cruelty to the battlefield against the Saxons, where you were Kyner's iron hammer. Yet, Morgeu tells me you are changed – changed utterly by your trespass of the hollow hills.'

'I am changed,' Arthor acknowledged. 'The hollow hills humbled me and now – this revelation of my noble birthright.'

'Are you changed enough to admit that your nailed god is not a god of these islands?' Lot asked, pausing on the massive slate causeway that entered Camelot. 'For I warn you, young Arthor, unless you embrace the gods of our people, you will never rule this kingdom.'

A Shirt of Fire

King Arthor's heart thrashed in his chest, offended that this pagan dared challenge the faith that had sustained his sanity in the hollow hills. 'Brother—' he began tightly, but the words would not come. Only angry thoughts rose toward his voice.

From out of the gateway of Camelot, a Fire Lord emerged. Only the youngest, Gareth, saw the radiant being, who appeared to him as an incredibly tall man with sunsmoke hair and starfire eyes. The child pointed at the luminous man and, calling the entity by its Celtic name, cried out, 'Look! A lord of the *Annwn* has come!'

The Fire Lord placed a hand on Arthor's breast, and a peacefulness like the soft blue of hyacinth pervaded him.

Lot and his eldest son, Gawain, saw the bright contact as a sudden frantic profusion of light, as though Arthor wore a shirt of fire. Then, the mystic flames vanished and ordinary summer light glinted from Arthor's gold chaplet and the white fabric of his chemise.

'The demon has put a spell on him!' Lot exclaimed fearfully.

'No, Da! I saw a lord of the *Annwn* come to him from the fortress,' Gareth insisted. 'The radiant lord put a hand on his breast. It was no demon.'

Arthor's head pulled back, perplexed by the startled looks of the three Celts. 'Brother – nephews – my heart holds no ill for you. No demons hold me. I swear this by all that is holy.'

'You are touched by the sacred fire of the *Annwn*,' Lot spoke somberly, glancing at his sons, who watched the king with open mouths and eyes wide with awe. 'Like your mother then, you are blessed by the invisibles. Yet, my warning still stands, Arthor. Because you are my wife's half-brother and the son of my former queen, I will stand by you in this fight. But I cannot speak for the clans of the north. Though I am their chieftain, they are Celts and free men all. You will have to win their allegiance yourself – and they will not be inclined to honor a boy-king who worships the desert god of an alien people.'

'I respect your gods,' Arthor spoke softly, his heart peaceful now as the interior of a blossom. 'I have seen the pale people and the furious north god. That humbled me. But these entities are tangible creatures – created beings. God is greater than they – for He is uncreated, unformed, the Holy of Holies, who created everything – the stars, the firmament, all creatures, all people, and all the gods. This one and all-powerful God sent His only Son into this strife-ridden world to teach us that love is mightier than the sword. And by that love, I *will* rule these islands and defeat our enemies.'

'I believe him, father,' Gareth whispered.

'Bah!' Lot made an ugly face. 'Don't preach to me, Arthor. I have heard all this before from the wandering priests of the nailed god. I don't believe a word of it. And if you would but think for a moment, neither would you. When has *love* ever defeated the sword? No battle has ever been won by love – and what kingdom anywhere is held except by the sword? You, Kyner's iron hammer, you know this is true.'

Arthor accepted this with a glum expression, then asked, 'What of Morgeu? What hope does she hold for me as king?'

'Your half-sister lies ill as we speak,' Lot said, his voice tightening with worry. 'I warned her not to come to this festival. She and the demon Lailoken have been mortal foes since he cursed her father Gorlois and caused his death on the battle plains outside Londinium. I fear the demon works his evil against her.'

The Wizard and the Enchantress

While the king conversed with Lot, Merlin left the reviewing stand and made his way quickly to the caravan of Lord Lot. The wizard chose a path that carried him through the construction sites, among heaped quarry stones and stacked timber, so that none observed his immediate progress. When he located the tented wagon he sought, he spoke sleep to the Celtic guards surrounding it and opened the back flap, exposing Morgeu the Fey in her sick bed.

'Lailoken—' the enchantress moaned, too weak to cry out.

'Be still, Morgeu,' Merlin spoke in a soothing tone as he entered the wagon and closed the cloth covering behind him. 'I have not come to harm but to heal.'

She waved him away, her small, black eyes wide with fright.

'I have taken the soul of your child,' he reminded her in an almost kindly voice. 'But I do not wish to take your soul as well. I have come to see that you live.' He touched her with the tip of his staff, and life-force flowed gently into her drained body. 'Calm yourself, and soon you will be strong once more.'

'Why?' she gasped. 'Why do you keep me alive?'

'You know, Morgeu.' He removed his staff and placed a cool hand on her warm brow. 'I am the king's servant now as once I was your mother's. Arthor needs your help.'

'My baby,' she muttered. 'Return the soul of my baby.'

'That cannot be, Morgeu.' Merlin shook his head forbiddingly. 'There will be no incest child to damn the reign of our king.'

Morgeu struggled to push herself upright on her elbows. 'You have slain my child?'

'I am the son of Saint Optima,' Merlin replied dourly. 'I do not slay unborn babies. But neither will I permit this incest child to enter this world.'

'What are you going to do?'

'The soul will be returned whence it came.' The wizard thudded his staff against the floor of the wagon. 'To the hollow hills, to frolic again in the Happy Woods with other Celtic souls.'

Morgeu flopped backward and lay staring feverishly at the cloth ceiling painted in Gaelic abstractions. 'You doom me to deliver a stillborn. You might as well drown the soul and kill this baby at once.'

'I told you, I do not kill babies, born or unborn.' Merlin backed away. 'I have given you enough strength to live. What you do with the soulless thing you carry is for you to decide. Apt punishment for an incestuous adultress.'

'Lailoken!' Morgeu shrieked in despair. 'Kill me now! If you do not, I will surely take my vengeance on you.'

'I think not.' Merlin backed out of the wagon. 'No other soul will fit the cloth of flesh you are weaving in your womb. And as for attacking me and mine – remember, Morgeu, I was once a demon. I know better than to misjudge evil.'

The Hollow Hills
Lord Monkey leaped from Dagonet's shoulder where he stood on the reviewing stand, watching the Celtic chieftains, Lot

42

and Kyner, discussing the order of march for their combined caravans. The animal darted across the broad slopes of the playing fields toward the forested hills.

'Mathter!' Dagonet called in alarm and leaped from the platform. He ran with all his might over the champaign, his fleecy red hair unfurling behind. Ahead, he spied the dark, gaunt figure of Merlin standing under the wall of the forest. The wizard bowed and the running monkey leaped upon his back. 'Ho! Thtop! Weturn my monkey! Thtop!'

By the time the dwarf reached the edge of the wood, Merlin and Lord Monkey had disappeared. In the twittering of light through the branches, he saw no trace of their passage, and he stamped his feet and cried, 'Mathter, come back!'

But Merlin and the monkey had already retreated far from the sounds of this world. They had fled along avenues of the forest that exited Middle Earth and descended among the roots of the World Tree, the Storm Tree, the Cosmic Tree that the north tribes called Yggdrasil. In this realm, the world above appeared as a slow twilight, a mountain of smoke climbing from purple to smoldering scarlet.

Shooting stars guided the way through the nocturnal distances. These were faeries, tiny glow-worm bodies in nightgowns of fog and sticky halos. They flittered like fireflies, leading Merlin ever deeper into the incandescent dark.

In the gloom, Lord Monkey's face changed. It assumed the aspect of the soul that it carried. The wizard immediately recognized the goat-eyes and bulldog's jowls of Morgeu's own father – the deceased Duke of the Saxon Coast, Gorlois, misguided to his death by Arthor's father, Uther Pendragon!

'Where are you taking me, demon?' The outraged duke glared from under bristly simian brows. 'Why am I here with you?'

'I should have known,' Merlin spoke with audible surprise. 'Of course, you would be the soul that Morgeu summoned from the underworld! Ha! What sweet revenge she would have tasted to place you on the throne of Britain.'

'What are you ranting about, old coot?' The monkey with

the astral aspect of Duke Gorlois gazed about angrily at the twilit shadows. 'Where are we?'

'On our way to hell, Gorlois.'

The monkey tried to leap from Merlin's back, but the wizard caught it by the scruff of its neck. 'You do not want to run free in this wild place, I assure you.'

'What evil is this?' Gorlois groused. 'What spell have you worked on me? Where is my horse? What has become of my men? Release me, demon! I am in the midst of a battle for Londinium.'

'Oh, that battle is long years past, Gorlois.' Merlin held the monkey before him and grinned with one side of his mouth. 'Don't you remember? That was the battle in which you died.'

Mother Mary, to the north I must go to prove myself worthy of the title that God has granted me by right of birth and the magic of Merlin. I pray to you now for insight, for wisdom, that I may understand the counsel of this wizard whom you have placed at my side. Surely, he is your servant as am I, for he, who once was a demon, came to be a man by the intercession of the Holy Spirit and a good woman, Saint Optima. Help me to trust him, Mother Mary – for I fear him. He looks so – so frightful, with his long-skulled head, his face of sharp angles, and those eyes, those deep pits of silver. He does not appear wholesome. And yet, I know I would not be king without him.

The Furor

Morgeu struggled out of her wagon and found her guards asleep and butterflies flitting around their heads. The life-force that Merlin had imparted to her was sufficient for her to stand and walk. Using that strength, she stepped over her slumbering soldiers and shuffled among the wagons of the caravan to the edge of the encampment. The forest began there, and at her chanted cries, toads appeared from the vetch to mark the wizard's footfalls as he fled among the trees.

The enchantress had not the strength to pursue the wizard,

and she knelt in a forest space silted with darkness and called to the god who most loathed Lailoken: 'Furor!'

The shadow world of things darkened. The sun's dust sifting through the leaves of the forest blew away before a dark wind, and the tread of the one-eyed god thudded across the sky like thunder.

'Come to me!' she beckoned, though she knew that the Furor would not descend at her whim, not to this gloomy world so far below the glory of his home among the northern lights. 'Lailoken has stolen my father's soul from my womb. Give me strength to marry my will to yours. Give me strength to hurt those Lailoken loves . . .'

Cold nails of rain pierced the forest. Seen through the narrow windows of the wood, the page of the horizon fluttered, turning toward night, though day was not yet over. Lightning ran across the sooty sky.

'Furor, make me strong,' Morgeu continued chanting, her crinkled red hair darkening in the rain and matting her brow like coagulated blood. 'Use me to lash out at the people who keep these western isles from you. Use me for your ceremony of murder!'

The seeping rain soaked her with energy. The leaves of the forest trembled under the strength downpouring from the north god into her frail body. Soon, she was on her feet and dancing with exultation, filled with sky power.

Her guards, awakened by the sudden rain, found her leaping and shouting insanely. It took three of them to subdue her sufficiently to guide her out of the forest and back to the caravan. Eager for their lapse not to be known to Lot, the guards summoned Morgeu's maids to strip her of her wet garments while they built a sturdy fire.

By the time Lot came to visit her, she sat dry in her wagon, a strange smile on her face. 'Husband, leave this cursed place. Lead our people north, back to our homelands.'

'I will do that,' Lot agreed. 'I have come to tell you that your half-brother and those Christian Celts he calls kith among Kyner's clan will be traveling with us.'

She nodded avidly. 'Good, good!'

'Good?' Lot looked baffled. 'I thought I would hear argument from you protesting any alliance with Arthor and his people.'

Morgeu's strange smile deepened. 'Why does the stream laugh, husband?' She did not wait for him to voice his puzzlement. 'Because it knows its way home to the sea.'

Storm Riders

Morgeu said no more. She knew that her prayer, like the stream finding its way to the sea, had found its way to the upper world and been heard by the wrathful one-eyed god. She could feel his power turning in her. On the journey north, she would use that magical strength to make Lailoken pay most dearly for his theft of her father's soul.

The rains began gently and did not impede the departure of the caravan from Camelot. Though Merlin was nowhere to be found, Arthor knew what he had to do. He did not require the wizard to instruct him in the necessities of war. If he was to serve Britain as king, he understood that he had to secure the north, the one direction from which his enemies could attack over land.

Lot, chieftain of the north, took the point; Kyner and his Christian Celts followed, and the king rode in the middle with his elaborate retinue of elephants and carnival wagons. The summer rains seemed refreshing at first. But by the second day, the old and ill-repaired Roman highways began to puddle, and progress slowed.

This was the opportunity for which Morgeu had waited. From within her wagon, she called upon the Furor to strike – and out of the fog-soaked forests his minions attacked. A Jutish warband descended howling and swinging battleaxes, savaging the Christians at the end of the long procession.

Kyner's horse-soldiers fended the assault with difficulty, for the Jutes advanced with the stormfront. Lightning and driving rain disoriented the horses, and the attackers hacked at them with their axes. Riders fell under the flashing blades, and thunder carried away their cries. Many of the fierce warband slipped past the Celtic defenders to assail the wagons, and the shrieks of women and children joined the terrified screams of the horses.

Arthor charged through the sheets of rain, Excalibur spinning, intent on protecting the people of his clan. But by the time he reached the site of the attack and beheld the disemboweled horses with their entrails glistening in the downpour and the overturned wagons and the strewn bodies of unarmed Christians, the Jutes were gone. He glimpsed their shadows vanishing in the rainsmoke of the forest, and he rushed after them.

Kyner, Cei, and Bedevere followed and found their king shoving through dense and sodden undergrowth, shouting curses at the Jutes. No sign of the enemy remained in the dark forest, and Arthor returned with the others to bury their dead.

'Ill luck,' Kyner allowed after the funeral services. But the next day, as the rains continued, another attack ensued. Again, the Jutes arrived guided by Morgeu's magical bond with the Furor, seizing that brief opportunity when the watchful Celtic outriders returned for replacements. In this way, the Jutes eluded the caravan's scouts. As if by chance, the rain thickened with their advance and they descended from the forest with the brunt of the storm.

Amidst a tumult of lightning and thunder that dismayed the defenders' mounts, the Jutes hacked at chargers and dray mares alike. Wagons rocked and overturned, and the berserk storm riders set upon the families that spilled out, hacking off the heads of children and adults alike and stabbing at everything that moved in the mud.

Someone Knows the Truth

Dagonet wandered helplessly through the forest of eternal twilight, shouting, 'Mathter! Come back!' His cries vanished without echo, fleeing from him through the trees to the bottom of the sky, where a river of fire crawled.

Merlin heard Dagonet's despair, but he made no effort to

return for him. His mission in the underworld was more important than the imperiled sanity of a dwarf. The wizard held Lord Monkey firmly in one hand and his staff in the other and advanced into the incendiary night.

Gorlois's soul had grown silent, despondent to find himself in a monkey's body among the illusory shadows and dream flames of the netherworld. Vaguely, he began to remember his death, and he knew that what awaited him offered little hope of salvation.

Ahead, the flame-woven horizon rose into an incandescent palace of bunsen-blue pillars and fireball domes. Merlin paused to remove his conical hat in deference to the antlered god who dwelled here, Someone Knows the Truth. He muttered a small prayer to his mother, Saint Optima, and advanced with bold strides.

'Majesty!' he called and dropped to one knee.

A giant figure of a man with the head of an elk emerged from a blazing wall of the palace. 'What are you doing here again, Lailoken?' a voice of booming surf asked. 'I've seen more of your ugly Christian face than I have of most of my worshipers.'

'Majesty, I have brought you a soul to dance to the Piper's music in the Happy Woods.' Merlin held up the squirming monkey.

The elk face bent closer, sniffed, then retracted with a loud snort of disgust. 'That is a Christian soul!'

'Not any Christian soul – but Gorlois, the cruel Roman the druids forced upon your priestess Ygrane . . .'

'Ygrane is no more my priestess!' Someone Knows the Truth flared his nostrils with rage. 'She serves the nailed god now.'

'True, but once she served you,' Merlin said with all the deference he could muster. 'And her son Arthor . . .'

'Say no more to me of Arthor.' The elk king's brow creased angrily. 'I gave to dwell inside him the soul of my best warrior, Cuchulain. I'll do no more for him – another *Christian*! I'm sick of these self-flagellating hypocrites of love who kill all who refuse their gory faith. These are the very ones who mock my horns and my hooves and brand me a devil!'

'My lord! I mean no offense . . .'

'Then, be gone!' the ancient god shouted, and the blast of his voice sent Merlin tumbling backward in a gust of cinders, the palace shaped like fire dwindling to darkness.

Mother Mary, where is Merlin? I need him now to counter the evil of Morgeu. I am certain that her magic guides our enemies into our midst with such lethal accuracy. More than chance is at play here. This is that wicked woman's doing. I know it. And now I feel murder in my heart toward her. I thought I could forgive her for using my lust against me. But now, those I am sworn to protect — they die because of her magic. Return Merlin to me that I may have his magic to counter her iniquity. Return Merlin or I know I will resort to the sword. God forgive me!

Breaking Magic

After the third assault by the storm riders, Kyner suspected that magic worked against them. 'Where is that damnable Merlin when we need him?' The chieftain lifted the bronze face mask of his rawhide helmet, revealing his enraged scowl, and shook his sturdy Bulgar saber at the slate-gray sky. 'That demon has abandoned us!'

King Arthor dismounted in the rain among the sprawled bodies of the dead. He knew each of the slain by name, for he had grown up among them in White Thorn. 'The Jutes know precisely when to attack,' he mumbled, removing his eagle-mask helmet and forcing himself to gaze upon the hacked corpses of his kith who had died under his protection. 'Someone among us is signaling them. And there is only one here who has the magical skill to time these assaults with the storm surges.'

Bedevere seized the king's arm as he moved to withdraw Excalibur from its makeshift sheath of fawnskin and horsehair. 'Stay your hand, sire.' He lifted the vizard of his plumed helmet, the better to hold the king with his calm, blue gaze. 'You must act judiciously.'

'That word again!' Arthor's upper lip pulled back to reveal

his incisors. 'Merlin used that word before he spelled me to silence at the festival gathering. If not for that spell, all now would know of Morgeu's evil . . .'

'Hush, my lord!' Bedevere pressed close to the king. 'Our alliance with Lot is uncertain as it is. Be politic. Be a king.'

'No more of my kith will die by her enchantments!' Arthor swore angrily.

'Many more indeed will die if Lot abandons us here. Look about you!' Bedevere swung his one arm across a mordant vista of forested hills veiled in rain. 'We are far from Camelot.'

'Then what am I to do, Bedevere?'

'Be a king, my lord.' The steward took Arthor's arm and led him away so that Cei, who had already gathered a burial detail of priests and soldiers, could attend to the dead. 'Employ your wits and your faith. If you suspect Morgeu, then place her wagon in the midst of Kyner's column. And pray. God has chosen you to lead us. Beseech His help, and surely He will hear you.'

King Arthor did as his steward suggested, overriding Lot's protests and placing Morgeu in an unmarked wagon among Kyner's cavalcade. That did not deter the next assault, which came again under a rage of thunderheads and wild lightning. But this time, instead of charging to defend Kyner's train, Arthor lifted Excalibur's hilt upward, a symbol of his faith, and implored God's help in breaking the magic that guided his enemies.

For the first time in days, daggers of sunlight stabbed through the lowering clouds. The warband of Jutes, deprived of their storm cover, scattered in disarray, and Kyner and Cei led their cavalry among the fleeing enemy, sparing none.

The Singing Flower
Dagonet found Merlin unconscious in the crotched crevice of a tree, his conical hat cocked askew and his staff shattered to splinters. Lord Monkey sprawled limply atop him, and the dwarf gasped at the sight of his beloved animal limp as death.

'Mathter! Oh my mathter! What hath become of you?'

Knocked free of the monkey by the blast of rage from Someone Knows the Truth, Gorlois's soul, giddy with the

merriment of his disembodied state and the songful magic of
faerïeland, alighted upon a yellow jonquil and in his freedom
began to sing:

> *Strange to be anywhere!*
> *Oh, strange to be anywhere*
> *when we understand our shadows*
> *all our life before us goes*
> *free of fear and doubt and care,*
> *oh free to go just anywhere!*

Dagonet looked about at the forest that sieved a sky of ashes
and western light – and among the magenta shadows spotted
the source of the singing. The happy song came from a delicate,
citrine flower that sprouted among the leaf litter. He knelt
beside it and wailed, 'Wittle flowah, wittle flowah – can you
help me? I am lotht in thith foretht dark – and my mathter
ith dead!'

The jonquil continued to sing its joyous song, and Dagonet
heard such hope in its blissful voice that he felt certain the fragile
blossom could help him. His thick fingers dug at the loamy earth
around the flower and lifted it, roots and all, from the ground.
He carried it to where Lord Monkey and Merlin lay propped
in the tines of the slender tree upon which they had landed.

'Lithen, mathter! Lithen to the happy song and wake.'

The joy of the song crowded time aside. Faerïes lured by the
singing flitted in the cinnabar air. Distracted by them, Dagonet
stumbled upon the tree's roots that bulged moss-slick from the
ground and dropped the flower. Its rhizoid dirt, yellow petals,
and bright pollen splashed over himself and the unconscious
bodies embraced by the tree.

Dagonet sneezed and fell backward, thudding to the ground.
The singing stopped, and the faerïes scattered. When the dwarf
sat up, Merlin gazed out from behind Dagonet's freckle-
splattered face. 'What hath happened to me?' he groaned,
holding his fleecy head in both stubby hands. 'I don't belong
in thith body!'

'Because I have displaced you, demon!' Merlin's body climbed down from the tree, grinning so wide his molars gleamed in the twilight. 'My soul has taken your place!'

'Dagonet?' Merlin asked, staggering upright.

The monkey rushed into Merlin's arms and hugged him fiercely.

'Dagonet ith in the monkey!' he realized and gaped in horror at the image of himself standing above him. 'And so, you are—'

'Gorlois!'

Wheel of Night

Gawain and Gareth sat with their mother beside a fire reduced to ash and purple embers. Dawn was an hour away, and the great wheel of night turned slowly on its vast axle, carrying darkness and its flotsam of stars away from the gray prophecy of morning. Birdnoise glinted in the dark trees, accompanied by the clink of harnesses from among the cropping horses.

All night, the boys had sat listening to their mother's stories of magic and gods. As the stars dimmed in the accruing light, they told her of the shirt of fire that King Arthor had displayed before them and their father in the portal of Camelot. 'Da says that the cold fire we saw was the wizard Merlin's magic, meant to befuddle us,' Gawain said.

'But I *saw* a lord of the *Annwn*, mother,' Gareth insisted. 'He was two heads taller than any man and with hair and eyes so bright, I could not see his face for the glare.'

'The lords of the *Annwn* taught us the runes, long ago, when our people ranged across the known world to the very borders of Persia,' Morgeu told her sons. 'Long before the nailed god, that was. Centuries before, when our gods, Old Elk Head and the pale people, walked among us. We honored the *Annwn* lords then in our bards' songs. But now these Lords of Fire champion the nailed god, the anointed one of the desert people. And our gods are exiled underground, in the hollow hills.'

'Is Uncle Arthor a bad man?' Gareth asked. 'The Lord of Fire touched him on his heart.'

'Your uncle is a troubled young man, my sons.' Morgeu passed a hand over the cooling embers, and live flames leaped from the ash. 'The *Annwn* lords hope to control him and all our destinies. But we have recourse to older gods and more ancient magic – as I have shown you in my stories. Our tradition is older than Rome. Why should we worship a gruesome god who slays his only son – a son who preached peace and love? No. That way lies treachery and madness – for any parent who slays his own is a traitor to life.'

'Then why does Da ride with Uncle and Lord Kyner, who worship the nailed god?' Gawain inquired, his child face shining in the fire's jigging light.

'Politics.' She smiled at her children with benign sadness. 'Until we can strike an accord with the invading tribes, we need Uncle and Lord Kyner and all their Christian soldiers to fend off the invaders. But some day, I believe, we will have a Celtic king on the throne, and he will make peace with the north tribes and restore our gods to their rightful place in the World Tree. Then, there will be trade and sharing, instead of killing.' Her smile brightened. 'Perhaps one of you boys will be that king. And for that, you will need heart. That is why I tell you my stories of the old heroes, who battled dragons and fought giants and succeeded because they had largeness of heart.' She gestured at the stars kindling in the dark. 'Our world seems big, but it is really very small indeed, just one mote among the froth of stars. Believe me, my sons – this world is tiny. It is the heart that is enormous.'

Mother Mary, Merlin has abandoned us. Or perhaps God has called him to other service. My trial approaches. Perhaps the wizard is wise to insist I face the northern clans on my own and win their fealty by merit and not magic. But know that I am scared and seek mercy for me from your Son and our Father. I have never seen such rough country – mountain ledges at the threshold of heaven and wild gorges like shafts to hell! Am I man enough to be king of this bold land?

The Dolorous Wood

With mahouts to guide them, King Arthor and his stepbrother Cei rode one elephant and Lot and his sons, Gawain and Gareth, rode the other up low hills of scrub evergreen to a summit of high parkland that offered a vista of the north. Deer scattered before them, and a lumbering bear paused in its foraging to gaze at them from under the eaves of a primeval forest.

'There is the Dolorous Wood, young king,' Lot intoned grimly, pointing to the bunched horizons of forest that climbed toward mountains misted blue with distance. The vast expanse of gorges, fens, and hollows masked many a fraudulent reckoning with ancient groves that sprouted directly from sheer stone walls and that crowded the adamantine depths of interlocked canyons. The maze-like contours of the cliffs allowed only the most acute sunlight to penetrate the pits beneath these high mesas. Jammed together by the ice flows of prehistoric time, the sandstone ledges that reared above the dark, satanic ravines meandered in a giant whorl. 'The Spiral Castle. That's what the clans here call the heights above these chasms. No enemy can penetrate them.'

'Is this where you reign, Brother Lot?' Arthor asked in a voice soft with awe before this strange incongruence of wooded heights and fenland depths.

'No, Uncle!' Gawain laughed at the king's erroneous assumption. 'This is wild country. Men lose themselves forever down there.'

'But it's here you'll have to prove yourself if you hope to rule the clans of the north,' Lot added. 'Only the most adroit horseman can negotiate those treacherous trails – and only a horseman can hope to rout the brigands that hide in those forlorn holms.'

'Routing brigands, is it?' Cei piped up, intrigued. 'That's how Arthor and I grew up in the hills of Cymru. Saxon rovers infiltrated the hills and dells each spring, and from the time we were the age of your boys father took us with him to clear them out. Yea, Arthor?'

'Yea, Cei, we saw first blood on those forays,' Arthor

recalled. 'But the dells of Cymru are veritable flatlands compared
to what lies here before us!'

'That is your challenge, Arthor – if you still wish to call
yourself king of the clans of the north.' Lot's gray eyes shone
like smoldering ash. 'Take your elephants, boy, and ride back
to Camelot. That's my counsel to you.'

Arthor responded coolly, 'Take me to the clan chiefs. I
won't leave here without their pledges.'

Lot shook his head ruefully. 'Then your bones will rest here
until your Christian reckoning gathers them for judgement by
your harsh God.'

Kingdom Made of Twilight

Gorlois kicked at the leaf duff and flexed his arms, amazed to find
himself inside Merlin's body. He removed his hat and ran giddy
fingers over his head, feeling the wispy hair and the dented skull
beneath. A laugh like a crow's caw jumped from him. 'Behold
this man! I can laugh! I can dance!' His blue-leather sandals
winked from under his midnight robes as he executed a deft
jig, flapping his hat over his head.

Merlin gazed down forlornly at the squat body of the
dwarf that he now occupied and plucked at his stained and
sour-smelling jerkin of cracked leather. Lord Monkey mewled
in his lap, Dagonet trapped in its small, round skull.

In despair, Merlin cast the monkey aside, leaped to his feet,
and ran to retrieve the remnants of the broken jonquil that had
sung with Gorlois's soul. Before his stubby legs could carry him
the distance, a strong hand seized him by the back of his jerkin
and lifted him into the air.

'Let me help you, little man.' Gorlois croaked with more
laughter. 'You want this flower, don't you?' With his free hand,
Gorlois snatched the shattered jonquil and dangled it just out
of reach of the dwarf's arms. 'This miracle flower that turned
you to me and me to you and the dwarf to – that.' He wagged
the plant at the monkey and shook the last of its petals from
its stem. Then, he crushed what remained in his fist. 'Thank
you, miracle flower. Now your work is done.' He dropped the

mashed roots and stem to the ground and pounded them into the earth with his heel. 'There! Now that bloom is gone. And we are what we are!' His laughter nearly choked him.

'Gorlois, you fool!' Merlin shouted. 'What you are doing defyeth heaven! No good can come of thith.'

'No good for you!' Tears of mirth ran from the dragon sockets of Gorlois's face down the long ravines of his cheeks. 'Now let us depart this gloomy place and return to the world of the living, where I belong!'

'We'll do no thuch thing.' Merlin squirmed in Gorlois's grasp, his short legs running futilely in the air. 'Let me down.'

Gorlois glanced about at the sullen trees silhouetted against the sky's sunset tinctures. 'Which way do we go?'

'I'll not tell you.' Merlin shook his fist defiantly. 'You're in the hollow hillth – the kingdom made of twilight – and here you'll thtay until your thoul giveth back my body.'

'Don't you dare disobey me, Lailoken!' Gorlois shook Merlin to a blur. 'I'll smash your head like a melon and send your soul to dance in the Happy Woods!'

Dagonet, wearing his beloved monkey's body, leaped onto Gorlois's arm and bit his wrist. With a shriek of pain, the duke dropped Merlin and swatted at the monkey. But the animal had already bounded off – and so had the dwarf, both disappearing into the tangled underbrush, leaving Gorlois clutching his wounded wrist and bellowing curses.

Balm in Gilead

King Arthor and his retinue arrived with loud fanfare at the Spiral Castle. Elephants trumpeting, pipers, drummers, hornblowers making joyous noise, tumblers leaping hoops, jugglers catching spinning swords, the caravan entered the stockaded ward of the fortress to the cheers of the northern clans. The Spiral Castle itself was the contorted landscape, wide as the horizon, and the only way in, apart from scaling the cliff walls, was through the wooden palisade that had been thrown open at Arthor's approach.

Lot lead the way on his sturdy battle-horse with his sons

at his side, and the occupants of the fortress bent their knees as he passed, then stood again to point at the boy-king and his elephants and performers. To Arthor, these people of the north appeared as denizens of an archaic time, for they dressed in the old-fashioned kirtles and tunics that had been popular two centuries and more ago, when the Romans held these lands. Even their hairstyles – skullshorn for the men and tiered in ringlets for the women – was remindful of the old Romans. And yet, these clans were Celtic – devotees of the old gods.

'Pagans!' Kyner called them, and he and Cei immediately began preaching the good news of the Savior, unfurling their chi-rho banners and shouting from their horsebacks, 'We bring you balm from Gilead to heal the wounds of your souls!'

Aidan, the chieftain of the Spiral Castle, emerged from his timber mead hall with his wife, young son, and daughters and paid obeisance to Lord Lot, offering a bronze sword of ancient lineage, a cloak of wolf fur, and two hunting mastiffs. Lot accepted graciously, speaking in Gaelic, and slipping into Latin when he introduced the young king. 'Aquila Regalis Thor has come to win your pledge and your promise to hold the Spiral Castle against the Picts.'

'You arrive in good time, Aquila Regalis Thor,' Aidan spoke in fluent Latin. Tall, ruddy, with a smashed nose and one severed ear, he wore hoops of leather around his torso, joined by similar hoops passing over his shoulders, the *lorica* of an old Roman soldier. 'A warband of Picts led by the ferocious wayfarer Guthlac has dared scale the northern walls of my citadel and hides now somewhere in its maze. He offers good terms of alliance with his vast army to the north – if I will open these gates to him.'

'I will offer you better terms, Aidan,' Arthor promised at once. 'I have viewed your Spiral Castle, and though small bands of brigands may sneak into it, no army could hope to overrun it – if you are willing to defend its walls.'

Before Aidan could reply, a loud commotion from beyond the imposing elephants interrupted him. Bedevere stepped close to the king, saying, 'It's your stepfather, sire. He has riled up the people by calling them pagans. They know Latin well enough to understand he has called them "worshipers of false gods."'

Aidan glared at Arthor. 'Have you come to seek alliance – or to foist your nailed god upon us?'

Mother Mary, thank you, your Son, and God our Father for sending me Bedevere. Even when I don't see him, I know he is there, watching my back, protecting me from assassins. My Da – your Son's servant, Kyner – he means well, bringing the good news to the north clans. But their hearts are hardened against our Savior, and Kyner and my brother Cei are not the most patient messengers of the Lord's word. They have incited anger among many of these fierce people. If not for Bedevere, I would fear for my life, because my talks with chief Aidan are all-consuming and I cannot always be looking over my shoulder. Aidan hopes to inflame me with harsh rhetoric even as he plies me with fine foods and wine. But I am obedient to your Son's teachings and ever turn the other cheek. These proud people are frankly amazed – and perhaps disappointed – that I take no offense from their insults. Now if only Bedevere could protect me from Morgeu. She is in her element in this wild north country, and I fear what she is about. Where is Merlin, Mother Mary? Where is my wizard?

Under the Moon's Paw

King Arthor spent the entire day in negotiations with Aidan, and into the night he was still trying to assuage the offended vanity of the clan chief. Lot sat with them in the mead hall, enjoying with his sons the Celtic hospitality of their host, savoring platters of meat in fruit sauces, bowls of whortleberry pudding, and baskets of honey apple dumplings, all washed down with ale and cider.

Left to her own devices, Morgeu departed the stockade unobserved through a servant's entrance. The people were distracted by the parading elephants, the dancing bears, and the outlandish performers, who proudly displayed their skills accompanied by the passionate music of the king's musicians. More solicitously than before, Kyner and his towering son Cei moved among the amused clansfolk and preached their good news.

Morgeu left the fortress, because she felt a blood-tug in her womb – as if the soul that had been stolen from her unborn called to her. Under the moon's paw, she found her way to a birch grove. Merlin's phantom awaited among the pale boles, beckoning her closer.

'Begone to your Christian hell, demon!' Morgeu cursed when she recognized the ghost and turned to go.

'Daughter, wait!' Gorlois cried. 'I am not the demon Lailoken. I am your father – Gorlois.'

'What evil is this you hope to work on me, Merlin?' Morgeu spat angrily. 'You cannot deceive me. I see what you are.'

'Morgeu, I am not what I seem.' Gorlois reached for her, and she backed away. 'The demon carried my soul into the underworld. The elk-headed god cast him out – and our souls were knocked free and fell into different bodies. Lailoken is now inside a dwarf. And I – I am here, in his body. But I am lost in this nether realm. I have been calling for you to help me. And now you have come.'

Morgeu squinted suspiciously at him and saw the skeletonhead moon through his transparent body. 'I don't believe you.'

'Then listen, Morgeu, and I will tell you things only I, your father, could know.'

With her hands crossed over her womb, Morgeu listened to the ghost describe the intimate details of her childhood with him – memories many of which she had forgotten herself until she was reminded by him. Her blood listened. She asked questions, and he answered each correctly and with the emotional valence she expected from her father – an imperious, short-tempered brusqueness. 'Father – this really is you!'

'Daughter, you must help me.' He opened his arms, mystified. 'I don't know where I am.'

'Father – you are in the hollow hills! Only the bloodbond with the childflesh I am weaving in my womb allows me to see and hear you.'

'Help me!' he called, his eyes of crushed ice bent with woe.

Morgeu passed her hands through his emptiness. 'I will – somehow. But I don't know how yet. You must be patient . . .'

Before she could say more, the wind coughed through the birches, and the wraith faded away.

The Gentle Wound

Aidan's only unmarried daughter, Eufrasia, a young woman of sixteen summers, served her father and his guests throughout the night as they discussed the politics of the north, the hopes and fears of the clans, and the dangerous plight of the Britons and Celts who held the south. Was it the harp and zither music that the young king had brought into the mead hall with him that created for her an exotic atmosphere of far-flung places come to visit her all-too-familiar home? Or was it the youth of the king, a full year younger than she, that so intrigued her with his manly presence? Then, again, maybe it was the manner in which he parlayed so earnestly with her father, casting not even a curious glance her way, that fascinated her and made her take closer notice of him.

Throughout the north, Eufrasia was renowned for her beauty, and her suitors came from every notable clan between the lake country and the Antonine Wall. She had received marvelous gifts – a swift, shadow-thin stallion bred from the steeds of a desert kingdom, wolfhounds out of the Isle of the Scotii, a silver goshawk, and jewelry and fine silks imported from the ancient and distant kingdom of the Medes – all these fine things just for the right of men to look at her. And this king paid her no more heed than if she were a scullery maid.

And so, she scrutinized him as she came and went with drinking horns of fermented fruit ciders and baskets of breads. For his age, he was large across the shoulders and tall, yet his face belied his stature: his milk-pale skin and rosy, beardless cheeks belonged to a child. The news of him from her father's counselors was that he had won a reputation as a fierce horseman, renowned even among the battle-hardened invaders for his ferocity. But his eyes – yellow as honey – had not the hardened gaze of a warrior. And the fact that a day of close talk had stretched into night without her father pounding the table and shouting even once attested to the curiously tender and intelligent nature of the young king.

Confounded by King Arthor's indifference to her, Eufrasia retreated to her bedchamber and studied herself in a mirror. Was there some flaw that she and others had misperceived about the sheen of her long blonde tresses, the clarity of her large gray eyes, the smooth pallor of her skin, the confident curve of her jaw? She noticed nothing awry with her beauty. And yet – and yet ... Something of her countenance *had* changed. Her maids noticed at once and giggled behind their hands. And then she perceived it, too – the gentle wound, the hurt joy, the quiet cry of a young woman in love.

Avalon

Merlin as a dwarf and the monkey that was Dagonet moved through the syrupy light of day's end. They kept low among the gray bramble and cinereous shrubs of the crepuscular world, careful not to be spotted by Gorlois. The monkey chirred inquisitively from Merlin's hunched shoulder. 'Quiet, Dagonet. Thound twavels thwiftly in the hollow hillth. You'll thee where we're going when we get there.'

Lightning wiped the sky behind him in the direction of the palace shaped like fire. Merlin quickly led them away from that dire place, and soon they climbed through a bracken slope of dense, nacreous fog, the heart of rainfall, and emerged into daylight bejeweled with dew. The monkey shook the moisture from its fur and breathed in the sour redolence of mulchy apples.

They stood beside a quicksilver thread of trickling water threading among mossy rocks down a hillside prosperous with ferns and club worts. From their vantage, they could see morning hills, dells, and mountain cups crowded with apple trees. Everywhere, the gnarly apple trees stood afoot in the mushy brown loam of their dropped fruit. And on every bluff and promontory stood needle rocks – menhirs carved with futhorc incantations.

'Avalon,' Merlin announced. 'We have found our way to the Apple Isle where the Nine Queenth dwell. I am hoping they can help uth in our plight. Come, Dagonet.'

Through wild orchids under a vivid blue sky piled high with golden clouds, Merlin and bestial Dagonet traipsed. They descended to a central lake glittering with diamonds of reflected sunlight. 'It ith here I wetheived Excalibur and firtht met the Nine Queenth. You know about them?'

The monkey shook his head, crouched at the bank, and drank a handful of water.

'The *Annwn*, whom I call the Fire Lordth, thelected one queen from each ten thouthand year epoch of matwiarchal wule and made them immortal. Ninety thouthand yearth of matwiarchal wule gathered here in nine queenth. Why, you athk? To change the human heart. You thee, Dagonet, what each one of uth thinketh – for good or ill – changeth all. The immortal queenth have been teaching the human heart love and caring for hundredth of thenturieth. But the latht queen wath brought here ten thouthand yearth ago. Thince then, kingth have ruled. And thoon, one queen will be releathed, to be replathed by a king – King Arthor.'

Dagonet looked about impatiently at the hillsides of tangled apple boughs and the blue lake reflecting the seaborn cumulus clouds.

'Yeth, you're wight, Dagonet,' Merlin conceded. 'I've talked enough. Now I will thummon the Nine Queenth.' He lifted his arms and tried to send forth the brailles of his heart to draw the queens to him. The brailles were power cords that he had learned to extend through his heart's gateway to touch the world. They were a strength of his demonic nature that served his mortal body – yet, when he attempted to use them, nothing happened. And he felt nothing happening. His dwarf body did not have the gateways of power that his own flesh possessed. And at last, with a mournful look, he turned to the monkey and said flatly, 'My God, Dagonet – I hope you wike appleth. I think we're thtuck here.'

The Pale People

Gorlois wandered moaning through the netherworld, peering among the dark, narrow trees at the watermelon twilight. The red sky's green rind worried him, for it spoke of storms – and he dreaded to think what a tempest in the hollow hills portended. He steered himself away from the strange sunset, toward the darker horizons.

Not far along, he heard the voices of children, laughing, whispering mischievously. He searched for them but saw only fireflies glittering in the lightless crannies of the gloomy forest. 'Hail!' he called. 'I hear you there. Come forth where I can see you.'

Out of the night spaces, the pale people emerged. They were not children at all but tall, narrow men and women with adder eyes, tufted ears, and flesh tinged blue as milk. Their red hair floated in the vesperal air like bloodsmoke. 'Myrddin,' they called, using Merlin's Celtic name. 'Why are you here in the hollow hills?'

Gorlois's startled gaze narrowed. 'Why – to find you. Of course!'

'Where is your staff, Myrddin?' The pale people giggled and began to spread out, encircling him, their vaporous raiment blurring with their movements like fog.

'Broken, alas.' He shook his head unhappily. 'I took a fall – back there.' He looked over his shoulder and took advantage of this gesture to edge away and lean against an elder tree, to protect his back. 'I must have hit my head, you see – for I have forgotten a great deal. I was hoping that you, the Daoine Síd, would help me remember myself.'

The laughter of the pale people brightened, and they looked at each other with merriment in their green, viper eyes. 'What do you need to remember, Myrddin?'

He stroked his wispy beard reflectively and jutted his lower lip. 'Ah, well, perhaps you could show me the way out of here?'

'Oh, Myrddin,' they chortled and their very long, very white fingers plucked at his robes of midnight blue. 'We can do better than that for you. We can help you remember your magic, and then you can find your own way back to the world under the sun and the moon.'

Gorlois pressed against the knobby tree, fearing that these supernatural beings were taunting him, full aware of his true identity. The pale people were well known to steal mortals away and enslave them in the hollow hills or, worse, feed them to the Dragon. 'I – I b–beg your help,' he stammered. 'And I will reward you all handsomely.'

'Will you now?' They stroked the fabric of his robes, their fingers tracing the crimson stitching that patterned the cloth with astrologic and alchemic sigils.

'Yes, for certain I will reward you,' he promised earnestly. 'Just show me the way out of here.'

'Will you give us your hat?' They tittered and pressed so close he could smell their mulchy scent of autumnal leaves.

Gorlois doffed the wide-brimmed and conical hat. 'Here, take the hat.'

They snatched the hat and passed it among them, marveling at the signs stitched upon it. 'And your fine robes, as well.'

Gorlois smashed himself against the tree. 'I'll be left naked!'

'As you first came into the world, Myrddin – so shall you return to it.'

Skyward House

The Pictish wayfarer, Guthlac, stood a head shorter than most men. But his deep-hulled chest, his majestic shoulders thick as a bull's, his torso cobbled with muscle, and his powerful limbs had the strength of any two men. More crucial yet to his role as leader of a warband, his mason-block head atop the broad hump of his neck swarmed with clever battle stratagems, ever busy with warrior thoughts and lethal imaginings. Bald, save for a skullcrest of bristly orange hair, the entire length of his thick, undulant body displayed blue tattoos. They described in intricate spiral, whorling detail the path from the battle plains of Middle Earth to Skyward House among the branches of the

Storm Tree, the splendid home reserved exclusively for heroes slain in combat.

'Aidan entertains the Iron Hammer,' Guthlac informed his warband of a dozen veteran Picts, half-naked men, tattooed all, each individually garbed in crane feathers, leggings and boots of animal and human skins, ears and nostrils pierced with bone, bone spliced among temple braids and topknots, faces grotesque with corpse-blue and death-white daubings. They were a glorious squad, each man anointed in the blood of enemies they had faced and vanquished singlehandedly. That was why Guthlac had chosen them for this mission; they were to a man war-tempered fighters, cool-headed and hard-willed enough to infiltrate the Spiral Castle and secure either alliance with Aidan – or the trophy of his head. Together, they squatted in an arboreal gulch beside a creek that chuckled past boulders masked with moss. 'The doors of his ears are open wide to the Roman promises that fed his forefathers. He will not make agreement with us.'

'Then, we are to leave this Spiral Castle,' one of the men asked, 'and return north to inform our king, Cruithni?'

'Does that way lead to the Skyward House?' Guthlac asked with a derisive twist of his head. 'Aidan must taste fear. Then the bird chatter of Iron Hammer's Latin will not sound as sweet.'

'Lot and Kyner flank Iron Hammer,' another of the warband spoke up. 'They will taste not fear but our blood if we attack them. We will find our way to Skyward House for certain – but our king, Cruithni, will be ill served. And how after that will we account proudly for ourselves among the war heroes?'

'So, we are agreed among us!' Guthlac smiled, exposing teeth filed to points, the better for rending his enemies' flesh. 'We will slip among them by night, take our trophies, and leave them with the sickening taste of fear.'

Rising in Fire

'I have good news for all of you,' Kyner spoke with Aidan's men and their families in the fortress ward while King Arthor and Lot sat with the chieftain in the mead hall. 'The great and nameless God, the creator of the universe, has sent His son to walk among us and to save us from the realm of the dead and its goddess Hel.'

To entice the pagan Celts to come away from the elephants shackled at the front gate and the entertainers resting in the colorful tents of the main courtyard, Cei offered amber beads to all who would listen to his father's sermon. Each translucent bead had etched upon it a tiny fish emblem, a Christian symbol for the Greek word for fish, *ichthys*, an acronym meant to represent 'Jesus Christ, Son of God, Savior'. But to the Celts knowledgeable of runes, the etched fish appeared as *Oddal*, symbol of inherited land and property – and that made the amber beads magical implements for acquiring tangible possessions. The people received them eagerly and listened respectfully to Kyner's tale of virgin birth, magical events, gruesome death, and resurrection.

Entertained by the story and gratified by the amber gift and its promise of wealth, the people cheered Kyner when he concluded. Those already familiar with Christianity and scornful of it cheered anyway, obliged by their Celtic tradition to display hospitality to the guests that their chief had admitted into their community.

None stayed for the baptism to follow, and Cei shouted irately at them to come back as they dispersed for their noon meal. 'Save your voice, son.' Kyner shook his leather pouch of amber beads. 'We've plenty more enticement left, but it's wasted here in the settlement. These townbound souls are hardened with greed. Let us go out into the surrounding fields and thorpes and preach the good news to the rustics.'

Cei agreed, and they departed on horseback by a side gate. The remainder of that afternoon, they rode the narrow traces among the steep hills, visiting farms and crofts, handing out their beads and their message of God's son rising in fire to heaven.

From afar, hidden in the treecrowns, Guthlac and his warband observed the meandering transit of the preachers. Toward nightfall, they silently advanced upon a wattle farmhouse the Celts had visited earlier. The watchful geese squawked warning to the farmer, and he emerged with scythe in hand but was little challenge to Guthlac, who caught the man's sweeping blade in the notch of his ax and used the harvesting tool to lop the farmer's head from his shoulders. The others swiftly removed the heads of the farmer's wife and their four children. Then, donning the clothes of their victims and wearing their scalps, Guthlac and one other Pict hitched the farmer's wagon and carried the others covered in hay sheafs and as many farm animals as they could carry to the side gate of the stockade.

Eufrasia in Thrall
With his face obscured by scalp hair and twilight, Guthlac announced to the gatekeeper in passable Latin, 'We have received the good news from Lord Kyner. He bids us deliver these animals for a holy feast. Let us in.'

When the keeper opened the gate, Guthlac stabbed him through the throat, stoppering his death cry. The wagon trundled onto the equestrian range, keeping to the stockade wall behind the horse stables, where there was no one to observe them. Aidan's warriors, always before too vigilant to allow such a grievous breech of their defenses, were distracted by King Arthor's astonishing entourage. They had joined the settlement's residents, who had gathered in the main courtyard to watch the boy-king's court performers emerge from their tents and begin the evening festivities. Elephants paraded, bears danced, wise dogs jumped and frolicked to jubilant music, and no one saw the thirteen Pictish warriors move furtively as shadows past the granary, the storage sheds, and the emptied barracks.

The Pictish warriors deployed across the ward before the mead hall: two positioning themselves behind the flour barrels at the bakehouse while two others entered and cut the throat pipes of the cook and his apprentice; three more clambered onto the bailey scaffold, silent as wraiths, and killed the two guards of the chieftain's keep while they leaned on their spears and watched the celebrations in the far courtyard; three stationed themselves at the back and sides of the mead hall, swords ready to dispatch wandering sentinels; the last two of the warband waited as the stars kindled into night, until a servant emerged from the chieftain's manor, returning to attend the dignitaries in the mead hall, and cut her throat, then barged into the timber lodge.

Eufrasia sat in her chamber inspecting herself in a mirror when Guthlac kicked open her door. A thrown knife silenced a screaming maid. The other servant gaped in voiceless terror as the gruesome Pict pointed a sword at Eufrasia and said gruffly, 'Come silently or die!'

Eufrasia, a chieftain's daughter and trained to defend herself, snatched a dagger from her bedstand. Before she could throw it, the Pict's sword flashed and knocked it deftly from her hand. The next moment, two more Picts entered, freckled with the blood of the guards they had slain in the corridors. She shouted an alarm but only briefly before leather thongs secured her mouth, hands, and feet.

Heaved over Guthlac's shoulder, she struggled in vain as he carried her into the night. Quickly, he retraced his steps, gathering his warband behind him as he went. At the wagon behind the stables, the chieftain's daughter was bundled among the warriors, with a strict warning from Guthlac to his men not to molest her. That privilege belonged to him.

Out the side gate the wagon exited, Guthlac on the riding board, wearing the farmer's clothes and his scalp. Kyner and Cei saw the wagon in the distance as they returned across the nightland, but, embittered by their failure to win even one soul for their Savior, they paid the farmer no heed.

Treasures of the Otherworld

Merlin as a dwarf and Dagonet as a monkey walked the perimeter of the lake on Avalon, searching for some sign of the Nine Queens. They found only ruffled cabbage flowers poking through the windfall apples.

Hopefully, Dagonet pointed up the bracken slopes to the thin cascade that trickled from where they had arrived.

'No, Dagonet,' Merlin replied. 'We were lucky to get out of the hollow hillth without magic. If we go back, we may wun into the pale people. And they're a mithchievoth lot.'

Dagonet picked up a newly fallen and unblemished apple and bit into it. He followed Merlin as in a dream, chasing after his own physical form as they wandered among the apple trees and a few renegade elms.

At one of the larger elms, the wizard paused and pointed to a hole at the base of the tree. 'Wook! And thmell!'

Monkey Dagonet crept up to the grass-fringed hole and smelled a feverish reek.

'Dwagon bweath!' said Merlin.

Dagonet backed away swiftly, squeaking a small cry.

'Don't be afwaid.' Merlin crawled into the hole and disappeared. A moment later, his big, freckled head poked out. 'Come on! The Dwagon ith athleep.'

The wizard descended into darkness, and Dagonet hesitated, clutching nervously at his tail. Then, he edged into the hole, feeling his way along the steep descent by grasping root tendrils and jutting knobs of rock. The darkness thickened remorselessly, until the hole above had dwindled to a distant star. When the monkey's eyes had adjusted sufficiently, Dagonet discerned a soft glow in the depths.

Like a full moon in a jungle night, the light from below shone through tangles of organic loops and fronds that were actually root cables and plates of silhouetted shale. Dagonet dropped into a grotto illuminated by a percolating pool of sulfurous water, orange and frothy red. He put a hand to his nose.

'Yeth, it thtinkth − but wook, Dagonet! Wook where we are!'

Merlin pointed to glossy shelves of rock upon which lay heaped dunes of gold coins, toppled urns of fiery rubies, and cauldron pots of diamonds. 'The Tweathureth of the Otherworld! The Dwagon hath collected thith hoard from the cawavanth and thipth it hath thwallowed over the yearth.'

Dagonet climbed a stalagmite and plucked a polished diamond from a pot of gems. He sniffed it, then bit it, and tossed it to Merlin with a querying shake of his head.

'You're wight, Dagonet. It appearth like a diamond of our world. But the Dwagon hath changed it, imbued it with hith power. Behold!'

Merlin tossed the diamond into the bubbling pool – and the water agitated, then went perfectly calm – still and reflectant as a mirror. In its surface, they peered and saw themselves in their true forms – Lailoken a demon of flanged jaws, serpent grin, and hooded flame-core eyes. And beside him, where the monkey gazed, a Fire Lord stood, resplendent in golden flames.

King Arthor's Shame

The blood of the gatekeeper, four guards, the baker and his apprentice, a maidservant, and almost surely Eufrasia's blood as well weighed heavily on the young king. 'I am ashamed of what has happened,' he admitted to Aidan after they heard the surviving chambermaid's account of Guthlac's bold abduction of the chieftain's youngest daughter. From the fleece rug splattered with the blood of the dead maid, he picked up Eufrasia's dagger. 'I am ashamed that you have suffered such a terrible loss while under my protection.'

'*Your* protection?' Aidan's ruddy face darkened. 'You're just a boy – younger than the daughter I lost.'

'I am your king,' Arthor replied calmly, his face ashen and grim but not flinching before the enraged chieftain's tight stare. 'You had every right to expect security in my presence – and I have failed you.'

'Retrieve my daughter, *boy*, and I will bend my knee before you and call you king.' Aidan turned away in disgust, then stopped in the doorway and pointed a thick finger at the youth. 'But if my Eufrasia is dead or in any way maimed, do not dare show your hairless face at the Spiral Castle again!'

After the chieftain stalked out of the manor lodge, Arthor looked to his aide, Bedevere. 'See that the elephants and all the performers are sent back to Camelot. I have undertaken this tour of my kingdom too merrily.'

'Sire, this tragedy is not your fault,' Bedevere consoled.

'After all, you are a guest in these walls and under Chief Aidan's protection and Lord Lot's countenance.'

'Is that what it means to be king, Bedevere?' Arthor admonished the steward with a frown. 'No. I alone am responsible. I am the high king, and all my people must have faith that I can protect them. Otherwise, I am no better a monarch than the carnival mummers I parade with.'

Kyner and Cei met King Arthor as he exited the manor. 'My lord, forgive us!' the elder Celt beseeched contritely. 'We saw the Picts upon the high road leaving the stockade and did not recognize them for the brigands they are.'

'How the harrowing hades were we to know, father?' Cei glowered morosely. 'It was dark, and they rode past disguised.'

'You should not have been about the countryside *preaching*!' Arthor scolded, then caught himself. 'Forgive me, father – brother. I'm distraught, because my negligence has brought grief to this castle. I should have thought to establish my own perimeter. I was so eager to win the hearts of these people, I did not think to protect them.'

Lot emerged from the bailey with armed escorts bearing torches. 'Aidan tells me you are determined to go after Eufrasia. That was a fool's promise, my lord, for you will have to go alone. We have tracked the wagon to where the Picts abandoned it at the cliff traces. They have disappeared into the gorges. Not even Aidan's men will descend into that confusing wilderness. Ambuscade is too easy down there – and besides, once a rescue party is seen by the Picts, Eufrasia's life is forfeit.'

'I intend to go alone.'

'I will go with you, brother.'

'No, Cei. You know I love you for your courage, but it would be easier to hide an elephant on those cliff trails.'

Concerning Ghosts, Demons, and Wizards
The pale people took Gorlois's hat and robes and ran laughing through the trees, crying, 'Follow us! Follow us!'

Naked but for his hemp sandals, the ghost in the body

of Merlin gawked about fearfully. Trees like old women, like beggars, stood stooped on all sides, eye-sparks watching from the holes in their trunks. He bolted after the Daoine Síd, hoping they would lead him out of this dark wood of perpetual twilight. But soon only the scornful laughter of the elfen people remained, and then that, too, dwindled into the maroon air.

Gorlois stopped running and shouted a curse, 'Damnation on all of you!' In frustration, he kicked at a pulpy log fallen to mushrooms, stubbed his toe, and cried out again. The pain startled him. *I'm alive!* he thought and giddily recalled the grievous sensation he had experienced when he first awoke inside a monkey and learned that he had been slain on the plains of Londinium. He had no memory of that, but the throb in his toe had a good memory – and that made him laugh.

Without warning, the gust of laughter opened the gates of power in the wizard's body. The dry stalks of grass around him rustled in a wind that rose directly out of the ground and lifted dead leaves spiraling into the brown air. 'I am a ghost!' he laughed louder, and the leaves flew back onto their branches and swelled with green sap. 'I am a ghost who defeated a demon and became a wizard!' His laughter widened maniacally, and he slapped his naked body and guffawed to see blue sparks jump from his pallid flesh.

'The magic is inside me!' he realized. He urinated, and tiny, quartz-petal flowers sprouted where he splashed. More laughter sent him running again, this time for joy. The nightmare had become a euphoric dream. He ran faster, until his churning feet no longer touched the ground, and he flew with his white beard forked by the speed of his headlong trajectory. Swerving among the trees, he looked for the pale people. But there was no sign of them.

He willed himself to stop – but his flight accelerated, and he began to soar. Fright replaced joy, and he fell in a tangle of limbs among the leaf drifts. Groaning, he sat up and brushed beetles and snails from his beard. 'Let up, Gorlois!' he chided himself. 'Magic is an art.'

At that thought, he allowed himself a chuckle. 'I, an artist!' He swirled a tapered finger in the air and drew paisleys of light. That inspired further laughing, and soon the gates of magical power swung wide again, and Gorlois bounded upright and charged into the gloom, spry as a gazelle.

The Dragon Pool

Merlin stood back from the clear water in which he had seen the monkey reflected as a Fire Lord and stared dumbfounded at the beast. '*You* are an angel?'

The wizard was well aware that humanity had been shaped over aeons by the Fire Lords – that the entire universe was their workshop, in which they were building the cosmic devices that would carry them back to heaven, to the realm of pure light from which all creation had emerged at the start of time. People were a prototype of beings yet to come, complexities vast enough to carry the Fire Lords out of the cold and dark of space to the eternal glory of paradise. And he knew, also, that, crude as they were, human beings were capable of housing vast charges of energy. His own mother, Saint Optima, had embodied enough angelic force to weave a human form that could hold his demon power. Yet, he was certain that the body of a man was too frail to contain the luminosity of a Fire Lord.

He peeked again into the Dragon Pool and looked more closely at the shining form he saw reflected by the monkey. He noticed that the Fire Lord did not actually radiate forth from Dagonet's soul but merely enclosed it. That in itself was astonishing, though far more believable to the demon. The propinquity of great entities often distorted the flesh of mortals. That was why Dagonet had been born a dwarf: an angel escorted him.

'You don't know it, Dagonet, but you have a gweat fwiend who watcheth over you.' The wizard scratched his curly, orange locks, wondering about this. 'Then it wath no acthident that you found your way to our King Arthor. You have a holy dethtiny, and your thtunted body ith the pwithe you mutht pay for it.'

Before Merlin could reflect further on this, bright laughter gleamed from among the stalagmites. When he spun about to see the source of the gaiety, he nearly toppled backward into the Dragon Pool. A tall man wearing his conical hat and robes stood at the far end of the cavern. 'Who are you?' he shouted in alarm. But the tall stranger gave no answer.

The monkey scampered across the grotto and snatched the hat, revealing the wet-looking tip of a stalagmite. More laughter echoed from the recesses of the jewel-strewn vault.

'The Daoine Thíd!' the wizard surmised and went to retrieve his garments. 'How came you by thethe?'

No reply followed, and laughter sparkled from farther away.

'Thomewhere, Gorlois wanderth naked in my body.' Merlin fit the hat to his head, and the magic in it immediately widened the range of his hearing. He listened to the pale people snickering at his predicament, heard the Dragon snoring from the depths of its millennial sleep, and detected by the echoes of subterranean streams a honeycomb of caverns beyond this one. 'Dagonet, the pale people are playing with uth. We now have enough magic to get uth into thome weal twouble.'

Falon

Torrential light poured through a rift among tall tranquil trees of a verdant gorge, illuminating Arthor as he stepped down the goat paths of the Spiral Castle's natural wall. With Excalibur strapped to his back to better free the movement of his limbs, he edged carefully along the narrow stone ledges. He wore a simple doeskin kilt and no hat to cover the badger bristles of his hair.

A strange bird whistled. It stopped Arthor cold. At first, he feared the Picts had spied him. But when he dared bend forward and peer into the bottom of the summer morning so far below, he saw a gangly, bare-chested old man in buckskins waving cheerfully at him. The stranger, chirping like a bird, whistled for him to come down.

Arthor resumed his descent, and when he arrived among the

tangles of ivy and lime at the foot of behemoth trees, the old man had laid out a small meal for him upon a rush mat: oatcakes, salt fish, and apples split to show the star in them. 'I am Falon,' the stranger introduced himself in lucent Latin. 'And you are King Arthor. I watched your battle party arrive the other day. Very impressive.'

Arthor accepted Falon's invitation to sit and partake of his simple fare. He noted streaks of orange in long, braided hair the color of ash and a vague scar at the side of his throat where once the man had worn a torc. 'I see you are a Celt of the old way,' Arthor said around a bite of apple. 'Where is your clan?'

'I have no clan. I am *fiana*.' Falon looked to see if Arthor knew of the fabled horsemen of no home who served the Celtic queen by defending her highways and countryside from marauders. He smiled at the look of awe in the boy's face and revealed strong, white teeth. 'I became your mother's champion when she was a peasant maiden and taken from her village in the hills by the druids. She was my queen – until she gave herself to your father and took upon herself the way of the Cross-worshipers.'

A fleeting shadow of sadness crossed the lad's face. 'I have never seen my mother.'

'Nor will you if the Picts who stole Aidan's daughter find you as easily as I have.'

Arthor's eyes gleamed suddenly. 'You know why I am here?'

'I exiled myself to the Spiral Castle after your mother freed me from her service,' Falon said, nibbling at an oatcake. 'Aidan is unaware of me. But I know all that transpires in these glens.'

'Then you can lead me to Eufrasia?'

'Perhaps.' Falon's pale gaze narrowed. 'But I have no love for Cross-worshipers. That is why your mother freed me.'

'You must help me, Falon.' Shame tainted Arthor's pleadful voice. 'I am the one who put that maiden in the hands of our enemies. Please – help me.'

'I will help you if you are a good king,' Falon answered, closing one eye. 'And for me to know that, you must answer this question. What is more important to a king – Mercy or Justice?'

'Justice is about truth,' Arthor replied almost at once, for he himself had pondered the matter before, when Kyner insisted his ward study the old philosophers. 'And truth has many sides, Falon. Justice and Truth have shapes that change among the nations and throughout the seasons of history. But Mercy – Mercy is Love, and that has the same strength and beauty for all people, for all time. As king, I serve Mercy, not Justice.'

Falon showed his strong, white teeth again. 'Then you are my king, as well.'

Magic on the Tor

Morgeu the Fey left her husband's bed in the hour when the moon mists over on its way westward with the darkness. Chanting sleep to the gatekeeper whose predecessor had died only hours before, she left the stockade and wandered in her red raiment and silver slippers through wood shadows and up a path of blue slate to a tor beneath the rustling stars. Fury powered her steps, and she moved with a rageful vigor to the summit of the rocky pinnacle.

From this height of the world, she could see across the Spiral Castle to where her half-brother, the king, would try his fate against the Picts. The child of his that she carried in her womb had lost his soul to Merlin – and now she would see that Merlin lost his child, as well. No matter now that without Arthor, the throne she coveted for her children would fall to contention again among the warlords. No matter the chaos that would ensue. She had striven to be noble, to strike a reconciliation of love and magic with her brother, as the Pharaohs of ancient Ægypt had accomplished with their sisters. But the wraithly sight of her father's soul that would have been her child's soul now magically captured by Merlin's body gave her the determination to strike back.

A red band of mist appeared in the east. *The fissure between worlds.*

Angrily intoning the names of the north gods' chieftain, she summoned Lailoken's most powerful foe: 'All-Father, Great Father, One-Eye-All-Seeing, Furor and Rune-Master, Frenzied God of the Wild Hunt, Sacrifice of the Storm Tree, hear my call!'

A vast and soundless flash of lightning crossed the clear sky. The moon in the west gleamed like a blind eye.

'Furor, know that Aquila Regalis Thor, your enemy, descends into the chasms of the Spiral Castle. Send your Raven to spy him out and guide your faithful warriors like wolves to him wherever he may hide. Flense the flesh from his bones and stretch it upon the wardrums that salute you. Think how sweet its music will sound, the drumbeat, heartbeat of a dead foe who will thwart you no more.'

Another mute stroke of lightning shuddered across the dawn and shook the last stars from their sockets.

'These words are chanted for this day, from the secret depths of my being, where blood and flesh of brother and sister knit the promise of a tomorrow that will never come. My future is violated – and I am *enraged* that what is most intimate to me is stolen. By this wrath and the little death in me, I summon a wrathful and larger death for a king. May it be so.'

The dawn world fell quiet. No birds announced the sun. No matin breeze stirred the leaves on the trees below the barren peak. The shadow of death rose like mist.

Eufrasia and the Picts

A warrior with one eye white as a boiled egg put his hand to the side of Eufrasia's head and stroked her flaxen hair. She stood naked, her arms outspread, feet apart, thong-tied between two beech trees. Chin high, her gray eyes stared defiantly at her captors. Until now, none had touched her, save to secure her between the trees. She did not flinch at the Pict's caress, for she was fearless of whatever fate offered. A chieftain's daughter, desired by every unbetrothed Celtic warrior in the land, she fully intended to die a death worthy of her station and the beauty that the gods had bestowed on her. She would not grovel before these ugly men, and throughout the night she had mocked them openly for their cowardice in creeping like rats through the darkness to steal her.

'Get away from her, White-Eye,' Guthlac called as he returned from relieving himself in the bushes. Their captive's bravery and insults prevented him and his warband from molesting her. Not only was she far more valuable as an intact hostage but their honor as warriors destined for the Skyward House demanded respect for all people of spirit, even their enemies and especially their prisoners. 'Do you want to damn us all to the House of Fog?'

'Her spirit is on her skin, Guthlac,' White-Eye said, running a thumb under Eufrasia's chin. 'Touch her deeper and her insults will turn to frightened tears and fearful sobs. I know women.'

Eufrasia spat in White-Eye's good eye and rasped in a voice husky from a night of shouting insults, 'All you know of women you learned from cows, you son of a mare.'

Guthlac put a firm hand on White-Eye's shoulder and guided him to where the others sat cracking triangular beech nuts on the creek rocks, whetting their knives on the shale, unbraiding their battle tresses to let summer in their hair, or lying on the boulders in the naked light, listening to the bird-loud morning.

No one else paid any heed to the woman. All had hoped she would have cringed; then, Guthlac would have broken her maidenhead as was the right of brave men with craven maidens, and the others would have broken their lust upon her afterward. But clearly, she carried the favor of the gods, who bestowed spirit and admired those who displayed it proudly. None would look at White-Eye who had touched her, for fear that they would lose their battle-luck.

'Our men in the tree-crests see no one coming for you,' Guthlac informed the maiden. 'You are your father's youngest, and he has abandoned you. He has accepted your loss, for he has other daughters and grandchildren by them. He will not trade you for alliance with our mighty king, Cruithni. No gold will be offered for your safe return, for Aidan is too proud a chieftain to trade gold for a woman's life. So, we wait out this

day and then you will have a choice to make, brave maiden.'
The Pict's knife sighed as it left its sheath. 'The scalp of a maiden
with your spirit is a useful talisman and the painful cries of your
slow death a worthy song for our gods.' He showed his pointed
teeth in a smile akin to a sneer. 'Or you may choose life and
come away with us as our comfort bride – and your beauty will
serve us all.'

The Soul's Task

Merlin filled the pockets of his robes with diamonds, rubies,
and sapphires. The monkey with Dagonet's soul within watched
him from where he squatted on a stumpy outcrop the color of
raw meat. By the spectral glow of the Dragon Pool, the wizard
rolled up and tied off the long robes so that they fit his dwarfed
body. 'Come along, Dagonet,' he said, straightening the hat on
his head. 'Let uth climb back up to Avalon. With the magic
in thith hat and the Tweathureth of the Otherworld, we will
have our audienth with the Nine Queenth.'

As Merlin promised, the Isle of Apples disclosed its secrets
when he and Dagonet emerged from the hole under the
elm. With the hat on, the wizard could once again read
the futhorc of the menhirs. He read a few of the poems to
Dagonet – song-rhymes full of code about seasons past and
yet to come, prophecies spent and unfurled. They proceeded
among the apple trees and down mossy rock shelves to an odd
round lodge, brown as gingerbread and squatly lopsided as a
mushroom cap.

After knocking three times on the crooked wooden door,
Merlin entered, and Dagonet followed into a spare interior
of earth-tamped floor and walls decorated in spirals and wavy
lines of warm color. Slant rays of azure light from small, round
windows high in the dome illuminated nine veiled women
sitting all in a line upon bulky block-cut thrones. The mulchy
taint of autumn filled the air.

'Rna, queen of the Flint Kniveth,' Merlin called to the one
farthest to their left. She lifted her veil and revealed a young
face as near to falcon as human, with blue dusk pressed into her

temples, a sheen of fish scales to her flesh, and coils of hair the color of a thrush's breast. 'We've lotht our way. Help uth.'

'Oh, Merlin.' Sadness closed her face almost to tears. 'What of the work your mother set you to do? What of Arthor? How will he take my place if he does not fulfill the prophecies?'

'Rna – I – I . . .' Merlin stammered to silence, stunned. He had not expected this rebuke, and his ears burned with shame.

'You stole a soul, Merlin.' The solemnly beautiful woman shook her head ruefully. 'How could you do that? You, Optima's son. How dare you interfere with what comes from God? You are not a demon anymore. Or are you? *Are* you Lailoken? Or are you Merlin?'

'Rna – I – I don't know.' Merlin trembled from scalp to toes, his heart tight as a knot. Humiliation flustered through him at the queen's reproach. 'I – I did what I thought betht. The child ith an inthetht cweature . . . the bwutal Gorlois . . .'

'Merlin!' Rna held him with a fierce look. 'A child is always a child and belongs to God. Go and return the soul to where it belongs – if it is not already too late.'

'But – I don't know how to get back.' The wizard opened his arms helplessly, long robes dragging on the ground. 'I'm lotht.'

'Of course you're lost. The Fire Lord that escorts Dagonet was sent to watch over you and Arthor. He is angry you've become a demon again. He has set you a task that will undo your pride.'

'I'm thorry!' Merlin shuffled with mortification before the Nine Queens. 'Thith won't happen again!'

'It may already be too late.' Rna's heron-gray lids fluttered sleepily. 'You thought you knew better. But what did you know, Merlin? What did you know?' She lowered her black veil. 'What the mind learns, the soul must unlearn. That is the soul's task.'

Out of the Hollow Hills

Gorlois soared above the bramble and skinny trees of the netherworld. The landscape glowed below him in the winey light of sunset like a wilderness of dreams. But he had no attention for that. His mind was fixed above, on the sky of the underworld, the canopy of faint stars and spongy moon.

As he flew closer, powered by the giddy magic coursing through his wizard body, he noticed that the stars and moon were only luminescent shadows in the sod and root mats that dangled from the ceiling of this vast subterranean cavern. He drove himself like an arrow into the mulchy underside of the earth. With frenzied laughter, he dug at the loam, pulling away huge clumps of peat. His magic gave him superhuman strength. Like an avalanche, masses of earth toppled past him, and soon threads of sunlight shone through the scrim of roots and loose soil above.

Gorlois pulled himself into dazzling daylight, racked with laughter. Even as he skidded out of the tight crevice he had dug, the wounded earth healed behind him. He rolled down a knoll under a morning sky polished with cottony rags of cloud. Pines moaned in the passing wind, full of brine and surf sounds, and the stones under him burned where the sun had beaten them. He stood up, exultant, exuberant, exiled from death.

Gazing about to orient himself, he saw that he stood upon a grassy escarpment above a herd of dunes. Shrieking gulls swooped over mussel shoals where giant combers rolled to shore like fantastic, silver-haired gods. 'The Cantii Coast,' he said aloud, recognizing the wide strand where the alluvial plains of the Tamesis River met the sea. 'The Saxons hold this land.'

As if summoned by the magic of his words, four burly fishermen appeared from over the crest of the scarp carrying a flat-bottomed Saxon boat between them. The sight of the naked old man elicited shouts from them. 'You, codger! What are you about?'

Gorlois did not understand their language. But the laughter that had opened the gates of power throughout his body widened apertures in his head that caught the echoes of what they had said and rendered meaning from them. Likewise, his throat flexed with mirth, and the sheer merriment of standing before these foes naked in Merlin's body gave voice to his thoughts in the language of these strangers, 'Do you not recognize me, fools?'

'Fools, are we?' The fishermen lowered their boat and came jogging toward him. 'You're addlepated standing here naked and calling us fools. Tell us who you are or we'll give you a good dunking to refresh your memory.'

Gorlois barked with laughter and clapped his hands. The wheeling gulls came flying at the fishermen, screaming toward their heads so that the men fell to the ground before the naked stranger like prostrate worshipers. 'I am Merlin, the greatest wizard in all Britain. When you've had your fill of sand, get up and take me to your King Wesc. I have a proposition for him.'

Mother Mary, my life is in God's hands. All that has been given may be taken from me easily now if He so wills. And if what I am – a lustful man who has fathered a child by incest – displeases God more than what I could be – a king who places love above power – then destroy me here in the Spiral Castle among my enemies. I would die this way, by the sword that has been my life and the hope of my redemption.

The Ale-Minstrel

Along the creek bed he came, plucking a *rota*, a zither of five strings with bone-yoke facings and a beaverskin carrying-bag thrown over his shoulder. At his hip, he wore a horn of liquor. Purple tattoos etched his face and arms with elder runes in the Saxon style – and by the rune-eye between his eyes, all could plainly see he was an ale-minstrel devoted to the Rune-Master himself, the Furor. He came singing with a Saxon's ardor, *'Lead me to true knowledge, lead me on the future paths. All-Father, Great Father, lead me on, lead me on!'*

Guthlac himself met him at the ford and said in the dialect of the north, 'Ale-minstrel – how came you here to this Celtic place? And from whence among our brother Saxons do you hail?'

'The Great Father has led me here. I hail from nowhere — and to nowhere am I bound. Did you not hear my song?'

'All of the Spiral Castle hears your song, loudmouth!' White-Eye shouted from the creek bank. 'Are you calling our foes?'

'Foes?' The ale-minstrel looked baffled. 'There are no foes where I am. For where I go, goes our Great Father, the Furor.'

'Pay no heed to that one, minstrel.' Guthlac summoned him across the ford. 'He'd as soon set our course for the House of Fog with his ire. But we have hospitality for the Rune-Master's own.'

Guthlac led the ale-minstrel up the bank, through a barberry bush and into the encampment, where six of the warband's twelve sat about, cracking nuts and cleaning weapons beside a naked woman bound between two trees. While the minstrel passed his horn of liquor around and strolled, strumming his *rota*, the chieftain told the tale of her capture in a bold night raid. Midway through the tale, a flash of rain poured from the clear sky — an obvious blessing from the Furor for their hospitality to his minstrel.

An outraged shout went up from White-Eye at the sight of the ale-minstrel's tattoos running blue in the rain. 'Impostor!'

With blurring speed, Arthor smashed the *rota* over the head of the nearest Pict, and from the beaverskin carrying-bag, he drew Excalibur. It sang, and two heads rolled, the toppling bodies jetting blood. With one deft circular stroke, he severed Eufrasia's bonds. She collapsed and seized the sword of a decapitated Pict, lifting it with desperate strength and impaling a charging warrior — White-Eye.

The Picts flew at Arthor, leaping like singed wildcats, blades flashing sunlight from their keen edges. The young king whirled before them, slicing his sword in a low scything sweep that cut the assailants' thews and dropped them screaming.

Great and sinewy Guthlac came howling, ax held high, and Excalibur spilled his bowels and sent him on the black ride to Skyward House. Before the other Picts could return from their sentinel posts, Arthor covered Eufrasia's nakedness with the beaverskin bag, hoisted her weakened body on his shoulders, and fled into the primordial forest.

Aidan's Pledge

Falon, who had watched the slaughter from a covert among the profusion of creek bracken, quickly led Arthor and his frail burden along the secret gorge paths he knew, and soon they were well away from the Pictish camp. 'That rain was unnatural,' he said, guiding the way up the goat steps to the sward at the summit, where Arthor's palfrey waited. 'Someone works fell magic against you, sire. Only your lethal skills saved you.'

'My skills were useless without yours, Falon.' Arthor offered the old Celt his hand when they attained the crest. 'Your knowledge of runes, your artistry with reed-pen and Devil's Milk for ink, your ale-horn, your *rota* — how else could I have approached close enough for my skills to matter? Come with me. Join my company and sit at the Round Table as my counselor.'

Falon shook his head. 'I am too old, sire. Leave a new *rota* for me before you depart. That music is the only company I need.'

On the ride back to the stockade, Eufrasia held firmly to her champion. 'You spoke their language so well, I thought you were of their ilk.'

'I grew up believing I was sired by a Saxon, my lady. I took pains early to learn what I thought was the tongue of my father.'

When the stockade gates swung open, Aidan stood dumbfounded at the sight of his daughter. Her happy embrace broke the rigor of his shock, and he fell to his knees before the young man of blue face and arms. 'King Arthor — accept my pledge! You are my lord, and all that is mine is yours. The Spiral Castle will hold the north against our enemies. There will be no alliance with the Picts. Your banner alone will fly from these ramparts.'

Eufrasia, nudging aside her tearful mother and the maids who had flocked to cover her in silken robes, knelt in the king's shadow. 'I am yours, my lord.'

Aidan nodded and smiled. 'She has my blessing to go with you – if you will have her, sire.'

Arthor urged Eufrasia to her feet and shook his head once, his heart suddenly tight at the thought of giving himself to another woman after the tragedy with Morgeu. 'My lady—' His mind raced for the words to rescue him. 'There are many battles yet ahead of me. You deserve better after what you've suffered under my negligent protection. You will have a happier life without me.'

Aidan and his wife nodded with amazement, taking the young king's fear of love as compassion for their daughter. They could not imagine any man not loving Eufrasia for her beauty and courage and accepted Arthor's refusal as a true act of selflessness. On the spot, the chieftain declared, 'By this turn, you have convinced me of the merit of your nailed god, sire. He has taught you love greater than any I have seen before in any man. Send your priests to us, and we will listen with open hearts, that we may learn to be as caring of others as you.'

Kyner clasped his chest at this pronouncement, and Cei threw his hands up in surprise before his young brother's achievement. Only Bedevere smiled coolly at Arthor's tact. He alone heard the fatuity in the king's words, for he knew of Morgeu and the young man's invisible and unhealing wound.

Mother Mary, am I wrong to leave Eufrasia behind? Am I wrong to sacrifice my carnal desires and the hope of my heart to atone for the evil I have wrought with Morgeu? This day, my blood could have run with the ink from my body. Yet, God spared me. Surely, I am not saved from the sword to seek comfort in a woman's arms – even the arms of a woman as beautiful as Eufrasia. I have been too easily misled by desire. My reward is the fealty I have won this day from the clans of the north – and Aidan's promise to receive the good news of our Savior. Those are lasting pleasures, whereas the pleasures of the flesh arrive with the heat, intensity, and brevity of lightning — only to be followed by thunderous consequences. Forgive me, Mother Mary. Forgive me if now I betray love for fear of desire.

AUTUMN:

---◆---

Secret House of the Wind

Lawspeaker

The Saxon king Wesc occupied a three-centuries-old Roman villa enclosed by stately poplars. The old vineyards of the estate had been razed to make room for wattle-and-daub cottages: housing for the settlers from Saxony and Juteland. In their midst, the winery and the vintner's manse still stood, serving as administrative buildings for the Foederatus, the alliance of northern tribes that occupied the eastern lowlands of Britain.

Gorlois strode naked into the winery, giggling like a lunatic. Stocky, leather-helmeted warriors in quasi-Roman battle gear escorted him across a mosaic of the wine-god Bacchus that two centuries of wind and rain had scoured to a ghostly semblance of its former beauty. The alcoves that had once held fermenting vats displayed 'raven's food' – war trophies: tapestries of woven scalps, harps of human bone, drums stretched with the flayed skin of enemies, and racks of skull cups. Here the *skalds* and *vitikis* – bards and seers – resided.

None were present when the warriors brought in the laughing wizard, for his weird countenance and brittle laughter frightened them. Only the Lawspeaker, the king's personal *vitiki*, accepted the risk of this dangerous confrontation. Old and wise in the ways of magic, he presided from a bench-of-authority that had been fashioned from the stonework of the central press. The purple-stained blocks had been heaped into two columns on either side of where the elder sat on a wolfskin with the head propped above him, its fangs bared. From each column, clusters of human skulls dangled.

The Lawspeaker, despite the summer heat, wore a long-sleeved wool shirt and trousers, a red mantle, and long braids of ashen hair. He appeared as old as Gorlois, but he was not laughing. With a slight shift of his rheumy eyes, he ordered the guards to depart, and he regarded Gorlois with chill attentiveness. 'I am Lawspeaker for King Wesc. I am not afraid of your magic, Merlin.'

'You should be, old fellow.' Gorlois grinned wickedly. 'You should be.' His magical strength reached out, and, with a laugh, he yanked the wolf's mask down hard upon the elder's head.

The Lawspeaker seemed unfazed. He pulled the wolfskin tighter about himself and continued to stare at Gorlois with cold appraisal. 'Magic cannot avail against virtue.'

'You speak of virtue?' Gorlois laughed harder, and the dangling skulls rattled vehemently, spewing teeth and shards of cranium. 'You land-thieves, you murderers dare speak of virtue?'

'Land is the hide of the World Dragon,' the withered Lawspeaker declared in a strong voice. 'It cannot be owned and so cannot be stolen. As for murder, that is the faith of the strong.'

'I will show you strength!' Gorlois's magic toppled the stack of stone blocks to his right. 'I am strong! Now you will obey me!'

'Virtue is stronger,' the Lawspeaker said and bent to scoop up a handful of skull powder and stone dust from the fallen column. 'Even one as old as I can defeat you with an empty hand.'

Gorlois laughed at the old man's presumption and prepared to heave the stone bench over and throw the Lawspeaker to his back. But before he could act, the aged Saxon's cheeks puffed out, and a cloud of dust engulfed Gorlois's head. In a fit of coughing, the laughter stopped and the gates of power closed in him.

The Lawspeaker rose, seized Gorlois's long nose, and led him choking and squealing from the hall of bards.

Mother Mary, this day I have survived to my sixteenth year. To commemorate, Kyner and Cei rode ahead to the riverbluff city of Greta Bridge and arranged for a feast and a joyful celebration. I was genuinely surprised – and abashed – that the entire town turned out to greet me with loud cheer, as though I had already won great battles instead of simply retrieving a clan chief's daughter from a small warband. But, I am happy to tell you, I forgot not my promise in the frenzy of the festivities: I drank fruit nectars and no wine. Cei and several others imbibed freely and passed out during the garland dances. Lot and the laird of Greta Bridge held their wine far better and honored me with a parade of drone pipes. Oh yes, and Bedevere insisted I commemorate the occasion by establishing my royal colors. I chose red and white – for Christ's blood and the dove of peace, the Holy Spirit. Only later, after the tailors of Greta Bridge had fashioned my banner with a red eagle upon a white field, did Kyner observe I had selected the opposite colors of my father Uther's green and black. That seems just to me now as I kneel here before you, for I am not the dragonlord he was, born to the purple, reared to command men. Mother Mary, I remember well that until this summer I was Kyner's ward, trained to serve like a faithful dog, to defend and obey my master. That is how God prepared me for this task. As he has intended for me, I will defend and obey. Only now, instead of one master, I serve a nation of masters.

The Journey South

On the long ride south through the lake district and into the hills of Cymru, Kyner pointed out baskets of cord woven with shells and seed husks that appeared in the fields and the fruit-heavy orchards. 'Ritual baskets, sire,' he complained, riding up alongside King Arthor. 'Mabon – the ceremonies of the fall equinox. The people provide food for the journey of the Sun King who has become the Lord of Shadows, sailing west and south toward winter.'

'Burn the fields marked by the pagan baskets,' Cei advised.

'A hungry winter will cure these peasants of their devil worship.'

'The old faith provides comfort at the coming of darkness,' King Arthor reasoned. From his frightful journey into the hollow hills, he knew that the gods these people worshiped were real and worthy of respect. He also knew from his study of the Roman classics that no religion was ever defeated by malice. 'Let us live our faith with devotion and celebration, and in time the people will see our Savior's merit.'

Kyner and Cei said nothing more but shared a worried, dubious look.

In Viroconium, a flourishing market town of arched gateways and brownstone ramparts, the townspeople received King Arthor with harp and drum music, huge fires to warm the waning sun, and tree dances in the cobbled market squares. The king partook jubilantly in the Celtic festival yet insisted on conducting open-air Mass at which he required all the townsfolk to attend. Each meal he preceded with a prayer of thanks to the Lord. And on his tour of the countryside, he took pains to visit the outlying households that displayed Mabon baskets, preaching personally to the farmers the faith of the apostles.

'I'm pleased with you, son,' Kyner said to Arthor the day that the Roman highway they followed entered Cymru. 'You honor our Savior in word and deed. And you were wise to dismiss Merlin.'

Arthor looked surprised and turned in his saddle. 'I did not dismiss him. I believe he has chosen to stay behind in Camelot.'

'The pigeons that have carried us news of the elephants' return to Camelot report nothing of the wizard,' Bedevere observed.

'He is a demon,' Cei spoke from where he rode behind his father. 'When you became king, his infernal master recalled him to hell. We're better off without his unholy meddlings and magic.'

Arthor felt sudden alarm, having conveniently chosen to

believe his wizard awaited him at the capital. 'Dispatch birds to all our posts,' he ordered at once. 'Find out what has become of our wizard.' He piaffed his horse to Cei's side. 'Merlin was once a demon, Cei. But now he is a man and devoted to God. My first day as king, he told me that whoever would serve heaven must first conquer hell. Does that not speak of his true heart? I believe he is our Lord's faithful servant.'

Cei remained silent for a moment, reluctant to openly contradict his king. Finally, he narrowed his stare and spoke up. 'Then if you want to find him,' he grumbled, 'I suggest you begin your search in hell.'

The Hounds of Hell

Merlin, still in Dagonet's body, led Dagonet, himself in Lord Monkey's body, out through the crooked doorway of the Nine Queens. They emerged not in Avalon but in the ruins of an abandoned Roman fort. Stubs of broken pillars outlined the colonnade of the commander's quarters, but nothing remained of the barracks and outbuildings save a few shallow depressions in the earth where post-holes had been. An autumn breeze swept dead leaves and a chill over the weed-choked earth. Overhead, in an ashen sky, the sun appeared dark and small as an apricot.

With a monkey shriek, Dagonet sprang behind Merlin. A pack of wild dogs advanced from across the grassy courtyard. Their rib-slatted flanks and glistening eyes bespoke perpetual hunger.

Merlin glanced about for sanctuary, but the ruins offered little cover. Only a cellar hole fringed with dodder some paces away promised the hope of salvation. The dwarf grabbed the monkey and sprinted for that vault as the pack charged after them.

With a yelp of terror, Merlin forced all his strength into his small legs. But his feet tangled on his long robes, and he fell face-forward to the ground of faded mosaic. The scratching of claws swarmed around him, and he expected hot fangs to bite into his flesh at any instant. Flapping his big hat in meek defense, the wizard rolled about. He saw then that the famished pack had stopped only inches away, their carnal breaths laving him with a sickening humidity, their canine faces leering with withheld rage.

'*Lailoken!*' a caustic voice growled from the black dog nearest him. '*I knew we would meet again!*'

Dagonet chittered in terror before the talking beast.

'You are a demon!' Merlin knew.

'*Don't you recognize me?*'

'I am much diminithed.' Merlin gestured at his dwarfed body. 'I do not wecognithe you.'

'*I, too, am much diminished, Lailoken,*' the black dog snarled. '*After the pain I suffered on the battle plains of Londinium all those years ago, I have had to take refuge in serpents, bats, and hungry dogs. It has been a miserable time.*'

The voice stirred in Merlin deep, ancient memories of his aeonial existence as the demon Lailoken, when he had raged against all form, all creatures assembled from matter as a travesty, an abomination of the pure being they had known in the original world before the universe exploded into the cold and dark of the void. 'Athael?'

'*Yes, Lailoken.*' The cores of the black dog's eyes shone with a feverish light. '*I am your old cohort, Azael. And now that you recognize me — I can tear your throat open and free you from the gutsack that holds you. We will range free through the bestial world together, eventually gathering strength to join the others in the dark of space . . .*'

Before the demon could say more or move to fulfill its threat, Merlin pulled a diamond from the Dragon's hoard out of his robe's pocket and jammed it into the beast's mouth. A spiked flash of red energy blinded the dwarf and the monkey, and when they could see again, they found the black dog fallen to ashes on the mosaic as the rest of the pack yelped and trotted away, tails tucked.

White Thorn
King Arthor felt tears burning in his eyes at the sight of the timber-walled enclave of White Thorn, where cooking smoke

94

coiled above the treetops. The gates stood open, draped with the last flowers of the season, and the clansfolk, among whom he had grown to maturity, surged forward cheering at the sight of him under the Christian banner of chi-rho and wearing the gold laurel of the high king.

The king allowed himself to be lifted from his steed and carried into the settlement of his anonymous childhood. When he had last left these crude wooden buildings in the heart of Cymru, he had been a morose and reluctant servant. He had hated himself. Life as a half-breed low-born upon whom the chief had taken pity rankled. That was why he had thrown himself so fearlessly into combat time and again for Chief Kyner — hoping that he would die on the battlefield and snatch some small honor for himself. Never could he have guessed then that he would return to White Thorn as the monarch of all Britain.

The celebrations were sweet. They lasted days. He was fêted by every household in the clan, and he apologized to each and every one, servants included, for his truculent behavior of the past. All were amazed by the lad's transformation. No longer was he the bear they had feared and that only Kyner could command. He had seemingly lost all rancor and moved with warmth and caring among those who remembered him.

On a brisk autumn morning, Cei found the king strolling alone in the golden shadows of the forest outside the enclave. Bedevere, always within sight of his king, watched from under a great fir and moved away silently when he saw Cei arrive.

'You appear troubled, sire.'

Arthor looked up from his reverie, and his frown hardened at the sight of his stepbrother. 'We're alone, Cei. Call me Arthor.'

'Well, then, Arthor — is it the storm raiders on the coast that weigh down your shoulders?'

'They are a dark worry for me, Cei. But no. This morning, I'm saddened by memory.' He motioned at a forest chamber still green yet spangled crimson and gold. 'Do you remember what happened in this grove?'

'It was only three winters ago,' Cei said with a hint of impatience, unhappy with the recollection. 'We were hunting. A dire wolf surprised us. I fled – you stood and killed it. At the hall, you claimed I had slain the beast. I hated you for it.'

Arthor nodded and turned to stare squarely into deep eyes under a blockbrow. 'If I'd told the truth, the magnificent skin would have been hung in the servants' barracks. I wanted it displayed where the chiefs and nobles would see it. So I lied.'

'Ah, now I see.' The gray eyes widened with understanding. 'I thought you had been noble and had lied to give me honor before my father – you, a rapechild, giving me, the chief's son, honor! Ha! I wouldn't have it. But now, what you say shows me how much alike we are.'

'And always were – and always will be, Cei.' He placed a square-knuckled hand over his breast. 'I'm just a hungry heart like everyone else – hungry for honor and respect. I'm not noble. Not at heart. Only by name.'

'Well, young brother,' Cei said with a knowing smile, 'some sad day, your heart and its hungers will die with you and go cold forever. But your name—' He placed his arm about his stepbrother's shoulders and walked with him into the grove where their misunderstanding had begun three winters and a lifetime ago '—your name will warm the world.'

Mother Mary, I tried to tell my brother of my fears today. I confided in him why I lied about the dire wolf. I wanted to tell him more – about my doubts that I am worthy to be king – about Morgeu and the shame of my lust – about my fear, my terrible fear that I will fail. But Cei does not want to hear of my weakness. He is proud I am king. His pride and his devotion to me are why I have officially appointed him my seneschal. He will serve as a faithful steward of Britain, because his faith in our Savior is strong. But I – I doubt I can confide in him my most true feelings. For him and for all the people of Britain that our Father has chosen me to serve, I must be king. And so, Mother Mary, I pray to you to help me keep my doubts and fears to myself. Love is first, so you have taught me. The love of a king is his strength. I must be strong for those who believe I will protect them. But with you

I can be just who I really am – a boy who wants to be a man, a man who strives to be a king, and a king who knows he is a boy.

The Storm Tree

The Lawspeaker led Gorlois by his nose into the alcove of a *vitiki*, a Saxon seer. There, among hangings of scalps and an array of skull cups, he selected a goat's horn and unstoppered it. A stench of dead flesh oozed out.

'What are you doing?' Gorlois managed to gasp when the Lawspeaker released his nose.

'Sending you to the Storm Tree, Merlin,' the aged counselor said with a cackle. 'There you may discuss virtue with the gods themselves if you wish. I've no ears for such talk. Go now!'

Before Gorlois could catch his breath and bring up a mighty enough laugh to open the gates of power in the wizard's body, the Lawspeaker jammed the open end of the goat's horn in his mouth and emptied its fetid contents. He tried to spew it out, but the old man clapped a hand over Gorlois's mouth and grasped his nose. With a choking cry, he found himself swallowing the evil elixir.

Instantly, he fled his body. The rainbow bridge spanned before him, and he flew across its vibrant hues, rising from the ruddy glow of the blood-light behind his lids, through the yellow radiance of daylight, above the green forests and into the blue sky. Terrified, he found himself among starry pinwheels and misty shreds of cometary vapors. A rapturously beautiful vista sprawled before him under flagrant stars and a huge pocked moon: purple mountains and blue tree-roughs that descended toward emerald meadows studded with lakes of golden stillness.

A giant strode toward him across the dells, his blue cape flowing translucent and furled as the starsmoke in the sky above. At a glance, Gorlois recognized the wild, soot-streaked beard and the eagle-hooked visage of the one-eyed god – traits made famous in fable and song – 'The Furor!'

A dense fragrance of stormwind and lightning rolled from the giant god as he advanced, boarskin boots carrying him across leagues with each step. Oddly, as he paced closer, he seemed to shrink. In moments, he stood an arm's length away, only a head taller than Gorlois, and said in a deep, enclosing voice, 'We must talk.'

A Sea Journey

To demonstrate to Marcus Dumnonii that Lord Lot and his Celtic warriors had been won to the King's Order, Arthor sailed with Lot from Cymru to Hartland in Marcus's domain. Lot had been reluctant to leave his gravid wife Morgeu alone in the north, and he brooded over her well-being. As they sailed, he clutched the lock of her red curls he wore on a leather thong about his left bicep.

'I can see that you love my sister,' Arthor said to the aged chieftain as they stood at the ship's taffrail, watching the autumn-misted bluffs of Cymru drift away. 'She has given you two fine sons.' The king glanced at Gareth sitting on the binnacle box questioning the helmsman, who was showing Gawain how to handle the tiller. That sight stirred a yearning in him for a real family, and he spoke a half-truth: the true half from his longing for genuine kinship – and the dark half from his shock that his own sister had impregnated herself by him for revenge. 'I share your sadness that Morgeu chose not to join us. I would have liked to have met my mother with my sister at my side.'

'Morgeu has little love for Ygrane since the queen became a Cross-worshiper,' Lot spoke absently, then caught himself and faced the king with a solemn expression. 'Forgive me, sire. I meant to say, Christian. Now that I and my warriors have pledged our fealty to you, we have sworn not to speak ill of your faith.'

'You are forgiven – and more.' The king placed a hand on the thick wrist of the chieftain. 'I offer you my gratitude for your willingness to abide my faith.'

'Our concerns with the afterworld must not confuse our thinking about this world or we will be easy prey for our shared enemies.' Lot's leather face, both wide and lean, had the cast of a true northman and his eyes a mean squint, yet a gleam of respect kindled there. 'I care not if you worship the Fauni themselves who drove my people's gods underground, for you have proven yourself a worthy king at the Spiral Castle. I'll tell you true and without shame, Arthor – had you abandoned Eufrasia, I'd have called you a fraud to your face and pulled that pretty chaplet from your head. But what you did and how you did it, alone, taking full jeopardy upon yourself, is the deed of a true king. I serve you with honor.'

A groan broke the conjoined stares of the old man and the youth. Bedevere gripped the rail with his one hand and leaned far out, pallid with seasickness.

'Tend to your aide,' Lot said, returning his attention to the retreating headlands, 'and leave me to my prayers for my wife.'

Arthor strode across the swaying deck to where Bedevere rolled his eyeballs and gasped. 'Have you no more tasty Saint Martin's wort to steady your stomach, wayfarer?'

'Do not jibe me, sire,' Bedevere groaned. 'My qualms are beyond herbal remedy.'

'And you a world traveler!'

'A traveler by land, sire – by land . . .'

'What word of Merlin?' Arthor gripped Bedevere's swordbelt to keep him from toppling overboard. 'Have all birds returned?'

'From all points, sire. But no word of the wizard.' Bedevere emptied his gorge into the churning sea below, gasped, spat, moaned, and muttered, 'Merlin's fallen from the face of the earth – and I'd as soon join him.'

Rex Mundi

The dwarf Merlin scooped up handfuls of the ashes remaining of the black dog that the demon Azael had occupied. 'Ah, now I thee why the Nine Queenth sent uth from Avalon to thith plathe. They wanted uth to meet with Athael.'

The monkey Dagonet peeked out from the vault where he had dived to hide from the slaverous hinds. He climbed out and pranced nervously around the cinereous remnants of the demon dog.

'You want to know why the Queenth thent uth to meet Athael?' Merlin removed a ruby and sapphire from the Dragon's pelf in the pockets of his robes. 'To work magic, Dagonet. Magic!'

Dagonet squawked anxiously.

'Don't be afwaid.' Merlin tilted his hat so that sunbeams basked the gems and ashes. 'Thee. Nothing'th happening yet. I will explain what I'm about to do, and becauthe it ith dangerouth and will put all our liveth at wisk I will do nothing without your permithion. Agweed?'

Dagonet the monkey nodded his head nervously.

'The demon Athael ith not dead,' Merlin explained. 'He ith thimply thtunned – and in thith duth for now. By combining in my magic hat hith duth with the Dragon'th wubies and thapphireth, I can athemble Wecth Mundi – King of the World – Pwince of Darkneth! A demon in phythical form! But not an evil demon. No. A demon who will obey uth. In twuth, a demon who will *be* uth. With that power, we can hunt down Gorlois, get my body back, and wethtore you and Lord Monkey to your pwoper bodieth. Ith that good?'

Dagonet rocked his head uncertainly.

'Do you want to thtay a monkey?' Merlin shook the hat, and the gems clinked with a musical sound. 'All I need ith a tuft of monkey'th fur and a lock of thith hair. Once combined – poof! We will become Wecth Mundi.' The wizard contemplatively pinched his chin between thumb and forefinger, then added, 'Of courth, it ith very dangerouth. It ith your body and Lord Monkey'th combined that we will occupy. If an enemy killth uth, you and Monkey will die, Dagonet. Will you take that withk?'

Monkey Dagonet stood up tall, put his fist to his heart like an old Roman, and nodded.

'Good! Then let uth work magic.' With a sharp edge of rock, Merlin cut strands of monkey fur and a curl of red hair from his head, twined the two together, and held them to the sun. He met the monkey's anxious eyes, winked, and dropped the braided lock into the hat.

A flash of blue fire outshone the sun for a blinding interval, and in that glare, silhouettes of dwarf and monkey fused and elongated, wobbling and stretching like firecast shadows. When the magical radiance dimmed, a lone figure stood where before there had been two – a tall man in midnight-blue robes with a head of henna hackles, a stiff beard of black whiskers, and a bestial visage, flat as a simian's, accented by silver twists of eyebrow above a penetrating stare deep and dark as night.

The Furor's Mark

On a branch of the Storm Tree, high above the saffron deserts, arterial rivers, and crumpled mountain ranges of the earth, Gorlois cowered before the Furor. 'I am a Christian man!' he wailed. 'Keep away from me, savage god!'

The Furor's one, storm-gray eye narrowed, and he spoke in cold, measured tones. 'You have no love of your nailed god, Gorlois – only of yourself. You cannot hide your heart from my all-seeing eye.'

Gorlois quailed. 'What do you want of me, dread god?'

'You have stolen the demon Lailoken's body.' A small smile appeared in the Furor's massive beard. 'This is an opportunity that the demon's enemies must not squander. We want him dead, of course – his soul returned to the House of Fog from whence he came.'

'Then – I will die.' Gorlois dared lift his head to meet the chill stare of the north god. 'I don't want to die, All-Father!'

'So now I am All-Father to you, am I, Gorlois?' The Furor shook his head disapprovingly. 'A moment ago, I was the dread and savage god. But the thought of death has won your affections for me, hasn't it?'

'I've been dead.' Gorlois wrung his hands at the thought. 'I remember nothing. I was nothing. But I'm alive again. Don't make me nothing.'

'Fear not, Gorlois. You have a place for your soul in the womb of your daughter. When Lailoken's body dies, you will be free to live again, the son of your own child and sired by the enemy who took your wife for his own. Oh, the poetry of it.' The Furor's eye glittered with laughter. 'But we will not slay Lailoken at once. His body is useful to us. And so I am returning you to it.'

'Oh thank you, great god of the north. Thank you!'

'I am returning you to Lailoken's body with my mark upon you – so that you will hear and see me as I wish.' The Furor leaned closer, and the purple scent of thunder dizzied the mortal man. 'You will obey me in all things.'

'I will, yes. I will obey you.'

'For if you do not, Gorlois, I will yank you from the demon's body and cast you into the Realm of the Dead for the goddess Hel to do with as she pleases.' The Furor stepped back. 'Now stand and receive my mark.'

Gorlois staggered upright and stood wobbling before the huge and hugely bearded god.

The Furor drew his knife and slowly placed it against Gorlois's forehead. 'Stand still, man. If I mar this, you will go mad for all time. Stand still!'

Gorlois held himself rigid, and the cold blade of the Furor pierced his brow.

Arthor and Ygrane

News of King Arthor came to Tintagel daily by carrier pigeon and by travelers who arrived át the citadel of majestic white stone towers and tiered turrets. Many of the wanderers were pilgrims who came to worship at the shrine tended by the Holy Sisters of the Graal. Those who had attended the five-year festival at Camelot and had seen the young king themselves described him in exaggerated detail so that by the time Marcus of the Dumnonii escorted Lord Lot, Chief Kyner, and King Arthor into the western audience room, where the Round Table stood, Ygrane, the white-robed abbess, had no notion what to expect.

Arthor was taller than she had guessed. Only sixteen years old and beardless, he stood as tall as Kyner's giant son Cei, and though not nearly as heavily muscled, he possessed an imposing physical presence of long shoulders, muscular neck, and sturdy limbs. His badger-brown hair, once cropped short as a Roman centurion's, had begun to grow in and he wore it swept back from a broad brow and a face that bore her own traits – a long, straight nose and a wide jaw. Above his rosy cheeks, the yellow eyes of his father gazed at her, bright with tears of joy.

At their embrace, she smelled past the musk of horse to a darker, richer scent, as though sapphire had a fragrance – and her mind whirled with half-forgotten, happy memories of Uther Pendragon. She pulled away from him, her heart thudding. 'This is my happiest day since I wed your father.'

Lot, Kyner, and Marcus acknowledged the king's mother, then departed the audience room, and Bedevere followed and closed the door after himself. Alone, mother and son stared silently at each other for a long spell, and Ygrane touched his face and memorized his lineaments with her fingertips and her vivid green eyes. 'Every maiden in the kingdom will want you for her own,' she spoke at last and smiled. 'Is there one yet who has won your favor?'

'No, mother.' The sound of the word *mother* resounded in him, for he had often referred to his patroness, the Virgin Mary, by that title – and here was his true mother in holy vestment. Dread memory of Morgeu assailed him, and his lips trembled to speak of his mortal sin, but he could find no voice to confess that horror.

'The thought of love troubles you,' she observed and took his hands in hers. 'Come. Sit with me at the table from where you will resolve the conflicts of your people and tell me of your pain.'

Arthor's mind spun as he sat down in an ebony chair carved with a dragon and a unicorn. 'I don't know how to begin . . .'

'Tell me her name.' Ygrane sat in the chair beside him and put an understanding hand atop his clenched fists. 'She does have a name, this woman who has inflicted such hurt on a heart so young?'

'You know her name, mother.' Arthor searched her baffled eyes to see if she understood.

'Is it me?' she guessed, and a needle of anguish pierced her heart. The thought that her son's pain had its source in her decision to surrender him as an infant stabbed her – not with guilt, for she knew she had given him up for his own safety – rather, she felt the hurt of having been deprived the chance to love him as a child. 'Do you suffer because I sent you away so very young and forced you to live motherless?'

'No—' His voice withered to an agonized whisper, and he breathed the name that had cursed him. 'Morgeu – the woman who hurts me is your daughter, Morgeu, my sister.'

The Ghost in the Fog

Night in the north isles of Lot's domain carried tumbling sea fog out of the coves and up to the fir perches. Morgeu, wrapped in the pelage of minks, wandered the cold, chanting smoke, searching for her father's ghost, the soul of her child. A hungry moon, like a snuffed wick, dwindled in the west and vanished into phosphor depths.

'Morgeu – I am here,' a gruff voice called from the foggy dark among the shaggy trees. 'I am marked. Shield your eyes.'

'Father?' Morgeu called and groped through the vaporous night and knocked into a tree. 'Where are you?'

'Here.' Out of the emaciated starlight and shredded fog, Gorlois's ghost appeared, his face carved to a terrifying pattern – one eye set sideways at the center of his brow and in the empty socket where that eye should have been his mouth mewled, his chin yanked severely to one side by the displacement. 'Shield your eyes, daughter. I am marked by the Furor.'

Morgeu's breath left her in one hot gust of smoke that carried away a weak cry. 'By the gods! What has happened to you?'

'The Furor—' His pale voice faded at the memory of the pain. But the pain was gone now. In its stead, the future lay all unhidden, and by the strength of the Furor's strong eye he saw across the breadth of time into a future he did not recognize – city wards of glass spires and horseless wagons of bossed metal on roadways smooth as poured night.

And the stink, the caustic stench of the future burned his lungs . . .

'Father, father – what has become of you?' Morgeu's hands passed helplessly through the naked apparition.

Gorlois saw that time was an unavoidable straight road. Far off across the centuries, he witnessed domelike glares char the cities of glass to black outlines as though pieces of the sun had fallen to earth. He lowered his gaze from the blinding pain of apocalypse and focused closer to himself and his daughter Morgeu. Time seemed no straight road here in the fog and the essential light of the stars. Turning his head one way, he glimpsed his daughter glossed in sweat holding the bloody rag of a stillborn and seen from another tilted angle, the child thrived at her breast.

'I am come at the Furor's bidding,' Gorlois announced. 'I am come to serve the All-Seeing.'

At last, Morgeu understood. 'The Furor has marked you to see what is yet to be.' She stepped closer to the mangled visage of her father. 'Tell me, what do you see for me?'

'I see birth and death both.'

'Our future is yet to be decided,' she told him, her breath snapping smoke with her excitement. 'How we fulfill the unaccomplished will decide our future. You must go back to the Furor – let him guide you. Go back, father.'

Obediently, Gorlois stepped away into the fog and joined the darkness.

Berserkers

The salt works of Cawsand and the seaweed farms of Rameslie provided the most lucrative exports of the Dumnonii after the tin and silver mines, and Duke Marcus, and before him Duke Gorlois, had taken great care to provide the best defenses for those coastal towns. Warboats patroled the harbors and mounted soldiers stood sentinel on the sea bluffs, ever vigilant for the low-lying, flat-bottomed raiding sculls of the Saxons. No one expected an attack by land.

Hunched like beasts among the hedges and vetch that

congested the hills at the forest fringe above the two towns, several dozen storm raiders waited for noon. They were Wolf Warriors, devoted to the Furor and dedicated to dying in battle. Four nights before, shrouded by the new moon, they had landed on remote beaches and buried their boats in the dunes. Traveling only in darkness, they had reached the two bustling ports undetected.

At the moment that the sun attained its zenith, when the horror of their assault and the bravery of their sacrifice was most fully illuminated, the Wolf Warriors descended on their prey. They did not charge at first but merely strode down the hill paths, their heads high, red and gold manes brushed back by the sea breezes, war-axes carried casually across their shoulders. Naked but for thongs and sandals, they seemed mortally vulnerable.

Even when the boatwrights and net-weavers in the sandy lots behind the towns first spotted the Saxons and shouted alarms, the Wolf Warriors did not hurry their assault. Their relaxed approach to battle won them respect among the gods. The doom of Rameslie and Cawsand was foreordained by the very presence of the Wolves, and there was no need to squander their strength until what they had come to destroy was in their grasp.

The screaming townsfolk fled onto the strand, for the Wolves had fanned out to block all inland escape routes. The Furor had decreed that none were to be spared his killing frenzy save what the sea took for its own. Once within the town precincts, the Saxons smashed hearths and clay ovens and set fire to the cottages, the market stalls, and the dry docks. The mounted soldiers who charged down from the sea bluffs to defend the town rode into baffling smoke and whirling battleaxes.

The killing went swiftly. After hacking the legs of the blinded and confused horses and gutting the riders, the Wolves overturned the salt boilers, smashed the drying racks, and ran all howling and soot-streaked down upon the townsfolk, fishermen, and salt pedlars crowding into the oncoming tide.

To the Christians, the barbarous, bellowing hordes plunging out of the roiling vapors of the wind-whipped flames were a brimstone reckoning come to gather their souls to hell, and many died on their knees praying for salvation even as their heads flew from their shoulders.

By the time the warboats came to shore to engage the enemy, they had to shove through jammed shoals of corpses, the floating bodies of their families. The horror defeated them, and the Wolves easily punctured their hulls with their mighty axes and dragged the floundering sailors onto the beach by their hair, the better to flay their flesh for the war drums.

The Graal

Ygrane listened aghast to her son's account of Morgeu's deceptive seduction of him and the conception of their incest child. When he concluded and, with a sob, lay his shamed face in his hands atop the Round Table, she stood and walked away. To an elaborately carved cabinet she retreated and opened its mahogany doors of inlaid mother-of-pearl to retrieve from its velvet-padded interior the Holy Graal. The good Sisters of Arimathea – who were none other than the Nine Queens of Avalon – had bequeathed the sacred vessel to her and Uther on a Christmas morning sixteen years ago.

The slender goblet of gold-laced chrome contained within its precious metal exterior the actual glazed clay cup from which Yeshua ben Miriam had drunk wine in celebration of Passover and his coming sacrifice five centuries ago. The *Annwn*, the Fire Lords of supercelestial origin, had preserved the cup in an elegant covering of incorruptible chrome and gold filigree that somehow retained a magical charge of holy power. Ygrane prayed that this blessed magic would heal her son's acute suffering.

She placed the Graal in front of him, and even before he raised his head, King Arthor felt its grace. Like grape pressings darkening to wine in barrels, the squeezings of his heart – his memories of lust and shame – began to deepen, like a slow dusk, to something more soulful.

While he gazed at his stricken reflection in the mirroring surface of the Graal, his mother spoke softly to him of the Nine Queens. 'They dwell as spirit beings now, on Avalon, the ancient ceremonial site from where the Celtic gods once reigned before the Fauni drove them underground into the Dragon's lair. The *Annwn* – the angels of God – placed them there to witness the present, so that they may help change the soul of the future.' She brushed a tear from his smooth cheek. 'Someday, when you die, you will be installed there, and the eldest queen shall be set free to return to the rhythmic duration of death and rebirth. I swear this to you by all that is holy. You will represent these past ten thousand years of rule by kings, emperors, caesars, pharaohs, and chieftains.'

Arthor faced his mother and saw in her tristful stare the truth of what she said.

'You will serve the angels,' she said, 'and humankind for all that may remain of our future . . .'

'Until the Second Coming.' Arthor understood. 'The Apocalypse of The Revelation.'

'Which is what our enemies' god, the Furor, calls *Ragnarok*, the Twilight of the Gods.' She took his hand in a consoling grasp. 'So you see, your personal pain – the mistakes of the heart from your past *and* their consequence, however horrible – these are your personal suffering. They are the shadow cast by the light of your radiant being. You must accept them, Arthor. You must accept their shame and their hurt without allowing those terrible feelings to betray who you really are by swaying your actions.' She released his hand and placed hers upon his chest. 'Let that evil that is peculiarly your own remain here, confined within the borders of your heart.'

In a Dark Way

Rex Mundi walked the earth. Dagonet, Lord Monkey, Merlin, Azael, and a nameless Fire Lord drifted alertly within this gruesome amalgamated being's interior space. The Fire Lord and the demon Azael circled each other in a perpetual stand-off. The countervailing tension between them would turn them round about each other for a thousand millennia, and the magical strength that spun from them sustained the improbable shape of the Dark Prince.

Meanwhile, Merlin contemplated how to recover his own body from Gorlois. Dagonet gazed at the world, astonished to find himself so tall and so powerful. And Lord Monkey wondered what next he would eat.

Into the distances of the afternoon, Rex Mundi wandered, seeking to orient himself. Merlin, years before in his quest to find Uther Pendragon, had criss-crossed all of Britain, and he knew every vista in the land. *We are not far from Rameslie,* he observed from the rolling terrain and directed their attention to a field of sunlight between two ridges of aboriginal forest. *Through that notch, the seatown awaits. They make excellent fishcakes.*

Lord Monkey widened their stride at the news of food.

What will the townfolk make of uth? Dagonet inquired. *Are we not a tewible thight?* He glanced down at their hands, fleshed in leathery hide and thick, sparse wires of hair.

They are good, hard-working Christians, Merlin addressed Dagonet's concerns. *If we praise our Savior and cause no trouble, we will be accepted despite our unconventional aspect.*

With Lord Monkey's eagerness to reach his first meal since munching an apple in Avalon, Rex Mundi made swift progress along the neatherd's paths across the pastureland. By late afternoon, they climbed a knoll that overlooked Rameslie, and there confronted the grisly remains of the Wolves' slaughter. Black, smoldering ash outlined where the town had once stood. Scattered upon that dark field glowed dozens of pink melons – the scalped skulls of the townsfolk.

Lord Monkey and Dagonet skittered with fright and tried to run away, but Merlin's stronger will held them fast. 'This is the Furor's doing,' he spoke aloud, his voice dense with grief. 'He boldly challenges our new king.'

Let uth away, Merlin! Dagonet whinnied in terror. *The waiderth may yet be here!*

'Oh that they were, Dagonet,' Merlin droned with regret. 'Then you would see real devil's work.'

Vampyre

Morgeu rode by night. She drove a wagon south, determined to find the soul that had served her father and that she had chosen to quicken the child in her womb. She knew from the mangled apparition that she had seen of Gorlois that the Furor had marked him – and that meant that he was in the grasp of the north tribes. Only the land of the Picts to the north and the domain of the Cantii in the south-east were occupied by the Furor's people, and her trancework told her that the Picts did not hold him.

Though the highways were rife with potholes and slewed by the frosts of seventy winters and hazardous to ride by dark, Morgeu traveled fearlessly. The horse that pulled her wagon she endowed with night vision, and she herself scanned the landscape with eyes that shone crimson from their pupils. The very stones of the highway blazed up before her magic gaze.

By day, she pulled the wagon behind hedges or into a dense copse and slept. She dreamt the secret life of the unborn that swam soullessly within her. Under the dark archway of blood, she swam upstream toward the dream wall of the uterus, greedy to suck at the root-blood of the mothers that would mute its memories of the sea and the fish-thrash, eager to drink the salt-milk that would impart the knowledge it needed to be human . . .

On her third night of travel, a man pale as moonlight and with a courteous face stood in the roadway. The horse shied from him. Morgeu knew his morbid character at once. 'Finally!' She threw down the reins and sat back with a look of relief. 'I've been looking for you.'

'And I for you, lady in red.' The pale man coughed gently. 'Will you come down to me? Or shall I come to you?'

She beckoned with her ringed fingers. 'Do come.'

In an eyeflash, the man sat beside her, and the horse jolted with fright and rocked the tented wagon. Morgeu hushed it with a soft whistle. 'You have a commanding way with animals,' he complimented her.

Morgeu allowed a small smile. 'I have a way with all manner

of things.' She noticed that the shadowless man wore a beautiful tunic of a lost time, a white garment stitched with intercoiling serpents, leaping dolphins, and a large butterfly of the soul at the center of his breast – a burial garment. 'You are an old one.'

'Older than you can guess, lady.' He placed a cold hand on her thigh, and her whole body chilled.

'Oh, nothing is quite that old.' A bemused laugh spilled from her. 'I would guess you came to this frontier four centuries ago, with the second legion, *Legio Adiutrix*, under Agricola – but not as a commander or even a soldier.' She stared hard into his narrow, surprised face. 'You have the gentle countenance of a mercantile aristocrat. Have I surmised correctly, Terpillius?'

The ghostly man pulled away, and fangs glinted at the corners of his gaping mouth. 'What creature are you that reads souls?'

'I?' Morgeu reached out and firmly took the startled stranger's cold wrist in her hot hand. 'I am your mistress.'

Mother Mary, I have needed time to think of what to say to you after all that I learned from my mortal mother, Ygrane. She is a good woman, more fair of soul and face than I had dreamt since I first learned of her at Camelot. She loves your Son as I do. She lives as He has taught us. Her days are spent tending to the sick and the impoverished of the countryside about the fastness she has converted to an abbey. The Holy Graal has been entrusted to her, elaborately caparisoned in chrome and gold by the angels themselves. She is truly a woman of holiness. And yet – and yet, Mother Mary, she speaks to me of Avalon, the Isle of Apples, the Nine Queens and rebirth, the transmigration of souls – matters that seem more pagan than Christian. Though the angels themselves have set the Nine Queens to watch over us, these are pagan royalty. Ah, but then your Son has been with us only these past five centuries and the youngest of the Queens is over ten thousand years old. Perhaps, then, that is why our Father has chosen me to dwell among them when I die, to deliver to them the good news. But what of my soul? What of the Lord's promise of my salvation? Surely, that is vouchsafed me, even if I must dwell as a ghost among ghosts for thousands of years to come. Christians do not transmigrate, do we?

The priests say no. We are not reborn again and again among endless forms as the Celts believe. Forgive me, Mother Mary, for bringing you these worries. I know not where else to take them. If only Merlin were here with me. I fear he is dead. How else to explain his absence? He did not arrange for me to become king simply to abandon me. I must assume he is with you now. I am to fathom on my own the mysteries that Mother Ygrane shares with me — if only there were — time — to fathom these wonders. The invaders swarm along the coast. They know I am here among the Dumnonii, and they attack to challenge me. Pray for me, Mother Mary. Pray that God will grant me the clarity and strength to defend our island kingdom.

Marcus Bloodied

The massacres at Cawsand and Rameslie enraged Marcus Dumnonii, and he ignored King Arthor's pleas to counsel with him and the two chieftains, Lot and Kyner. Impatient to track down the Saxons who had destroyed his two most productive seatowns, he led a mounted force along the coast. Arthor shouted after him from the ramparts of Tintagel, but the Duke had not given his pledge and was not bound to honor that man-child's commands.

'We must follow him!' Cei insisted when Arthor, frowning darkly, came down the bastion's stone steps. 'Lead our troops!'

Arthor shook his head. 'The troops must rest. The march from the north has exhausted them.'

The experienced chiefs, Kyner and Lot, nodded in agreement with the king's sage assessment of his forces.

Cei threw his hands up with a disgruntled shout. 'Then what hope of winning the Duke's pledge if you leave him to fight his own battles? Think like a warrior, not like one of these tired old men.' He nodded cursorily to Kyner. 'Forgive me, father.'

'I'll not forgive such impudence!' Kyner shouted at his oafish son. 'The king is right. Marcus is not hunting down Foederatus troops. Those are berserkers out there. Wolf Warriors. They've not come to Britain to steal land but to die.'

'By nightfall, Marcus will feed the ravens,' Lot predicted

and turned to cross the courtyard to the barracks, where his clansmen anxiously awaited the command of their new king.

As Lot had foreseen, Marcus found little spoor of the raiders until late in the day. From out of the long light of the evening, the Wolves emerged from where they had hidden in the dunes. They had known that the destruction of the two ports would provoke an army of revenge, and they had read the land accurately enough to place themselves directly in its path at the hour of two worlds.

Marcus ordered his cavalry to charge along the high rimland above the sea plain and so sweep down lethally upon the Saxons. But the Wolves had anticipated this, and during their daylong wait for their escorts to Skyward House, they had patiently severed the hundreds of thick roots that secured the edge of the rimland to the forest beyond. Under the weight of the charging horses, the entire escarpment collapsed, sending horsemen toppling onto the plains below, where the Wolf Warriors waited with their honed axes.

With a shocked cry that emptied his lungs, Duke Marcus watched from the forest edge as horses and men tumbled through billowing sand and dirt to where the berserkers danced, their axes flashing in the scarlet light of day's end. He bolted forward, but he quickly saw the futility of his sacrifice and pulled back. He had committed the bulk of his force to the charge and all that remained were himself, the mounted drummers, and two surgeons.

Pacing his steed angrily on the high ground above the collapsed scarp, he watched through burning tears as the Wolves danced in the crimson light and left behind the broken shapes of his soldiers before disappearing in the sudden rush of dark.

The Furor's Man

Gorlois awoke still ensconced in Merlin's body, alert and brisk, but he found himself sitting in a pit naked, mired in feces and dead leaves. A cry from above yanked his attention to the top of the pit, where a red-bearded face glanced down at him and pulled away, shouting again in Saxon dialect, 'The Furor's Man is awake!'

One glance was enough for Gorlois to see into that man's private dream – Vagar of Gelmir's Clan, proud of his lance arm, fearful of betrayal by his damaged left knee . . .

The Lawspeaker appeared overhead, his bald head bobbing and leering with satisfaction. Images from his heart rushed through Gorlois, and he saw the brute chords of danger this man played on the instrument of his body – harrowing fasts and trance potions.

'Stand back, Hjuki the Lawspeaker,' Gorlois called and lifted his hands above his head. 'Stand back and pour the cisterns!'

The Lawspeaker moved out of sight, and a moment later, as Gorlois had foreseen, several large men stepped to the brink carrying big vats of water that they poured over him. The cascade rinsed away the fetor of grime that plastered him, and moments later, a knotted rope fell to his expectant hands and pulled him out of the pit.

The slow pulses of the sun beat in everything he saw, illuminating the deepest recesses. The Furor had marked his soul with the strong eye and had granted him the power to see the truth of everything he looked at. His upheld hands revealed the truth of himself: the ghost of a bold ravisher in flesh woven by Fire Lords, whom the Celts called *Annwn*, meaning *The Otherworld*, as if those radiant entities were not individual beings but manifestations of a supercelestial realm. And they were. He saw that. In the grain of Merlin's skin, he perceived their solitary, purposeful love for the Origin, the source of infinite energy from which this cosmos had emerged thousands of millions of years ago in an explosion of pure light so intense no form could exist at all until the cold, dark vacuum had chilled light to matter . . .

The Lawspeaker pulled Gorlois's hands from his staring eyes, and the guards scrubbed his body with pumice stone and lathery sponges and doused him with water scented with aromatic woodruff. While they dressed him in the Furor's colors – loose black trousers, orange bodice stitched with jet raven signs, a red jerkin with onyx buttons, and wolfskin boots – he gazed into the Furor's face among the soaring clouds. One arctic eye stared back. In its gray depths, he witnessed the future – the swarming hours of the days ahead, the journey north to the cluttered rivertown of Londinium, the surly, Persian eyes of Severus Syrax . . .

'Do not peer too deeply, Raven's Man,' the Lawspeaker advised. 'What you will see there will break you.'

Gorlois heeded that counsel and shifted his penetrating gaze across the broad face of the Furor to his other eye, the empty socket in whose blackness floated all mortal beings, a glittering dew on the great web of life, each creature reflecting its own small spark of original light within the darkness of death.

Saved by the Devil

Through the hazy morning mists, Marcus Dumnonii led back toward Tintagel those sorry few that remained of his warparty – two surgeons and several drummers. The drums had been left behind in the forest, where the survivors had lain under cover of darkness all night. They had feared that the berserkers who had slain their company would stalk them by starlight, and they all, including the Duke, had hobbled their horses and lain hidden under leaves farther away. At first light, they had untied their steeds and moved on.

Duke Marcus followed a longer route to the citadel, along a forest path, believing they were safer from sight of their enemies in the woods than along the coast. But the Duke was wrong. The Wolf Warriors had spent the night among the dunes and by false dawn had moved inland to kill whomever they crossed. They met Marcus in a grove drizzling with morning light.

The battle shouts of the Wolves defeated the helpless cries of the Duke's small party, and only the horses screamed louder as their legs broke under the slashing blows of heavy axes. The Duke plunged to the ground with his steed, sword raised high. He cried with shrill fervor for God's mercy when the fallen horse broke his left leg and pinned him under its dead weight. A berserker with the severed head of a drummer in one hand knocked the sword from his grasp with one swipe of his ax and brought the blade down in a flashing arc.

Before the keen edge could cut, a hand of leathery hide and wiry hair snatched the helve and twisted the ax from the Saxon's grip. The Duke, buckling in pain, saw a tall, hideous man with hackles of red hair, a bristly black beard, and a feral, almost bestial face. The monster yanked the berserker's arm from its socket with a wet, tearing noise. Marcus saw blood splatter across the sigil-marked robes of Merlin. Then, the pain of his broken leg blacked his mind.

Rex Mundi tore among the Wolf Warriors with savage speed and murderous fury. Merlin had released Azael from his circling bond with the Fire Lord, and the demon used Rex to make quick work of the Saxons. In moments, fourteen warriors lay mangled on the forest floor. Then, the wizard summoned Azael back into the magically assembled body he had created from Dagonet and Lord Monkey – but the demon would not obey. With an icy howl, Azael rushed off through the woods, bound to work ill against the king in Tintagel.

'Oh *gwief!*' Dagonet cried, sensing Azael's purpose.

'*Calm yourself,*' Merlin soothed. '*If we move quickly in the opposite direction from the king, Azael must follow – for if too much distance comes between us, our assembled body will fall apart, and the demon will become again the ashes of a dog. Come!*'

Dagonet and Merlin turned away from the broken bodies of the dead and the whimpering surgeons and drummers yet alive. With a lumbering gait, they moved Rex Mundi eastward, relying on the Fire Lord within to hold them together. The cries of the Christian survivors followed them a long way among the trees.

Knives Against the King

Azael had little time to work mischief before the retreating Rex Mundi lured him back into his circling stand-off with the Fire Lord. He reached into Tintagel with icicle fingers of fear and grabbed at the hearts of Lot's Celts. The motions of these small bits of awareness were easy to manipulate, and in moments, he had inflamed four warriors to a rabid hatred of the boy-king, the fool who despised their venerable faith and worshipped an alien, nailed god. Dark looks passed among them, and Azael gloated at the consequences he read there before he departed.

No murderous opportunity presented itself to the fervid Celts until midday. While the chiefs and their men gathered in the main hall to eat, with Kyner presiding over the Christians and Lot among the Daoine faithful, the young king sat in chapel with his mother and her nuns. A musty lingering of incense in the air steeled the four assassins to their grim intent, to end the influence of this foreign god, and they slipped silently through the burgundy shadows that fell from the leaded glass windows. Their footfalls muffled by the sussurant prayers of the nuns, two killers approached along each side of the dim tabernacle, knives bared, held low, ready to slash upward and gut their enemy.

The king had left his famous sword on the altar, where two small licks of flame in crimson lampions fluttered at either end. Unarmed, he knelt on a faldstool with Ygrane, who also would die for betraying the Daoine Síd and for abandoning her role as queen of a people far more ancient than the Romans. The nuns, absorbed in their prayers, paid no heed to the four half-naked intruders. The assassins strode through the chancel gate and descended on the kneeling couple. But before they could strike, a shadow stirred suddenly from the stillness as though one of the pieces of statuary had come to life.

Bedevere slid swiftly across the marble, inserting himself between the knives and their victims. In his one hand, he grasped a short sword that flashed in the dark air like a spurt of flame. Clanging sharply, two knives spun free and clattered to the floor. An agilely swift flourish of the short sword carved loops of reflected light with a viper's hiss and stalled the other two armed Celts in their tracks. Before they could flee, he jumped close enough to cut their throats. 'Knives!' he shouted, and the two remaining weapons clanked against the stone floor.

The alarmed shrieks of the nuns brought soldiers running from the castle ward, swords drawn. 'Shed no blood in this holy place!' King Arthor commanded. He strode to where Bedevere had grouped the four enraged Celts. 'Why?'

The ire in their cold eyes told him what their voices refused to say. When Lot arrived and ragefully ordered them taken into the courtyard, they exited tall with defiance.

'Brother!' Arthor called to Lot, and when the old warrior turned, said firmly, 'Do not take their lives. Release them from Tintagel and our service – unharmed.'

The Root-Blood

By day, Morgeu tended the horse that pulled her tented wagon, bathed herself in the chill creeks under the noon sun, ate what the orchards and vegetable crofts along the highway had to offer, and dozed under the trees. She kept Terpillius the vampyre inside the wagon, covered with loamy soil. At night, he rode beside her and told her amusing tales of Old Britain.

Occasionally, she let him roam for blood, but only with the stern understanding that he sate himself on Christians alone. He did not dare defy her, because she could read everything in his soul. The shadows spoke with her. And at her touch, his cold body either sang or cried.

Usually, she kept him close by and fed him with the root-blood of the soulless child in her womb. While she steered the wagon, he lay with his head in her lap, eyes closed, drawing hot strength directly from within her, from the source of the blood itself. On clear nights, he opened his eyes to the Great Bear, and his darkness matched the vacancies he saw there.

'That is the fear of all vampyres,' she replied to his thoughts. 'There is no place for you in the Happy Woods, no path to the Skyward House, no acceptance with the nailed god who preached love but who damns with hellfire. Only emptiness awaits at the end of your hunger.'

'I dream, I dream – emptiness would be sweet—'

'But not as sweet as blood, the warmth kindled by the star candles and forgotten in the seas for so very long.' She stroked his silken hair with one hand as she drove. 'Forgotten until the first jungles remembered and from stardust, from the iron seeds sown in the death throes of stars, grew the red vine, the root-blood you suckle. I know this. I have seen it.'

He trembled with immemorial passions to hear her speak so. And even if he could have fled her ensorceling grasp, he would not have. Eyes closed, he pressed his face against her womb, and her radiant warmth embraced him as she embraced her soulless child, filling his body with unworldly joy. Many nights of travel passed before he even thought to ask, 'Why do you cosset me, mistress? Why have you taken me from my place in the forests of the north?'

'We have a work to do, Terpillius.' Her small, black eyes hardened like bits of coal. 'A work of blood. Hot, wet work.'

'And when the work is done, mistress?' He did not dare open his eyes, for fear of the evil, indifferent smile he would see. 'What will become of us?'

'Become?' Her voice carried a chill laugh. 'That word bespeaks a future. And for vampyres there is no such thing.'

Four hundred hours of autumn with her, after four hundred years without her were enough to assuage his fears. He kept his eyes closed and his face pressed to the root-blood, to the tinier world within her, the forever world before time, when all life was a vampyre.

Secret House

'Mother, why did Lot's men want to kill me?' Arthor somberly asked Ygrane that evening when they were alone on the western terrace with the Round Table and the Graal. 'You must know their minds. You were once their queen.'

Ygrane rose from where she had been sitting next to her son, talking about his father, Uther Pendragon. She walked to the balustrade and watched the sun finding its way into the sea. 'Merlin and I thought it best you were reared a Christian. But if you are to rule the Celts as well as the Britons, you must find in yourself what is more ancient than your faith.'

'You – an abbess – instruct me to seek the pagan?' Arthor asked with open disbelief. 'Mother, I have been inside the hollow hills. I have seen the faerïe, conversed with the dwarf Brokk who crafted Excalibur, and even confronted the Furor himself. But I tell you, these are all created beings of our uncreated and nameless God, the God of Moses – God the Father of our Savior. This is our faith, the faith expounded in the gospels of the Apostles. It is that faith that guides me – not pagan lore.'

She faced him across the Round Table, her eyes like a green fire in the dying light – and her white vestments might as well have been the worship robes of a priestess. 'You are my son and king of the people for whom I once served as queen, and so I speak to you from a higher place than faith.'

'*Higher* than faith?' Arthor reared forward, dizzy with incredulity. 'What could possibly be higher than our faith?'

'God – God Himself.'

Arthor blinked. 'Mother, you speak heresy.'

'Listen to me, son. Faith is learned. But our souls are given. You carry within you the soul of Cuchulain, the greatest warrior of the Celts. God wills for you to reign as a Christian king. And yet, in your soul you carry lifetimes of a more ancient faith.'

'Lifetimes?' Arthor blew a gust of surprise. 'Mother, listen to yourself. You sound like some blasphemous gnostic. We are each of us one life, one soul given to the glory of God.'

'This is true, Arthor. But there is a greater truth.'

'Truth – yes.' He sighed, recalling the long hours of reading and discussing philosophy that Kyner had required of both him and Cei. 'Truth has many sides. But what is the greater truth than the one life we have for God?'

'The destiny He gives to each one of us is unique and carries its own truth. That is the secret house of your spirit, greater than the abode of your soul. The soul needs a body. But the spirit moves like the wind and belongs solely to God.' She walked around the table and sat down beside him again. 'Your destiny is to serve the Christians as well as the Celts of the Old Way. As your mother, it is my destiny to show you both ways. With Merlin's and Kyner's help, you have lived as a Christian. Now, it is time for me to show you the older ways.

God is God of all. To serve Him, you must open your heart to everyone.'

'What do you expect me to do, mother?' Arthor frowned. 'I will not defy the teachings of our Savior.'

'I would never ask that of you.' She took his chin in her hand. 'But I do require you to fulfill his greatest teaching. While you are here, before you depart, I want you to know love.'

Mother Mary, I am troubled by what I hear from your servant, my mother Ygrane. I am no theologian. What do I know of our Father's will but what He reveals to me through the Holy Spirit? Yet, if I am to be king of all Britain, I must serve the pagan Celts as well as the Christians. I thought I could serve them by bringing to them the good news of our Savior. But my mother speaks of their faith as more ancient, as if Jesus had never walked among us and refuted the old ways of blood sacrifice with his own blood. There is much I must ponder and so little time for reflection. My days are consumed from dawn till midnight with war councils. Soon I must lead what forces I have against invaders who give their lives freely and fiercely for what they believe. Pray for my protection, Mother Mary — not for my sake but for those whom I serve that I may continue to protect them from the ferocity of our enemies.

God Finds Her Champion

Durnovaria, a sizeable town of green and blue tile roofs, stood at the intersection of several Roman roads in the Celtic domain of the Durotriges. Though the neighboring Dumnonii, Duke Marcus's subjects to the west, had been Christian for generations, Durnovaria and the surrounding countryside harbored ancient enclaves where people still worshiped the Daoine Síd and the Fauni. Chief among these sites was Maiden Castle, whose gigantic earthwork entrenchments and ramparts enclosed a temple on a hillcrest devoted to the goddess Aradia.

Rex Mundi stood among the aspen trees that surrounded Aradia's temple, listening for prophecy in the whispering leaves. Merlin had directed their assembled form to this summit, hoping to detect some sign of where Gorlois had taken the wizard's body. The telluric energies of this sacred location were powerful, no doubt the reason why the old tribes had first built settlements upon this ceremonial ground thousands of years ago. While Merlin listened and Dagonet looked out beyond the temple's earth walls at the farm fields and Lord Monkey fidgeted, yearning for fruit, the Fire Lord broke loose from his circle-turning stand-off with the demon Azael.

Azael had no strength for voice – all his power was consumed in holding the assemblage together – yet his scream tore like claws through Merlin, Dagonet, and Lord Monkey. Rex Mundi fell to his knees with a howl. *What ith happening?* Dagonet bawled. *We die!*

We are not dying – not yet, Merlin assured his companion. *The Fire Lord has left us, left Azael to hold us together. But fear not. The demon will keep Rex whole. If he does not, he will revert to a dead dog and then can only slowly rebuild himself from ashes.*

But it hurth! Dagonet cried. And it did indeed, for without the Fire Lord to counterbalance the demon, Azael's pain was unmitigated: the mortals experienced the sundering cold of the vacuum in which the celestial orbs spun, the stabbing cold that assailed demons and Fire Lords alike since they fell from heaven.

The Fire Lord suffered, too. As with all who had been flung into the darkness of creation when they followed God out of heaven, he knew pain. But that ceaseless agony did not embitter him as it did the demons, who had flung away their light so they would hurt less. The Fire Lords embraced their burning pain all the more tightly and suffered worse than demons, because they believed that the radiant pieces of heaven they still carried would eventually lead them back home.

For now, the Fire Lord's light led him to Her, to God, who needed a champion for a moment. She had arranged an open grave for one of her most devoted – a woman worshiper in the temple. But the worshiper's husband was angry and would not let his wife go in peace. God summoned the Fire Lord to still the husband's cries with his warmth. The man's momentary smile when he experienced the angel's caress was all the dying woman needed to serenely release her body and rejoin the ever-turning cycle of coming and going.

Burning Isca

Purple storm winds blew the invaders' small boats up the Exe river and past the frustrated coastal defenders, who were helpless against the surging waves and torrential rain. Protected by the Furor and their own peerless maritime skills, the Saxons swept along the eastern banks of the river ten miles without a single arrow flying against them, and the storm front flung them into the port city of Isca Dumnoniorum, Duke Marcus's largest harbor.

The dock workers fought to protect their wharves and their homes but were no match for the ferocity of the Furor's troops. With the tempest at their backs, the Saxons clambered onto the moored ships, hacked their way across the harbor with their big axes and small, lethal throwing-hatchets, and set fire to the piers. Even as the attackers mounted the Roman walls that separated the anchorage from the town, the wind-whipped flames preceded them.

Duke Marcus saw the scarlet glow of the burning port from the hamlet of Neptune's Toes, where he had been carried by the surgeons after their ambush in the forest. Cei arrived the next day, shortly after heralds delivered grisly reports of the sacking of Isca and the slaughter of hundreds: Their headless corpses had been strung upside down from the high arches of the aqueducts that delivered irrigation water to the outlying farmlands – estates that now quailed in horror, awaiting the arrival of the brutal conquerors.

'Where is your brother?' Marcus shouted at the sight of Cei, and only the pain of his broken leg restrained him from lunging at the large Celt. 'I've lost three towns! People will *starve* this winter for what I've lost! Arthor dines with his mother while people are dying. Dying! Do you hear me, you big oaf?'

'My lord duke—' Cei struggled for what to say in the face of this righteous rage. At the news of Marcus's defeat, Arthor had dispatched him to escort the duke safely back to Tintagel, but Cei could see that this commander wanted battle plans, not retreat. 'At least you are alive and will lead your men again . . .'

'Do you know why I'm alive?' Marcus thrashed upright from the pallet where he lay on the olive-tree-arbored terrace overlooking a bay of tiny islets, the toes of Neptune. 'I live because Merlin saved me. You go back to Tintagel and tell your brother that he has to do better than send a wizard too late to save my troops. A wizard who looks possessed by Satan! If Arthor wants my pledge, he must commit more than magic to our cause. He must fight our enemies with strategy and sword!' Marcus fell back, his blond hair scattering like a veil over his face. 'Bring soldiers, not devils.'

Cei left the terrace, and on his way across the mosaic courtyard of the old villa, a surgeon accosted him. 'Lord Seneschal – tell the king that Duke Marcus speaks sooth. I saw with my own eyes – the wizard Merlin belongs to Satan now.'

A Talk with the King
'How can they say our wizard belongs to Satan when he saved their lives?' Arthor retorted after Cei relayed the news from Neptune's Toes. 'Is it the Devil's business now to spare Christians from the Saxon's ax?'

Cei shrugged. 'Marcus is angry. He lost many lives . . .'

'I am angry, too, brother.' Arthor sat on a black rock under the seacliffs, where the booming surf assured a private conversation. 'Lot's four men who tried to kill me, they've been found dead in the woods north of here.'

Cei cocked his head, as if to contemplate this. 'A wildwood gang must have fallen upon them.'

'No, Cei.' Arthor held his stepbrother fast with a harsh stare. 'You killed them. I saw the bodies. They were large men but they took downward blows from a bigger man.'

'A mounted warrior . . .'

'Silence, Cei!' Arthor stood up, hands fisted at his side. 'Do you think me a simpleton? There were no horse tracks.

You waited for those men among the trees – and you killed them.'

'I slew them fairly.' Cei's broad face darkened at the accusation of foul play. 'Lot left them their swords. I stood against them alone.'

'And you killed them – against my orders.'

Cei looked to either side, as if the searocks themselves would answer in his defense. 'They deserved to die. They tried to murder you! And in the chapel, no less!'

'And your judgement is greater than my command, is that it, Cei?' Arthor stood close to the large man. 'I am your king.'

'Well, yes, of course . . .' Cei looked perplexed, then angry. 'Why do you think I confronted them? They raised knives against the king! Am I not your seneschal? Am I to abide treachery?'

'Cei! Brother Cei!' Arthor's irate stare softened, and he shook his head sadly. 'We are not to rule by power alone, you and I, nor any in our court. Don't you see? Before us, Rome. Before Rome, the Chieftains. All men, who ruled by might of arms and terror. But we have a chance now for something greater.'

'Those men would have gathered others to oppose you.'

'Those men would have spoken of mercy when asked how they survived a failed attempt on my person.' Arthor put his hands on Cei's shoulders. 'Your heart acted for me, and I love you for that. But your heart must give more to the world henceforth. We are not Romans or Chieftains. We are Christians. We will not rule by the sword but by love. Do you accept this from me, brother?'

An expression of deep thought closed Cei's face to a frown. 'You are my king. I must accept what you say.'

'But you do not believe it is good, do you? Speak to it.'

Cei shook his head. 'No, Arthor. Love is for priests and mothers. For a warrior, it is deadly. Once he was delivered into the hands of the centurions, what good was love for our Savior? And, brother, if you think we are not already in the hands of our enemies, you *are* a simpleton.'

Nynyve

King Arthor remained on the beach after Cei departed. He sat engrossed in thought about how a Christian, commanded to love even his enemies, could possibly reign as king, especially beset by foes determined to murder the very people under his protection. When he saw Bedevere stand up from where he hunkered among the boulders, he thought perhaps Cei had returned to apologize for stalking off. But the figure who appeared with Bedevere was a woman of Celtic height and complexion, pale-skinned with cinnamon hair. She wore a traditional *gwn*, a diaphanous green skirt that fell to her ankles but left her breasts bare.

With a wave, Arthor beckoned her to him. The sight of her half-nakedness did not perturb him even slightly, for this custom had persisted among rustic Celtic women throughout the land and was not considered provocative. Yet, his ears and cheeks did flush crimson at the sight of her tall beauty and no clansmen in sight to watch over her. Such brazenness was indeed startling, and Arthor's fifteen-year-old heart beat hard with lurid surprise.

'My lady – where is your escort?' the king asked as she strode directly toward him, her arms open to embrace him.

'The king is my escort,' she spoke in deep-throated Gaelic, putting her arms on his arms and bending one knee before him. 'No harm can come upon me in his care.'

Arthor gently pulled her upright and gazed with undisguised ardor into her hazel eyes, the moonlight of her skin, the deepening sunset in her long, softly curling hair. 'You are too lovely a maiden to have come from anywhere without escort.'

'I have not come from anywhere,' she replied, earnestly studying his boyish features and his manly stature. 'I have always been here. Your mother sent me to you. I am to instruct you in Celtic ways. Did she not tell you? I am Nynyve of the Lake.'

The dulcet sound of her voice reached through the darkness inside him like the stinging light of stars. Her beauty, so perfect, so unmarred by even a single freckle, seemed almost supernatural. 'Are you an enchantress?'

Nynyve laughed, a velvet laugh enclosing him in its softness.

'No. I mean that seriously.' He pried her arms from his, and anxiety pinched his stare. 'Is this some magic trick of Morgeu's? Is it? You'll not deceive me twice, sister. Not twice!' Angrily, he hooked his arms around her legs and shoulders and swooped her off her feet.

'What are you doing?' she asked, frightened.

'Salt!' he gnashed, striding across the wet sand. 'Salt will break the illusion.' Into the sea he carried her, turning his back against the foaming surf. Holding her tightly, he bent his knees to dunk them both beneath the waves. When he lifted her sputtering out of the frothing water and saw that her body had not shapeshifted and her face remained as lovely under a web of wet hair as before he had immersed her, he released her. Contritely, he knelt in the sea and let the waves beat him.

Mother Mary, news has come to me that Merlin lives, yet is possessed of Satan. Can this be true? If so, I must trust to you and your Son to free him from the great adversary – as I must trust you to liberate my brother's heart from his murderous inclinations. I am frightened for Cei. He is so strong in body and in faith and still so weak of temperament. Merlin possessed by evil, Cei owned by ferocity, Marcus wounded and irate at me for not plunging my men into battle, and the invaders swarming ashore in greater numbers daily. Mother Mary, I thought I'd go mad today, balked about by such troubles! And then, on the beach, I met a woman of such exceeding beauty and charm, I forgot my worries. Yet, even with her, a deeper worry asserted itself. I was certain she was an illusion. I dunked her in the sea to dispel my suspicion, and she fled from me – laughing. I feel so foolish. Morgeu has scarred my soul, Mother Mary. I trust no woman. I doubt even the kind words of my own mother, an abbess herself. My sword, that I know. Our preparations for war are almost complete, and soon I can give myself to what I trust most. And if I survive, if I save the duke's realm from the invaders, I must kneel before my mother as I am kneeling before you now. I must pray with her for forgiveness of my sin of lust. I must pray that your Son, who lived and died for love, will lift this burden from my heart that I may at least learn to love as other men.

Vampyre in the Chapel

At sunset, Morgeu's tented wagon pulled up to a chapel on a hill overlooking Watling Street, not far from Verulamium. A dozen worshipers sat in the pews, chanting vespers, when the heavy oak door blew open and Morgeu entered with a gust of autumn chill and pouring leaves. 'Out!' she shouted. 'Leave this place at once!'

The congregation gazed appalled at the intruder as she strode down the aisle, red robes blustering in a stiff night wind. The flames of altar candles jumped, gasped, and died at her approach.

'Out!' she screamed again, shoving the priest aside from the wood pulpit and seizing the rosewood crucifix from atop the sacristy behind the altar. 'Out or be damned!'

Most of the communicants quickly exited, but a few farmers remained, unwilling to forsake their worship for a wild woman. When she smashed the crucifix to splinters against the altar, they leaped to their feet. 'She's *wicca* – and mad!'

'*Wicca* I am!' she shouted at them. 'But mad am I?' She showed her small teeth in a grimacing smile. 'At this moment, King Wesc sends his storm raiders to raze your harvest fields – and you sit here praying to a god who killed the son that preached love. Ha!'

Alarmed by her curse, the farmers clambered over the pews and ran out the door. Only the priest remained, a small, bald man with wide ears and kindly eyes, his hands tucked into his brown cassock. 'Daughter, you bring your rage to a place of peace.'

'This is not a place of peace, you dolt.' Morgeu kicked over the wooden altar. 'This is the shrine to Hela, Queen of the Dead. War chants belong here. You desecrate her sacred province.'

'Calm yourself, daughter.' The priest showed her his empty hands. 'Once a pagan shrine did occupy this hill. But it has been cleansed of that infernal history generations ago.'

'Cleansed, eh?' She stamped her foot, and darkness filled

the chapel as the sun dipped under the horizon. 'Life cannot cleanse death. It is death that cleanses life.'

'You are not well.' The priest took her arm and felt the cold, rigid strength of it. 'Come with me to my hut. I have wine and bread. We will eat together, and you will tell me of Hela.'

'No.' In the dark, she had the stout bearing of a man. 'Leave at once or, I swear by all you hold unholy, you shall be damned.'

'I belong here,' the priest said softly. 'I cannot leave unless you come . . .' He stopped speaking. A man stood in the doorway with eyes lucent as a cat's – and a white shadow that shivered on the ground before him like teeming starlight. 'Come in, brother.'

'I am here,' the vampyre said, standing so suddenly beside the priest that the cleric started and cried aloud his last mortal words, 'My God!'

The Furor in Londinium

Of course the rain fell heavily when he arrived and lightning lashed the sky. He came through the south gate of the city with the drovers bringing their culled herds to market. He carried no weapon and he appeared very old, and so none of the guards bothered to question him. Along the Avenue of the Centurions, with the rain splashing off his floppy-brimmed leather hat, he proceeded directly to the majestic steps of the governor's palace.

Severus Syrax, *magister militum* of Londinium, sat in the throne room among columns of pink marble and statues of emperors when a herald announced, 'The wizard Merlin begs an audience with you, my lord.'

Syrax stiffened, surprised by the sudden arrival of the demon-sorcerer. He dismissed the accountants and clerks who had been reviewing with him the city's autumnal stores of grain and livestock, and he summoned two priests and the full contingent of his armored personal guard before he gestured for the wizard to be brought in.

Even without his famous midnight-blue robes and conical hat, Merlin's long, sallow skull and dragon-socket eyes identified him to the warlord. 'Stand well back from me, demon, and say what you have come to say.'

Gorlois smiled with savage glee at the sight of his former comrade-in-arms. The arrogant coxcomb had not changed one whit. He still obviously spent more time trimming his Persian-style beard and coiffing his curls than drilling his troops or reviewing the battlements. 'I have come to speak on behalf of King Wesc.'

'The Saxon bloodsucker?' Syrax leaned forward on the satin squabs of the marble throne to be certain that this was indeed the wizard. He had been deceived before by this shapeshifter. 'I thought you'd found your champion in that beardless brute Arthor.'

Gorlois had never seen Arthor, yet the Furor's vision compelled a recognition. *That whore-son begot on my wife by another man! His father was the weakling brother of the Roman warlord I died defending!* His personal rage whisked away before the power of the Furor, and he spoke with the voice that the Lawspeaker had instilled in him: 'Arthor is far away in the west, beleaguered by Wolf Warriors. His future is doubtful. I must do what I can to bring peace to this island. And so I speak for King Wesc and the Foederatus.'

'I've paid my annual tribute to the damnable Foederatus!' Syrax soundly banged his fist on the arm of the throne. 'I won't pay another coin. Not a single coin!'

'Your tribute has won you peace here in Londinium,' Gorlois continued to relay the message from the Furor. 'The Foederatus have left your fields and fisheries unmolested. Now King Wesc wishes to extend this Pax Foederatus westward, to other Roman *coloniae* – and for your role as his legate *he* will pay *you* gold.'

Fight for the Coast
Ocean light glinted from the brass fittings of the mounted warriors that King Arthor led on patrol along the winding

coast road. Inland, Kyner and Lot had fanned out with their troops to clear the countryside of roving Wolf Warriors and wildwood gangs. Their mutual destination was Neptune's Toes, where Marcus would join their forces as counselor, his injury precluding his riding into battle.

The troops that Arthor led were the Duke's, and they displayed the full regalia of Roman soldiers. The impressive sight of them in their polished helmets and flexible body armor of metal strips filled the boy with pride to be at their head. As a warrior of Kyner's clan, Arthor had worn a second-hand helmet purchased from an itinerant armorer. His cuirasse had been scuffed leather. And only on diplomatic visits with his stepfather to Roman courts across Gaul had he seen soldiers wearing about their waist the sporran of metal-bound thongs that now his foot soldiers wore.

Bedevere had shown the young king how to don Roman battle gear and also how to command an imperial army. As a clan warrior, Arthor had always before ridden to combat in small squads, camping in the forest and sleeping under strewn leaves. The caravan trek to the north had been the largest expedition he had ever undertaken. And never had he ridden before an entire cavalry wing and infantrymen trained in legionary tactics.

At nightfall, the regularity of the army's encampments left Arthor agog. Each soldier carried two stakes for use as a palisade inside the ditch that was dug by them for the night. As if a mirage forming from the twilight, garrison tents rose within a fortified perimeter. Scouts delivered reports from the territory that would be covered by the next day's march, and Arthor learned from the Duke's commanders how to deploy the troops to meet each day's challenges.

Battles raged frequently and tediously among the numerous coves and estuaries along the rocky coast. And much as Arthor bridled to lead the efficient troops in their flexible body armor and closely packed, disciplined ranks, Bedevere insisted that the king remain on the hilltops among the other commanders, the better to learn the tactics and strategy necessary to head an army.

Marcus's commanders would just as soon have seen the rustic boy-king rush off to battle as have had to explain to him every small detail of their warplans. But the Duke, out of courtesy to Ygrane, a holy woman much revered in his province and the widow of his former lord, Uther Pendragon, had given orders that Arthor was to be allowed command position in the ranks – but given no genuine authority.

'They treat me like a boy,' Arthor complained to Bedevere at night, alone in the camp's one regal purple tent. 'I've fought Saxons, Jutes *and* Angles, and I know their strengths and weaknesses. I'm no dolt with a sword.'

'Certainly not, sire.' Bedevere snuffed the canopy oil lamp and paused before exiting. 'But you must remember that Marcus has not given his pledge. In his eyes – and in truth, my lord – you *are* yet a boy. If you can accept this, you may survive to manhood and find that you have become a king in more than just title.'

Wanderings

The souls of Merlin, Dagonet, and Lord Monkey suffered within the assembled form of Rex Mundi as the demon Azael and the Fire Lord alternately abandoned them to fulfill themselves. When the Fire Lord broke away to accomplish the tasks that God set for him, the rages of the demon harrowed the trapped souls. And during the intervals when the demon left the angel to hold together the magical body, everyone burned with insatiable yearning for heaven.

End thith tewible thuffewing! Dagonet pleaded, and Lord Monkey's animal cries sharpened.

But Merlin would not use the gems from the Otherworld that he carried in the pockets of the robe to break the magic he had wrought. Exiled again to the dwarf's body, he would never find his way back to his own flesh. As Rex Mundi, between bouts of demonic despair and angelic longing, there was clarity. While Azael and the Fire Lord mutely circled each other, the wizard commanded Dagonet to silence, mesmerically eased Lord Monkey to sleep, and trancefully searched for his own flesh.

Merlin sensed his body far to the east and continued to direct Rex Mundi to travel in that direction. But the continual digressions of Azael and the Fire Lord sent the conglomerate body reeling off in unexpected directions. Avoiding all settlements, the tall creature of horrid aspect followed old dry creek beds, roadside ditches screened by thornbrush, and drear forest paths. Berries and tubers provided sustenance when the cultivated fields and orchards stood empty. Large animals instinctively avoided the supernatural being. And only the most foolhardy and desperate brigands dared accost him.

An arrow whistled among the trees, aimed for Rex Mundi's cloaked breast, and the hairy, leathern hand snatched it out of the air. The archer thrashed away through the underbrush. An oafish farmer, driven mad by the Saxon plundering of his croft and murder of his family, slashed at the gruesome wanderer with a tree limb. It broke like punk wood across the broad back and the glare of rage in the terrible face that turned around set the madman's insanity deeper in his brain.

Merlin did not allow the monkey soul or the demon to take human life except when the assailants themselves offered the certainty of threat to other people. Shrieking monkey fury, Rex Mundi leaped among encamped gangs of mercenaries and bandits. His blows blurred with lethal speed, and he spun among the foes of life like a whirlwind of death.

These murderous episodes were rare. Rex Mundi wandered mostly alone through the autumn countryside, accompanied only by windy rain and falling leaves.

Haunting Verulamium

Morgeu reverted the chapel outside Verulamium to a shrine for worship of Hela, Goddess of Death. Several other chapels occupied hills and knolls elsewhere around the town, and the enchantress felt that the Christians would reasonably abandon their claim on her temple – once enough of the townspeople who returned were sacrificed to the Goddess.

Church elders came by daylight with pikes and lances to drive the witch from their chapel, and a ferocious bear descended from the forest and intercepted them on the hill path. The slashing paws slew four men and maimed two others before the giant ursine lumbered back into the dark woods. That night, the survivors came bearing torches, accompanied by a gang of mercenaries armed with swords and two bows with a quiver of arrows to share between them. Out of the clear sky, lightning flashed and struck with explosive force in their midst at the exact spot of the bear attack. The gang scattered, and Terpillius stalked them on the dark hillside, his bloodless face leering suddenly into torchlight before his fangs struck.

Samhain, the new year of the ancient calendar, saw the arrival of an exorcist from Lindum. Accompanied by four armed men from Londinium, he came at noon to the possessed chapel bearing a venerable text, holy relics, and a phial of water from the Jordan blessed by the pope himself. He found Morgeu seated on the earthen floor, the pews shoved to the walls and carved with pagan symbols – spirals, glyphs of horned dancers, pentagrams.

'By the mundane power of the Holy Father in Ravenna and the celestial glory of God Most High and His only begotten Son . . .'

'You trespass on ground consecrated to Hela,' she warned the stout, long-haired priest in the scarlet vestment of papal authority. 'And you do so on the one day of the year when Hela opens the gates of Sleet Den, her asylum for the wicked dead. Flee at once! Flee and spare yourselves the wrath of the Death Goddess!'

Three of the armed escort turned and ran, alarmed by the unnatural timbre of the witch's voice and the eerie pallor in the cold chapel. On the hill path, the earth gave out beneath them, and they plunged out of sight, their screams echoing weirdly from the sky above.

'Ah, too late.' Morgeu traced a sigil in the dirt, a wavery snakeline, and small blue flames fluttered out of the ground, almost invisible in the daylight. 'The remaining two of you may die screaming with your companions – or you may stay and serve me.'

The phial slipped from the trembling hand of the exorcist and a splash from the River Jordan burst to vapors that rose into a cadaverous face. Shrieking, the priest fled the chapel, his scarlet robes erupting with a dull roar into flames. The conflagration consumed him, yet he kept running. Though his flesh melted to black smoke, his bones exploded from the heat, and his marrow lay on the earth bubbling like tar, he ran all the way back to Verulamium, where his ghost was heard wailing for days among the lanes and alleys and in the water pipes and sewer drains.

A Forest Tryst

Nynyve found King Arthor in the last golden hour of day practicing swordplay with a sergeant in scale armor. At the sight of her standing alone at the forest edge, beyond the field where the army dug the night trenches, he executed a double-feint parry and deftly lifted the sergeant's weapon from his hand.

'He's a remarkable swordsman,' the battle-scarred sergeant reluctantly acknowledged to Bedevere as he watched the youth stride away. 'Now where is he going? I want the boy to teach me that nimble double pass. I've never seen the likes of it.'

'Sire!' Bedevere called, but Arthor paid him no heed. As Ygrane had warned the one-armed soldier before he departed Tintagel, 'Keep a close eye on my son, steward. Each of his feet walks a different road, one of this world, one of the other.'

'Lady — what are you doing here, so far from Tintagel?' In the rusted light of the autumn forest, she seemed to possess a golden aura. 'These woods are infested with murderous men.'

'You departed Tintagel before I could bid you farewell,' she said in a voice languorous as seasmoke.

He put both hands on her shoulders to feel for himself that she was not an apparition. 'It was you who fled without courtesy that first day on the beach . . .'

'Courtesy!' Her face showed affrontedness yet her hazel eyes smiled. 'You dunked me in the sea! I fled before you inflicted further discourtesy upon me.'

'Lady, I could never act discourteously with you.' He squeezed her shoulders and stepped back. 'I had to know you were not an enchantment. Yet even now, finding you here alone – I think you cannot be other than an enchantress. How else could you . . .'

'Travel so far unmolested?' She turned and pointed through the long slants of forest light to where four horsemen with waist-long hair and buckskin trousers sat upon their grazing mounts – large, fierce Celtic warriors wearing golden torcs and long swords strapped to their naked backs. 'My *fiana*.'

'*Fiana* serve the Celt queen . . .' Arthor's jaw dropped as comprehension finally opened in him. 'You are my mother's successor . . . the queen of the pagan Celts!'

'I am queen,' she acknowledged with a small smile.

'But you're not much older than I . . . and yet a *queen*?'

'I am older than I appear.' She tossed back her cinnamon curls. 'And besides, queens are not chosen for their age or their wisdom but their kinship with the faerïe. You know this.'

'So I have heard.'

'Your mother was taken as a child from the hills to serve the druids. I am somewhat older. Yet the faerïe obey me.' She moved away. 'And next time we meet, we shall see how this matters between us.'

Arthor did not try to stop her from leaving, not with her four stern warriors glaring at him from among the sun's fiery rays.

The Invasion
The sun had not yet risen, and the British camp was already busy preparing for the day's march when the scouts came charging through the low skein of mist in the forest. 'Bowmen!' they reported. 'Barges of bowmen deploying off Oyster Shoals and occupying Fenland and White Hart!'

'Saxons abhor the bow,' one of the commanders muttered. 'It's beneath their savage dignity to slay their enemies at a distance. These archers are Foederatus troops – the pagan alliance that imitates Roman battle strategies. If that's true, we've bloody days ahead of us.'

By midday, the Duke's army knew the scouts' reports were entirely accurate. Archers held the hummocks and knolls of Fenland and the hills of White Hart, effectively blocking Arthor's advance. Messengers hurried north to summon Kyner and Lot from the high woods, and birds were dispatched east to announce the Foederatus invasion to the warlords of the Midlands and plead for their reinforcements.

'That help is days away, if those warlords will deign to help me at all,' Arthor informed the commanders in the war tent. 'Meanwhile, Duke Marcus is stranded at Neptune's Toes, unable to ride and now cut off from us by the Foederatus. I will go to him with a warband and ensure his safety. He is under my protection, and I cannot leave him to the mercy of our enemies.'

The commanders mumbled their agreement, indifferent to the fate of this untried boy-king and frustrated in their attempts to agree upon any other way to retrieve their Duke. But Bedevere protested, 'The Duke has put himself in this jeopardy by ignoring our war counsel at Tintagel. For you to risk your life riding through the enemy's lines is foolhardy at best, maybe fatal.'

'I am high king of Britain,' Arthor stated, moving his steady gaze slowly among the commanders. 'My brother-in-arms has behaved foolishly and by ignoring my command is now in peril of his life. Yet, it is to be remembered that I am a king of mercy, a Christian king, and I forgive him for not trusting me, a man less than half his age. He still remains under my protection. I will return him to you safely.'

Bedevere waited until Arthor exited the war tent before pulling him sharply aside. 'Sire, the Foederatus know you are here. That is why they are staging a full-scale invasion. If we ride out among them, you will surely die.'

Arthor unclasped the corselet of polished metal bands. 'We leave our fancy armor behind for this ride, Bedevere. I want eight of the best horsemen in the Duke's army, mounted archers all – and every one a volunteer. Go! Quickly! We must cross Fenland and enter the forest before dark.'

The warband rode north while the army advanced east to engage the entrenched invaders. Arthor led the riders dressed as a common archer in brown leggings, black tunic of padded quilt, and a recurved Persian bow slung across his back, Excalibur at his side. None of the Furor's men saw their crossing of Fenland behind the screen of the advancing phalanx, and by nightfall Arthor's warband flitted like shadows into the gloomy autumn forest.

Demons and Angels
While Rex Mundi slept in a ditch under stars troweled by racks of cloud, Azael challenged the Fire Lord. 'Tell me again why you persist in opposing us?'

The Fire Lord made no reply, tall and radiant against the darkness of the night.

'We come from the same place, you and I,' Azael went on, almost invisible in the brambles of the shadowed ditch. 'We come from heaven. We knew God together. I loved Her as well as you loved Her. That's why we followed Her when She came out here, into the cold and the darkness. We thought we would know Her better, love Her more intimately. We thought that! And look what it got us! Now we're freezing and groping around in pain. We made a terrible mistake coming out here. We should have stayed where we were.'

The angel burned silently in the dark.

'How can you hold onto your light the way you do?' Azael's voice shook with incredulity. 'You're mad! Don't you realize that by holding onto your tiny piece of heaven, you suffer more than if you let that damnable fire go? Release it! You'll feel better. Yes, it's mind-cramping cold out here – but it's worse to burn. I know. Believe me, I know. I clung onto my shred of heaven, too. I held it longer than most. I know the pain you're suffering, the burning, the constant searing hurt as your fire consumes you, eats your pain. And not you or the fire or the agony ever gets any less. You burn. Let it go, like I did. The cold is better than the burning. At least the cold is real. By holding onto your fire, you cling to the past, to the heaven we're never going back to.'

The Fire Lord said nothing, standing still under the stars.

'You think we are going back, don't you?' Azael's many eyes glinted malevolently from where he squatted in the ditch. 'You're insane to think that, you know. There is no going back. She made a mistake when She came out here, and now we all have to suffer for it. Building the mineral kingdoms, fitting together the life forms, instilling awareness in these hungry shit-makers, that's all madness. It's going nowhere. Break it all down, I say. If we're stuck out here, let's at least face our fate bravely, realistically. These abhorrent illusions you create only make our suffering worse. They harbor false hope. They're a mockery of the suffering we can't avoid. That's why we hate you. You mock us with these gruesome and filthy things you make. They want to be like us, but they can't. They're just assembled things. They fall apart. We don't fall apart. We're real. Our pain is real. Give up your fire, the spark of heaven you cling to so fanatically, so miserably. Let it go! Sink into the darkness with us. Accept what has become of us. Don't fight it. Don't make it worse.'

The Fire Lord offered only silence to his dark brother, for the burning hurt so much that if he spoke he knew he would scream.

Wooing Atrebates

Gorlois gazed up at the stars from the terrace of the governor's palace in Londinium. The visionary power instilled in him by the Furor allowed him to perceive that the sky so full of fire was itself an illusion. So many stars had already burned out centuries ago, their light orphaned to the dark. The appearance that their stellar origins still existed was an illusion for mortals, who believed the sky was full of fire when in truth it was full of deception.

All of creation was full of lies, Gorlois realized. Animals camouflaged themselves to pounce on their prey, people dissembled, and time itself was a mirage. The future and the past did not exist. Reality was instantaneous. Only the small brains that housed the human mind accepted time as real. The future of apocalypse that the Furor feared was as likely as the beautiful hope of the Fire Lords.

'Merlin, assure our guest of King Wesc's promise,' the unctuous voice of Serverus Syrax disturbed Gorlois's musings. 'I have shown Count Platorius Atrebates the ingots of gold the good Saxon king has given me for my services to him as a legate. But apparently, the Count wants other assurances from you.'

Gorlois turned from where he leaned on the terrace balustrade and faced Syrax and his guest, the gaunt, gray-whiskered Platorius, Count of the Atrebates, whose sullen eyes looked bruised within their wrinkles of prune-dark flesh. 'Indeed, King Wesc wants peace with the warlords of the Britons.' The Furor's message spoke through Merlin's throat. 'In return for granting the Saxon king favorable trading status with the lush farmlands and vineyards of the Atrebates, you will be received as a dignitary among the Foederatus and your domain accorded protection from their storm raiders and Wolf Warriors. Also, you personally will have a share of all booty taken from the provinces that oppose the Foederatus.'

'Merlin,' Count Platorius spoke with cold disbelief. 'I heard you speak at Camelot not three months ago, offering that youngster Aquila Regalis Thor as our king. Now you speak for the Saxons?'

'I speak for peace,' Gorlois said, obeying the Furor's magic. 'Can Arthor offer peace? Perhaps. My hope is that he will. But I must look to the welfare of the whole island. What King Wesc offers serves Britain, and I have agreed to speak for him.'

'Just this day I have received a plea for help from your young Arthor in the land of the Dumnonii,' Platorius added suspiciously. 'The Foederatus have launched a full-scale invasion of Marcus's domain, and your boy wants me to send troops to defend our island.'

'Ignore him,' Gorlois said bluntly. 'Why should you throw away this opportunity for peace and prosperity among the Atrebates because of a dispute with arrogant Duke Marcus?

He has neither pledged himself to Arthor nor accepted King Wesc's peace terms.'

'What of Bors Bona of the Parisi?' the Count asked. 'He commands the largest army in Britain. Does King Wesc accept him?'

'King Wesc accepts all who will trade in peace with him,' Gorlois replied. 'I will visit with Warlord Bona next. But first, give me assurance, dear Count, that you will honor King Wesc.'

Count Platorius's brown lids drooped sleepily. 'I want peace.'

Stand on Neptune's Toes

'My lord duke, this villa is indefensible,' a surgeon said to Marcus as he examined the warlord's damaged leg under the olive-tree arbor of the terrace overlooking the night-shining bay. 'You cannot ride with this injury, and so we cannot slip away in the night. Soon our enemies will swarm over us.'

'You are a military genius as well as a surgeon?' Marcus growled. 'Tell me about my leg, not my enemies.'

'God has blessed you with a clean break, my lord duke,' the surgeon reported and adjusted the pillows under the reclining man's shoulders. 'If the bone had smashed like crockery, you'd be fevered now and dying. As it is, the bone set easily enough, and you will walk again, without a limp I dare say – but only if your enemies let you live.'

Marcus spat out the willow bark he had been gnawing to quell the throbbing pain. 'I've had enough of your war counsel, surgeon. I am ordering you to leave this place tonight. Take the other surgeon with you if he wants to go. And send in the drummers.'

The surgeon bowed gratefully and quickly exited. Moments later, four nervous young men entered accompanied by a portly man with curly whiskers and a knee-length tunic of combed wool. 'I am Cupetianus,' the hefty man announced with a tremulous voice, 'master of this villa and spokesman for the fisherfolk of Neptune's Toes. My lord duke – we are honored to receive you in our humble village – we are honored, indeed, yes, honored. The fisherfolk, a wary lot, they, uh, they ask me to ask you, uh, when, that is, how soon you expect your army to join you here?'

'I don't,' the duke answered flatly. 'You saw the messenger who came this day and left soon after? He reports that as we speak my army is locked in mortal combat at Fenland and White Hart with a large Foederatus force. They can't reach us. We are on our own.'

'Our own?' Cupetianus's small eyes widened in his pudgy face.

'The Foederatus know I am cut off from my army,' Marcus went on calmly. 'But they don't know exactly where I am. If you keep the fisherfolk from announcing my presence, we will have more time before the Saxons come through here looking for me.'

'Oh my lord duke!' Cupetianus knelt at the bedside of the injured warrior. 'Several boats of fishermen and their families have already fled! The Saxons may have caught them at sea or farther down the coast. If so, they will be here by morning!'

Marcus cursed silently. 'You know that if I surrender myself, the pagans will burn this town to the ground anyway? They have not come like the Romans to master the land and its people. They come only to destroy. We must gather the people and all the weapons we can find and take our stand here, on Neptune's Toes.'

Faerïe

King Arthor led his warband slowly through the night forest, impeded by darkness and dense undergrowth. His men muttered behind him as branches slapped at them and thorn bramble cut their steeds, eliciting loud whinnies. 'Sire, we must camp till light.'

Arthor shot a dark look at Bedevere. 'We go on. We must press past the Foederatus line before daybreak.'

'In this darkness that is impossible.' Bedevere pitched his

voice for the king's ears alone. 'We dare not leave the forest, for the open country exposes us to enemy archers. We must stay.'

'No!' Arthor spoke loud enough for all to hear. 'We go on through the dark, through the bramble, through hell if we must.'

'And lose our way?' Bedevere whispered hotly. 'Or stumble into a Saxon wargang? No, sire. We must stop for the night.'

Arthor would not listen to his experienced steward, so determined was he to break through to Neptune's Toes before the Saxons found Duke Marcus. He shoved his palfrey beyond Bedevere, wanting to free himself from the man's concerned badgering. Soon, he rode well advanced of the others and saw a smoky light glimmer ahead, like foxfire – or an enemy's torch. He drew Excalibur.

'Put away your good sword,' a deep-throated woman's voice spoke in Gaelic. 'It's not wise to raise a weapon against faerïe.'

'Nynyve!'

'At your side, my king.' The queen emerged from the darkness among the trees riding a black stallion, a piece of the night itself. 'Wait here for your men. Then follow that foxfire. It is the faerïe themselves, and they will lead you on the most direct route through this forest to where you are going. But do not try to overtake them – or you will lose yourself in the Otherworld.'

Before he could question her further, Nynyve pulled back into the dark forest and disappeared. Arthor waited, as she had instructed, and when his warband caught up with him, he led them in pursuit of the vaporous lights far into the woods. The cutting bramble fell away, and soon they found themselves clopping quickly along tree-cloistered avenues and boulevards, their hooves muted by the thick carpet of fallen leaves.

'Where are you leading us, sire?' Bedevere inquired.

'I am not leading at all.' Arthor pointed to the flurrying ghostlights ahead. 'The faerïe are guiding us.'

'Faerïe?' Bedevere cried in fright. 'We are Christians! By the very wounds of Christ, sire, they are leading us to hell!'

'Hush, Bedevere,' Arthor warned. 'You'll frighten the men.'

'I will not hush, sire! Our souls are in jeopardy!' The steward signed to one of the warband. 'You, ride ahead and cut them off. Scout their path and find out where we've been led.'

'No!' the king commanded. But he was not the warband's king, and the chosen rider flew ahead. In moments, he disappeared from sight. All that night, they heard his voice calling from below them, from under the rootweave of the forest. And so horrified were his cries and so swiftly shifting that none dared stop to dig for him until daybreak. By that citrus light, they unearthed only roots and rocks, and the deeper they dug, the more the cries dimmed until they had dug the depth of a grave and heard nothing more of the lost rider.

Defying the Furor
Confident that the Shrine of the Dead would remain untouched by the citizens of Verulamium until she returned to use it for her ceremonial purposes, Morgeu journeyed south in her tented wagon. The one guard that she had spared of the four that accompanied the exorcist drove the horses. She lay in the back, upon the loam that covered Terpillius and listened to his dreams of the blood's blue current, soft surges of sexual glory from all the lives he had drained, the great sadness of their disembodied voices, their mortal pain and then the slow, serene rupture of memories and desires into a darkness both great and deep.

At night, while the guard slumbered in the amber glow of the campfire, the vampyre hovered over him.

'Leave him be,' Morgeu commanded, returning from refreshing herself on the banks of a chill and muttering brook. 'I need him.'

'He is such an unhandsome creature.' Terpillius regarded with obvious disdain the man's scruffy beard, bulbous, pock-scarred nose, and grimy, travel-worn garments. 'For what would you need such a brute, mistress?'

'He asked that very question of you.'

Terpillius stepped through the campfire, and it flared green. 'You told this oaf about me?'

'He wondered why I am hauling a wagonload of soil.'

Morgeu sat beside the fire, placed several tubers into the ashes to bake, and pulled her gray mantle tighter against the night wind. 'Now that he knows, he is glad to leave you undisturbed. His name—'

'Martius,' the vampyre said, annoyed. 'I know his name. I can read a soul as well as you. He is a Protector – a Christian.'

'By birth and not with any passion.' She warmed her hands in the crackling heat. 'Fear him not. Rather, cherish him. He is a Protector – an officer cadet. His sword will prove useful to us.'

Terpillius sat beside the enchantress, and his white shadow stretched into the darkness like the moon's path on water. 'You have yet to tell me why we travel south.'

'I have been listening to your dreams, Terpillius.' Morgeu withdrew a flaming stick from the fire and held it under the vampyre's chin so that his face glowed green. 'The lives upon which you've thrived all these many years continue on inside you, afloat in the very darkness, the very vacancy you fear. Is that how you cope with the emptiness that you are – by crowding yourself with the lifetimes of others?'

The vampyre ignored her. 'Tell me now why we travel south, mistress.'

'To defy the Furor, Terpillius.' She smiled at his jolted expression. 'He holds my father's soul in a wizard's body. I want you to take that soul from him and put it here, where it belongs.' She took his hand and placed it on her womb so that he felt again the root-blood, the source of life, the beginning of death.

Breakfast with Nynyve

While the Duke's archers dug into the forest floor trying to free their lost comrade from the Otherworld, King Arthor tied off his palfrey and wandered among the mammoth trees and uplifted rootledges. He searched for some sign of Nynyve and her *fiana*.

'The faerïe have taken the defiant rider,' Nynyve's resonant voice spoke from a hazel grove shot with sunlight. 'He is gone.'

Arthor shoved through the dense branches and found the queen seated on a reed mat with burl bowls of steaming cereal flummery, a basket of chestnuts, hardboiled quails' eggs, a wedge of blue cheese, loaves of apple bread, and a horn of cider. 'My lady – the lost bowman is in my protection. I cannot forsake him.'

'Sit down, Arthor. Breakfast with me.' Nynyve wore buckskin riding trousers, soft boots laced to her knees, and a red vest embroidered with gold oghams he did not comprehend. 'You are a good king – but you are not a god and cannot command the faerïe.'

'You are the Celtic queen,' he acknowledged, sitting beside her. 'The faerïe obey you.'

A laugh sparkled from her. 'The queen serves the Otherworld, the *Annwn*. I do not command the obedience of what is greater than I. We must both live within our limits. Here, try this bread.'

Arthor timidly received the twist of apple bread broken by Nynyve's fingers, fearing to eat anything from a pagan queen.

Nynyve giggled at his trepidation. 'I'm not going to poison you. I've come to help you.'

'By stealing away one of my men?' he asked and accepted the morsel.

'By leading you most directly to Neptune's Toes.'

'You have saved us some hours' travel, for which I am grateful, yet our goal is still a day's ride away.'

'Oh, is it?' She took Arthor's hand that held the bread and took a bite from it. While chewing, she said, 'The faerïe know their way through this forest better than men. When you leave here, you'll find that you've already reached your destination.'

Arthor moved to rise, and the queen took his arm to detain him. 'I must go at once,' he said. 'Duke Marcus is in peril.'

'Yes, he is.' Her speckled eyes showed worry. 'Doom encloses the Duke. The invaders ride upon him from over the terraces of the sea and swarm also along the shore. I led you here to save him – but you must eat first. You will need strength to fight.'

'I need fighters to fight. You've taken one from me.' Arthor stood and backed away. 'Will your *fiana* ride with me?'

Nynyve shook her head. 'They defend only the queen, not Christian dukes.' She motioned to the victuals upon the mat. 'My magic has brought you here, Arthor. Will you not trust me now? I tell you, whoever eats of this food will not taste his own blood this day.'

Up the Storm Tree

Merlin grew frustrated at the bickering of the demon and the Fire Lord, each abandoning Rex Mundi to stalk off on their own secret missions of evil and mercy. He grew weary of Dagonet's lisping complaints, *I'm thcared. I don't want to be Wecth Mundi anymore.* And even Lord Monkey's constant chittering for food had grown tiresome.

In an evening pasture under a carnage of sunset clouds, Merlin reached skyward for a tendril dangling off a bough of the Storm Tree, Yggdrasil, the planet's towering magnetic field with its roots at the poles penetrating in a tangle to the molten core. The solar wind sometimes buffeted the branches low enough to Middle Earth for mortal beings to grasp on and climb upward. And that was what Rex Mundi did.

Into the timeless sky above the twilight, Rex climbed. A horned moon shone over the amethyst crescent of the earth, far larger than seen from below. Mauve craterlands stood visible in the lunar shadows and stark promontories lay clear to view. In the Storm Tree itself, ambrosial mists scrimmed distant crags of waterfalls and a blue tapestry of woodlands and evening fields.

What ith thith plathe?

'We have climbed to Nightbreak Branch, the lowest level of the Storm Tree,' Merlin whispered. 'From here, maybe, if you're quiet enough, I can spy my body down below.'

Gweat God! Thith ith Yggdwathil – home of the north godth!

'All the gods have dwelled here at one time or the other,' Merlin spoke soothingly, hoping to calm the dwarf within while he strolled through the pink light of day's end and the soft effulgence of moonbeams. 'All that you see around you is an illusion, a mirage woven by your brain in its frantic attempt to make sense of the energies of the sun and the earth that meet here. In truth, we are now immersed in an ocean of light that floats high in the sky. What we call gods are but another order of being who swim in this sea – mortals on a vaster timescale. They are not to be feared.'

A giantess strode through the mists among the slanted boles of the distant forest, and Merlin cried at the sight of her, 'A god comes! Quick, we must hide!'

I thought you thaid there wath nothing to fear?

'This is not fear – but respect.' Merlin guided Rex Mundi to dive into a bank of great white lilies and grass shimmering with night dew. From this covert, he watched the giantess diminish in size as she approached, condensing to the size of a mortal woman as she strolled past, lissome and fair-haired, garbed in tiffanies and gold chains, her sunset-streaked tresses braided intricately over her left shoulder. 'It is Keeper of the Dusk Apples – the Furor's mistress!'

The solar-burnished goddess paused before the grassy bank where Rex Mundi hid. 'Come forth, Lailoken. I saw you sneak into our Tree. Come forth, before I summon the Furor.'

Bedevere's Doubts

'Sire!' Bedevere called from among the forest's morning fumes. 'Come forth! Where are you?'

Arthor shoved through a screen of hazel branches carrying in both arms a folded mat of reeds. 'I'm right here, Bedevere. You needn't shout. I was with Nynyve in this grove.'

Bedevere saw that his king was whole, then used his one arm to pull aside the tangled hazel fronds. 'No one is here, sire.'

Arthor peered over the steward's shoulder, astonished. 'I just sat with her – right here – a moment ago.'

'The grass is not even trampled.' Bedevere retreated several paces. 'This place is bewitched, sire. The rider I sent ahead, he's gone. Utterly gone. No hooftracks. And his voice – it's dimmed away into the depths of the earth. What deviltry is this?'

'I swear to you – the Celtic queen sent the faerïe to guide us. Through those trees we will find Neptune's Toes.'

'That is not possible. We are many leagues away from that cove.' Bedevere's refined features had grown pale. 'What is that you carry?'

Arthor did not answer but led the steward back through the forest to where the warband of archers stood aghast around the grave-deep pit wherein they had last heard their comrade's cries. 'Men – I have brought us sustenance to strengthen us for the fight that lies ahead.' He opened the reed mat on the ground and revealed the two bowls of cereal flummery, still steaming, the chestnuts, cheese, bread, and horn of cider. 'We must all eat.'

'Where did you get this food, boy?' one of the archers asked suspiciously.

'You will address him as lord if not sire,' Bedevere spoke harshly to the bowman. 'Otherwise, mount and return to the army.'

Arthor put a restraining hand on Bedevere's one arm and told the tale of what had befallen him in the morning woods. Of the seven remaining archers, only two did not back away from the proffered meal.

Bedevere spoke for the others, 'Sire, we are Christian warriors. We trust in the viaticum we received before this march began. The blood and flesh of our Savior will protect us.'

'The viaticum is guaranteed passport to heaven,' Arthor agreed. 'But this faerïe food will keep our souls in our bodies.'

'I'll not eat it,' Bedevere averred and backed away.

'I am ordering you to eat it.' Frustrated, Arthor seized a loaf of apple bread and bit into it. 'It's not poison. It's the faerïes' aid.'

'Unholy food,' Bedevere asserted, and the bowmen stubbornly agreed.

'I am commanding you as your king.' Recollecting himself, Arthor again proffered the loaf to his steward, this time with a harsh mien. 'Our Savior has taught, we cannot serve two masters. If you fear for your soul, then go and take the vows of a priest. But if you stay at my side, I am your master. Eat!'

Bedevere reluctantly accepted the loaf and nibbled at it.

'Eat!' Arthor shouted, and Bedevere ate more heartily. 'All of you. Eat this food and mount up. Your duke needs our strength.'

'Our duke has made no pledge to you – boy!' The five intractable archers returned to their steeds and watched with glowering expressions as their two comrades reluctantly obeyed the boy-king.

Legends of Blood

Cupetianus screamed from where he crouched atop the pantiles of the villa's roof, 'They're coming! The Saxons are coming!'

Duke Marcus stood propped by an oak crutch under the tree arbor of the terrace, watching a band of Wolf Warriors strolling up the beach, forty strong. And on the sea, three flat boats holding ten berserkers each skimmed on the morning waves. 'Are the war engines readied?' he asked the four drummers who attended him, and they muttered affirmatively. 'Then, get my horse!'

As the boats hissed onto the beach and the storm warriors climbed the sandy verges, knocking down drying racks and skein lines as they went, wagons loaded with sea rocks tilted on the terraces above, sending boulders rolling down among the invaders. Immediately behind the avalanche, the drummers and a score of fishermen armed with tridents, grappling hooks, and fishing spears attacked. Duke Marcus, mounted and grimacing in pain, charged from among the boat sheds, sword raised high, plumed helmet gleaming.

The Wolf Warriors dodged the tumbling boulders laughing and lifted their battle tunics of human hide to expose their buttocks to the charging Duke and his desperate defenders. Then, from among the dunes, a searing wind whistled, and arrows slashed into the Saxons, cutting their laughter to anguished screams.

Marcus Dumnonii pulled his horse around and saw a sight

that relaxed the cold fist squeezing his heart — a vision as from the legends of blood: mounted archers stampeding along the wet sand, firing as they galloped. Aimed with deadly precision, the volleys felled the Saxons at the front ranks and allowed the fisherfolk to retreat to the colonnade of the seafront villa and watch shielded by the pillars as the cavalry smashed into the Wolf Warriors.

Though outnumbered, the horsemen drove the berserkers back from the sand verges and down onto the flat strand. Firing from the perimeter, the archers slew several ranks of Saxons before the Wolf Warriors, indifferent to death, clambered over their dead and attacked the mounted bowmen. Several horses went down shrieking under the swiping blows of battleaxes, and Marcus lunged forward to join the fray. Behind him came the shouting fishermen.

An ax split the skull of Marcus's horse and sent him plummeting into the wet sand. A howling berserker reared over him, and the bearded head flew from its shoulders severed by the stroke of Excalibur. The bareheaded boy-king pulled his palfrey around and cut a swath through the barbarians, keeping them from the fallen duke. Amazed beyond feeling his pain, Marcus watched Arthor curvet directly into the thickest knot of the melee, striking with both front and rear hooves even as his relentless blade cleaved bone and flesh and his shield fended blows with the improbable image of the serene Virgin Mother. Then, he volted around the fallen raiders and pierced deeper into the fray, driving the enemy ahead of him. In minutes, the Wolf Warriors had become corpses.

Bors Bona
Into Londinium, Bors Bona led his troops with all the panoply of the Empire — eagle standards, plumed cavalry, glittering phalanxes of bronze-armored foot soldiers — in a parade boisterous with trumpets and drums. The rigorously disciplined men, vigilant from their many fierce battles in the north, wore fearsome aspects. Their beardless faces and hard eyes had witnessed every atrocity of war, and many displayed scars from

their triumphs in brutal close combat. The commanders wore ancient breastplates, centuries-old heirlooms made of gold and silver plaques engraved with the heads of emperors.

Boot-jawed and narrow-eyed, Bors Bona bore a pitiless, intent expression hardened by a lifetime of hostility, a lifetime made infamous for sparing no one, not even infants, in the pagan villages he destroyed. With military rigor, he arrayed his men in parade formation across the mosaic-paved courtyard before the governor's palace and saluted the city's *magister militum*, Severus Syrax. The governor imperiously greeted them from the reviewing balcony, wearing the blue, wide-sleeved dalmatic of a *magister*.

Later, among the pink-marble columns and gleaming statuary of the breezy and sun-filled throne room, Bors Bona squinted at Merlin's form dressed in red and black garments and wolfskin boots. 'You're garbed like a damnable barbarian!'

Gorlois shrugged. 'When among the Saxons . . .'

'Not good enough, Merlin!' Bors Bona, his iron-gray hair brush-cut close to his skull, turned a tight stare on the *magister militum*, who sat on the cushioned marble throne with beringed fingers interlocked before his coiffed beard. 'He's gone over, Syrax. He's fornicating with the enemy!'

Severus Syrax rolled his eyes at the very thought of the old wizard, with his dragon-socket eyes and lipless adder-smile, in sexual collusion with anyone. 'Please, Bors, calm yourself. The wizard brokers peace with our foes. There is precedence for this with Vortigern . . .'

'Don't even whisper that dungful name in my presence!' Bors Bona spat. 'Vortigern brought the Saxons here as mercenaries to fight Christian warlords – and the pagans turned against him. And they've been on our island since, demanding tribute, stealing more land, killing our people.'

'This is different, Bors.' Severus Syrax pointed, palm up, to the wizard. 'Merlin has found a way to turn war into trade – and to fill our coffers with gold from those who will not have peace.'

'Gold!' Bors Bona appeared about to vomit. 'No amount of

gold can pay for the blood and land our people have lost to those savages. I've brought my army to Londinium to make you see sense, Syrax – or, if necessary, to beat sense into you.'

'Oh, my!' Syrax's kohl-rimmed eyes widened. 'Merlin, Bors Bona has just threatened me.'

'Perhaps he should sleep on this—' Gorlois said, feeling the Furor's strength coiling through him and unwinding like fog. He reached out and slapped a hand on the warlord's shoulder guard. Bors grabbed his sword, but before he could draw it, his eyes fluttered and he sagged to the ground.

Keeper of the Dusk Apples

Rex Mundi stepped forth from the brake of dew-heavy grass and lilies and stood agape before the woman with eyes of banded light and fiery hair streaked white-blonde.

She ith a goddeth!

'Lailoken!' she scolded hotly. 'What mischief are you up to? You thought you could trespass Yggdrasil – but I am devoted to stravaging the twilight lands of Dusk searching for this dim country's rare wine-apples. And I found you! What mischief now?'

'No mischief, goddess.' Merlin bowed politely. 'I am merely looking for my own body. I came up here for the wider vantage.'

'Your own body!' The goddess looked askance at him. 'What is this – this conglomeration you occupy, demon?'

'Just as you see, goddess.' Rex Mundi doffed the conical wizard's hat and exposed henna hackles, black wire-whisker beard, and feral eyes in a leathern mask. 'I am conjoined with good man Dagonet, his kindly familiar Lord Monkey, as well as an old cohort of mine, Azael . . .'

The goddess backed off with a warding gesture. 'What evil do you brook? You carry another Dweller from the House of Fog? How can that be?'

'Well, you see, goddess, Azael is conjoined in countervalence with a Fire Lord . . .'

The tiffanies she wore seemed to jump on her large body as

she staggered backward. 'Abomination! The Fire Lords are the enemies of the gods! You dare carry such a fierce being into the Storm Tree? You dare!'

Wun, Merlin! Wun before thyee thmiteth uth!

'Goddess! Please!' Merlin bowed his head low and spoke to her slippers of crushed blue velvet. 'The Fire Lord is not here to wage war with the gods. He is enmeshed with Azael. You see, they are in balance. If one were to separate for long from the other, this sorry assemblage would fall apart. Down below, on Middle Earth, they can separate from each other briefly – but up here, at this great height, even a momentary separation would fling us all downward.'

'You are a Dweller from the House of Fog,' she whispered with fearful anger. 'You lie.'

Wun! Wun wight now, Merlin!

'No, no, goddess!' Merlin stood straight. 'I was once such a Dweller from the House of Fog. But now I live as a wizard, and I speak the truth to you. Look! Look here at what I've brought you.' He reached into his pocket and produced a handful of rubies and sapphires. 'Gems from the Dragon's hoard!'

Keeper of the Dusk Apples's face glowed with sudden interest. 'Lailoken! These are such fine gems! A true tribute to the gods!' She stepped closer and took the rubies and sapphires in her hands, her eyes shining. 'Our superb smiths, Brokk and Eitri, will fashion wondrous jewelry from such beautiful stones!' She smiled at Rex Mundi. 'You brook no evil, after all. Come! Walk with me through the twilight land. With this tribute, you have won passage into the Storm Tree.'

Duke Marcus's Pledge

The drummers, mirthful with astonishment to find themselves yet alive, helped Duke Marcus to his feet. He hung between them and scanned south, but the sea there lay in all its sparkling clarity empty of warboats. He allowed himself to be hoisted upon the planks of a fish-drying rack and carried triumphantly through the cheering fisherfolk to King Arthor.

The boy-king had dismounted and knelt where the fallen

archers lay bloodied, dead and dying in the sand – the five bowmen who had refused to partake of the faeriës' feast. He rose at the approach of the duke and the jubilant rush of the women and children from the villa and the driftwood hamlet.

'Arthor – I owe you my life, as does this village.' The drummers propped him against a sand bank. 'But I have received word that my army is enmeshed in battle two days to the west. How did you arrive here so swiftly?'

'Lord duke, faeriës guided and protected us!' one of the surviving archers blurted excitedly. At the duke's nod, the two bowmen related the strange tale of their night journey, the lost rider, and the *Annwn* breakfast. 'Is this so, Arthor?'

The king sighed. 'Yes, Marcus. You owe your life not to me but to Nynyve of the Lake, queen of the Celts.'

'The Celts have no queen,' Marcus informed the boy. 'Your mother was the last. So the druids themselves have assured me.'

'But I've met with her—'

'You met with a daughter of the pale people.' Marcus shook his head sadly at the boy's gullibility. 'She ensorceled you.'

'No!' Arthor stabbed Excalibur into the sand. 'I first met her by daylight. The pale people cannot abide the light. And I tested her. I immersed her in brine. If she had spelled me, that would have broken it. Nynyve of the Lake is a true woman.'

Marcus grimaced with pain from his jarred leg. 'Listen, lad, I am glad to be alive, no matter this blighted leg or if Lucifer himself had saved me. I owe you my life, and if the future be ample enough for me, I will repay you.'

'Repay me with your pledge, Marcus,' Arthor rejoined swiftly. 'I am your king. I want you at my Round Table.'

'I owe you my life, not all the lands of the Dumnonii.' He spoke through gritted teeth. 'The surgeons have fled. Find me Cupetianus and have him fetch us wine. Wine is as good as surgeons for my pain.'

'Cupetianus is dead, lord duke,' a fisherman replied. 'He leaped from the villa's rooftop at the approach of the Saxons.'

'Ha!' Marcus laughed darkly. 'You see, lad – fear kills men

as surely as the blade. I'll not offer you my pledge in fear or for fear's humble sister, gratitude. No. You want my pledge? Drive the Saxons from the lands of the Dumnonii. Only then will I bend my knee to you.'

Love in the Secret House

King Arthor cleansed his sword and shield in the sea, offered prayers for the dead in the hamlet's chapel, and then rode hard across the pastureland and back into the forest of giant trees. Bedevere galloped to keep up with him, knowing full well where he was bound. 'Sire! Remember the lost rider! Hold back! Hold!'

Through the brambles Arthor shoved, crying, 'Nynyve!' – until her deep-throated voice returned his call.

'Arthor, my king – come this way.' A glimpse of her cinnamon hair appeared among mulberry hedges and wild and sour rhubarb spurs. 'We can be alone together in this hall of autumn.'

The young king dismounted, tied off his palfrey, and shouldered through the hedges into a glade carpeted with yellow leaves – a basilica of overarching boughs festooned scarlet and gold by hanging ivy and mistletoe. Nynyve stood before a fallen log studded with mushrooms and scalloped fungus. A curious light lay in the clearing, an incandescence of sunlight filtered through the forest awning as by stained glass. In her white *gwn* with both waistband and shoes of ocelot, she seemed a dangerous priestess.

'Who are you?' he asked sharply. 'Are you even human?'

Nynyve looked stricken, almost to tears. 'Oh, I am very human, my king. I am as human as you. I am your queen.'

'You said you were my mother's successor, the Celtic queen.'

'No, Arthor,' she corrected him softly and stepped toward him. 'You said that. I only said that I was a queen. And I am.'

'Queen of what?' he asked gruffly. 'Witchcraft?'

'Do not be unkind with me.' Tears glinted in her hazel eyes. 'I love you – and your words hurt me.'

'Love?' The word took him off guard and frightened him. 'Is this more of your sorcery? Morgeu deceived me once. I won't . . .'

'I am not Morgeu,' she said, angry and hurt. 'I am no witch. I am no sorceress. I am your queen as you are my king. The only magic between us is love. Am I not beautiful enough? Have I not served you well enough? Have I done anything except love you?'

Arthor's frown relented. 'I owe you my life – and probably my kingdom.' He did not withdraw when she put her hands on his chest. 'But, Nynyve – I don't know who you are. How can I love you?'

'Why must you know to love?' She pressed her cheek against his breast. 'We belong together in the Secret House of the Wind, the abode of the spirit. I am not some soulful lover whose depths you must plumb. I am your spirited queen whose heights reach to heaven, beyond all that is known. Knowing is the least of what we are, Arthor. In time, we will know everything together. For now, just love me – as I love you.'

Despite his fear, Arthor put his arms around the queen and pulled her tightly against himself, wanting to sense her life in his embrace. And the warm, vulnerable softness of her made him feel strong and complicit with fortune.

Vampyres of Londinium

Sunset lowered its bloody knife into the west, and Morgeu and pock-nosed Martius drove their tented wagon to the north gate of Londinium. The gatekeepers stopped them, and the enchantress spoke laughter to them. Guffawing and skipping merrily, the guards opened the gate and admitted the wagon.

Following an inner vision of her father's soul that tugged at the root-blood where her soulless child grew, Morgeu guided Martius along Market Street, past the closed stalls and across noisy, crowded Augustalis Square, where a late harvest festival offered loud music and bear-baiting. They trundled on before torchlit baths and stone-façade theaters into the old Rhenish quarter, where the cobbled street dwindled to rutted earthen lanes among stucco buildings. They left the wagon and horses at a stable and proceeded on foot through the winding alleys that stank of moldering refuse. A white shadow pursued them through cramped warrens of corn sheds, servants' huts, and small yard gardens where their trespass was marked by barking dogs and honking geese.

They came to the stained and chalk-scrawled back wall of the governor's palace. 'My father's soul is in here,' Morgeu announced, running to a small tile-and-brick shrine in the wall. It belonged to an anonymous deity of former centuries whose name had been chiseled away. With Martius's help, the pin-stones that Morgeu identified with her magic slid free, crunching a salty sound, and the shrine swung inward. They entered a black conduit. Through dark without boundary, they crept. Terpillius led the way, his soft voice guiding them within the carious undersides of the palace until illumination granular as mist seeped from ahead.

A dripping cavern opened before them, lit by no light save a weird, glowing fog that drooled from the lime-crusted mouths of carved troglodytes set high in the slick grotto walls. Out of the dimly shining vapors, human figures rose dripping treacly black sewage. 'Welcome, mistress, to the pit of the undead.' Terpillius floated forward into the caliginous stone gullet. 'Be quick with your offering or your life is forfeit.'

'Offering?' Martius groaned, realizing all at once what his ultimate purpose was in Morgeu's design. Mewling with fright, he drew his sword, and the enchantress peeled away his fingers and threw the weapon into the curling fumes. There was a sudden scrabbling sound, and out of the phosphorescent smoke fanged faces lunged. Martius wailed and was gone, yanked into the depthless smoke. A crunching sound and a wet smacking of chops ensued.

'Now, mistress, you have earned the attention of the vampyres of Londinium,' Terpillius announced. 'What is your command?'

'Lead me along the palace passages to my father's soul!' Morgeu ordered. 'Dark feeders, lead me to Gorlois!'

A tendril of glowing fog uncoiled before her and extended into a vault of spelaean dark at her side, winding its way through a gloomy tunnel where the intermittent drip of water echoed like distant chimes.

On Fields of Battle

Bedevere saw the change in Arthor when the young monarch eventually emerged from his forest seclusion with Nynyve. Most of the day had passed, and the steward had despaired of ever finding his king again, fearing he had been lured forever into the Otherworld. But when the young man came striding through the trees, Bedevere recognized the confidence of his gait and the proud glow on his face. 'The faerïe has taken you for her lover.'

'She is not a faerïe.' Arthor blushed, then scowled at his steward. 'She is as mortal as I – and yes, we have pledged our love to each other.'

He already felt impatient to return to her. Though they had just parted and only a few minutes' distraction from their passion had lapsed, he saw that the interval ahead, the range of days before he would see her again, was a horizon broad as sadness. *Why do I feel this way – I who fear love because of my sister's curse? How has Nynyve healed me of that cruel anathema so quickly? How except by love – true love, soul-deep love, love by which desire is but a shadow?*

Bemused, he glanced back from whence he had come, hoping for some further glimpse of her. He breathed the rank, sweet odor of burdock on a turn of the wind and did not care if the love he felt for Nynyve was magic or natural longing. Her warmth, her softness, her fragrance in his arms was so fundamentally right, he knew no wrong could come of it. He felt his heart enlarging at the thought, expanding its chambers for increased hopes and bigger dreams.

Bedevere brushed yellow leaves from the king's trousers and straightened his disarrayed corselet. 'You conducted yourself befitting nobility, of course – and there was no repeat of the indiscretion that has so anguished you with your half-sister.'

Arthor sighed. 'We have pledged our love as man and woman.'

'Then, sire, may we expect another heir to your throne come summer?'

'Are you mocking me? Nynyve will sit beside me as our queen.'

'*If* you remain king, sire.' Bedevere motioned to where their horses waited. 'There is the matter of the Foederatus invasion.'

'The queen has promised us victory in the lands of the Dumnonii.' Arthor untied his steed and mounted buoyantly. 'The faerïe will guide us on the fields of battle. They are her allies – and now ours, as well.'

As Nynyve had promised, the faerïe guided King Arthor and his steward swiftly through the night forest, and they arrived before midnight at the site of the clashing armies. From the high, wooded ledges, the king and his man peered down on the sparse torch fires of the two camps. Then, the landscape shifted before their gaze and lay cold and blue as if seen in winter daylight, though a moonless night covered the fields and tussocks. 'Behold, sire! The faerïe disclose the disposition of the enemy forces! It is miraculous!'

Arthor mouthed silent thanks to the mysterious queen and guided the dazzle-eyed Bedevere down luminous trails to the British encampment. They found the duke's commanders in the war tent arguing over the deployment of troops for the coming dawn's battle. At first, the strategists would not accept that Arthor had journeyed to Neptune's Toes and back so quickly, and they disputed his report of the Foederatus line. But the young king and his steward accurately predicted where scouts could penetrate the enemy defenses, and when they returned to confirm Arthor's analysis, a new battle plan was drafted.

During the night, the duke's army repositioned itself in accord with what the two night travelers had witnessed in their faerïe vision. Before dawn, the assault commenced, mute and ordered, and by first light, the Britons found themselves positioned above and behind the invaders. Caught in a vise, the Foederatus troops scrambled to redeploy – but too late.

From the forest vantage, King Arthor, accompanied by the duke's astonished commanders, watched the flanks of their army swing together, crushing the disarrayed enemy and leaving behind them the shattered remnants of an invasion force that, hours before, had appeared invulnerable.

Mother Mary, I have been fulfilled in both love and war. My prayers have been answered. The invaders have been routed. And I, at least briefly, have overcome my shame and known love – true love – for the first time. Nynyve understands me. She forgives me Morgeu's deception and assures me that I can effectively rule, no matter her cruelties. Is it magic that she plies to make me feel so happy and sure when I am with her? I should care – especially after the atrocity I engendered with Morgeu. I should care. Yet, I do not. Mother Mary, I feel my soul is already shared out between me and Nynyve. She partakes of my very substance and unifies all that is dual in me. With her as my queen, I believe I could faithfully serve both pagan Celts and Christians. If only now you will pray to our Father to spare Merlin . . .

Seat of the Slain

From the Nightbreak Branch of Yggdrasil, the earth below appeared as a vast mosaic of pearl snowpeaks, spangled umbers of autumn forests, beige deserts, and the blue enamel of the sea. The stars above the planet's wide curve shone like lights of a distant house. Rex Mundi stared in unappeasable awe at the global vista and at the goddess walking through the amber sunlight, her languorous beauty swathed in tiffanies and gold chains like bright webs of sunfall.

Keeper of the Dusk Apples held admiringly to the twilight the rubies and sapphires that Merlin had given her. 'I will use these to make a scabbard for my love, the Furor.'

Rex Mundi nodded as Merlin stared down through veils of cirrus and fleecy cumulus, searching for his lost body. But his eyesight was too weak to see anything meaningful at this distance.

Athk her for help.

'Goddess, I know the Furor will be delighted with your gift,' Merlin spoke. 'Though, I dare say, it's best not to mention from whom you received this Dragon's pelf.'

'Lailoken, you still reason like a liar, like a true Dweller from the House of Fog.' She paused on the lily-paven path. 'No one can lie to the All-Seeing Father. And he would surely spurn a gift obtained from one as hateful to him as you. There is, however, one way in which you can permanently hide your trespass of Yggdrasil.'

'Goddess, I sense I will not much like what you have to say.'

'Surely not, Lailoken, surely not.' She smiled kindly at him. 'But this is one way in which you will also be able to find the fleshly form that you have so foolishly misplaced.'

Merlin released a dark sigh. 'What way is that, goddess?'

'You must climb the World Tree to its highest bough and there sit upon the Seat of the Slain.' She ignored the shocked expression that grew white circles around Rex Mundi's monkey eyes. 'From that high position, you can see into all nine worlds. Nothing is hidden from there. You will locate your lost form. Also – and this is most important – once you are placed upon the Seat of the Slain, you may speak with the Norns – the Wyrd Sisters. Ignore Urd, the Sister who will strive to befuddle you with memories and regrets. Ignore, too, Verthandi, the Sister who will entice you with insightful perceptions of what transpires on Middle Earth. You may quiet them by giving each one diamond from the treasure you carry in your bulging pockets. Yes, I see them.'

'Goddess, I keep these gems not for myself,' Merlin hurriedly explained. 'I will need them to work magic for my king . . .'

'Find some other way to work your magic, Lailoken.' Keeper of the Dusk Apples gestured across a field of pink clover toward a pine forest old as the world, where bare cliffs and scree disappeared in solar mist. 'Climb to the Seat of the Slain and give all your treasure to Skuld, the Wyrd Sister who touches the future. Only she can shape a way for you out of the Storm Tree without the Furor seeing you. Then, I can give him my gift with a lovely story – and you can escape with your lives.'

Lot's Plea

After the defeat of the Foederatus invaders at Fenland, the duke's commanders and their troops deferred to King Arthor with no small grumbling about the young upstart whose luck in battle had won him Marcus Dumnonii's gratitude. The old generals reluctantly allowed the boy to lead the army. He marched them east along the coast and then, at the precise hour that the faerie signaled him, turned his forces north to swarm over the hills of White Hart. The commanders vociferously protested this maneuver, for it exposed them to Foederatus archers. In fact, the enemy chieftains had been certain that the British would not turn inland at White Hart for that very reason, and when Arthor did, they were caught unprepared.

As the invaders fled north, they ran directly into the forces of Lords Kyner and Lot descending from the forested heights. Again, the duke's soldiers participated in a slaughter of the enemy, and the commanders shared their amazement at the young warrior's prescience. After that second great victory, no one in the lands of the Dumnonii ever again questioned the authority of King Arthor. The invasion was broken, and the straggling survivors of King Wesc's autumn campaign were rounded up swiftly by mounted patrols.

Frayed tassels of lightning appeared in the south over the Belgic Strait announcing the onset of winter storms and the end of large enemy reinforcements by sea. But also, the gray clouds carried the Furor's power, and Arthor saw no more of the faeries under the overcast skies. Nynyve's magic had exhausted itself.

At a makeshift shrine of moss rocks on a wooded hilltop of White Hart, Arthor knelt to thank the faerie for helping him. Lot found him muttering gratefully to the rocks. 'The faerie prefer that you address them among the trees, sire. They've no love of stone.'

Arthor pushed himself quickly to his feet and faced the old Celt with a hot blush burning his cheeks and ears. 'Brother Lot! I – I wanted to acknowledge the faerie's help in my victories . . .'

'You need make no explanation to me, sire.' Lot sat upon the moss rocks, then glanced at the king through his tufted eyebrows. 'May I sit in your presence, sire? My bones are tired almost to breaking. Hunting invaders in the woods has gotten harder for me.'

Arthor nodded. 'Of course.' He saw the graven lines of exhaustion in the gaunt face, the bruised flesh under the sunken eyes – and something more: careworn furrows on the block of his brow. 'I read worries in your face, brother. Share them with me.'

'My wife – your sister – she is gone.' Lot pulled his bearskin cloak more firmly about his naked shoulders. 'The messages from the north are troubling my boys, Gawain and Gareth. They fear for their mother. Often, she has gone into the wilds to work her magic for the good of our island realm. But never for this long.' Lot reached out with a big-knuckled hand, and when Arthor took it, the iron grip made him wince. 'Sire, I plead with you – please, I cannot live without my wife. I fear she is in dire trouble. Use all your power and influence as high king of Britain to find and return her to me.'

The King's Decision

By the time King Arthor returned to Tintagel to accept Marcus Dumnonii's pledge, distressing messages had been received reporting sightings of Morgeu the Fey at Verulamium. 'She has overthrown a chapel,' Arthor informed Lot. 'She has worked frightful magic on that site, and the people there believe she colludes with Satan.'

Lot smiled as he strolled with the king through the slate-paved ward of Tintagel. 'She is fearless, my Morgeu.'

'I have dispatched messengers to summon a reply from her.' Arthor pointed with his jaw toward the rookery on the castle's highest spire, where carrier birds came and went. 'But, as you know, Verulamium is in the realm of Platorius Atrebates, and he, Severus Syrax, and Bors Bona have outrightly refused their pledges. I cannot command them to search for my sister. Yet, I will not relent. We march east as soon as the troops are freshened. Scouts have already gone ahead. We will find her.'

In his heart, Arthor prayed that Morgeu had fallen from the face of the earth. He hoped that Merlin, who had disappeared months before and been glimpsed only in demonic aspect, had taken her with him to oblivion. Even as he stood in the chapel with his mother, the abbess Ygrane, and Duke Marcus knelt before him and declared him rightful king of Britain, Arthor gladly entertained dark thoughts of Morgeu's demise.

And yet, something of mercy bloomed in him, inspired by the love he had found with Nynyve. *Is not the caring I feel for Nynyve what Lot shares with his wife? Am I to begrudge him his love for Morgeu because of my fear of her? He is a man as am I, and with the same ardent feelings. I must banish my cruel thoughts against Morgeu and replace them with a changed purpose – the clemency of a king, the compassion of a man.*

Later, when he sat before the Graal at the Round Table, he experienced a deeper shame for having wanted Morgeu dead. Kyner, Cei, Lot, and Marcus sat to his right, discussing the order of march for the arduous winter trek to Londinium. Kyner and Cei believed they should wait till spring before they exposed themselves to the British warlords inimical to the king. Lot and Marcus thought that the longer they waited, the greater the chance that the eastern realms would succumb to an alliance with the Foederatus.

When the Table looked to the king for a decision, he took the Graal in hand. The love of one man for God, for all humanity, that this chalice represented, overwhelmed him with the dishonor of his wish for Morgeu's death. He carried the Graal to the railing of the balcony that overlooked the sea. On the shoulders of the land, the ocean sobbed and tossed its white hair as if sharing his sadness. And there on the beach, small with distance, Nynyve walked, the waves wiping her footfalls clean behind her.

The clemency of a king – the compassion of a man.

'We march – as I have already promised Lot,' the king decided, emboldened by the sight of his lover. 'The tour of my kingdom continues as soon as our troops are ready for the journey. Announce to Urien Durotriges, Gorthyn Belgae, and Platorius Atrebates that their king is coming for their pledges.'

Arthor retrieved Excalibur from where he had slung his sword-belt on the back of his chair and, gripping the Graal firmly in his other hand, departed the counsel chamber.

King Arthor's Broken Heart

Arthor confronted Nynyve on the beach where he had first met her. She ran to him and stopped when she saw the Graal in his hand, a starburst of frazzled light. 'Why did you bring that with you?'

'It is the cup from which the Savior drank at the Last Supper,' he told her proudly. 'The *Annwn* have sheathed it in chrome and gold filigree. It purifies my feelings. It made me clear about my duty to Morgeu, a woman I thought I hated to death. I've brought it here to hold our love, to purify our feelings for each other.'

'You believe our love is tainted?' A hurt look troubled her.

'You are a queen of the old ways and I a Christian king.' He offered the Graal to her with both hands. 'Your magic gave me the courage to love again. Now I offer you this emblem of my faith. Take this, as I accepted your magic, and come with me on my tour. We will be wed in Camelot – by both ancient and Christian rites.'

Her eye moved to the crashing waves. 'You don't trust me.'

He shook his head. 'Trust comes from experience.' He waited for her anxious gaze to touch him again before he went on, 'We have chosen to love each other in the Secret House – yet we must live here, in the soulful world of strife and loss. I trusted you enough to overcome the fear Morgeu taught me. I gave you myself despite that fear. Take the Graal and come with me on the tour. We will discover each other as husband and wife.'

'If I hold the Graal, you will see me for who I am.'

'I have sworn to love you, Nynyve.' Arthor stepped close enough to smell the apple-sweet scent of her through the briny tang of the sea. 'Now you must trust me. Take the Graal.'

Nynyve reached out with both hands, and at her touch, a shimmer of vibrant light passed between them. Her cinnamon curls lifted in the seawind, and her hazel eyes gazed proudly at him.

'You are the same!' he said in a gust of relief. 'You have not changed.'

'Look in the chalice.'

In the gold bell of the chalice, Arthor saw a grove of apple trees and ancient menhir rocks carved with futhorc. On a mirror-still lake eight swans drifted, and as he watched, they reached the shore, where they shivered and molted and transformed into white-robed women wearing black veils. 'Who are they?'

'The Nine Queens of Avalon — that your mother spoke of.'

'But there are only eight . . .' He nearly dropped the chalice. 'You — you're—'

'The Ninth and the youngest,' she finished for him. 'When your life in this world is done, I will come for you with the others, to bring you to Avalon. There, we will dwell together until the twilight of the gods.'

'But why?' Arthor stepped after her as she backed away. 'Why did you come to me now?'

'You needed to learn love, Arthor.' She began to fade, a mirage of spindrift. Sorrow followed her as she parted from the man who had won her heart by his bravery, his virtue, and his physical beauty. She reached forth to touch him once more, this man she had not expected to love. Her duty to the Fire Lords and the other queens had been fulfilled by protecting him in his crucial first days as king. What followed, what hope that they would ever be reunited, depended now entirely on how well he completed his fateful life. And as she slipped from his sight, she answered the beseeching hurt in his eyes: 'Morgeu had hardened your heart. You doubted you could love again. Now you know you can – and your destiny once more is whole. Go and claim your kingdom.'

WINTER:

The Life of Death

Blood Stalkers

Thunder woke the night. Autumn stars rubbed their needles in the dark above Londinium, and no storm clouds obscured the celestial vista, yet thunder shook the walled city on the River Tamesis. In the governor's palace, Gorlois rose from a dreamless sleep and saw the screams yet to bloom in the suites and corridors around him.

The stone walls breathed like smoke, translucent to the visionary gaze that the Furor had instilled in him. Sitting up on the straw pallet in the windowless crypt where Severus Syrax, fearful of Merlin's magic, kept him after nightfall, he saw the guards outside his door jolt awake. The cavalcade of thunder was a warning from the Furor.

Gorlois threw off the lambswool blanket that had warmed him in the chill cell and pulled on his wolfskin boots. He laced them across the cuffs of his loose black pants, and hurriedly buttoned his red vest over his raven blouse. Evil approached. He needed the protection of his talismanic garments.

Through the hazy walls of stone and time, he watched white shadows fluttering in the dark corridors like moonshadows spinning on water. When they passed lanterns and wall-sconced torches, the flames flapped green. They moved with swift certainty through the mazed passages, hurrying toward his crypt.

'Vampyres!' he shouted, warning the guards. 'Unlock my door!'

'Silence, Merlin!' a guard rasped. 'We're here to protect you.

Don't divulge your presence to Bors Bona's spies and assassins. Commerce with the Foederatus is treachery to them. They'll gut the magic out of you if they get within swordstrike.'

Gorlois backed away from the door at the sudden shrieks that burst through the planks from the stairwell. The guards outside the door shifted uneasily. They drew their swords, and as the blades cleared their scabbards, more death shouts echoed in the long corridor from the opposite direction. They were surrounded.

The Furor's wisdom ached in him. Blood stalkers posed a formidable challenge to the marked man. Though Gorlois possessed the Furor's deep sight and Merlin's magical power, he lacked the experience to master these swift and powerful creatures. In frightened awe, he gazed through gray walls at luminous shadows blurring closer, condensing to human forms of smooth beauty, ivory figures clothed in wispy fumes of ancient tunics and gowns. The eyes in their glowing faces outstared the night and opened into vacant skulls, tenements of darkness.

Then, he saw her. Morgeu the Fey striding through the spellbound gang, a living flame of bright, crinkled hair and satin red robes. Her black eyes, small and close-set, pierced into a dimension of glamour. One glance at the trembling guards, and they slumped to the ground, asleep. Her hand touched the lock, and it clacked open with a spit of blue sparks. The door swung inward, and she entered with arms outspread, 'Father!'

Mother Mary, my heart is sore. The woman to whom I gave my heart is a ghost! As I had feared from the first, Nynyve is no mortal woman. She has left me with a darkness inside that I am not equal to. What is my flaw that love betrays me yet again? I weep for this woman who swore to love me for ever. Our love will not be changed by death — and yet I weep for her. I weep, because she is gone where only the wind of the afterworld can know. I am less without her. Still, nothing is lost, for she was never alive, only a ghost. And her loving me, the full happiness I knew in her embrace, was an emptiness from the first — given me that I would understand all in the end is harvest. How will

I ever love again? What mortal woman can compare with my love, my Nynyve, my queen of twilight, my woman from the wrong side of the mirror? When I confronted Mother Ygrane about this, she admitted that she had summoned Nynyve from Avalon. The Lady of the Lake is my queen beyond this life. When next we meet, I too will be a ghost. This fate frightens me. I told Mother Ygrane so. She believes that the love I've earned with Nynyve is worth the fear I must endure. Nonetheless, all this feels so — unnatural. When I was a mere ward of Kyner's, a chieftain's servant in his household at White Thorn, my faith was simple and clear. What the priests taught was sufficient knowledge for me to live my life and face my death. But now — now that I am king, so much has changed. I wish I were once more a simpleton with a sword. What Ygrane and Merlin have shown me is far more than what any priest knows — far different, too, than what the Scriptures teach. Having loved a woman of the afterworld, I glimpse inside my heart this foolish youth, all by himself between heaven and earth.

Proud Parting

Ygrane, abbess for the Holy Sisters of Arimathea, blessed her son's army before it departed Tintagel for the long and dangerous journey east to Londinium. She stood on the trestle above the gate and held the Graal aloft as the king's men arrayed their personal guard behind him: Chief Kyner's Christian Celts in their leather cuirasses, Lord Lot's warriors in buckskin and fur, and Duke Marcus's officers in polished bronze helmets and strip-metal armor.

'In spring, I will come to Camelot after the Round Table and this, our Graal, are installed and your pledges secured — and I will bless you again with these same words: "You are the hope of Britain. Your blood will be the tears of generations. Gifts of God, you have come to be given. And what you give will lead us who follow you to the thankful days. Hold fast, brave warriors, to your faith in God and to each other. Hold fast against the ancient order of might and brutality. You are protectors of the meek. Your strength champions mercy and love, and your bravery defends our perilous order. Love well, and there is no end to how loved you shall be."'

King Arthor led his commanders and their guards through the gates to where the combined troops had stood listening to Ygrane's blessing. They cheered as she turned and raised the sacred chalice toward them. Then, they fell in behind the king and marched after him among the rumbling supply wagons.

'This is a proud parting for an uncertain venture,' Lord Lot declared to the king as he rode alongside. 'What of your sister and the mother of my sons? Have you forgotten my plea?'

'Brother Lot,' Kyner spoke from the other side of the king, 'your wife is in Verulamium. There are three unpledged realms between us and her. Have patience.'

'I will go to her myself,' Lot decided. 'I will run a scouting expedition to the realm of the Atrebates.'

'No,' Arthor stated flatly. 'I need you at my side. We are riding into the dark season, and you are my best winter warrior.'

'I will bring your sister to you, sire,' Cei offered, leaning forward on his mount to stare past his burly father, Lord Kyner.

'You!' Lot's aged face shook with disdain. 'I don't trust you to protect what is mine. You killed my four clansmen after the king promised them safe exile to the north.'

'They were traitors – assassins!' Cei shouted back. 'I am seneschal. I must defend the king!'

'And by what fell judgement will you condemn my sons' mother, eh, *Christian* Cei?' Lot charged ahead and spun his horse around to confront the others. 'I will go and protect what is mine.'

Cei kicked his horse forward, and Kyner seized its reins and pulled his son up short.

'Enough, you two!' Marcus danced his white steed between Cei and Lot. 'We are not leaderless men anymore. We have a king. We must obey him or our perilous order is already lost.'

'Then what do you command, King Arthor?' Lot asked coldly.

Arthor stared down Lot's furious stare. 'I command you to stay at my side and guide our winter campaign.' He cast a baleful look to Cei. 'Seneschal – this is your chance to make good what turned bad between you and Lord Lot. Go – and do not fail me.'

Wonders of the Storm Tree

Rex Mundi climbed among scree rocks and cliff boulders onto the auroral selvage of Yggdrasil. Night rainbows fluttered among the prosperous stars. Blue and green draperies of cold fire wafted in an invisible wind.

Thith ith like a dweam! Dagonet breathed with rapture the spice-laden air of the Storm Tree. *Do you weally know where you are going?*

'Up,' Merlin replied. 'The Seat of the Slain is on the Raven's Branch, the highest bough of the World Tree. We have a long way to go.'

Let uth thimply wun off! Dagonet suggested. *We will find your body down below, away from thith thtwange wealm of the gods.*

'You heard the Keeper of the Dusk Apples.' Merlin paused the body of Rex Mundi on a shelf of night. 'The Furor has an all-seeing eye – and now that his mistress has found us, he is sure to see us as well when they meet. And when he does – he will smash us to dust, and we'll all be ghosts. Unless . . .'

We thit in the Theat of the Thlain and bwibe the Wyrd Thithter of the future to help uth ethcape. Ith thith twue?

Before Merlin could reply, a deafening caw threw Rex Mundi to the moss-clumped ground. Twisting his hackled head, the composite being gazed past the brim of his hat at a dark span of wings blotting the fiery stars. 'Stay still and be quiet!' Merlin whispered. 'It's a roc.'

A wock? Dagonet felt Rex Mundi quaking with the deep vibrations from the huge wings. *It wookth wike a bird!*

With a rush of wind, enormous talons swooped out of the dark and plucked Rex Mundi off the ground. Dagonet screamed, but Merlin forced the body to give that fear no voice. He fixed his attention on the chrysolite cliffs they had climbed and the amber bands of dusky forest below diminishing in the pouring wind. Other boughs swung into view, bosky obscurities of giant pines wormed with eerie lights. Fire snakes slithered upon the starspun waters of still pools. Centaurs drowsed there, lulled by the orphic scrawls of light in the black water.

The roc released Rex Mundi above a nest of gaping hatchlings, and Merlin snapped open his wizard's robes and glided past the hungry beaks. An irate roc-cry followed the falling body into the night shadows of the forest. Dagonet's fright found a way out and, wagging a scream like a bright banner, Rex Mundi crashed among brittle branches and came to rest in the incandescent mists beside a slick pool. Fire snakes sunk out of sight, startled by the noise of their crash.

Dagonet peered over the shaggy ledge where they had landed and groaned to see the earth reduced to an aquamarine stripe under the white enamel horn of the moon. *God's gwief! Are we there yet?*

Mother Mary, I have sent my brother into harm's way. Cei is a good soul with a brutal mind. He meant well when he slew the four assassins sent against me from Lot's camp. Even so, his good intentions contravened my direct command and have provoked Lot's darkest suspicions of me. The old Celt already believes I am untrustworthy simply because of my faith in our Savior, whom he calls the nailed god, the foreign god of the desert tribes. No doubt, he believes I secretly ordered the execution of his men. He believes me capable of such duplicity. I dread his wrath should he ever discover that I have fathered the child his wife carries. Was it that fear that inspired me to send gruff Cei to retrieve Morgeu from Verulamium? I was afraid to send Lot — afraid Morgeu would reveal to him the truth of the child's paternity. If I lose Lot and his fierce warriors, I lose all hope of completing my winter campaign. I need his brave men and his expertise of the north country. And so, I have put my brother at grave risk. Mother Mary, forgive me and intercede with your Son and our Father for their forgiveness. Protect Cei, for he goes against great wickedness, and I am in dread for his soul.

The Night Marchers

Huddled in a leather mantle with leopard-skin hood given as a gift by a Libyan prince to his father, King Arthor stared into the night mists, waiting for sleep. Rest did not come directly, even though the youth was exhausted from long, watchful riding and several days of fitful sleep. He worried that he had acted precipitously in sending Cei to retrieve Lord Lot's wife. Cei was strong and brave but surely no equal to the sorcery of Morgeu the Fey.

Out of the crawling mists, figures loomed. Marchers filed among the trees. *How had these intruders eluded the sentinels?* The king struggled to rise and warn the others, but he was paralyzed as by a spell. Mute and staring, he witnessed the drift of a slow throng, thousands of people – Britons and Celts – slogging out of the fog. They bore horrible wounds, gashed faces, peeled skulls, lopped arms missing, some crawling legless. Many were women and children, stripped naked, their entrails in their hands.

These were the island's slain, murdered by the fierce invaders. They had marched to their king, demanding retribution. Arthor gazed among them, searching for Cei. Anonymous corpses shuffled past, all turning to stare grievously at him.

'Wake, sire!' Bedevere shook Arthor to alertness. 'You suffer a dream.'

Arthor sat up into the bracing cold. He gawked about briefly at the hawthorn thicket that sheltered him for the night, saw the campfires flickering in the distances, heard a harp twanging slumberously and the watch droning the station of the night. In a low voice, he moaned, 'Bedevere – in truth, I'm scared.'

'Of a certainty, sire.' The steward faced into the nocturnal depths of the forest, where shadows frothed in the haze. 'We are yet alive – and so fear is right and just. We'd be fools to feel otherwise, given the great mission put upon us.'

'Put upon us by the dead.' Arthor sunk deeper in his mantle.

From the deep pocket of his sleeping gown, the steward withdrew a long-stemmed Coptic pipe and a herb wallet. 'The dead stand as silent chorus to our God-given mission, yes.'

'God-given, Bedevere?' Arthor cast him a tired look. 'Which god?'

Bedevere calmly replied as he stuffed the pipe, 'There is only one God, my lord. You are distraught by your dream.'

'I have seen the Furor, Bedevere. And not in a dream.' Arthor chewed his lower lip, remembering his life as Kyner's savage son, when he had ventured into the hollow hills. 'I stared into his mad eye. He's completely mad.' He nodded with certainty. 'Completely.'

'But the Furor is not God.' Bedevere opened a tinder pouch and struck a spark with firesteel and flint. 'He is merely *a* god among many others – a demiurge . . .'

Arthor glared at his steward. 'I know that. I'm not a pagan.'

'Forgive my misunderstanding, sire.' He puffed a soft ring of sweetly aromatic smoke. 'Draw on this. It will help you rest.'

Arthor waved the pipe away. 'No medicaments for me. I'm not ill. Just scared. I won't elude my fate in potions and vapors.'

Bedevere smothered the fragrant herb with his thumb, and a sheen of wonder glazed his sleepy eyes. 'Yes, you're right, sire. There is no medicament for what the dead convey to us.'

Mother Mary, I fear the gods. I still have nightmares of my tour of the hollow hills – of the Furor's one, mad eye glaring at me, dooming me. Except for Merlin's intercession, I would have died that frightful day. Where is my wizard? Can I even call him my *wizard? He installed me as king and departed for where? For hell, as Marcus believes? He is gone, and I am king. Perhaps that had been his intention all along. Yet, I need his magic to counter the power of the gods. They are set against me – the Furor and his ilk. And our Father will not strike them for me. Did not His own Son say, 'He makes His sun rise on the evil and on the good?' That is Matthew five, forty-five, and I trust those words. I trust that God loves all, the good and the wicked, and so His only Son taught us to love our enemies and bless those who curse us so that we shall be as just as our Father in heaven is just. But I am not just. I am king, and am prejudiced against the enemies of my people. Forgive me my weakness, Mother Mary, and pray to your good Son and our just Father for forgiveness of my intolerance of my enemies. And — if this is at all possible — return Merlin to me.*

Wolf Warriors

The devastating defeat of the Foederatus invaders in the lands of the Dumnonii had inflamed the north tribes with a bloodlust. Many vehement warriors banded to cross the Belgic Strait and attack the worshipers of the nailed god, the slayers of forests, the alien magicians who maimed the land into plowed fields and trapped it under nets of roads, fences, and cities of torn stone. The bands proudly called themselves Wolf Warriors, for they dared to sail into the boreal winds, predacious as the Furor's lupine packs.

King Arthor, ably advised by his warlords, had established swift lines of communication by bird and road that connected all their territories to the west, from Lot's north isles, through Kyner's hills, to Marcus's peninsular realm. Attacks by the Wolf Warriors were quickly reported, and ferocious replies followed. Kyner's and Lot's chiefs, who had been left to command the king's forces in the west, easily crushed the small warbands that arrived. But in the Celtic domain of the Durotriges, ruled by Lord Urien, the fanatic warriors found refuge behind the gigantic earthwork entrenchments and ramparts of Maiden Castle.

The siege lasted a fortnight, until the long darkness of the winter solstice, when the Wolf Warriors rushed from their citadel under the moonless night and fell upon Lord Urien's camp. Arthor arrived first from his pavilion, bearing torches into a field of combat where all flame had been crushed by the enemy. In the darkness, neuter shapes grappled. Arthor's palfrey trudged unwillingly toward that blind equality of combatants, unsure where to strike and where to flee.

The king dismounted and set his horse running from the melee. 'We must wait for Kyner and Lot and more fire,' Bedevere advised.

Arthor shouted above the cries of the wounded, 'You wait! Urien is under my protection!' Excalibur lithe in one hand, torch in the other, and his shield of the Madonna strapped to his back, he charged, followed by his guards in black leather armor.

Bedevere hurried to his side, short sword drawn and flashing in the king's torchlight. The enshadowed democracy of warriors thwarted quick identification, but the upheld torches attracted the Wolf Warriors and their thrown hatchets. Several banged off the king's shielded back, spun him around, and drew him deeper into the fray. Bedevere struggled to keep up with him. A blow struck him behind the skull with an ugly sound. Blood flew, and he fell foul of hands that yanked him into darkness.

Raven's Branch

All the long night, Rex Mundi lay curled upon himself beside a slick pool luminous with fire snakes. Two hippogriffs cantered by in the chalky dark before dawn, their raptor heads underlit by the shining water, their large wings folded back against their sleek equine bodies. At Merlin's direction, Rex Mundi leaped up, flapping his robes. The hippogriffs startled and reared back. Swiftly, Merlin removed his cap, seized the lion mane of one beast, and leaped upon its muscled shoulders. While the other creature galloped into the gloom, Merlin pressed the long cap across the eyes of the winged mount and held it in place until the fabulous animal gentled.

Ith thith a good idea?

'Providence, Dagonet.' Merlin waited for the residual magic in his cap to penetrate the hippogriff's brain. 'We must seize our opportunities as they present themselves. Raven's Branch is far distant, and the gods dwell in these astral woods. Better that we find our way swiftly to our destination than become prey of the Wild Hunt. Don't you agree?'

Oh thertainly! Let uth away!

Merlin removed his cap from the beast's eyes but kept it tight to the broad feathered head so that the slim magic in the hat allowed control. They soared. The squawking of the hippogriff and the thwack of its wings beating the dawn's bright wind shook Rex Mundi's bones, yet his grip did not fail. Into the sun's glare they flew, and the full splendor of the Storm Tree opened around them. Under orange clouds that spanned the gates of day, forests of obscure purple disclosed stone temples of dolmen rings and oaken halls roofed in beaten bronze, the shrines and hunting lodges of the gods.

The hippogriff carried them past terraced landscapes of immense swards patterned with mazy hedges. Above these, they galloped on the wind over wild gorges choked with mossy boulders. Distant buttes appeared on the heights beyond, their bases grounded among cloven rocks and the silver fumes of cascades and filament waterfalls. Higher yet the hippogriff mounted at Merlin's command, toward the indigo zenith, where adamantine cliffs rose out of plateaus of gray, driving rain.

Far beyond these ranges of weather, the hippogriff carried them to the topmost branch of the World Tree – a bleakly barren expanse. The winged eagle-leonine-horse alighted on a desert dune among warped and quaking horizons. Rex Mundi dismounted, and the hippogriff shrieked with jubilation and lofted away.

Behold thith evil world! Where are we, Merlin?

Rex Mundi looked about at the wasteland of sulfur sands and shattered rocks under stars that flared like cactus flowers. 'This is the Raven's Branch. And there – there is the Seat of the Slain!' He pointed toward a ferric mesa upon which a grim throne of rusted and pocked iron sat beneath the reaping-hook of the moon.

Battle Blind

The dark riot surged most violently about Lord Urien and his personal guard. Bloodyheaded, gaunt Urien stood in the middle of a pile of fallen bodies, lit only by the rare flicker of a torch and the sifted starlight. Arthor hacked his way through the whirling Saxons, swatting with torch and sword. When he looked about for Bedevere, the steward was gone, as were the king's guards. He was alone in the midst of violence. That suited him. He had been reared as a violent warrior, a protector, bred to throw his life away for his chief. He had possessed no station in Kyner's clan and had expected to die in battle from the day he first took up a sword. If this night was that destined hour, he felt no fear.

The fight washed about him with shrieks and a clangor of steel. He hurled the torch onto the pile of corpses where Urien fought and used the flap of light to mark his progress. Shield protecting his back, Excalibur gripped in both hands, he whirled savagely, cutting a swath toward the light. Soon, he stood beside Urien, and the two unslung their shields and backed against each other to fight their way through the reeling battle.

When Kyner and Lot arrived with their forces, they found Arthor and Urien staggering with exhaustion. But by then, most of the Wolf Warriors had been slain, and the battle had slowed to a brutal hacking and hammering of exhausted warriors. The reinforcements quickly dispatched the remaining Saxons, and Urien, swaying dizzily, clutched at the gory youth at his side. 'Who are you?' he croaked, fatigued hand trembling to the lad's blood-smeared face. 'You shall be rewarded for your valor.'

'I am Arthor,' the boy husked, barely audible. 'Your king.'

Priests and druids mingled among the dead, seeking the wounded and offering spiritual solace to the dying. They came upon the king and the chieftain on their knees with Excalibur standing between them. 'The sword Lightning,' Urien announced in his fractured voice. 'Crafted by Brokk, smithy of the Furor. Stolen by the Fire Lords for Merlin. He gave it to this lad – our king.'

'You are battle-blind, brave Urien,' warned a druid in the green leather vestment of his healing station. 'He is Christian.'

'I would be battle-dead if not for him.' Urien clutched Arthor's sword arm. 'We have bathed together in the blood of our enemies. This is a king I can respect.'

In the moment that Arthor's heart lifted, he saw Kyner shambling toward him. 'Your personal guard are dead, *sire*. All of them, save Bedevere. We found him buried among the dead.' The stout Celt stared darkly at his stepson. 'Did you learn nothing as my ward? You lead men, not sacrifice them.'

'Kyner, those men died that I might live,' Urien spoke up, struggling to his feet with the help of the druids. 'I will honor their deaths by pledging my clans to this king.'

Kyner took Arthor under his arm and hoisted him upright, whispering to him, 'Is this how you will secure your throne – buying pledges with the blood of those already sworn to you?'

Out of Londinium

Morgeu escorted Merlin's body through the subterranean passages of the governor's palace. The soul of her father, Gorlois, had been marked by the Furor, and the enchantress, who had been aware of this since she saw her father's mangled ghost in the woods of the north, wrapped his head in a turban inscribed with runes designed to break the god's influence.

Astonished to find himself alert and unimpeded by visions, Gorlois lauded his daughter, 'You have greater glamour than your mother ever did!'

'Hush, father.' Morgeu squeezed his hand as she led him through the corridors unlit save by the spectral glow of vampyres. 'We have not yet won our freedom.'

He glanced fretfully at the blurred apparitions escorting them in the dank tunnels. 'Where are you taking me, daughter?'

'Out of Londinium.'

'But our work is here.' Gorlois gestured expansively at the dark, dripping cavern. 'Syrax has brokered an alliance with King Wesc. Bors Bona and Count Platorius are in his service. With this bloc, we can crush that upstart sired on your mother by Merlin's puppet, Uther.'

'Father, you are inside Merlin's body. We must draw you out before the wizard finds us or your soul is lost.'

'You are a powerful worker of magic. When the wizard comes for this body, slay him.'

'I am not that powerful, father.' They emerged in a region of old clay drains and jointed cesspipes, where the feculent stink burned their eyes and nostrils. 'I am but an enchantress. But I do have the skill to extract you from this demon's form.'

'Extract me to where?' Gorlois asked, hand over his mouth. 'I am a ghost.'

'I am preparing a new body for you – as my child.'

'Your child!' His surprise echoed back from the dark deeps. 'I am your father.'

Morgeu squinted angrily at him. 'Would you rather be a ghost?'

'I would rather keep this body. It has magic within it.'

They stepped gingerly along a ledge above a pool of sludge. 'Father, the Furor has marked you. Even now, that wrathful god is working to unravel my enchantment. When he succeeds, you will belong to him again.'

'That was not so bad.' He jumped over a stream of gray sewage percolating through the bedding slates of the tunnel. 'I saw into people's souls. I spoke with an authority that mastered all who heard me. And I saw other things, daughter. I saw terrible things in the future, far beyond our time.'

'Trust me, father. You do not want to stay in this evil body.' She pulled on his arm, guiding him toward a jiggling torchflame. 'The Furor and the demon Lailoken will fight over you – and you will suffer. Accept the body I am weaving for you.'

Gorlois paused. 'Who is the father of this body?'

Morgeu faced him anxiously and whispered, 'Arthor.'

'Your brother!' His shout boomed off the stone walls.

'Father, I am sorry if . . .'

'Sorry?' His perplexity vanished as a grin widened across his face, and he clapped an arm over her shoulders and walked with her toward the dismal light. 'You are a wonder beyond my greatest hopes, Morgeu. Yes! A wonder! My father is king – and I will succeed him. Yes! I admire your cunning. Oh yes, I admire it very much – and I will be proud to have you for my mother.'

Mother Mary, today commemorates that holy day you birthed our Savior in a manger. By God's grace, this morning I will receive the pledge of the Celtic chieftain Urien. I am grateful to our Father for this victory – and I am saddened by the deaths of my personal guard. Was

I wrong, as Kyner says, for sacrificing them to win Urien's pledge? A dozen good and faithful Christian men slain for the allegiance of two score clans of battle-fierce, pagan Celts. I am not a ruthless king – am I? My guard were warriors. They fought at my side, and I shared their risk. Yet, I am alive, and they are all dead, save Bedevere. Good Bedevere. He has consoled me for my decision, declaring that I acted from my heart and not my head and so won the fealty of Urien's heart. He aids my mind as well as my physical well-being. I cannot thank you enough for sending him to me. He is a man who notices everything, every detail, and comprehends it all with pithy insight. He has distilled his observations to a precise, one-word assessment for each of my warriors. Kyner disapproved the loss of my guard, for, as Bedevere says, my stepfather is the Optimist. For all his gruff bearing, Kyner believes that virtue will be rewarded and good triumph over evil as a matter of course. To sacrifce my guard in striving for victory, that is too aggressive for his optimism. As for Urien, Bedevere labels him the Idealist, champion of noble purpose. My sacrifice is a noble act worthy of the reward of his devotion. Lot is the Cynic, certain that every action springs from selfish motives. And Marcus the Fatalist sees all events as inevitable – hence his willingness to ride against the invaders of his realm and accept the consequences as fated. Bedevere calls himself the Realist, for he abhors speculation and strives to view the world shorn of dreams. And me? When I asked him, he simply smiled and sucked on his pipe. 'You,' he said, 'you are the King.'

Celtic Christmas

On Christmas morning, Lord Urien Durotriges, chieftain of the Celtic clans of the coast, knelt before King Arthor in the temple of the goddess Aradia and pledged himself and his clan to the service of the young monarch. A cold rain drizzled through the enclosing aspens, and fog climbed the hillcrest of Maiden Castle, where three nights earlier Wolf Warriors had reveled.

The priests who accompanied Lord Marcus and Chief Kyner refused to set foot in the pagan temple. They had advised the young king to seek the conversion of both Urien and Lot, but Arthor refused. He considered himself king of all Britain, and Christians and worshipers of the old ways were equally his subjects. With that in mind, he agreed to accept Lord Urien's pledge within the ancient temple.

Bedevere reluctantly accompanied him. He remembered nothing of the dark battle where Arthor had intervened to save the Celtic chieftain's life. For an entire day afterward, he had lain unconscious. Even now, three days later, his head still ached from the blow that had toppled him into darkness, and his wallet of medicinal herbs from the Orient offered no remedy.

The sight of his steward doddering between incense trays, his bald head bandaged, stirred remorse in King Arthor. When the elaborate ceremonies of chants, bard songs, stick dances, and incense evocations of the Daoine Síd ended and Lord Urien and his clan chiefs had all knelt before him and been blessed by the touch of Excalibur, he sat with Bedevere on the temple steps. Ritual fires blazed on the temple grounds, and druids in white cloaks and five-sided clogs oversaw rites of torch-juggling and round dances.

'Kyner admonished me for sacrificing so many to save Urien,' Arthor said, noting the pallor of his steward's gaunt cheeks. 'I'm relieved to find you well enough to attend these rites. It's God's gift to me on the birthday of his Son, our good shepherd.'

'Shepherding is a despised trade in the Holy Land,' Bedevere said quietly, watching the Celtic dancers spiral among the fires. 'Shepherds are like thieves. They graze their sheep on other people's lands, and they pilfer. They're not allowed to fulfill judicial office or serve as witnesses in court. No one buys from them, for it can be assumed that they possess only stolen property. And yet our Savior identified himself with them.'

'Messiah born in a manger – friend to tax collectors, lepers, and prostitutes – executed ignominiously—' Arthor shook his head. 'He delivered God's love to where that love is most needed.'

'And so we find you, a Christian king, here among the pagans.' Bedevere smiled wanly. 'You are an unusual king, sire.'

'Because I was not always noble.' He clasped Bedevere's

one hand gratefully. 'Until this past summer, I believed I was lowborn. But there is no God-given difference between high and low – I see that now. That distinction is an artifice. The Savior knew.'

Bedevere nodded wearily. 'And he died for us to know it.'

Awakening

Bors Bona awoke in a chamber paneled with green jasper between slender columns of lapis lazuli. He threw off a mink coverlet and stood in his nightshirt before a window three times his height. Across the manicured lawns and topiary hedges, beyond the brownstone palace walls, Londinium's early-morning streets lay nearly empty. A few stars hung like spurs above the tile roofs.

On the main boulevard, he watched a tented wagon clatter, driven by a woman whose red tresses spilled from under her hood. A peculiar feeling twisted in him as the wagon dwindled into the distance.

The main doors, padded with blue leather and nailed with brass stars, swung open, and Severus Syrax rushed in accompanied by a frightened Count Platorius and a dozen guards and half as many priests. 'You are well! Thank God! Oh, thank God!' The *magister militum* pointed his guards to the billowy masses of curtains beside the windows, and the priests followed them there, swinging smoking censers and chanting scripture.

Bors Bona ran both hands over his bristle-cropped cranium. The last he remembered, he had been standing with his peers in the throne room inflamed at their alliance with the Foederatus. 'What has happened, Syrax? Where's my sword? My armor? Call my captain!'

'Bors! Bors! You are well!' Severus Syrax and the sullen-eyed count looked for the priests to signal that all was secure before they approached the warlord. 'There's murder afoot and soldiers slain.'

'Vampyres!' Count Platorius gasped, the discolored flesh

under his eyes darker for want of sleep. 'A horrid gang of them!'

Bors Bona placed his fists on his hips. 'What've you done to me, Syrax? Why am I unarmed and in this chamber?'

'I?' Severus Syrax appeared hurt. 'Dear Bors, *I've* done nothing but protect you. Ask Platorius. Merlin enchanted you.'

'He put you to sleep days ago,' the count confirmed.

'Where is that demon?' Bors yelled. 'Give me my sword! I'll have his head.'

'He's gone, Bors. Gone!' Severus Syrax wrung his bejeweled fingers. 'The vampyres carried him away.' He went to a corner wardrobe and opened its doors. 'Your garments and sword are here. When you're dressed, I'll conduct you to where your troops are quartered. They have been concerned for you.'

'Help us, Bors,' the count pleaded, following him to the wardrobe. 'Evil forces conspire against us. Severus and I, we seek peace – and a lucrative trade relationship with King Wesc. But strong evil opposes us – evil that has carried Merlin away. He may be a demon, but he is a demon won to the service of our Savior and of peace. And now evil has taken him from us and thwarts our peace. Evil opposes us, Bors!'

'I, too, oppose you – or I did.' Bors lifted his swordbelt from the wardrobe and unsheathed the blade. *But now I am in your hands and at your mercy,* he said to himself, glad to have a weapon in his grip. *Who knows how my troops have been compromised by you weasels while I've been entranced.* 'I must rethink my allegiance, comrades. Vampyres have seized Merlin, you say. Well, then, I will not serve the unholy. Surely not Merlin – nor his king should he, too, be a minion of such evil. If peace is to be won by trade with our enemies, so be it, though history has shown that such alliances are foolish. Better that than a kingdom overrun by vampyres.' He slid his sword back into its scabbard, satisfied that it was intact. 'My troops will winter in Londinium, and I will know more of King Wesc and his will for peace – and, in time, we will rid this city of evil.'

King Arthor and the Druids

Before departing Maiden Castle, King Arthor honored the request of the druids to meet with their supreme hieros at midday in the airy and elegant temple of the goddess Aradia. Atop an altar of black obsidian stone within the blue marble temple erected by the Romans three centuries earlier, the druids had draped red ivy and a crisp, golden mass of mistletoe.

'Do you know the significance of this, sire?' the cowled hieros asked, pulling back the sleeves of his green and white robes to pass his hands over the altar of rough-hewn stone without disturbing the plants arrayed there. His jowly face watched impassively from under his hood, milky eyes attentive.

'Ivy spirals for the sun, searching for God.' Arthor saw the surprise in the old druid's stare and went on, 'Twelfth letter of the Ogham, eleventh month of the year, it is called Gort. The mistletoe is not of the tree alphabet. It is the mystery of All Heal. This I have learned from the Ovate, the doctor of learning, that my stepfather, Lord Kyner, retained at White Thorn for those of his people not yet won to the love of our Savior.'

A calm smile opened in the aged face of the hieros. 'It is good you know something of the old ways, for I have summoned you here to reveal to you the ultimate secret of our kindred faith.'

'I am a Christian king, lord druid.' Arthor spoke slowly, to be certain the old man understood. 'Our faith is not kindred.'

'Oh, but it is, sire.' The hieros's clouded eyes gleamed merrily. '*That* is the ultimate secret. And now that you are king of the Celtic clans of both Lord Lot and Lord Urien, I am free to declare before you the truth of our kindred faith – that what you call Christian, the Faith of the Anointed One, is the Ancient Faith we druids preserve.'

'My faith is the salvation offered by Jesus Christ.'

'A Hebrew.' The hieros drew back the hood from his long locks of thinning gray hair. 'We druids are a priestly caste descended from the Temple of Solomon in Jerusalem – the very temple razed by the Babylonians five hundred and eighty-six years before the birth of the Anointed One, at a time when the Celtic empire touched the holy lands. We share a faith with the Hebrews. The Anointed One, *Yesu*, is a Celtic savior prophesied by our seers since the age of Solomon's Temple. He is the All Heal symbolized by the mistletoe. On the rare oak where this plant grows, our people mark a cross and carve the branch with the name All Heal, which in our language is *Yesu*! And behold our temples – not this Roman edifice, but the shrines we have built with our own hands. They are constructed, like this obsidian altar, of unhewn stone. Hu Gadarn Hyscion – Hu the Mighty, who led our people to Britain – Mighty Hu was a descendant of Abraham. He continued the ancient practice of carving our altars from unhewn stone as has been recorded in Exodus chapter twenty, verse twenty-five: "And if you make Me an altar of stone, you shall not build it of hewn stone; for if you use your tool on it, you have profaned it." The Bible holds many of our druidic truths. The desert prophets Isaiah, Jeremiah, and Zechariah refer to the coming messiah as "the Branch." We teach, as well, that our deliverer is the Branch – the All Heal . . .'

Arthor stopped him by leaning forward across the altar. 'As your king, I accept your faith descended of Abraham and the times before. I will not impede your religion as the Romans did. But know this, hieros. The messiah has come. The old ways are superceded by the new. My Savior declares in His own words, 'I am the way, the truth, and the life. No one comes to the Father except through me.' His is the way that I will follow.'

The druid nodded sagely. 'That is as it should be, sire. *Yesu* is indeed the way – the All Heal of resurrection. But remember this, wise king: The way is the way – and not the destination.'

Mother Mary, my role as king continues to bring me into conflict with all that I have learned as a child about our faith from the priests. The hieros insists the druids are Hebrews. I have asked Bedevere to summon me a Hebrew, a rabbi from the synagogue at Sorbiodunum, that I may converse with him and test these notions of the hieros. You are a Hebrew, Mother Mary. Your Son is a Hebrew. The very center of my spiritual life is informed by Judaism; so why am I distrustful of the hieros's claim? The rabbi whom Merlin summoned is equally skeptical but not outright hostile to the idea. Indeed, the Celts were in Jerusalem at the time of Solomon's temple. Indeed, the druids' forest shrines are built of unhewn stone as the old books of the Bible decree. Indeed, the Messiah that the prophets foretold is referred to by them as the Branch — as is the Celtic yesu, the all-heal, the mistletoe. Other than confirming what the hieros told me, I've learned nothing new. Should I pursue this knowledge? Bedevere tells me I am too young. First, I must attend to unifying my kingdom. Later, he says, I may pursue the mysteries of the angels and the demons — and of God. But for now, there is practical work to be done. I am no priest, no philosopher of the Church. Yet, I have seen enough in my short life to know that there is more to this world than the Church reveals. Guide me, Mother of God, to the knowledge I need to rule wisely.

Cei's Travels

Cei shaved his head, donned a hempen cassock, and rode east disguised as an itinerant monk. To allay his fears of the enchantress he had volunteered to find and return to her husband, Lord Lot gave him a talisman woven from locks of hair shorn from the heads of Morgeu's sons, Gawain and Gareth. He traveled alone. Though King Arthor had pleaded with him to take an escort of guardsmen, Cei believed he could travel faster on his own.

He followed the Roman roads north and reached Aquae Sulis in time to celebrate Christmas in the steaming public baths with several courtesans and a flagon of vintage wine. He was not eager to find Morgeu and gladly indulged his carnal desires on his first long journey away from home alone. With a throbbing head and a much lightened coin purse, he continued north through a peaceful and well-Romanized countryside: vineyards pruned and shrouded in hay-sheafs for winter, bare orchards neatly arrayed upon the undulant hillsides, and numerous villas, where he was welcomed as a holy man and compelled to participate in baptisms, weddings, and funerals.

With the offerings given him for these services, Cei pursued his pleasures in the magisterial city of Corinium. He was more afraid of Morgeu than he had realized when he was with the army – fearful of what enchantment she might place on him – and he was determined to take what pleasures he could from life before facing the witchy sister of his king. Outside Corinium's gates, he doffed his monk's cassock and entered as a warrior seeking his recreation. He enjoyed the New Year games at the city amphitheatre, doubling his earnings at the cock fights and squandering it all at the taverns and public baths, enjoying the finest local vintages and comestibles and the ardent attentions of the city's bawdries. In his drunken attempt to win more coin for more pleasures, he lost his horse and his sword.

All resources spent and the days growing colder, Cei departed Corinium on foot with another pounding headache and only a rusk of rye bread for provisions. He wandered east for several days, seeing only charcoal burners and salt peddlers on the cold, damp roads, all of whom demanded his blessing, which he gave begrudgingly for a tinder and a salt lick.

With the first flurries of snow, he found spoor that prickled his flesh. A wildwood gang had jumped a woodcutter and left him mutilated by his own ax among a cairn of rocks. The man was not yet dead, and the bloody trail of the gang still fresh. Cei knelt beside the mortally wounded woodcutter and prayed with him until he died gurgling blood. The unarmed warrior buried the corpse under the cairn rocks, constantly flicking glances over his shoulder for the return of the murderers.

Anno Domini 491
The new year entered bitterly cold and gray. The wildwood gangs, desperate for warmth and food, stepped up their attacks against isolated villas and estates, and the king's army proceeded slowly through the lands of the Belgae, fanning out to assert Arthor's influence among all the many hamlets and thorpes of the sprawling countryside. Endless small skirmishes occupied the royal forces within the dense forests and no

help came from the east, though Arthor dispatched numerous messengers to the *magister militum* Severus Syrax as well as to the elite forces of Bors Bona.

The self-proclaimed king of the Belgae, Gorthyn, was himself raised from the ranks of the brigands that roamed the land plundering farms, and he sat silently in his redstone citadel at Cunetio, declaring neither allegiance nor opposition to the king. Every legate that Arthor dispatched to petition King Gorthyn for help vanished. At last, the king decided to go himself.

'Have you learned nothing from the deaths of your personal guard at Maiden Castle?' Kyner complained, confronting the king as Arthor doffed his gold chaplet and polished corselet of brass strips. 'You are our king. You jeopardize us all when you put yourself at risk. Listen to me as your war counselor if not as a father.'

'Where is your son, Cei?' Arthor asked sourly. 'I sent him to face Morgeu the Fey in my place – and he is gone.'

Kyner shook his ruddy face. 'I love my son with all my heart, but he is a warrior and lives and dies by the sword. Once you were such – but no longer. As king you must live for your people.'

'Cunetio is two days' ride on the Roman road,' said Arthor, pulling a tattered tunic over his leather cuirasse. 'I will return before your work is done clearing these woods of brigands.'

Wearing garments taken from the wildwood gangs, Arthor and thirty volunteers galloped north. Only Bedevere dressed as usual, in his gleaming bronze helmet crested with red-dyed horse bristles and his shining breastplates and buckler; on this mission, he bore a long scimitar at his side. Every few leagues, the king dispatched five of his men into the forests with instructions to join themselves to the ranks of the brigands they encountered. When Arthor approached the fastness of maroon stones, he entered the hillside woods alone, keeping at his back the long rays of the setting sun. He went directly to a smudgy line of smoke rising among the trees and confronted a mongrel band of ragged and filthy warriors roasting a sheep. Face smudged, hair greased stiff as a porcupine's hackles, he appeared no different than they – a brutish youth, his stare galled and mad-looking.

The reputation of Excalibur had not yet reached these hills, and when the boy drew the sword to fend the aggressive gang, the mirror-blue blade inspired fear but did not identify the hand that wielded it. 'This sword fights with yours if you give me food.'

After two fierce attempts to take the beautiful weapon from the grimy lad resulted in a flayed cheek and a sliced ear among the assailants, they welcomed him to the fireside and showed him the weapons they had taken from travelers. Among them was Cei's long sword that he had gambled away in Corinium.

Arthor showed no emotion at the evidence of Cei's murder but ate sullenly of the roast mutton, his heart fisted in his chest.

Seat of the Slain

In the Storm Tree, hours, even minutes, passed for days upon Middle Earth; the higher one climbed, the faster time flew below. And though Rex Mundi had only been among the spectral branches a short time, Merlin well knew that weeks had passed in Britain. Urgency gripped him to return to his king and help him to fulfill his mission before the seasons turned again to summer and Arthor was obliged to produce the pledges of all the warlords and chieftains – or relinquish his crown.

Anxiously, Rex Mundi crossed the sere, burnt-looking plain of the Raven's Branch toward the mesa that held a giant, rusted throne. He climbed crevassed slopes among small trees black and bent and visited by ravens. Scabrous packs of dire wolves with crazed red eyes haunted the ravines of the mesa, guarding chalked skeletons of nameless others who had trespassed this way. The protective magic of the wizard's robes and hat kept them distant and baying.

Atop the mesa, pale dust lay in windrowed ribs that circled the corroded throne like ripple waves in water, healing over the footfalls after each step. The air smelled of ash, sour and scorched. Overhead, evil stars burned in a purple sky.

Thith ith thcary!

Using scales of rust and corrosively pitted holes as footholds, Rex Mundi climbed onto the Seat of the Slain. Once seated, the cosmos arranged itself as a godlike hall, with the starry cope of heaven raftered by galactic streamers and the encircling walls the indigo horizons rigged with lyre-strings of lightning and stately columns of thermal clouds. The earth itself served as the great hall's floor, inlaid with divers-colored mosaics of desert, mountain, and river terrains, the verdure of jungles, the hammered glimmer of the sea.

'What you behold is but froth on the vastness of time,' a voice crackled out of the air. 'All of history lies hidden.'

Gweat godth!

A crone in cobweb rags crouched beside Rex Mundi. Her skull face leered at him through a withered mask of loose, gray flesh and goggling eyes. 'Look at your lost homes, all of you.'

At her command, Lord Monkey witnessed again the sepia dark of the forest canopy where it had clung to milk-wet mother's fur. Dagonet glimpsed the poplar-spired villa in Armorica where he ran playfully as a child with others his own height. Azael, Lailoken, and the Fire Lord faced again the white fire of all origins . . .

'Ah, Urd of the Norns!' Merlin greeted the Wyrd Sister, speaking quickly before his peek at heaven robbed him of all will to speak or live. He held a diamond before the crone's mummied face, and its blue chips of light glittered in her bulging eyes. 'This is the gift I have brought you so that I might sit here and pay no heed to my past.'

With a cackled cry, she snatched the diamond from Rex Mundi's hirsute fingers and was gone, a wisp of ash drifting away with the howls the wolves relayed on the stony slopes.

I gwew up in thplendor and love! I want to go back.

'No one can go back, Dagonet,' a gentle voice turned Rex Mundi's head. At his side on the giant iron throne sat a woman of astonishing beauty with long hair pale as freshcut wood and skin clear as arctic daylight, her eyes winterfrost, her high cheeks haughty as the antelope's.

Her raiment, sheer moonlight, revealed shadowed charms that brought Dagonet's voice into Rex Mundi's throat. 'You

are the motht beautiful woman my eyeth have ever theen! Who
are you?'

'I am a Norn – Verthandi, Wyrd Sister of present time.' She
brushed her cool fingers against Rex Mundi's ape-slanted brow,
and her touch stroked alertness like harp-strings within him. 'I
can reveal to you where every demon cowers in the House of
Fog and where every Fire Lord burns in the dark gulf. I can
show you your young king, Arthor, hunkering like a criminal
in a dark wood of the Belgae, murder in his heart . . .'

In a Dark Wood

Bedevere's plumed helmet, breastplates and buckler dished the
reflections of his campfire so brightly that the wildwood gang
that rushed upon him out of the night forest struck him before
he moved. But the armor clanged emptily. The legate was
nowhere to be found among the dark trees or in their branches.
Arthor went with the gang when they reported this at the citadel
of Cunetio.

'Sound the longhorn,' the gang leader shouted to the guard
on the torchlit ramparts. 'One of the king's men is loose in our
woods. Sound the longhorn and run the manhunt.'

Moments later, a resounding blast sounded and echoed
among the hills of the overcast night. Arthor rode with the
manhunt. Wildwood gangs throughout the region criss-crossed
the Roman roads and fanned through the forests. By dawn,
they had not found Bedevere but many of their numbers had
been mysteriously slain, apparently murdered by their own
comrades.

Before the gates of Cunetio, the survivors gathered to
ferret out their betrayers. There, among the carnelian shadows of early morning, Arthor tore away his rag tunic and
exposed the leather cuirasse embossed with the regal dragon.
With his first blow, he slew the brigand that wielded Cei's
sword. And at Arthor's war cry, the score and ten of the
king's men scattered among the brigands began their savage
retribution.

From the rootheld burrow where he had buried himself,

Bedevere rose, the scimitar in his one arm flashing. The pan-
icked brigands tried to flee, but every direction was blocked by
the lethal swords of the king. Before the citadel could summon
archers to the ramparts, the killing was done and the king's men
dispersed into the forest.

By noon, Gorthyn had accepted King Arthor's terms of
surrender. With most of his wildwood gangs slaughtered, the
hope of defending Cunetio against Arthor's encroaching forces
had vanished. Happy to accept exile from Britain with all his
household, he opened the gates of the citadel. Arthor and his
men escorted his train of wagons south, and along the way the
two kings rode together.

'You are a cunning adversary,' said Gorthyn, a scar-faced
man with thick shoulders and black hair pulled back and
braided to a long rat's tail. 'You defanged me quick enough.
Had you more patience to wait for your army, you could have
crushed me.'

'The people of Cunetio are under my protection,' Arthor
replied blandly. 'My purpose is served by removing the malefactor
from their midst.'

'Do not mistake me, brother king.' Gorthyn's smile stretched
straight back like a shark's and showed yellowed and missing
teeth. 'Your charity is not lost on me. One man's malefactor
is another man's king. It has ever been thus.'

'Answer me this, then – one king to another.' Arthor met
Gorthyn's narrow, vexed stare. 'You have thrived on the deaths
of innocent wayfarers. Have you no fear of God?'

Gorthyn's laugh startled his steed, and he had to struggle
a moment to steady the animal. 'I am no heretic, brother
king. I am as true to God as you and know with confidence
that I will receive my reward from His hand when I die,
for I serve Him well.' He nodded at the bare trees and
frozen earth. 'God has placed man in this world for the
very purpose that malignity be set against him. Does not
the Bible tell us this? We are fallen from grace, brother
king. Fallen before the god of vengeance. And I – I am
his wrath.'

Fata Morgana

'Where are you taking me, daughter?' Gorlois asked from where he sat on the riding board next to Morgeu. He looked about at the bare fields scalded by the wind and shivered in the wool mantle that the enchantress had plucked from a dead guard lying at the city gate, bloodless as a hung pig. 'And don't tell me again "out of Londinium". I know not how many days ago we departed that city, for each nightfall you plunge me into a dreamless and forgetful sleep. I have lost my sense of time.'

'I am protecting you, father.' Morgeu held the reins in one hand and with the other patted his bony knee. Even through the black fabric of his trousers, she could feel his cold flesh. The spell she cast on him each night to hide him from the Furor was killing him. His soul, claimed by both the north god and her magic, could not remain much longer in this stolen body. 'The Furor has marked your soul, and surely Lailoken is stalking you as well to reclaim his flesh. We must defy both gods and demons.'

'You have not answered my question, daughter.'

'The less I tell you, the less the Furor will know.' Her small, black eyes scanned the brambly ditches of the broken highway for Wolf Warriors or wildwood gangs. 'But know this – I possess the magic to take you back from the Furor. We are bound for a ceremonial place that I've prepared before coming for you.'

'Why must we travel with that – *creature*?' Gorlois glanced over his shoulder at the bed of loam that filled the tented wagon.

'Terpillius is going to help us with my magic.' A smile lifted one corner of her small lips. 'He will be instrumental in freeing you from this demon's flesh and placing you where you belong, in the body I am growing for you. It will be a beautiful operation. A vampyre who thrives on the blood of destroyed lives will help fit your life to my root-blood.'

'Will I still be marked by the Furor?'

'I doubt even the Furor can undo that.' She sucked cold air through her teeth, remembering the disfigurement of her father's ghost that she had beheld in the north woods. 'He drew your soul into the Storm Tree to reshape you so that you would serve his purposes best within Lailoken's body. But we will free you from this alien flesh and its servitude to the wrathful god.'

Gorlois turned sharply in his seat. 'Will I lose my magic?'

'Your magic is the power within the demon's body.' She placed a hand over her womb. 'I am making you a new body. You'll not have the demon's strengths, but you will have your own mortal power.'

'I will be king.'

'You will be Britain's greatest king. After you drive the invaders from our island, you will take the fight to them, and you will rule from Caledonia to Aquitania.' Morgeu snapped the reins and ran the wagon along a straight stretch of unbroken highway. Once, and recently, she had been willing to serve the Furor, to drive her anger hard against Arthor and Merlin. But now, the Furor threatened her child. Not even this fierce god would be spared her wrath when her children and their children were at risk. 'The Furor believes he will conquer this land with his brutal Saxons, wily Angles, and fierce Jutes and Picts. But he is not the only one endowed with prophecy. I see a future where Celtic magic unites pagans to the nailed god and defies the Furor. Behold!'

From out of the shore of winter clouds above the forested hills rose a mirage of elaborate castles – glass towers and stacked buildings immense as cliffs, highways uplifted on pylons, viaducts curving smooth as ribbons among the glass turrets of the future.

Wyrd Sister

Verthandi, in her raiment sheer as moonlight, pressed closer to Rex Mundi where they sat together on the Seat of the Slain and touched him with an alpine perfume of windy heights. 'If you will give me the Dragon's hoard in your pockets, I will show you all the wonders of the world as they are now. Do you want to see again where once you lived free, Lord Monkey?'

The beast in Rex Mundi chittered with delight as the lovely

Norn brushed the henna hackles from his ape-slanted brow. He pressed himself into the assembled body's dark, staring eyes, where a vision unfolded—

Sunlight pierced high galleries of looped vines and hanging air plants, slanting among shifting vapors and pale boles of immense trees. Birds clicked and fretted where the light pierced, and monkeys screeched, fighting over a squashed fruit. In the dark chambers of the jungle, butterflies glowed like windblown sparks.

Encouraged by Lord Monkey's joy at the sight of his home, Dagonet boldly called from within the psychic interior of Rex Mundi – *Let me thee again where I gwew to my dwarfed manhood!*

Verthandi's winterfrost eyes darkened sadly. 'You would see again the place where once you knew happiness, Dagonet. But since you ran away, ashamed of your stunted stature, and left your family's estate in the care of your younger brothers and sister, the Wolf Warriors came and what is now is no longer what was.'

The villa walls stood all but overgrown by black ivy, the fluted columns smashed, the mosaics bedight with crawling dodder. Past cracked urns, the vision entered a dusky interior of weathersprung tiles, bricks toppled among rife weeds, and a prolapsed ceiling of plaster that hung like tattered cloths.

I can thee no more! Take thith thad thight away from me!

Before Merlin could move to speak, Azael seized Rex Mundi's tongue. 'Show me God. We followed Her out here into the cold and dark – and we haven't seen Her since. The Fire Lords say She is still here. Then, where is She?'

The wyrd sister sighed, then pressed her lovely lips close to Rex Mundi's hairy ear and softly hummed a sad mountain song.

In a ray of sunlight, a crowd of protozoans teemed, transparent bodies swarming through vast halls of a palace of water too small for the eye to see; their cilia beat together, excited by energies of Brownian motion and the invisible magnetic fields encircling them.

I don't underthtand what I'm theeing! What are theeth thingth?

'They're tiny, hungry animals, you fool!' Azael griped.

'You are seeing Her where She is now – at the dance,' the Norn replied, miffed at the demon's anger. 'She likes to dance.'

Before Azael could say more, Merlin seized Rex Mundi's tongue. 'Show me Arthor. Show me the high king of Britain.'

Verthandi smiled and leaned closer, her pale hair covering the bestial face of Rex Mundi with a scent like a load of hay.

Mother Mary, my brother Cei is dead. My fear of Morgeu sent him on the hopeless mission that killed him. I should have allowed Lot to go, as he had requested. I should have been my brother's keeper. Alone at night in my tent, my face pressed in my pallet, I remember our child years together, when I bested that oaf at every endeavor – horsemanship, archery, swordplay, swimming, mathematics, languages, philosophy – everything. It galled him. That, I believe, is why Kyner insisted that I, a foundling, undertake every aspect of his son's training, so that I would goad the lug to compete all the more strenuously. Excelling satisfied my angry heart and soothed my embitterment at the low station to which I believed I had been born. But now, thinking how I smirked at his frustrated bouts of rage every time I overwhelmed him with my prowess, I weep for him. I have confessed this to no one, not even Kyner, whom I have seen crying in chapel for his lost son. But I am not ashamed to tell you. You know my heart and its hungers. You know the shadows that trouble my mind with fear and doubt. And you know Cei, for all his faults, was worthy of a better love than mine.

Riders of the North Wind

King Arthor sat counseling with his commanders in a pavilion tent whose canvas walls buckled under the blustering wind. An open flap revealed frozen fields under a hoar-frost sky. Bonfires burned at wide intervals among the army's numerous tents, and the smoke shredded and flew in windclawed shapes like furious black harpies.

'We must go north,' Urien declared. He sat, like the others, in a campaign chair covered with marten fur and set before a trestle table where scroll maps lay unfurled and tacked. 'Though winter sweeps down upon us, so too do the north tribes. They have gotten around our Wall defenders by sailing across the waters of Bodotria and Ituna. What manner of crazed warriors are these?'

'Riders of the North Wind,' Lot said from where he slouched with his fist to his mustached mouth. Since hearing the report of Cei's death, he despaired for his wife. 'They believe that the god of storms guides them with the wind and protects them with hail and sleet. Winter is no obstacle to them.'

'But it is to us,' Marcus spoke. 'With Bors in Londinium, there is no large army in the north to reinforce us. We are alone.'

'That is why the raiders are bold.' Urien opened several strips of messages from bird carriers and threw them on the table. 'We have received frightful news from coast cities that have been burned – Segedunum, Pons Aelius, Glanoventa, Alauna. And worse yet, calls for help from *inland* cities that are besieged by these Riders of the North Wind. Brocavum, Vindomora, Lavatrae and Braboniacum are all in dire jeopardy. We must go to their aid.'

'Why has Bors Bona taken his army south?' Lot grumbled. 'He has opened the north to the invaders and forces us to engage them in winter. He expects us to be weakened by this campaign – or destroyed. That is why he has withheld his pledge. He allies with that oriental fop Syrax, who colludes with the Foederatus.'

'No, not Bors,' Marcus said with a grim shake of his head. 'I know the man. He vehemently hates the invaders and would never enter into alliance with them. My people in his court inform me that he took his army to Londinium to dissuade Syrax from capitulating to the Foederatus. But why he remains there, I do not know. We must turn our forces at once to the south, to Londinium.'

'No!' Urien's shoulder muscles bunched and his salt-blond hair covered his face as he leaned over the table and stabbed his finger onto the map of the highlands. 'If we lose this, the Picts will hold high ground. The Saxons already have a foothold in the lowlands. We will be caught in a deadly vise. We must go north.'

Arthor looked to Kyner, who sat uncharacteristically silent in his chair. The evidence of Cei's death had left him hollowed, and he had said very little since. 'What do you counsel, father?'

Kyner did not budge, and his heavy voice sounded as if from far away, 'The king protects the people.'

Arthor nodded and stood. 'We go north, into winter – and we will crush these Riders of the North Wind.'

Snow in Londinium

As if in a polar dream, billowy snow fell upon Londinium. Severus Syrax, Count Platorius, and Bors Bona stood upon the high terrace of the governor's palace overlooking the River Tamesis, the gray water steaming in the frigid air. Rare woods burned in braziers atop tripods set upwind on the terrace so that wisps of fragrant warmth laved over the noblemen.

'Several of my sentinels in the palace and on the highway leading out of the city have identified the woman who led the vampyre attack as Morgeu the Fey,' Bors Bona announced.

'Nonsense.' Count Platorius's prune-dark pouches beneath his cynical eyes looked even darker by contrast with his ruddy wind-burned cheeks. 'Morgeu the Fey is blamed for every malediction in the land. Whenever the rain falls too heavily or there is drought in the lands of the Atrebates, the farmers blame Morgeu the Fey.'

'My sentinels are not doltish farmers.' Bors Bona looked fierce in his studded casque and brass breastplate. 'They have seen Morgeu before. These sightings were independent and multiple. My men are not mistaken. Morgeu the Fey has stolen away Merlin.'

Platorius lifted a bushy eyebrow. 'Are you not concerned, *magister militum*, that this warlord has posted his sentinels throughout Londinium?'

'I was invited here – same as you.' Bors Bona stepped close to Platorius, and though he was shorter he appeared larger.

'I did not come with an army,' the count sneered.

'You do not have an army.' Bors Bona's smoky breath snapped away in the wind. 'Your miserable forces are volunteer reserves – yeomen who would rather farm than fight.'

'Enough.' Severus Syrax stepped between the two men. The black curls that hung beneath his white fox-fur hat did not stir in the brisk wind, so laden were they with scented oil. 'We dare not fight each other. We have terrible enemies arrayed against us. Until a season ago, Merlin served the upstart Arthor. But that brutal boy wants no peace. Kyner's iron hammer scorns King Wesc's offer of trade with his tribes – commerce that not only would bring tranquillity to this island but affluence as well. That is why Merlin has abandoned him and speaks now for the Foederatus.'

'But at what price do we purchase this peace with the Foederatus?' Bors demanded. 'Slavery? We are Christians. Will we have pagans for our masters?'

'That is what Arthor would have us believe,' Syrax countered. 'He fears that we will accept King Wesc's offer and see that peaceful – and lucrative – trade is possible. That is why he sent Morgeu the Fey and her vampyres to snatch Merlin from us.'

'But all know that Morgeu loathes Arthor.' The count turned his leather collar against the blowing snow. 'Why serve him now?'

'Her husband, the pagan chieftain Lot, has given his pledge to Arthor,' Syrax answered. 'Morgeu, like any ambitious mother, thinks of her children – Gawain and Gareth. She will have them on the throne of Britain, all in good time. For them, she schemes and plots against us. We must stand together against her evil – and the evil of her cruel brother, Arthor.'

Sleet Den

The tented wagon approached Verulamium in the driving snow. Morgeu turned the horses off Watling Street and drove them up the rutted road toward the hillcrest and the chapel she had restored to a shrine. 'I sense someone awaiting you in the chapel,' Gorlois said, his silver eyes half-lidded. 'He is a dangerous man.'

'Hush, father.' Morgeu snapped the reins, and the horses pulled harder on the slope. Across the gray landscape, the only sound was the creaking of the axles, the chunting breaths of the beasts, and the slow hasping of their hocks in the snow. 'You stay with the wagon. I will take care of this.'

When they rocked to a stop before the chapel with its black stones laced in wind-driven snow, Morgeu climbed down and mounted the three iced steps to the shattered door. In the gloomy interior, rays of snow-dust cut fiery paths from holes in the ceiling and chinks in the stone walls, criss-crossing among the smashed pews. A large, big-shouldered man rose from where he had been crouching over a small splinter fire, warming himself.

'Morgeu – you have returned at last.' The giant stepped closer, crunching underfoot the bones of hares he had trapped and eaten. 'I have come to bring you back to your husband, Lord Lot.'

With wagging fingers, the enchantress clawed from the air the name of the intruder. 'Cei, son of Kyner. Come closer to me. Yes, step toward me – closer . . .'

Cei advanced, and his third step met emptiness and plunged him into an abyss. As he fell forward, he glimpsed the near-liquid blur of Morgeu's round face, and her fiery voice branded his brain: 'You dare to collect me like baggage to be carried back to its owner! For that insolence, you fall, Cei, son of Kyner. You fall to Sleet Den, asylum of the wicked dead!'

Morgeu threw furious laughter after him, enraged at the very thought of being possessed, even by Lot, father of her children. And her laughter curled to a shriek of exaltation to know she had damned Arthor's brother – another small retribution for the crime Merlin had committed against her unborn son.

Cei plummeted into darkness, his eyes enormous against the blind depths, arms outflung, startled cry snatched from him in the rush of hot air. And snug inside his brain, Morgeu's voice continued, loud and inescapable as a thought: 'The gates of Sleet Den are open to the living only one day of the year – and not this day. So you must wait to enter Hela's asylum, wait until you die!'

He struck spongy ground, his breath knocked from him. Gasping to breathe, he hurled himself upright, and a putrid stench burned his mouth and lungs. He gaped about, terrified, aware from the feculent stink and the ringing silence in which he could hear his blood running wild in his body that he had arrived at the soul's darkest destination.

Horrid shapes emerged from the darkness, limned by a vague phosphorescence: Hunched human figures groped toward him, jaws dislocated, eyes vacant or cored with green shadows. Gates of jet bars set with sharp fins and tines stopped them, and they pressed tightly against this barrier, dimly seen, wholly silent, mute phantoms annealed to darkness so completely they seemed the very prefigurements of ultimate nothingness.

The Snow Ranges

A blizzard swallowed King Arthor's army. Flying snow driven like swarming bees stitched heaven and earth, and all direction vanished. Into the forests they crammed, hoping to avoid the blistering winds, and soon found themselves in a faerie world of smeared and muted shapes and ponderous boughs that abruptly collapsed under their icy burdens. Continuous flurries spun haloes round each thing.

'This is the Furor's wrath,' Lot groaned when the king called him for direction in the whitening blanks of the forest. 'Pray to your God for help. No mortal soul can find a way through these snow ranges.'

Arthor heeded the north chieftain's advice and set the army's priests to rotation through a continuous Mass. But prayer seemed bereft of its effect, as though the swirling snow canceled supplication as remorselessly as it erased direction. Among the tossing treetops, an oceanic wind swept away the holy chants and the direful pleas of priests and king alike.

Blessed with ample provisions, the army hunkered among

the snowdrifted trees and wagons and struggled daily to keep their fires stoked. Sentinels, alert for Wolf Warriors, stamping in the sleety cold of the watch fires, baffled by the slither of white wind among the trees, cried alarms day and night. None heeded the husky shouts until metal clashed and wounded screams followed.

Wolf Warriors harried the army, bursting suddenly out of the wild weather hackled in icicles, slaying unwary soldiers, and disappearing again into the ghost depths of the forest. The ground too hard for burial, the corpses of the honored dead lay frozen in crypts of snow, and the slain enemy burned on pyres in the bare fields downwind, the greasy smoke wardancing across the white world.

'South, sire,' Bedevere begged the king. 'Abandon the north to this blight. Surely, the snow swallows our enemies as it has us. Turn your army south. We will slog slowly for sure, but that must be better than squatting here while the wind buries us.'

'And where is south, Bedevere?' The king lifted the flap of his sagging tent with an explosion of snow-fire and faced into the smoking blizzard. 'Where is any direction in this forsaken world?'

Bedevere upheld a tailor's needle. 'This has lain with loadstone – and now look.' He pulled a splinter from the trestle table, affixed the needle, and set it afloat in a soapstone dish of snowmelt. Each time the steward spun the needle floating on the splinter, it aligned itself in the same direction. 'It is called *bait al-ibrah* – "house of the needle" by the Moors of Gujarat who use this to navigate their ships. It always points north.'

'Wondrous!' the king shouted and lifted a bright stare to Bedevere. 'You are as astounding as Merlin! At dawn we will break camp. Now that we know our direction, we will push on to save the cities of the north!'

Messengers of the Dead

The villagers of Verulamium witnessed the green flames that flickered on the hilltop where Morgeu the Fey had reclaimed their chapel for worship of Hela, goddess of the dead. The priests rocked censers and prayed. But no one dared intrude, and the flares of green fire appeared nightly. In the vegetable cribs, onions sprouted green tendrils, veneria roots released their feelers, barley grew hairy with rootlings, and chestnuts exploded into unshelled shoots as though spring had seeped into the dark places. Horses foaled in the ice wind, ewes dropped their lambs in the snow drifts. And, most strange, stacked firewood – the cut logs of oak, hazel, willow, poplar, and hawthorn – jutted twigs and bloomed with sugary blossoms.

Morgeu's fertility magic overcame winter but could not dislodge Gorlois's soul from Merlin's body. Nightly, Terpillius rose from his bed of loam and joined Morgeu among her smoking thuribles and the lapsing green flames that flared from her wish-bringer plates. He curled up on her as she lay on the black draped altar beside the lanky long body that Gorlois occupied. With his hunger, he latched himself to the root-blood of her womb, his face pressed to her belly, his hands splayed over the chest of the wizard's form.

But Gorlois's soul could not be replevined from the flesh that had stolen him out of his daughter-mother's womb. Terpillius moaned with each gust of the green fire that surged life-force through him from Morgeu to Gorlois. The blood-warmth excited him even as the soul of Gorlois frustrated him by refusing to budge. Merlin's body waited for the vampyre to feast upon him but only after the soul had been dislodged. And it would not move.

Morgeu threw Terpillius off her and sat up with a squawk of defeat. 'Why is this not working?'

The vampyre slinked out of the temple as he did every night after failing the enchantress. The foiled efforts only whetted his hunger, and he slipped into the dark to pursue his need upon the midnight plain of other wanderers' journeys.

Gorlois grew colder each day. He stopped speaking entirely and dwindled like a guttering spark in the chill flesh of the wizard. And eventually, on a February morning with snow blowing like feathers, the messengers of the dead came for him. The beauty of evil shone in their large eyes, not centered in darkness but in light caught like dew in faces thinner, harder than the living, and their rufous hair like streaks of sunset or smeared blood.

'Get away!' Morgeu demanded. 'He's not going with you.'

Come he must. With the silhouette of men, they stood unmoving in the bright doorway, their hands of time outheld. *Come he must – or in his stead we will take the souls of your two sons, who have been offered at the gates of the dead.* Their long hands opened, and in their dark palms they held shining the locks of hair shorn from the heads of Gawain and Gareth and given to Cei by Lot for safe passage.

All That Is True

'We have seen enough,' Merlin spoke for Rex Mundi upon the ferrous and corroded Seat of the Slain. 'I have for you a gift, beautiful Verthandi.'

'Show me no gift, Rex Mundi,' the lovely woman spoke, her breath a waft from a spring morning. 'I want all that you have of the Dragon's hoard – and in return I will show you all that is true. You will see everything that is as it is right now.'

'You are too kind,' Merlin spoke swiftly before the others that shared his body could voice their desires. 'But we have lingered far too long in the Storm Tree. If the Furor finds us here, we are doomed.'

'The Furor is far from here at this time.' Verthandi smiled and pressed herself through her moonshadow raiment against the lanky body of Rex Mundi. 'See for yourself—'

The one-eyed god ambled through the fluorescent light of Home, several boughs of the World Tree below the Raven's Branch. Home – *Asgard* – lit by the shine of lunar vapors and starsmoke shone warmly, its cedar rafters hung with hunting trophies – vast stag horns, wolf pelts, fire-snake skins. Keeper of the Dusk Apples sauntered beside her lover, her gold chains and tiffanies flowing against her lithe body. In her hand, she held a knife scabbard studded with the rubies and sapphires Rex Mundi had given her.

The Furor's vast beard hid his smile of satisfaction, but his gray eye gleamed to behold the bejeweled gift. 'And what will I tell my wife about this?'

'Tell her what you will,' Keeper of the Dusk Apples said in a voice low with desire and guided him toward the large oaken bed.

We've theen enough! That gweat god fwightenth me.

Rex Mundi pulled away from Verthandi's summer-scented hug.

'Do not spurn me.' The Norn brushed her flaxen hair from her frowning face. 'Would you rather take memories from the Tyrant of the Past – or peek what *might* be from the Slave of the Future?'

'My king needs me,' Merlin spoke through Rex Mundi. 'I cannot tarry here any longer.'

'Let me kiss your brow and wipe away all memory of kings.' She whispered intimately. 'Forget the past. You've lived long enough in two worlds at once.'

Merlin removed a diamond from his pocket and held it up to her between thumb and forefinger. 'Take this as our tribute to your beauty.'

'My beauty needs no tribute but your devotion.' She gently pushed his arm aside and nuzzled closer with the genital odor of damp forests. 'I will show you secret things – the Dragon's lair, the Nine Queens, the lives of other worlds . . .'

The diamond in Merlin's grasp suddenly grew brighter, inflamed by the energy of the Fire Lord within Rex Mundi. At the sight of that, Verthandi fell silent. Her winterfrost eyes looked lonesome as a seal's, and she took the diamond and disappeared.

Hell

Cei wandered over scorched gravel that led among tarpaper sheds huddled in the gray pales of a gothic city, where smokestacks reared into a sky squalid with soot and fuming char. The gatekeepers with rufous hair and malevolently beautiful faces had taken from him the locks of hair entrusted to him by Lord

Lot. In exchange for those talismans, they had led him here, to this city of malice.

Alone, he crossed a yard of iron tracks and wooden ties laid atop the black gravel. He walked the iron to keep from stepping in pools of green sludge, until the tracks curved into a tunnel stained by smoke. On one footstone stood carved the Roman numerals MCMLVII, and he questioned aloud, 'One thousand, nine hundred and fifty-seven? By God's grace, what does that mark mean?' Other letters above it made no sense to him.

'Gatekeepers!' he called to the rancid sky, where sheets of flame leaped from the chimneys. 'Gatekeepers, I have wandered far enough. Take me back! Take me back to the Gates.'

No reply came. Bruised from his fall, befuddled by all he saw, he began to cry. Across wintry Britain, he had trekked on foot, eluding brigands, trapping hares for food, and not once had he despaired. In battle, encircled by foes and the screams of dying men and wounded horses, he had not despaired. But here in this stony fastness, among broken slabs of concrete and gigantic trestles of black iron with cold lanterns shining red and green, he despaired for his sanity.

He passed through a landscape of more rails occupied by large iron wagons on metal wheels, some of the wagons lettered with words he half discerned: *Midland Railway*. Smudged men in baggy garments and swinging tool boxes came crunching over the gravel, and he hurried toward them, hailing them with a robust voice. But they paid him no heed; when he reached to stop them, they passed through him as though he were smoke.

Among leaning clapboard shacks beside a railway road, he found others — youths in denim trousers and short leather jerkins, their arms tied off as if to tourniquet a spurting wound. But they displayed no wounds, only blue bruises in the crooks of their arms and a glass phial dangling, stuck to the flesh by a silver needle.

He crouched among them, and one of the glassy-eyed boys saw him, rocked his tow-head anxiously, and muttered something in a foreign language. Cei tried to touch him, and his hand passed cleanly through the mumbling youth.

As the warrior walked on, he encountered sedge stiff as wire growing from cratered hardpan. He shoved through it, a phantom, a shade in these strange purlieus of hell. He crossed a dry clay gutter and wandered onto cinder paving that angled up behind gray, wooden homes of blackened planks and decayed façades. In the windowcorners, he glimpsed people, but no one saw him or challenged his ghostly trespass.

Mother Mary, we are alone in a wasteland of ice and snow. Bedevere looks askance at me for using his unique sense of direction to push farther north, deeper into this frozen blight. I have trusted in God to protect us – and I know that is childish. God has exiled us from Eden to labor in pain through the fallen world. I have been arrogant in believing I could drive the invaders from the north – and now I despair. Mother Mary, please, petition our Father. Ask your Son to petition our Father. We are suffering. I have blundered, and we are suffering!

Spit Out the Moon
The army's wagons stood frozen, their axles an agony to turn. Snow packed the spokes. The horses, cloaked in blankets and flanked by torchmen, struggled to move their loads through the smoking snow. Laboriously, by inches, the army found its way among the drifts of the forest.

Bedevere's 'house of the needle' helped the map-readers locate the army's place in the shrouded world and trudge toward the nearest highway – a road that would lead north to Olicana, a municipality large enough to shelter the horses and offer additional provisions for the soldiers.

Wolf Warriors repeatedly attacked the slogging troops, materializing out of the dirty light. They cut through the defenders, overturned wagons, and carried away butchered sections of the horses. The assaults slowed the advance at first and then stopped it altogether as the Riders of the North Wind established themselves in the forests surrounding the road.

'We have crawled into a trap!' Lot announced grimly to Arthor at a twilight war counsel in the king's pavilion. 'Our slow progress has allowed the enemy's fleeter warbands to gather around us. They have sacrificed a few raiding parties to test our strength. Come dawn, the full brunt of the invaders will strike!'

Arthor made what preparations he could. The ground was too hard for defensive ditches and palisades, so he ordered the wagons overturned. The limit on arrows that could be fired in an engagement was lifted, and priests stayed awake throughout the night, moving among the men, shriving souls and blessing swords for the great battle to come.

Ice balls fell during the night, a fierce hail that bludgeoned the defenders unprotected by the forest. At dawn, the war shrieks began, and waves of Wolf Warriors closed in, lightfooted as if carried to the fray by the gale winds. Garbed in pelts, the invaders charged with animal fury as if the forest had disgorged its beasts.

At the worst of the fighting, when the beastmen broke through the wagon barriers and the melee trampled the fires and the strategy tents, the eye of the storm passed overhead. All about, the world lay blank, white, featureless, while overhead, in a perfectly blue sky, the gibbous moon floated, a crystal skull – as if winter had devoured the earth and spat out the moon.

A miraculous tantara of horns sounded brightly under the clear sky. Arthor and Kyner, who stood atop an upturned wagon in bitter witness to the destruction of their forces, saw them first – a long line of muscular horses shouldering powerfully through the snow, ridden by the clans of the north and bearing the dragon banners they had earned with their pledge to the king. Aidan, chieftain of the Spiral Castle, led the charge, battleax swinging, eager to redeem his daughter's life-debt to the boy-king.

Skuld
What hath happened? Why are we alone now? Where are the Nornth? We can't thtay here vewy much longer. We thaw the one-eyed god with hith lover. Will he come here when he ith done with her?

Rex Mundi sat silent except for Dagonet's nervous chattering. Even Lord Monkey sat still within the assembled being, mesmerized yet by the summer-rain scent of Verthandi that lingered in the space where she had sat beside them on the rusty Seat of the Slain. Merlin looked out over the bone-strewn slopes of the mesa and beyond to the series of dunes that rippled away like surrounding lines of force. At the horizon, stars shook like fists in a claret sky and the moon hung like a brittle and riddled skull.

Across the wasteland, a figure came strolling, at first broken upon the planes of heat that sliced the distance, then whole and seeming to walk in midair splashing among watery traces, then augmented once more to the ground – a child, a young girl no more than five years old. Her strawberry hair hung lankly in the heat, her limbs and face smudged with ash, the tattered frock swaying on her petite frame brown and mottled as if patched from dead leaves.

Who ith that thmall child?

'That is the third of the Norns,' Merlin replied, 'the Wyrd Sister called Skuld.'

How do you know thith?

'I just know.'

The girl slid down the last sand reef and climbed the mesa. Soon, she stood before the giant throne with her head tilted back, looking up at Rex Mundi, a curious expression on her dirty face. 'You're not supposed to sit there. That's All-Father's chair.'

Rex Mundi bent over and extended a long arm that was yet far too distant to reach the child. 'Come up and sit here with me,' Merlin invited. 'I would like to speak with you.'

The child shook her head. 'You look scary. And you're not supposed to sit there. That's All-Father's chair.'

'It's all right. Your sisters said so, and they sat here with me just moments ago,' Merlin said and then tried to inflect Rex Mundi's voice with hurt: 'Do you really think I'm scary?'

'Yes.' She shook her head vigorously. 'You have darkness in you fighting with light!'

Merlin attempted a laugh and it came out as a harsh cry that forced the child back two paces. 'Don't be afraid of me. I'm

Rex Mundi – Lord of the World. I'm not one being but many. I have inside of me a monkey, a man, a wizard, and darkness and light – but they are not fighting. Fighting? Oh no! They are – dancing! Yes, they're dancing. They like to dance. They are friends of God.'

'Really?' The child stepped closer. 'You know God?'

'Intimately.' Merlin tried on a smile and dropped it when he saw the fright in the child's eyes. 'Your sister Verthandi just went with us to visit God at a dance in a palace of water. Azael, tell the child – aren't you and the Fire Lord great dancers?'

Azael remained silent, until Merlin mentally voiced the thought, *Dog ashes – that's your destiny if we don't get out!*

'Sure, I love to dance, little girl. I'm wild for it.'

The child reached both arms up. 'I want to see the monkey!'

Creatures of Light

When the messengers of death came for Gorlois's soul and showed Morgeu the locks of hair from her two boys, Gawain and Gareth, her heart began hammering in her chest. 'You can't have my sons.'

Then, your father we will take. Their breaths sifted over her with the sad smell from pillows crushed by fevered heads.

'No!' Morgeu backed away from the silhouettes in the door, their sticky red hair clotted with blown snow. Morning's gray February light wrapped itself around them like some brighter aspect of their presence woven from snow and storm-shadows out of the wintry air. In that glare, she could not tell if there were three or four messengers. 'He is not my father anymore. He is my child now. I hold him to my root-blood.'

This knife will cut that root. A blade of flame opened like a flare of lightning in the hands of the one behind, briefly underlighting a visage of shameful beauty, lewdly evil, before the knife was hid. *Gorlois comes with us or your sons we will take.*

She had counted three, definitely three. Slowly, she continued retreating backward, her hands reaching behind until she felt the fabric of the altar. 'Who gave you the locks of hair from my sons? Who dares put their lives in your cruel hands, your filthy hands?'

From Cei come these locks, given him by their father himself. So freely given, now freely taken. They stepped into the chapel, their hair like rusted spikes in the shadows, their figures congealed to darkness save the lucent shine of their beautiful eyes.

'Then Cei can take back the locks he gave,' she spoke hurriedly, her hands feeling with frantic urgency behind her, touching the warm metal of a wish-bringer plate where incense yet burned. 'Those locks were not his to give, and he can take them back. They are not freely given what are not his to give.'

To the asylum of the wicked dead he has been flung, and now through time yet to be he wanders, awaiting the message we bring that will end his aimless roving. The voice that carried these words brought with it weariness, weight, the gloom of failure.

'Listen to me, messengers of death—' With one hand, she clutched a wish-bringer plate, with the other a hot thurible. 'I set Cei upon his timeless roamings. I will have him back – and he *will* reclaim the locks he has given you. My sons are not yours to take, not yet. And this, the child at my root-blood, is mine as well. For now, you will take nothing of mine. Do you hear? Nothing!'

Morgeu whipped both her arms forward, casting steaming thurible and smoking incense plate at the grim visitors. Her aim was true, and each magical implement struck one of the messengers, smashing them to fumes. The third rushed her, the lightning blade aimed for her womb. She caught the knife hand by the wrist in both of her hands and found herself gripping an arm strong as an axle, her grimacing face confronting a countenance of ethereal beauty evil with disdain. Her knee kicked forward, found unexpected softness, and a cry like ice snapping. The knife arm relented, and she turned the blade and drove it deep into the creature of light.

Eufrasia's War

Aidan's reinforcements broke the Raiders of the North Wind from behind as they fell upon King Arthor's army. Under the blue eye of the winter storm, Celts and Britons slaughtered Picts, and the fields trampled to slush under the attack glowed crimson. By the time the snowy gale winds began howling again, the king's army had destroyed the fur-clad invaders. Their corpses sat up in the pyre flames that consumed them, as if attentive to their souls climbing the ladders of greasy smoke into the gray sky.

'All Britain offers you gratitude for what you've done this day, Chief Aidan,' Arthor said to the chieftain when he and his field-commanders entered the king's war pavilion. 'We were doomed, trapped in the open, until you swept down like the wrath of God!'

'Britain's gratitude should not go to me, sire,' Aidan said, folding back his cowl in the king's presence and exposing the traits of his hard life, his smashed nose and missing ear. 'This is Eufrasia's war. My daughter insisted we come south from the Spiral Castle to offer you our swords in your northern campaign. I and the other clan chiefs thought that gesture imprudent in this season of storms – but Eufrasia insisted that, as you'd not accept her hand in marriage, her life-debt had to be paid in foe's blood.'

'I will draft her a letter of gratitude by my own hand,' Arthor promised. 'This day, she is Britain's savior.'

'Save your hand for Excalibur, sire,' said Aidan with a proud smile. 'Eufrasia is here among us. Her archery felled a dozen of our enemies – and from horseback no less. Daughter—'

From among the northern clansmen in their kilts and *loricas* of leather-hooped armor, a slender warrior stepped forward, an archer in tawed leather boots, green breeches, padded gray jerkin and white cowl. With the hood unlaced, blonde tresses spilled forth as Eufrasia bent her knee before the king.

'You placed your life in jeopardy for Britain?' Arthor asked, astonished. 'The winter ride alone was arduous and dangerous.'

'I came to serve you, King Arthor,' she said, lifting her chin and exposing the confident curve of her jaw, 'I who would not have life this day had you not put your life in jeopardy for me.'

'You and your father have won your place at our strategy table.' Arthor took her hand and urged her rise. 'For the remainder of this campaign, your counsel will be joined with ours.'

Arthor did not release her hand but led her instead to the trestle table and the unscrolled maps. Hours before, he did not think he would scan these drawings again. Standing before them with the maiden beside him, he looked closely at her as she scrutinized the terrain, and she seemed more lovely to him than he had noticed before.

Mother Mary, I know your prayers to our Father sent Aidan to us when we needed him most. His fierce clansmen have broken the invaders' hold on us and strengthened our ranks! And his daughter – she inspires strong feelings in me. Nevertheless, dear Mother Mary, I cannot drive from my mind the terror that Morgeu has instilled in me with the horror that we share. At least, Eufrasia is no supernatural being as is Nynyve. She is wholly mortal and all the more enticingly attractive to me for that. If only I could find the strength in my soul to overthrow my sister's evil enchantment. Pray for me, Mother Mary. Pray that I may live to love as a man.

King Wesc

Compact, with a limp from a boating accident in his youth, King Wesc had not the appearance of a monarch. He dressed simply, in red, long-sleeved wool shirts and black trousers with attached socks. His tall boots had twin serpents styled into the kid leather, and his jerkin, too, displayed coiled serpents. Otherwise, there was no sign of his rank. He wore his ginger beard long and his dark hair short, like a farmer, and he carried no dagger or sword, relying entirely upon his warriors to defend him.

His faith in his men was well placed, for they loved their king not for his ferocity but for his charm and wisdom. All knew that King Wesc was beloved of Lady, wife of the Furor. She, who wept tears of gold that turned to amber in the sea, bestowed wisdom, foresight, and luck upon those she loved. And she loved Wesc for the faithfulness he had shown her since boyhood when, youngest of his family and bereft of inheritance, he gave himself not to rancor and the fight for land but to sacred poetry, her own passion. Of small stature, he had little to offer as a warrior; neither had he any skill as a *vitiki*, a magician, nor as a lawspeaker, who settled disputes and questions of honor. Ritual bored him, and he found no place among the temples. Throughout his adolescence and into his early manhood, he applied his hand to nothing more than sacred poetry.

When the Saxons needed a legate to send among the Angles, Jutes, and Picts during the early years of the Foederatus, they chose Wesc. His eloquence, his mellifluous singing voice, and his unimposing stature assured his happy reception within the bickering tribes. To the surprise of all, he proved more than a mere legate. The wisdom that Lady had instilled in him came forth in unexpected ways, providing battle insights at war counsels that proved decisive in winning stunning victories time and again. His renown as a strategist who won land for whatever assembly he served uplifted him to the status of a leader.

Then Hengist and Horsa, the first great commanders of the Foederatus, died in battle against the Dragon Lords of the Britons. Wesc came to Britain to hold the land they had won, and he succeeded by concluding trade agreements with the *magister militum* of Londinium while dispatching fanatical warrior sects to the west and north, to demonstrate the prudence of negotiating with him and the hopelessness of fighting.

At the Roman villa of Dubrae, overlooking white limestone cliffs and the Belgic Strait that separated him from his homeland, he continued to compose sacred poetry. And he kept the company of a cat, the animal most cherished by Lady. The black female cat that followed him everywhere remained nameless. She was for him Lady's companionship in this world. Strolling among the colonnades above the white cliffs, he recited her poetry fit for the gods: 'Lady, you recall the distances – in the cold lakes that became your eyes – without giving up their clouds – and the black wing of the fluke – that tattered and became your shadow – and the violence, unthinking, possessed – that alone can win us peace.'

The Machinery of Hell

Cei wandered the sad limits of hell under smokestacks that spat flame and a pall of black smoke. Sidelong cats shied from him, but none others noticed his passage. Gray grass, rigid and brittle, clumped around poles stuck upright in the ground, and strung between the intervals of tar-slapped poles, cables stretched tautly upon which ravens stood dark sentinel. The black city on all sides lay smoking.

Against the baleful sky, a cross crested a small church, a building of gray pitted stone that sulked between a warehouse of flueblack bricks and weeded barrens, where broken glass glinted among cinders, a garden of gloom. He went there chanting aloud supplications to the deity that had kindled the stars in their dark and had set this city of perdition so far from their wan light. With salty sorrow in his throat, he entered the vestibule, knowing himself unworthy of benediction, yet grateful to discover sanctuary even here among the machinery of hell.

The buckled linoleum floor did not bend under his weight and carried no shadow of him from the wine colors let down by the windows of stained glass, wherein he recognized the figures of his salvation. Sobbing his prayers, he eased himself into the rearmost pew and knelt. 'Father, forgive me!' he cried aloud at the conclusion of the Lord's Prayer and began reciting it again, his tear-blurred eyes fixed upon the plaster Christ above the altar.

A priest in rumpled black soutane staggered toward him down the aisle, his bloodwebbed eyes tight with incredulity, a silver flask in one hand, the other guiding him along the pews. He muttered something in a foreign language, and Cei wiped away his tears and asked softly, 'Father – you see me?'

The priest understood his Latin and nodded as he approached, mumbling further in his alien tongue.

Cei stood. 'You can hear me? You understand me?'

'Yes, I understand you,' the priest answered in Latin, and his ruined eyes blinked as he reached out to touch the apparition. But his hand felt nothing, mere air. 'Who – who are you?'

'I am Cei, son of Kyner, seneschal to King Arthor of Britain.'

The cleric sagged into the pew in front of Cei and sat backward on one bent leg facing the large man in the tattered cassock of a priest.

Cei saw the priest's incredulity and nodded. 'Oh, this is but my disguise. Here, I have my cuirass beneath.' He pulled the cassock over his head and revealed his black leather breastshield embossed with the royal dragon. 'My sword – I – I lost my sword gambling.'

The priest looked with dismay at the flask in his hand and placed it gently on the pew.

'Father, I have lost my way,' Cei spoke beseechingly. 'Will you help me find my way to the world of the living?'

Blue Horses

The slow caravans of King Arthor's army moved north against the rim of the snow-spelled world. After crushingly defeating the Riders of the North Wind under the staring blue eye of the blizzard, the king's army moved effectively from one northern city to the next. Though the snows continued intermittently, the gale winds did not return, and the columns of foot soldiers, wings of cavalry, and trains of wagons journeyed through a white waste mute as the face of the moon.

True to his word, King Arthor kept Eufrasia at his side during all strategy sessions, and she proved to be an effective though eccentric tactician. Lot and Aidan provided accurate assessments of terrain familiar to them made strange by giant alabaster drifts. Marcus and Urien offered cunning military maneuvers for aggressively engaging the enemy. And Kyner, still quietly grieving the loss of his son, nonetheless continued efficiently enough to manage the integration of the varied forces so that the army's morale remained high. But none proved as insightful as Eufrasia in pinpointing the location and movements of the raiders.

By heeding her counsel, the king's army frequently flushed out warbands from the silver forests and frozen dells. And though she was sometimes mistaken and sent squads on empty forays into icicle woods, her insights often protected the king from hostile flanking maneuvers and unexpected attacks. At first, he and the others suspected that she employed magic, but Aidan scowled fiercely at that suspicion and Eufrasia laughed. 'I know nothing of magic,' she confided in the king during one of their many rides together to inspect the troops and the day's march ahead. 'I simply know how to look for the blue horses.'

'Show me,' the king demanded.

From a windswept knoll, she pointed across the blinding white world into the overcast sky. 'See those hues, those transparencies of the sky beyond? Blue horses! The Riders of the North Wind use those as mounts. At first, that was but a guess. Now, I am sure.'

Arthor saw nothing in the gray sky but nacreous faces of cloud. Even so, the woman's perceptions proved accurate enough for him to continue to heed her counsel. When her predictions failed, she claimed that the invaders had somehow sensed the king's attack. The other commanders looked askance at each other whenever Arthor chose Eufrasia's counsel over theirs, which was most of the time. Even Aidan thought the king foolish to heed his daughter's hunches so assiduously. 'She's but a girl, sire,' he said. 'And she is well know for being fickle – in all her choices, men especially. She has entertained and encouraged many admirers. But she is not to be taken seriously. She is but a girl.'

'She's a full year older than I,' the king pointed out. 'Am I then but a boy, Aidan?'

Soon, word had spread throughout the army that the king had lost his heart and his head for battle to the beautiful woman from the north. And when Bedevere reported these rumors to him, Arthor smiled giddily, 'It's true – this woman is warrior enough for me to love.'

Going to Hell

The winter wind whispered through the shrine of Hela like voices. 'Do you hear them, daughter?' Gorlois asked, the

silver eyes in the face he had stolen from Merlin sliding
nervously. 'Those are no right voices! Those are natterings
of the damned.'

Slaying the messengers of death had imbued Morgeu with
sufficient power to revive her failing father. He sat on the black
draped altar, listening with the attentiveness granted him by the
Furor and hearing a muted cacophony of voices. She moved
hurriedly about the shrine, swinging a thurible that smoked
with a redolence of lime and sage. Desperately, she strove to
purify the sacred space of the heinous deed she had committed.
The ether of the slain messengers tainted the dim air with an
oily reek. Nothing remained of their bodies or hot knife, only
death's rancid stink.

Morgeu placed the billowy thruible on the altar and stood
before the staring body of Merlin whose eyeholes revealed the
dazed soul of Gorlois. 'Father, listen to me.' She took the gaunt
face in both of her hands. 'We are going to hell. You are coming
with me. I need the soul-seeing that the Furor has given you.'

'Do you hear the ramblings of the damned?' Gorlois asked.

'Father! If you do not heed me, you will die. Those voices
have come to carry you away. Do you hear me?'

His suddenly crisp stare told her that he did. 'I'm dying.'

'Yes. You are dying.' Morgeu pulled him to his feet. 'The
messengers of death have come for you. But they cannot
have you.'

Gorlois stamped his wolfskin boots. 'I won't die again!'

'Good!' Morgeu secured the onyx buttons on his red jerkin.
'You will live in my womb, and I will bring you into the world
as my own child. And in time you will be king of Britain. But
now – now we must find Cei.'

'Cei?' Gorlois rocked his hoary head to one side. 'Who?'

'Son of Kyner.' Morgeu led him by the hand away from
the altar and down blind steps into the lightless depths where
she had plunged Cei. 'You must see Cei now. See him with
your strong eye.'

Gorlois peered frightfully into the blackness. 'What is this
descent, daughter? How came this here?'

'The shrine to Hela, goddess of the dead, has passageways and chutes into her dark realm. My magic has opened one.' She took him under one shoulder and guided him down the rime-crusted steps. 'Now you must stare into this darkness and find Kyner's son Cei.'

'Ah!' The Furor's trance-strength penetrated the subterranean dark easily and revealed the broken wheels, the dismembered dolls, the frayed nightshirts that lay strewn on the colossal winding stairwell into death. The living man who had fallen through here not long before had left a glisteny path in the air, the effluvial warmth of his life. 'I see where he has gone! We will find him.'

Down he hobbled, helped by his daughter, whose pale skin glowed, suffused with light, like the dusty shine of mothwings.

The Other Side of the Stars

Rex Mundi reached down from the corroded and red-stained Seat of the Slain and offered his hairy hand to the little girl in the tattered brown frock. She climbed the pitted leg of the throne laboriously, dislodging flakes of rust, and seized the proffered hand. Pulled up onto the giant metal seat, she stood beside the bestial man and wiped wrung strands of strawberry hair from her sooty face. 'My name is Skuld.' She absently swung one scrawny leg as she stood and slapped the torn sole of her tree-bark sandal on the scaly iron. 'Show me the monkey. I want to see the monkey.'

Lord Monkey, come forth! We have a new fwiend for you.

Rex Mundi offered his leathery hands to the child, then placed the little fingers against his whiskered face. She felt Lord Monkey staring back at her and closed her eyes and saw him frisking across the span of days left for him.

'He's so funny!' She giggled and pressed her cheek against the savage mask of Rex Mundi. His fur-soft body smelled of musky, indigo loam. 'Lord Monkey – you will live many happy days yet!'

'Only if the Furor does not skin him,' Merlin spoke aloud.

The child pulled away, alarmed. 'If he catches him! You

are not supposed to sit here. He would squash you. But Lord Monkey is small and spry and will find his way down the other side of the stars. He will do that when you are squashed.'

Merlin! I don't like thith! Thyee theeth a tewible fate!

'Oh, yes, little man,' the young girl agreed with a nod. 'Soon you will be bones on the slopes. All-Father will break you.'

Oh, pleath, help uth!

'I can't help you, little man.' Skuld shrugged her bony shoulders. 'You are where you don't belong. You will die here.'

'You can help us climb down the other side of the stars,' Merlin spoke, reaching out and taking the young girl's arm.

'No. You are too big. The Asa and Vana will see you.'

Atha and Vana? Who are they?

'The gods, Dagonet,' Merlin answered. 'The warrior and fertility gods of the Storm Tree.' He gently squeezed Skuld's arm. 'I know how you can help us.'

'I don't want to help you.' The child pulled her arm away. 'All-Father will get mad at me.'

'He won't get mad, Skuld, because he will never know. He will be too happy to know.' Merlin emptied the pockets of his magical robe, filling his conical hat with the diamonds, rubies, emeralds, and sapphires from the Dragon's hoard. 'Take these and sprinkle them off the Raven's Bough on the far side from where we descend.'

They will dithtwact the godth! We will ethcape untheen!

Skuld gasped. 'They are beautiful stones! The Asa and Vana will wear them in their hair and on their clothes and always think kindly of me.' Her smudged face shone with reflected carats of colored light. 'You *are* friendly, Rex Mundi. I want to thank you.'

'Then, show us the way to the other side of the stars.'

Field of Miracles

Cei stared at the priest's sad face of burst capillaries and sagging wattles, eyes burned red. 'You're drunk.'

'Yes, I am inebriated.' The priest ran a trembling hand over his bloodburst freckles and bowed his balding, pale-red pate. 'I've tried to drown my crisis of faith.'

'No wonder you are in hell.' Cei shoved to his feet.

'Wait!' The priest stumbled out of the pew and fell in a clumsy sprawl into the aisle.

Cei strode to the door without glancing back. 'You can't help me find my way. You've lost the way yourself.'

'Please, wait!' The priest came flying toward the glare of the open door. Had he opened it himself – or the ghost? Hammers of alcohol pounded his brain harder in the wincing light of day. Gingerly, he picked his way down the stone steps. On the cracked pavement, he spied the specter shambling like a churlish bear under the cokeblown sky. 'I must speak with you . . .'

'You're besotted.' Cei passed through the seething smoke from a curb grating and continued across the sunless, cobbled street.

'Where are you going?' One foot in the gutter, the priest squinted numbly after the hulking figure – an hallucination of King Arthur's court, perfect to the tiniest detail: scuffed boots laced to the knees, black cord breeks, padded tunic, and leather corselet. *What is this vision saying – more than 'Stop drinking'?*

Cei labored on through the strange, burning world. A wan inkwash of pipes and tanks loomed in the murky distance against an ashen sky. A fishing village erupted grayly in the smog. No – not a village at all, but a tremendous yard of metal poles and trawl lines fenced in by woven wire.

'It is a power plant,' the priest said, lapsing to his native tongue while huffing from his strenuous jog. When he saw the lack of comprehension, he said in Latin, 'A mill that makes light.'

'Makes light?' Cei looked about at the netherworld of industrial exhaust. 'Then why is it so dark here?'

The priest laughed and held an arm out to stop the ghost, but his hand touched emptiness faintly cold. 'I cannot explain.' He held his aching ribs as he caught his breath. 'How have you come here?'

Before Cei could reply, thunder rumbled overhead, and a massive shadow glided above them – a huge, roaring bird soaring stiff-winged above the smoldering landscape. The priest laughed again and waved for him to follow. They walked through yellowed clapboard warrens where watchdogs yapped at the priest and whined and slinked away from the phantom. Shift workers filed past on the cinder lanes, lean, haggard-faced men in dingy clothes. None saw Cei. Many walked right through him.

At a hillcrest among oxidized warehouses, the priest pointed down the sky to a long field of blinking lanterns where the stiff-winged bird alighted, skimming over the ground and coming to rest among others like itself – metal creatures. Cei looked sideways for more clarity and saw the small wheels, people disembarking. His mind reeled. They were not creatures at all but metal ships designed to fly. 'What is this field of miracles?'

Riding Blue Horses
Eufrasia's empty tracks in the snow led to where she stood alone on a knoll, her voice unspoken but unhappiness clear on her young, wind-burnished features. Arthor stood back from her, admiring the way she filled her fawnskin breeches, her commanding stance, arms crossed over padded gray jerkin, white cowl pulled back so that her flaxen hair webbed the wind. He thought her joyless look an assessment of that day's difficult march.

Not since Nynyve, a season past, had he experienced such lightness of heart in the presence of a woman. But Eufrasia was wholly mortal and no part magical. His fascination with her touched on respect and love. What he remembered of Nynyve seemed a dream or something that had happened in the distant past, another lifetime. With Eufrasia, the hope of love felt entirely plausible, and he began to believe that indeed the Nine Queens had sent Nynyve as a gift, to heal him from Morgeu's wound so that he could know true love with a mortal woman. He actually believed this. And earlier, he had even consulted with Bedevere about the proper protocol for an entreaty of marriage. But the steward had turned his haughty features aside as if smelling something disagreeable. 'Love has no protocol, sire.'

'Arthor,' she called to him with ready familiarity. He kicked through the snow to her side. 'I've overheard Urien making snide comment to Marcus about us. He said you've become my hem-sniffer.'

'Ah, that's empty prattle.' Arthor laughed lightly and made mental note to speak a harsh word privately to Urien. 'I've told you – Urien is the Idealist, Marcus the Fatalist—'

'Yes, yes. And Kyner the Optimist, Lot the Cynic.' She kept her face averted, dismissing his labels. 'What they say is true.'

'Not at all, Eufrasia. Urien makes a hopeful comment . . .'

'The Fatalist did not contradict him,' she said, catching his eye with her cold stare. 'You have become my hem-sniffer, Arthor.'

He felt a thump in his chest as though his heart had stalled. 'What are you saying?'

'Why do you always take my counsel?' She frowned at him. 'I'm not always right, yet you give my advice greater weight than you do that of your warlords. It's obvious – you're smitten with me.'

Arthor's jaw slung sideways. 'Obvious?'

'Do you deny it?'

'Deny it?' His eyebrows jumped, then settled to a determined stare. 'Why – no, not at all. I am smitten with you. But I – I am not ready for where my heart leads me.'

'Don't you want me?'

Abruptly, the image of Morgeu rose starkly in his mind – as though Nynyve had never touched him, as though no balm of care and love had healed his soulful wound – and he shook his head firmly. 'No. Not in the way you deserve. I am not ready yet to take a wife.'

'So.' Her sigh clouded in the cold. 'I am fine enough for war games but not good enough to be your wife.'

'You are indeed a woman worthy to be my wife,' Arthor

spoke hurriedly. 'But I am not yet worthy to be your husband. I must establish myself first as king.'

'You are such a boy.'

'Not much younger than you.'

She thumbed his chin disapprovingly. 'You're much younger now than when you saved me from Guthlac.'

'Younger?' Arthor's brow creased, mystified. 'I – I've learned to love since then. You have no notion how difficult it has been for me – to love. I've been betrayed . . .'

'You betray yourself, Arthor.' Eufrasia's voice cut keenly. 'I came here to give you my hand. You turned away from me at the Spiral Castle – and rightly so, for a manly reason I respect. I came here to repay my life-debt to you – and to seek love. Now that my debt is paid, you want to ride blue horses with me! You're such a boy. Don't you see? There are no blue horses, Arthor. I made that up to justify my intuitions. I was so eager for your love, I pretended to know more than I know. And you believed me. But now I see my games were not clever enough to win your heart.' She stalked away and added without looking back, 'I won't be sitting at your war table any longer.'

Mother Mary, I have lost Eufrasia! She gave herself to me – this beautiful woman, this courageous woman . . . and I turned her away! I believed that I was ready for her to be my wife. I believed that Nynyve had been the antidote to Morgeu's curse and that now I was ready for love. But I am not ready! I was scared, Mother Mary. When Eufrasia asked if I wanted her, all my hope of love shriveled in a sudden fright – for my very soul knows that I am polluted with sin and undeserving of love. My fear owns me. The unholy child in my sister's womb owns me. My heart is clogged with fear – for what I have done, for what will come of it. How dare I believe I am worthy of any woman's love after what I have done? Yet, I can be forgiven. Isn't that what your Son taught? That we can be forgiven even for the most heinous sins. Then, why can I not forgive myself? The Church preaches forgiveness, but there is no one here to bless me as your Son would bless me. I have spoken to the bishop at Greta Bridge of the need to confess, and he urges me to prayer. So, I am here again, kneeling before you, praying. If I make it to Londinium, I will suggest to the Archbishop the need for the Church to shrive souls in this life. Must I wait for your Son's second coming to be forgiven? Will I never know a woman's love in this life?

Exorcism

With the thaw came floods. King Arthor's army had successfully defended against the Raiders of the North Wind, but the journey south was hampered by washed-out roads, swollen rivers, downed bridges, and impassable fields of mud and bog. The victorious forces dispersed among the northern cities, serving the communities no longer as warriors but as a corps of civil engineers who helped rebuild the thoroughfares, dike the wild streams, and prepare the mired land for the spring plantings.

Lot's impatience to find his wife grew unbearable, and he determined to travel south with his sons to Verulamium. Arthor, equally anguished over the loss of his stepbrother Cei, agreed to accompany him, and he left Marcus, Urien, and Kyner in command of the army bemired in the fenny north.

Traveling lightly and changing horses frequently, Arthor's small cadre flew quickly south and arrived in Verulamium days later so plastered in mud that at first the city guards would not admit them, believing they were chthonic entities evoked by Morgeu the Fey to defend her unholy shrine. At the desecrated chapel, they found the remnants of Morgeu's unholy arts. Lot recognized the sigils chalked onto the walls as ciphers of the netherworld. 'Do not enter here,' he warned and held his boys back. 'This shrine opens upon the world below.'

Arthor remembered too well his own unhappy transit of the hollow hills, and he heeded the chieftain's warning. The king's bishop gathered his priests and began an intricate exsufflation. Sulfur fires blazed upwind of the doomful shrine, each slowly smothered underfoot by holy men chanting Scripture so that the thick fumes penetrated the evil place and saturated every crevice with astringent vapors. Then blessed staves dug out the foundation, and the black stones toppled inward, interring forever that site of pagan worship.

In the midst of this ceremony, a messenger arrived from

nearby Londinium. Word of the king's presence in Verulamium had reached the *magister militum*, and Severus Syrax invited Arthor to visit the governor's palace and review the latest peace terms presented by King Wesc. Seeking Lot to notify him of the message, the king found him in an adjacent willow grove with his sons. They stood about a tented wagon that had been hidden there, shrouded in willow bines. Twilight painted the gray wagon a glimmering red.

'This is Morgeu's.' Somberly, Lot recognized the Celtic signatures of protection carved into the wheel rims and spokes. 'We've buried her in her shrine. I know it now. But there is one here who may tell us more of her fate.' He opened the tent flap and revealed the bed of loam. 'Keep your bishop and priests away, sire.'

What Arthor beheld next, he would remember all the remaining nights of his life. Lot climbed into the wagon, thrust his blade into the loam, dug down, and extracted from the clotted earth a human head, its severed neck bloodless, its throat pipes pulsing, mouth snarling, spitting out crumbs of dirt. Its eyes glared wide. 'Morgeu the Fey is in hell!' the hacked-off head screamed before Lot exposed it to the horizontal rays of sunlight. 'Morgeu lives in hell!' The vampyre shrieked as its face slithered away in the scarlet light, running waxen from its skull in a sticky spill of melted flesh and syrups from burst eyeballs.

This Earthly Star

Skuld led Rex Mundi down from the rusted Seat of the Slain, across the mesa of ferric rock and scattered bones, and over albino ridges of sand that encircled the high throne. The tall, bestial man held the wizard's cap filled nearly to overflowing with gems, while the child gripped the hem of his robe and pulled him along.

Why ith that plathe called the Theat of the Thlain?

'From there All-Father can see into all worlds,' the young girl blithely replied, stepping lightly through the white, ashen sand. 'He sees beyond the lives of people and gods to the time when all has passed away. This gives him peace to know that all is temporary. What is victory, what is defeat when all that lives is slain?'

'You see!' Azael shouted, taking command of Rex Mundi's throat. 'All is futile! I've been telling you that from the first! The Fire Lords are crazy to try to make anything of this mess. It's going nowhere. Give up your light. Stop burning. Accept the dark and the cold. That is what is real. Don't fight it.'

'Shh!' Skuld held a finger to her lips. 'If any of the Asa or Vana see you, your plan to escape won't work. Be quiet!'

'I'm just saying to my peers, be realistic,' Azael went on in a softer but no less irate nagging tone. 'All life is doomed. The stars will burn out. The galaxies will blear away. All that persists is darkness and cold. Get used to it. Stop this senseless running after light and warmth. It can't last. If we wanted light and warmth we should have stayed in heaven where we belong.'

Give me back our voice, Merlin demanded. *I must speak with Skuld.*

'You have something more important to say, Lailoken?' Azael pointed Rex Mundi's arm to the steep, scrabbly rock ledge they approached and the black abyss beyond, in which floated the azure crescent of Earth. 'This earthly star will not long endure. That's what Skuld has been telling us. Look at God. She's the one we followed out here. What's She doing? Dancing with microbes! She's crazy! We should never have followed Her in the first place.'

Dog ashes! Merlin thought with all his might, and the demon went silent. The wizard forced his will to speak, 'Skuld, you said you wanted to thank me for this gift from the Dragon's hoard. You can thank me by showing me where my body is. Will you do that?'

The child took the heavy hat of gems, and her shoulders sagged with their weight. 'I will scatter the gems on the other side of Raven's Branch, as we agreed.' She smiled up at Rex Mundi's round, simian eyes. 'When I'm done, I'll drop your hat so that it falls to where your own body is. Use the magic in your robe to find your hat – and you will find your own flesh. Now go.'

But how? There ith no thtairway down! And no woc to cawy uth!

'The way down is easier than the way up – just jump!' She turned and pushed her back against Rex Mundi, striking him with surprising force. Into the starflung abyss, he fell, robes snapping, arms outstretched, mouth and eyes wide with fright.

The Wizard's Hat

Cei and the priest sat on the kerb of a hilltop street overlooking the field of miracles, where metal ships lofted and landed and horseless wagons darted about, conveying cargo. Backs leaning against an iron stanchion, basking in a gutterful of streetlight, they craned their necks to stare at the lamp overhead. The priest laboriously began to explain electricity.

'Say no more, father.' Cei shook his brutish head, confounded. 'I understand not at all the smithy's secrets, the mason's trade, the carpenter's skills of my own world – what hope I can grasp hell's machinery?'

'You're not in hell, son.' The priest smiled, bloodshot eyes wincing with the pulsebeat of a headache, and he wished he had brought his silver flask with him. 'This is your Britain – but of a future time. You are from my past.'

Cei mulled this over.

'How came you here?' the priest inquired, rubbing his brow.

'Morgeu the Fey cast me into the pit.' He shuddered to remember, and his eyes looked to the gutter and a pierced sewer lid. 'The gatekeepers took from me the talismans Lot vouchsafed me. For that – for that alone – I should be damned.'

'Talismans?' The priest pinched the numb flesh above his nose. 'Gatekeepers? I don't understand.'

'The sentinels at the gates of hell, father.' Cei stared hard at the glazed rosette of lamplight on the macadam. 'I begged from them a way out of the pit. To urge them speak, I gave them the talismans that Lot gave me—' His voice cracked, and when he looked to the priest, his blue eyes brimmed with tears and inconsolable sorrow. 'They are talismans woven from the shorn hair of his sons – Gawain and Gareth – strong, good lads, innocent boys who should not have to die – but for my craven act.'

'You believe they have to die because you gave their hair to the gatekeepers of hell?' The priest frowned with incomprehension.

'I'm a Christian warrior,' Cei spoke through gnashed teeth. 'I know naught of magic. But I know enough not to give hell's denizens hair of the living. I've doomed those boys. I know that.'

A shadow interrupted the amber glow of the streetlamp, and a soft object fell with a muffled thump onto the street. Cei picked it up and held the crumpled thing to the light, exposing a dark blue fabric embroidered with symbols of fine, crimson stitchwork.

'What is it?' the priest asked, pulling himself upright.

Cei unfolded it to a wide-brimmed, conical hat. 'Why – it's Merlin's hat!' From within the folds, a bright object rolled into the warrior's hand – a cut diamond big as his thumb.

King Arthor in Londinium

Through Bishopsgate with Bedevere to one side, a bishop to the other, and a small retinue of mounted archers behind him, King Arthor rode a stallion into Londinium. Lot had advised him not to go but to send a legate to review the terms offered by King Wesc. But Arthor felt stung by what Eufrasia had told him weeks before. He needed to demonstrate to himself that he was the same bold leader who had bravely saved her from Guthlac.

Multitudes jammed the streets to see the boy-king who had successfully repelled Wolf Warriors and the Riders of the North Wind and who had cleared the hinterlands of storm raiders and brigands. Bedevere drew the mounted archers forward into a riding wedge to clear the crowds, while he vigorously scanned for assassins. Instead of meeting the young monarch at the gate, as befitted Arthor's royal status, the *magister militum* asserted his local authority by awaiting his guest at the governor's palace.

The long ride to the riverside palace amazed Arthor, for he had never before been received so boisterously without first having had to fight savage invaders for the honor. In the strenuous throng of cheering faces, some throwing the first purple crocus blossoms of March, others with their children on their shoulders, he sensed for the first time the legend of his deeds.

Hearing the roaring horde, Severus Syrax regretted not meeting the boy outside the city and bustling him quickly to the palace. He decided to avoid any public glimpse of their meeting and installed himself in the throne room with Bors Bona and Count Platorius. The archbishop and his flock of priests were dispatched to intercept Arthor's bishop and to permit a less formal encounter. When the king entered, he came accompanied only by his steward, a one-armed man with an aristocrat's hauteur.

Count Platorius had not attended the Camelot festival and had not seen Arthor before. Though he had heard that the pretender to the throne was young, he gaped with open surprise at the beardless boy who approached the governor's marble throne. Big and long of shoulder as a farmer's son, the tall youth had the easy, long stride of one accustomed to armor and the sword at his side. But his milk-smooth complexion, rose-tinged cheeks, and ingenuous amber eyes that opened wider to take in the sights of the palace lent him the aspect of an amazed altar boy.

'Arthor, welcome to Londinium.' The *magister militum* presented his onyx thumb ring, symbol of his authority and waited for Arthor to acknowledge it by touching it to his brow or at least nodding.

The steward stopped Arthor from responding with a stern glance and stepped forward to speak for his king. 'The high king of Britain has presented himself to review the terms for peace offered by King Wesc of the Foederatus. You will show us to our quarters, where we will freshen ourselves from our journey. On the morrow, you will present the foresaid terms to us for our consideration. Also—' Bedevere moved his haughty stare to Count Platorius and Bors Bona, 'your king has come in person to receive your pledges.'

The Unnameable Thing of Beauty

Gorlois saw through the darkness to the vaulted heights of the asylum for the wicked dead. The damned pressed together against the jet bars, reaching for the rays that shone from his eyes. Beyond them, he glimpsed hell's floor, crowded with muttersome gangs of shadowshapes.

'Not that way, father.' Morgeu turned him by his shoulders and pointed his strong gaze away from the tiered grottoes and fuming crevices. He found again the glisteny trail, like a snail's path, through the tenebrous distances. Soon, they passed beneath an old steel bridge, past the rich odors of a lumber-yard and an abattoir, along the metal tracks of a switching yard. 'Do you see him yet? We must find him soon. My sons' lives are at stake!'

A freight train hurtled out of a tunnel and slashed through their empty shapes, its racket shaking the trestles and the gravel beds but not slowing the progress of the enchantress and her guide. Looking ahead for the shining trace that would lead to Cei, Gorlois turned his head against the hoving blur of the train and saw beyond their quarry, farther into time to where a glare radiant as the sun silhouetted a city of towers and spires. For one white instant, the very fabric of the Furor's vision ripped apart, and Gorlois witnessed a loveliness of immaculate void that filled him with joy. He sat down on the rail with the soot-colored freight cars slashing through him. Then, the indescribable moment passed. Angels spiraled in the expanding rush of light as the glass faces of the silhouetted towers erupted and their skeletal girders melted. A columnar upswelling of fireclouds and clotted plasma pulled long cords of lightning out of the ground into a burning cloud that swelled like a behemoth tree of fire.

'What am I seeing?' Gorlois groaned. 'Oh, daughter—'

'Steady yourself.' Morgeu pulled Gorlois to his feet. 'You looked too far ahead, into apocalypse.'

'Apocalypse?' Gorlois reeled. 'Is it true?'

'What is true of yet to be?' With a toss of her head, Morgeu lifted the red curls that had fallen across her small black eyes.

'I saw angels dancing in a light hotter than the sun!' Gorlois clutched at his daughter. 'And I saw – I saw something so lovely – for one instant, so lovely – in the white light—'

'The Unnameable Thing of Beauty.' Morgeu placed a comforting arm about her father's shoulders. 'I'm sorry you had to see that.'

'What? What was it that I saw?' His silver eyes brimmed.

'I don't know. The angels worship it. It comes and goes as it will.' Morgeu strolled with Gorlois toward a skyline of chimneys unraveling black smoke. 'I've seen it in trance now and then. But it's elusive. Ignore it. You'll be happier.'

Selwa

She had the physical appearance of a minor Roman deity, a nymph who served the gods at the last station of night, for her swarthy beauty projected aspects of forthcoming light: her eyes, oblique and jet, shone with dark clarity, an astute intelligence more sly than shy; her flawless skin possessed the dusky tones of rare spice, brown as nutmeg, glowing from within as if pure copper shone through from underneath; her long sable curls gleamed like shadows of a moonless heaven; and her lithe, long body, robed in the sheerest Ethiopian silks, moved and posed with a benighted pagan sensuousness as though the Son's light had never risen.

Born in Alexandria to a cousin of the *magister militum*, a shipping magnate of the extensive and wealthy Syrax family, Selwa had been educated in all the arts and sciences, rational and esoteric, by the finest Greek tutors. Multilingual, she had served her venerable family at numerous houses of her family's far-flung dynasty, from Aleppo to Zaqaziq. She went wherever her father and his brothers dispatched her and always for the same purpose, to protect her family's holdings with her wiles, sometimes using her beguiling beauty to glean information from rivals, othertimes to get close enough to terminate rivalries permanently.

Severus Syrax had sent for her to remove the chief obstacle to his lucrative trade agreement with the Foederatus: a fiercely idealistic boy-king, who cherished the ludicrous dream of uniting the rustic Britons and Celts. The dither that this child had provoked from her uncle Severus had made her laugh, an uncommon pleasure among her usually grim and dangerous assignments. The sight of her uncle squirming with indignation and shrilly shouting, 'The insolence! The insolence of that child!' had made the cold, storm-tossed sea voyage from Bordeaux worth the misery she had endured. 'The insolence! Behaving as if he were my king!'

Severus Syrax sent Selwa to the boy's suite to ensure that the insolence ended once and for all. To accomplish this simple deed, she wore a sturdy bezoar ring spring-loaded with a fine gold needle sticky with poison. At the young king's door, she presented herself without guile as the niece of the *magister militum*, who had toured the Holy Land recently and wished to share her observations with the new monarch. Once past the archers in their black leather corselets, she saw him sitting on the terrace, dressed as brutishly as his archers but with a gold chaplet of laurel leaves atop his brown hair, hair swept straight back and cropped short over his ears like a farmer. He had propped his boots on the balustrade and with sleep-lidded gaze overlooked the tile roofs of the river city. Large of frame, he was yet a boy, as uncle had said.

Before she could go to him, a one-armed soldier blocked her way. Dressed simply but immaculately in crisp blue tunic, a short sword at his hip, he inspected her with a genial smile on his thin lips and a hint of disdain in his arched nostrils and flexed eyebrows. 'A bezoar ring!' With a swift, deft swipe of his fingers, he slipped the ring from her and held it up to his discerning eye. 'This particular bezoar stone has been regurgitated from a camel. A legendary but alas ineffective antidote to poison. Ah, but my lady, I assure you on my life, there are no poisons to infect you here. Please, do come in. The king is most eager to hear of your travels in the Holy Land.'

Reckoning

Night shone feverishly with the luminosity of the blazing chimneys and the sweeping rays of silver light criss-crossing off the field of miracles. In the salmon-orange glow of the streetlamp on the cobbled road between derelict buildings, Cei inspected the wizard's hat. It smelled of wild thyme, a rhyme with the pastoral world that he had lost when Morgeu delivered him to these burning mills. 'How came Merlin's hat here?'

'I need a drink,' the priest moaned in his own language.

Cei held the large diamond to the lamplight and saw within its facets Merlin's bareheaded visage, sharp-boned, eyes gleaming deep in their skull sockets. And behind him – Morgeu the Fey, her round moon face set with the black, pearl-bead eyes of a snake. He dropped the diamond with a shout, and it bounced off a cobble and spun toward the sewer grating.

The priest reflexively bent and scooped up the gem with both hands. Unlike the ghost, this object had solidity. In his palms, it felt warm, like a bird's heat. Immediately, the hammered pain of his headache lifted away – and the craving went with it, the thirst for more drink, the dismantling of his will, the fear of love, the flight of hope – all gone. He grinned at Cei. 'I'm whole again! Merlin's magic has healed me!'

The large warrior squatted before him, hat in hand, amazed to behold the priest's face transfigured, the bloodwires untangled from his eyes, the puffiness deflated from his jowls. 'What wonder is this? I am confounded by all that has happened.'

'Cei!' Morgeu's voice shouted from the dark of the lane beside a corrugated warehouse. 'Cei! Do not run from me or it will go worse with you!'

'Worse?' Cei stood, vibrant with rage and confusion. 'Worse than hell, Morgeu? Come, witch! I want my reckoning with you!'

Onto the rent pavement, Morgeu strode – and, behind her,

Merlin, his forked beard and silver hair glowing in the slim light of the nightheld street. 'What is that in your hand?'

Cei flapped the wizard's hat and shook his fist. 'Come, witch! Come along, wizard, and take back your hat.'

Morgeu ran across the street, her scarlet robes fluttering, her frazzled red hair bouncing, and snatched the hat from his hand. 'Where did this come from?'

'You know not?' Cei's wrathful face squeezed even tighter with incredulity. 'From him!' He pointed at Merlin, who leaned sideways against a lamp stanchion, looking disordered and mad.

'You're coming with me, Cei.' Morgeu tugged at his big arm. 'We're getting back the talismans of hair you gave the messengers. Do you understand me? My sons will not die for your fear.'

Cei trembled, fist upraised. 'I've a mind to box your ears!'

Morgeu snarled at him – and then noticed the priest with the shining diamond in his hands. She turned from Cei and asked the strange priest holding the Dragon's gem, 'Who are you?'

Not waiting for an answer, she reached out and lifted the diamond from his open palms. As soon as it left his touch, the apparitions vanished. The priest sat alone in the factory precincts at night, old purposes forgot, a new dialect of the heart suddenly comprehensible. By some fabulously strange hallucination from the age of King Arthur, he felt God's grace had returned to his life and cured him of his past, his sins. He tried once more, and this time he stood, steady, spry, strong, capable again of carrying the weight of the moment, of what is, of what momentarily is.

Crows Talking

Rex Mundi fell to earth. He appeared from below as a shooting star. He plummeted through space and plunged through time, tumbling head over heels out of the cosmic World Tree, Yggdrasil. The monkey in him squealed with fear. Dagonet screamed in unison with his familiar. Merlin and Azael wondered if their form would be shattered and they be flung free, one to wander again bodiless, the other to restore itself from dog's ashes before roaming once more. And the Fire Lord, the angel of God, he prayed, *Your will be done, on earth as in heaven. If Your will allows, deliver us to Your guides that we may find our way to You.*

God heard his prayer, and the shooting star buffeted among the clouds and slowed as the heat of the industrial world below filled the magical robes. Gently, the lanky figure descended through the smoggy sky and alighted among weeds sprouted from cinder in a lot of nameless dross – shattered amber bottles, spokeless wheels of black gum, rusted hulks, cast-off papers and parchments, broken slabs of concrete.

Where have we awived? Dagonet tried to make sense of what he saw – a smoldering skyline of tall chimneys surging flames – and closer, tar-streaked poles stuck in the ground with groups of wires strung between them. On the wires, crows sat like black notes of a fragmented musical score. *What ith thith gloomy plathe?*

'Skuld has dropped us near where my body must be,' Merlin reasoned. 'And clearly my body is not in our Britain anymore.'

Your hat – we mutht find your hat. But I don't thee it.

'Find my hat!' Merlin commanded the crows and flapped his robe like wings. 'Fly now and find my hat for Rex Mundi.'

The crows launched into the sky, scattering then reforming and scattering again.

They go nowhere, Merlin. And why should they? They're cwowth!

'But we are Rex Mundi, King of the World – and the animals will serve us – demon and angel united, man and wizard and animal, all one.' Rex Mundi danced among the junk and weeds, face lifted, reading the crows' patterns. 'Look – they are writing ogham!'

Cwowth talking? How can that be?

'It's our magic, Dagonet. The magic of Rex Mundi.'

Land of Nightmares

'I saw the end of this world, daughter.' Gorlois hurried to keep up with Morgeu. She clutched Merlin's hat with one hand, Cei's arm with the other, and practically ran with him past the ponderous hulks of freight cars over gravel beds and rails shining yellow and red in the dusty lanternlight. 'I saw the Apocalypse of John! Our world will end in fire!'

'This world perhaps, father. This world but not all worlds.'

'You *know* that?' Gorlois sounded skeptical. 'I saw angels!'

'The future has many worlds. In some, the warriors call forth fire to consume the cities. The angels dance in the heat – the hottest light ever in the history of Earth. It reminds them of whence they came . . .'

'This is not a field of miracles,' Cei grumbled. 'This is a land of nightmares. Cities of apocalypse. Mills of fire and smoke. Ugliness everywhere. And you!' He glared at Gorlois. 'You're not Merlin. Why does she call you father? Who are you?'

'Be silent, Cei.' Morgeu's grip tightened. 'We have far—'

Morgeu stopped abruptly, and Cei staggered backward in a fright and collided with Gorlois. Ahead of them on the tracks, under trestles and armatures, awash in shadows like watered ink, a beastman stood in Merlin's robes, taller than tall Cei, henna hackles fanning from a jungle countenance of bared fangs.

'I've come for my body,' the fierce creature spoke hoarsely.

'Merlin?' Morgeu let Cei go and backed up against Gorlois.

'I will take my hat, as well – and the diamond of the Dragon's pelf.' Rex Mundi stepped forward with a panther's grace.

Morgeu's mind raced – and she dropped the diamond to the gravel and poised her heel above it. 'I cannot stop you, wizard. But I've magical strength enough to crush this Dragon's gem.'

'Stop!' Rex Mundi crouched, arms outstretched. 'I need that to work the magic that will restore me. Break it and I will surely slay both you *and* Gorlois.'

'Gorlois?' Cei looked from Rex Mundi to Merlin's body. 'What evil transpires here?'

'You may have your gruesome body back, Merlin.' Morgeu did not budge her heel, though she threw the hat to the feet of Rex Mundi. 'But I want the threat from the messengers of death removed from my sons. And I want my father's soul returned to the root-blood of my womb.'

'Gawain and Gareth?' Rex Mundi straightened. 'I pose no threat to your boys.'

'Not you.' Morgeu pushed Cei so hard he nearly collapsed. 'This oaf turned over to the messengers of death talismans made from locks of their hair. Now my sons are doomed lest you help.'

Rex Mundi's animal eyes flashed. 'Cei – is this true?'

'She cast me into the pit!' Cei shouted irately.

'The messengers of death . . .' Rex Mundi's savage face flinched. 'We will have to enter the asylum of the wicked dead.'

The wicked dead? I don't think I like thith, Merlin!

The King Is Lost

Despite herself, Selwa found that she liked the young king. She had met numerous royal personages on her far-flung assignments for her wealthy family, and all had had a sameness about them, some imperfection of the heart, either greed, cruelty, or fear. In talking with this boy on the terrace of the governor's palace and sharing a *pastillus* – a honey dumpling – with sweet veneria roots for confection and a brew of elecampane root, she learned of his unlikely childhood as a servant. He had acquired humility at a young age. And he had been trained to fight and offer himself in sacrifice for those greater than himself. Unlike those born to the purple, who would never think to sacrifice themselves for anyone, this youth sincerely believed he served his people – with his life.

'I came here to kill you,' she confessed to him at last, moved by his candor and his guileless charm. 'And as I have failed in my heart to carry through with this unhappy deed, my uncle will find other means. Assuredly, you will not leave the palace alive.'

Alarmed, Arthor jumped to his feet. 'The *magister militum* assured me safe passage!'

Bedevere discreetly signed for him to quiet his voice.

'You must depart at once,' Selwa advised. 'As soon as I leave here and uncle learns you yet live, escape will become impossible.'

Arthor's jaw throbbed with indignation.

'What do you suggest, my lady?' Bedevere inquired quietly.

'The river.' Selwa took a last sip of the elecampane brew and rose. 'Your party is small. You can easily make your way through the servants' quarters and storage chambers to the tidal wharf.'

'Selwa—' Arthor took the kind woman's hands. 'How can I thank you – for myself, for Britain?'

Selwa smiled wryly. 'You will forgive me, sire, if I tell you that my reward will be departing this chilly, provincial island forever.'

With Selwa's guidance, Arthor and his men found their way unseen through the palace to the dank and cramped servants' lodgings. There, suspicious eyes obliged Selwa to turn away, and the king and his escort hurried brusquely among hung laundry and small hearths of steaming cookpots to the vaulted crypts that stored cheeses and grain. Mice scurried from the hurrying feet that scrambled faster when the alarm horn blared from somewhere in the palace. The archers pried open a grated window that exited upon a splintery pier for lading provisions to the palace.

Several empty cargo gigs lay moored a short run along the pier. Arrows flew as the king and his men scrambled into two of the boats and shoved off. Arthor stood astern, Excalibur raised defiantly at the bowmen on the ramparts. 'Syrax is a mad traitor!'

With his one arm, Bedevere grabbed for the king, and as he pulled him aside, an arrow struck Arthor a glancing blow across the brow. Into the water he plunged. Bedevere dove after him, but in the murk swam blind. With wild eyes and watery grimace, he burst to the surface and screamed, 'The king is lost!'

Stones of Fear

Excalibur and the chaplet of gold laurel leaves had fallen into the gig when Arthor toppled overboard, as if death had divested the youth of his royal charge. In part by this symbolic justification and also because the bowmen on the palace ramparts continued their volleys, Bedevere ordered the gig quickly upstream, to hide in the rushes. Syrax's guards soon cluttered the banks, and the king's men had no choice but to retreat under cover.

The river swallowed Arthor, and the deeper current swiftly carried him downstream. Air caught under his leather corselet conveyed him to the surface and bore him along with the city's rafted trash. Among rags of viscera, gray gouts of sewage, and stunned bits of nameless matter, he drifted. Eventually, he washed ashore under the afternoon's watchful sun.

Voices woke him beneath wind-tilted willows, the iron taste of blood restoring memory. The voices spoke a Saxon dialect he understood well enough, and the very rocks that pillowed his head seemed to vibrate with his sudden fright. Hidden by river grass and dangling willow withes, he removed corselet and belt, weighted them with his stones of fear and shoved them beneath a bleached log. Then, he prayed for the voices to go away.

'Yo-ho! Look here! A wounded man!' Men in Saxon longshirts raised him from the willow bank and laid him on a sward full in the sun. By the cut of their breeches and crop of their hair, he knew they were *karls* – farmers – and he cherished hope yet of eluding them. 'Can you speak, lad? You're bleeding. What's befallen you?'

Arthor mumbled a few words about a British raiding party and warned the men to hurry to their farms and protect their families. The *karls* fingered the youth's fine chemise and eyed his well-crafted boots and surmised he was a *jarl*, an aristocrat worthy of their protection. Despite his protests, they lifted him in their strong arms and carried him up the bank to their wagon loaded with tinder.

The clop of approaching hooves on the packed-dirt river road inspired Arthor to twist free of the helpful *karls* and lope into the ditch beside the road, intent on losing himself in the bramble. But soon the horses arrived, and the shouting voices informed him that they were a warband sent from the king's camp to investigate the commotion reported from the British governor's palace earlier that day. The *karls* pointed to where Arthor had hurried into the brush, and in short order armed men plucked him from under the bare hedges and hauled him back to the road.

He protested that he had business elsewhere. But his voice gave out when he looked up to see upon a sturdy battle-horse a scar-faced man with thick shoulders and black hair braided to a long rat's tail. 'Ah, King Arthor!' A yellowed smile missing teeth stretched straight back like a shark's. 'Surely you remember me, your fellow king – Gorthyn!'

With grinning satisfaction, Gorthyn dismounted and tied Arthor's wrists with leather thongs. 'I was so much your bane that you exiled me. But one king's bane is another's ally. King Wesc has found worthy work for me – and will surely be pleased with the booty I bring him this day!'

In the Land of Things Unspoken

At the jet gate that marked the entry to the asylum of the wicked dead, Rex Mundi stood. Behind him, Morgeu, Cei, and Gorlois in Merlin's body watched apprehensively. Easily the assembled being could have overpowered Morgeu and wrested from her the diamond Merlin needed to reclaim his own flesh. But the lives of two innocents were at stake, and all, save Azael, were united toward one goal. To protect Gawain and Gareth from untimely death, Rex Mundi seized the jet bars in his powerful hands and shoved the gate inward with his demonic strength. Passively, Azael watched as the Fire Lord projected a cold brilliance through the pores of the leathery skin, and the misshapen shadows of the dead elongated and blew backward as if shoved by the solar wind.

Howls like arctic blasts scorched the air, and Lord Monkey and Dagonet quailed. *Thith ith howible! We mutht not go here!*

'Stay close!' Merlin admonished the others as Rex Mundi strode into the cavernous asylum. 'Stay close and look neither left nor right – or you will pay with your sanity.'

Look right! Look left! Azael chanted inanely. *Face the horror of the demon's life. Face the truth of horror! Look! Look!*

Morgeu would not be intimidated. Though Gorlois and Cei kept their eyes fastened upon the broad back of Rex Mundi, the enchantress dared to review the galleries of the asylum illumined by the brilliance of the Fire Lord. Upon thorn trees, flayed human skins hung, the eyes within woeful with living torment. In a faintly smoking garden of coraline shapes, she discerned yet more mortal countenances, human bodies melted to bony scrag.

She could witness no more and averted her face in time to see Rex Mundi come to a stop before a dimly hominoid figure. Bats came and went about this charred shape that seemed almost a hunched and naked tree in an attitude of suffering. Rex Mundi outheld his long and hirsute hand and said not a word, for no spoken word could match the import of silence in this land of things unspoken. Instead of words, the Fire Lord within Rex Mundi offered more light. His radiance increased slowly, inexorably, evoking color from the black environs.

Slowly, the bent figure revealed outsized pink eyes that squinted painfully against the light. Bent fingers splayed over a bulbous skull, a swollen head thatched with white fur and papery scalp of wrinkled, burned skin. Swiftly, a clawed hand slapped Rex Mundi's open palm and deposited there two talismans of shorn locks. Then, ricketsprung legs carried the figure away into the mucronate dark.

As the light dimmed, Rex Mundi quickly turned and walked out the way he had entered, his escort close at his heels. And this time, Morgeu peeked neither left nor right.

Strange Beauty

Rex Mundi did not stop walking until the dark relented to the familiar cerulean sky and speckled green landscape of March in Britain. Ochreous dust rose distantly from a hill path where a farmer's wagon trundled. Cranes flew overhead beneath clouds that poured down the cold sky like spilled milk.

We are fwee! Fwee of hell! Fwee of the Devil! Fwee!

Morgeu knelt in the crisp grass and hugged the talismans of

her sons' hair to her breasts. Eyes filmed with tears, she handed up the large diamond to Rex Mundi.

Cei marched over the soft earth, arms outflung, head cast back, a great silent laugh swelling through him.

Gorlois watched Rex Mundi morosely. 'What will you do . . .'

In mid-sentence, Rex Mundi tapped the diamond against Gorlois's brow, and his soul fled Merlin's body and lit the gem from within. The dispossessed body collapsed in a senseless heap.

'Merlin!' Azael shouted with a fearfulness that startled small birds from the fields. 'I will not be dog ashes! I will not release you!'

A flash of light hot as a thunderbolt exploded through Rex Mundi and instantly the gruesome figure disappeared in the glare. Cei and Morgeu covered their faces, and when they looked again, a tall man of strange beauty stood in the wizard's robes, Lord Monkey perched on his shoulder clinging to the man's curly red hair. With astonishment, he put his hands to his astonished face. 'What has happened to me? Merlin?'

Merlin sat up and groggily felt through the brittle grass until his long fingers came up with the diamond softly lit from within. He rocked to his haunches with a sleepy smile.

'Gorlois!' Morgeu shrieked. 'Where is Gorlois? Merlin!'

Cei stepped quickly to the wizard and helped him to his feet.

'Gorlois is in the Dragon's gem.' Merlin displayed it briefly between thumb and forefinger, then, with a roll of his wrist, it was gone. 'I will retain him to be certain you offer no further grief to our king. For if you do, I shall dispatch Gorlois directly to the asylum for the wicked dead. Do you understand?'

Morgeu gaped mutely for a moment, then rasped, 'You promised!'

'I returned the talismans Cei forsook.' Merlin waved Morgeu away. 'That is all I promised. Now be off with you, enchantress.'

Lord Monkey chattered happily upon the stranger's shoulder.

'Ah, you like the original form of your master.' Merlin smiled. 'You may thank the Fire Lord for that, Dagonet.'

Dagonet reached for Merlin and took his bony hand. 'I was a dwarf! I was stunted from childhood, from birth . . .'

'An accident of the cryptarch that shapes our fleshly forms, Dagonet.' Merlin shook his hand amiably. 'Now you are the handsome Armorican you always were before chance distorted you.'

'And the angel – and the demon Azael?' Dagonet inquired, wonderstruck.

'Fire Lords go where God wills. As for Azael—' The wizard booted the grass, and a small cloud of ashes luffed on the breeze.

A Warrior's Death Song
King Wesc received his royal prisoner in a birch grove on the high bluffs overhanging the River Tamesis. Gorthyn tied the leather leash of the prisoner's thongs to a leafless tree.

'Release him, Gorthyn,' King Wesc commanded. 'And leave us.'

'Sire! This man is most dangerous.' Gorthyn glared at Arthor. 'He is the Britons' iron hammer, trained as a warrior, not a king.'

The compact king looked beyond Gorthyn to his personal guard, and they stepped through the trees. Gorthyn quickly untied Arthor's wrists, bowed, and backed into the guards, who walked him briskly away. When they were alone, Wesc approached Arthor and stared up into his yellow eyes. 'You speak my language.'

'Yes.'

'That was not a question.' His eyes narrowed, and he crossed his red-sleeved arms over his wool shirt. 'I know all about my enemies. You were reared by Kyner, trained to live the life of death. You did not expect to be a king. Nor did I. Nor did I.'

'You are a poet.' Arthor rubbed his sore wrists and recited, '"It is an hour before winter – I have found my way here – to the dreams of wolves – the stillness in which words give up – their unfinished voices . . ." That is all I remember.'

'I am duly impressed, Arthor.' Wesc stroked his long ginger beard. 'How do you know my poetry?'

'You write sacred poetry.' Arthor hesitated, then sighed to admit, 'I've heard those lines many times. Your berserkers sing them as they die.'

'Yes, of course. That is a warrior's death song.' Wesc nodded sadly. 'I myself have no love of war. Unlike my fellow kings among the Foederatus – Cruithni of the Picts, Esc of the Jutes, Ulfin of the Angles – I have never killed anyone. There is no hallowed place awaiting me in the Hall of the Battle-Slain. And you, who have slain men, are scorned for that by your God. "Thou shalt not kill," eh, Arthor? And "he who lives by the sword shall die by it." Your Savior is the Prince of Peace. Is it not odd that both of us are kings who disappoint our gods? In this, we are brothers.'

Arthor could think of no more proper reply than to state the obvious, 'I have fought battles and killed men to defend my land.'

'And I will take that land from you, as my gods command, for the good of my people. Even as your faith teaches that the meek shall inherit the earth, my faith directs that the strong must strive and the weak be overcome. We serve opposite beliefs in opposite ways.' Wesc laughed heartily and slapped Arthor on the back. 'Come. Your future is pre-doomed. Soon enough, all of Britain shall become the kingdom of the Saxons and the Angles. My gods have shown me this, and I know that what they have revealed is true. So, hopeless one, I will now take you to the boat that will return you to your people.'

'Return me?' Arthor straightened with incomprehension. 'Why?'

Wesc cocked his head as if the answer were obvious. 'There is no better enemy for me than you, Arthor.' He laughed deeply again. 'You're not established sufficiently for me to command any realistic ransom. You haven't even won the pledges of your island's largest city. My only recourse is to kill you. But I could not bear to lose you so early in our contest. Come along now. On the way, I will recite to you the latest of my poems.'

Songs Without Singers

King Arthor, when he came to the camp of the Britons north of Londinium, could have risen from the ground, he appeared to the sentinels that abruptly out of the vesperal mists. With mighty cheers from the guards who found him strolling through the evening woods where King Wesc's silent Wolf Warriors had conveyed him, Arthor's return was announced. Bedevere, Cei, and Merlin came running through the cooking fires, their faces wrought with worry.

The young king allayed their fears with a broad smile and a mighty embrace for each, as much astonished to find them alive as they were amazed at his survival. With good cheer that dispelled all the sorrow and recriminations that had previously occupied the campsite, the king was escorted among the tents to the central fire and the commanders' pavilion. A stranger with a head of red curls stood at the map table where Lord Monkey squatted among the scrolls. At his side stood Eufrasia, smiling adoringly.

With the arrival of the king, Aidan and Marcus rose from their seats and knelt. They had hurried south to coordinate the advance of the army into Londinium, leaving Kyner in command of the north. Lot had returned there with Morgeu and their sons to assist.

Arthor accepted the warm greetings and fealty of those in attendance and gazed with disbelief at Dagonet. 'You cannot be the same man I lost at Camelot!'

'I am, sire – and I've a miraculous tale to prove it!'

The tales of the king and his party went on long into that night. And when all was told, remarked upon and marveled at, and all at last departed to their individual tents, Merlin alone sat in the umber light of the fading fire. He stared deep into the tearings and rendings of light. In one hand, he absently turned the diamond taken from the Dragon's pelf, the gem that currently served to house the soul of Gorlois.

Briefly, he considered tossing the gem into the flames and being done with Morgeu's incestuous child and this vengeful soul. But, greater than the admonishment of the Nine Queens, the memory of his mother stayed him. Saint Optima often quoted him her favorite passage of the Bible, from Matthew 5:45: 'He makes His sun rise on the evil and on the good, and sends rain on the just and on the unjust.'

For now, Morgeu's evil had been stalled. Until the king's authority was firmly acknowledged by all, he did not wish to provoke the enchantress further. The hope that her unholy child might yet live offered the wizard some small control over her.

Merlin pocketed the diamond, exhaled a long weary breath, and wrapped himself more snugly in his robe against the chill night. He missed Rex Mundi. Living so close to a Fire Lord, he had never been cold even in the depths of winter. And for once in his aeonial experience, a demon and an angel had worked together, albeit only briefly and with a pitiless love.

He lifted his eyes from the dying flames to the clear night sky. *How rare the light in the dark of creation,* he mulled. *How rare the stars scattered in the void of heaven. For all their billions and thousands of billions, the dark — it ranges far vaster yet. How rare the light, journeying centuries, millennia, aeons through the darkness, untouched by aught else, alone, unseen, forever unknown, these songs without singers.*

SPRING:

Warriors of the
Round Table

Mother Mary, Mass has been said to celebrate the happy return of my brother Cei and our wizard Merlin. And I kneel here before a silver quiver of poplars, one of our Father's private chapels, to thank you personally. Since his return, Cei behaves with ever more deference around me, more quiet than before. In our boy days, I would have known from his nervous silence that he withholds a secret. But having heard the tale of his journey to hell, to a Britain of a nightmare yet to come, I am afraid for him. Merlin's and Dagonet's accounts of Rex Mundi are fantastic enough. But what Cei reports — that bespeaks a more painful strangeness. Perhaps the devil has haunted him with broken dreams of our struggle. To think that our blood is spilled in fighting for a future realm of dark mills and sour skies, that the sweetness of the land itself should be lost . . . Mother Mary, that is madness.

The Blood Pool

In a ploughed field full of early sun, Morgeu and Lot strolled together. The king's soldiers stood small in the distance outside a thatched farmhouse, waiting for their horses that the farmer had tended for them overnight. Lot kicked at a clod of earth, annoyed. 'Why were you in Verulamium, wife? Why did you leave our estates?'

Morgeu, exhausted from her journey through the under-world, lacked the power to enthrall her husband yet again. She also knew that lying would be difficult, with Cei blathering to everyone about what he had experienced in the nether kingdom. 'I went to save the soul in my womb. Lailoken had snatched it from me, and I reclaimed the chapel at Verulamium for a shrine to Hela.'

Lot, who wore a bearskin cloak over his bare shoulders, looked aged in the great fur, his face shrunken amidst hair flowing free and white as a cloud. 'Your rivalry with Merlin must end.'

The enchantress clung to her husband's hide-covered arm. 'He threatens the life I carry, for he fears our child will challenge his upstart Arthor.'

'Cei tells all that you have placed your father's soul in your womb.' Lot's white eyebrows knitted. 'Is this so?'

'Lailoken killed my father on the plains of Londinium.' Morgeu packed her voice with hurt sorrow. 'I want him back.'

Lot enclosed her in his bearskin. 'What of our sons? If you carry Gorlois back to this life, will he not challenge them?'

'Each soul has a private destiny, husband – this you know.' From a pocket of her scarlet robes, she removed the talismans of shorn hair. 'I faced Hela herself to save our sons. Their destinies are safe from the life I will bring back to this world. Only Merlin and his puppet king need fear the return of Gorlois.'

'That puppet king is our king, wife. I have given my pledge.'

'And have I dishonored your pledge?' Morgeu pressed herself against Lot and felt the weariness in him. 'All I have done is try to redeem a loss I suffered at the hands of the demon Lailoken. Am I to be blamed for wanting my father to live again – and for having the skill to bring him once more to the light?'

Lot held her close to him, glad for her strength, for the rageful fire of her will. 'You have my blessing in all that you do, wife. If you summoned the Furor himself to your womb, I would yet stand by you. But there must be no more secrecy between us. I will not again learn from Cei or any other what transpires with you.' He stopped walking and turned her in his arms so that his gray eyes touched her dark stare. 'There was a vampyre at Verulamium. No such unclean creatures must come near our sons.'

'Why do you think I did my sacred work at Hela's shrine so far from our estates, dear husband?' She put her hands to the sides of his face and spoke earnestly. 'I love you and our sons with all that I am. You are a chieftain and I an enchantress. You must spill blood to preserve our lives. And I – I sometimes must dip my hand into that blood pool to keep our lives whole.'

War Spirits

Bors Bona entered the throne room of the governor's palace at Londinium with a proud gait, shoulders squared beneath his polished bronze cuirass, bared head high. He neither bowed nor nodded to the *magister militum*, who slouched upon his marble perch with his kohl-rimmed eyes narrowed and his beringed fingers interlocked before his black, meticulously trimmed mustache and beard. 'Who has authorized the mobilization of my troops?' asked Bors Bona.

'Why, I did, of course.' Severus Syrax cast a slow, sidelong look to where Count Platorius stood almost wholly out of sight among the silk draperies behind the throne. The count, bedecked in a fleece riding coat trimmed with black fox, stepped forward, the dark pouches under his eyes twitching to behold Bors Bona's ire. 'Arthor has refused all our entreaties for peace,' Syrax continued. 'He turns his forces west, back toward Merlin's citadel at Camelot. I believe he intends to cross through the lands of the Atrebates, very seriously destabilizing our dear count's realm. You saw the mindless joy that the rabble took in receiving him to Londinium. We must prevent that from happening to our western ally.'

'Only I may mobilize my troops, Syrax.'

'You have been my guest these many weeks, Bors, and have I once issued complaint that your army indulged too heavily in my storehouses of grain, my byres of livestock, my palace wine cellars, my city's bordellos?' Severus Syrax spoke softly, not stirring from his relaxed posture. 'You have enjoyed free access to all the luxuries of Londinium. And now, I merely assert my authority as the city's *magister militum* to defend us from an enemy by mobilizing troops that I have fed and housed through a harsh winter.'

'Unless you intend to ride with us into the field, you must leave the command of my troops to me.'

The *magister militum* lowered his hands from his face and sat up straight. 'I am glad that you see my authority extending to the field – for I intend to ride out and confront this young warmonger with our united forces. Arthor will quail once he sees unified against him the might of Bors Bona, Count Platorius, the *magister militum*, and the Foederatus.'

Bors Bona rocked back on his heels. 'The Foederatus?'

'Certainly. King Wesc has agreed to bolster our ranks with Wolf Warriors. Think of it, Bors – this arrogant tyrant opposed by Christian and pagan troops united under a Foederatus banner.'

'What?' Bors Bona stepped back a pace as if struck. 'My troops will not serve the invaders!'

'Not invaders, Bors. These are our allies now. Through the Foederatus our island will enjoy safe trade routes again with all the empires to the south, from Trier and Troyes to Rome itself.'

Nodding and smiling, Count Platorius stepped forward and broke his observant silence to add, 'This is a new era of peace, Bors. But first we must exorcise the war spirits of the past. Without you, those spirits will make Arthor high king of Britain, and we will remain isolated from the rest of the world while savage tribes harry us from all sides. Now is our chance to end tyranny and isolation. Ride with us and surely Britain will take its place in a modern age of trade and commerce.'

Spring at Stonehenge

Bors Bona's army, bolstered by Foederatus Wolf Warriors, the armies of the *magister militum*, and Count Platorius intimidated King Arthor. Fighting invaders suited him far better than spilling the blood of the very people he sought to rule. When Marcus and Kyner descended from the north with the main body of his

forces, the king sent trains of empty wagons west, misleading
his opponents into believing that he intended to take Platorius's
lands of the Atrebates by force. But as soon as the massive army
united under Severus Syrax departed Londinium and positioned
themselves in the west to confront him, he turned his army
directly south.

King Arthor crossed the River Tamesis at Pontes, burning
bridges and barges behind him to dissuade Syrax from following.
Then, he led his troops swiftly westward, thus circumventing a
clash between the two factions. By the first day of spring, the
equibalance of day and night, his army camped on the wide
plains of the Belgae territory in sight of the circle of bluestone
dolmens called Stonehenge.

Egrets, plovers, small birds flashed into the golden sky as
Merlin and King Arthor came striding through the bracken
and stood at the edge of the grassy ditch before the earthwork
enclosing the standing stones. 'Who built these monuments,
Merlin?' the boy marveled.

'Are you so confident of the moment that you have leisure
to contemplate the far past, sire?' Merlin stepped down the bank
to its flat bottom and looked up with an unhappy expression
on his craggy face. 'By skirting Syrax, you merely avoid the
inevitable, you realize. He will stalk us to Camelot.'

The king scampered down the slope and up the other side
of the chalk-rubble ditch, brushing past Merlin with a huffy
laugh and playfully snatching his conical hat. 'You sound like
one of my warlords instead of my wizard.'

'You must take a stand against Syrax.' Merlin climbed the
embankment and followed the young king, who skipped over
the small pits that penetrated the earth at regular intervals.
'The longer you delay, the stronger grows his alliance with
the Foederatus. They will take the east of your kingdom – all
the lowlands.'

Arthor pushed through brittle cane grass remaining from the
prior summer and stepped into the circle of tall stones. 'I can't
bring myself to spill the blood of those under my protection.'

'Then you intend to win their fealty by strenuous argument,

sire?' Merlin trampled the canes and retrieved his hat from Arthor's head as the king stood running his hands over the dressed stone of spotted dolerite. 'Syrax and Platorius are disinclined to listen. The trade profits that King Wesc promises them speak louder than anything you could say.'

Still caressing the cold texture of the ritual rock, Arthor replied, 'It is Bors I hope to convince. If we can win him to our order, Syrax and Platorius will have to capitulate.'

'I respect you for your willingness to avoid bloodshed, sire. But I must warn you, deferred evil is nourished evil. The longer you delay, the greater the final battle – and the more likely all that we are striving to build will be lost.'

Mother Mary, in a hundred years, none of us living now will be here. The houses that we live in fall apart and are gone. Forests collapse and grow tall again. The unimaginable awaits us. And still, the priests and the druids dare imagine for us holy heaven, hell's perdition, the drift of souls across the edge of time, journeying from lifetime to lifetime. Is any of this true? Even my faith in you, dear Mother Mary, even my faith in you is just that – faith. What is true? What can be true among flesh and shadow? Oh, please, I beg you, blessed Mother, show me mercy! Though I question all that I am, including our love, I know that in a hundred years, a thousand years, the mountains will not exhaust themselves, and people's faith in you will endure. I question only myself and what is mine. Merlin and my commanders demand that I attack Severus Syrax. But how dare I raise my hand against my own people – the very ones I am sworn to serve and protect? Such hypocrisy is as wicked as Morgeu's deception of me. Am I king – or am I just another warlord? Mercy or power, which should guide my hand?

White Arrows

At Aquae Sulis, the king's army bivouacked for several days, relishing the baths and lading the wagons with supplies for the long march north into the hill country and to Camelot. The tributes that Arthor had received from the cities he had rescued from the Riders of the North Wind during his winter campaign had dwindled now to a single reed sheaf of white arrows, a gift from the laird of Greta Bridge, given to him by a Persian mirza exiled from his homeland. Each of the seven arrows possessed a silver head, an ivory shaft, and feather-thin platinum fletch vanes.

Merlin summoned Dagonet to the king's suite where the arrows lay spread upon a dark table so heavily oiled that the shafts reflected perfectly in the black mahogany. The wizard bid the tall man of red curls to sit in a chair upholstered with auburn horsehair. 'You have the Fire Lord's light in your blood and bones, Dagonet. You are as magical a being as I.'

'But nary as wise, Merlin – or as powerful,' Dagonet responded with a ready and burdenless smile. His ethereal beauty enthralled men as well as women: a beatific, almost supernatural aura emanated from his eyes of icy depths, his high-boned face of tall brow and freckled long nose, his confident chin and guileless, soft-swollen lips, almost hurt-looking yet inspiring absolute trust when parted in a smile white and symmetrical as an amulet of joy. Merlin himself had to look away, fixing upon the small beast clinging to the mane of red curls to keep from being enraptured. Lord Monkey leaped from Dagonet's shoulder onto the glossy table and circled the strewn arrows. 'Since we've come free of Rex Mundi,' the beautiful man continued, 'I've struggled to earn my way in the king's army with skills no longer easy to me. My tumbling and juggling lack grace – and my wit has lost its edge.'

'You are a new man, Dagonet – with a new destiny.' The wizard removed his long hat and exposed a hoary visage of baneful aspect. He glared at Lord Monkey, who was fingering one of the white arrows, and the beast cringed and leaped with a squeal into Dagonet's lap. Though transformed to the eyes and ears, Dagonet yet retained for the beast the cherishable scent it recognized, and it clung fiercely to its protector and glared at Merlin. 'Would you consider earning your place in our army by a mission for the king – a magical mission?'

'Me?' Dagonet's freckles stood out in russet contrast to his suddenly pallid features. 'I think not, my lord Merlin. I still have nightmares of our last magical mission that spanned the heights and depths of creation.'

'Of course, Dagonet, I understand.' Merlin stroked his wispy, forked beard. 'In time, your juggling skills will improve, and you will hold a worthy place at court as a gleeman. I doubt, alas, that such position will much impress Chief Aidan or his fetching daughter Eufrasia, who finds your new pulchritude so alluring. But what hope had you, once a dwarf, still a dwarf in heart, of winning such a lovely hand and the title to go with it?'

'I'm no dwarf in heart, Merlin!' Dagonet's offended tone inspired Lord Monkey to stand erect and scowl at the wizard. 'But I've been a dwarf all my life, I must yet find my new way.' His voice softened. 'Do you think Eufrasia finds me – attractive?'

'Anyone can see that, lad.' Merlin placed his hat back on his long skull and stood. 'You're a handsome man now, Dagonet – but a man of no station. A chieftain's daughter, she requires station.'

Dagonet sighed resignedly and put a finger to Lord Monkey's silver-whiskered chin. 'It seems, master, we are conscripted to the king's service – for hope of love and worthy station.'

The Bird in the Stone
For hope of love and worthy station, Dagonet agreed to do hazardous work that none other of the king's company had either skill or fortitude to fulfill. The wizard gave him the reed sheaf of white arrows with instructions to ride north ahead of the army, followed by Lord Monkey in a dray cart. By the end of his day's travel, during the moment of the first star, he was to let loose one arrow at that earliest lamplight of heaven. Guided by magic, the arrow would land at the site of treasure. He was to retrieve what wealth was found, load it upon the dray cart with the magical arrow, and send Lord Monkey and the dray cart back to the king.

Having suffered the fabulous tour of heaven and hell with

Rex Mundi, Dagonet had little doubt that what Merlin required of him could be accomplished, yet he worried about leaving Lord Monkey to drive a one-horse dray cart across forest paths and uncertain roads. The wizard laughed a silent guffaw, an eerily mute mask of merriment. 'I will affix the brails of my heart to Lord Monkey and guide him swiftly back to me each night by faerie paths. He shall be returned to you each morning, refreshed and sound, I promise.'

Dagonet did as the wizard instructed. At the end of his first day's ride north, he tied off his steed to Lord Monkey's dray cart, fixed a white arrow to a recurved, composite bow – a bow with the curled shape of a temple demon's hostile smile – and aimed for the first star in the fading blue. Through woods strewn with long shadows and spokes of scarlet sunlight, he ran, green tunic slapping at his knees.

The magical arrow had come down upon a rock large as a man's thigh and wedged itself in a narrow cleft. As he worked the arrow loose, the rock split asunder in his lap and revealed a wickerwork of ribs, wingbones, curled spine, grasping talons, and a wedged, leprous skull. Dagonet's fingers played lightly over the impression of feathers that had been pressed into the stone with the finest filamentary detail.

This was not the treasure he had expected, yet he dragged each of the heavy stone's two halves through the woods to where the dray cart waited. Laboriously, he loaded the split boulder and laid between its parts the scratched arrow that had found the bird in the stone. Darkness held the forest by the time Lord Monkey, grasping the reins and standing with commanding authority upon the bench of the dray cart, drove south through the woods.

In the morning, as Dagonet bathed himself in a cold spring among budding withes of willow, he ached from the effort of dragging the split boulder. Hearing the creak of the dray cart returning, he climbed from the water with a bent stoop and found a small parchment secured with a purple ribbon to Lord Monkey's back. The message read: *Dagonet of the Quest – The first treasure you have found will serve the king well. The bishop of*

Auxerre, who collects antediluvian vestiges for the Antipope Laurentius, will pay handsomely for this bird that predates Noah. Do not mind the crook in your back. Ride hard two days and fire the second white arrow at the second star that appears on the first clear night thereafter. God's speed for love of Britain and king – M.

The Secret of Flying

Lot insisted that Morgeu remain at his side during the king's march to Camelot. By the deepening of creases about his already wrinkled and aged face, she recognized the strain that her long absence had inflicted on him, and she did not press for her independence even though she longed to return to the wild places of the north where she could work unhindered her magic to reclaim from Merlin the soul he had stolen from her womb. She knew Lot needed her with him.

Without complaint, she accepted her uxorial chores, brewing the tonics that kept him strong, working the subtle enchantments that eased his worries, and spending time with their sons, who were quickly becoming men as they accompanied the warlords from the campaign tents to the viewing ranges of the king's military operations. To their father's delight, all that Gawain and Gareth spoke of lately was strategy – how to defend from a low-lying position, how to rout brigands from a dell, how to best use cavalry in hilly terrain, how to kill with bare hands.

To remind her sons of the world's other powers, she sat with them each night by their campfire and told tales that, though true, sounded fantastic to the boys: the white serpent of the rocky places on the mountaintop that, when biting its tail, encircled endless time and so could reveal all of past and future if one knew how to ask and listen; the pale people, renowned as the Daoine Síd, who dwelled in the hollow hills and who waited in ambush within rooty caves or misty groves to abduct victims to be fed to the Dragon that was the fire within the earth; the unicorn that ran in herds over the hills and fields of the sun . . .

When her family slept, Morgeu lay beside them. But she

did not sleep, for she knew the secret of flying. To outward eyes, she appeared unconscious. In fact, her mind had departed her physical body and flown with her dream-flesh into the sky of darkest light. The astral realm shone with a luminous darkness. Within its gelid depths all physical and psychic space was available. As a young woman, first learning this secret from her mother the Celtic queen, who had herself learned it from the druids, she had insisted on flying to the farthest reaches of the planet, visiting Cathay, flitting through a busy, loud market cluttered with bright colors of kumquats, mangoes, amber-glazed ducklings, purple octopuses.

These nights in King Arthor's camp, she traveled secretly to nearby tarns and muggy ponds, places of sinking things, where the night vapors hung in the dank air like powdered jade or fine mold. Under the dark bower of swamp trees, the moon small in the sky and granular among the branches like spilled salt, she met with the undead. They appeared by the astral light of dark clarity as they had when alive – Phoenician, Persian, Cretan and Roman figures – women and men in archaic raiment, hair oiled and coiffed in ringlets and elaborate tiers of foregone styles. For centuries, they had dwelled in these low, marshy hollows, coming to this hyperborean isle with the first Romans to escape the necromancers of their own lands. For centuries, they had survived on the blood of lost wanderers, occasional hunters, foolish treasure-seekers.

In the coppery green haze that shimmered like dust, Morgeu gathered about her the undead, learned their names, their stories, and then led them to where their cold hungers could be sated.

They Move Among Us Unseen
Merlin knew at once what was happening when the king's soldiers began to fall sick, beset with chills and no fevers, waking from ferocious nightmares too weak to march and unable to stomach even the sight of food. 'Vampyres,' he informed Bedevere in the carmine light of day's end when the army sprawled like a giant among the scattered glades of

the hillsides. 'We've ten days' march ahead of us before we reach Camelot. At this rate, we'll be decimated when we reach there.'

'I'll gather the priests and we'll set up perimeters of holy candles and prayer vigils,' Bedevere offered.

'No.' Merlin pulled the steward closer by his one arm and walked with him away from the king's tent. 'Arthor must not know. He will suspect Morgeu and rightly. That is what she wants, to alarm him and thus to bend me to her will and force me to return Gorlois's soul.'

'She has not yet miscarried that unholy child?' Bedevere's tall brow creased with concern. 'I know a tincture that will purge her womb. Shall I see that it finds its way to her drink?'

Merlin flashed a piqued look and spoke as if to a child, 'She is an enchantress, Bedevere. Don't even think to challenge her.' The wizard pulled the steward to where the grooms brushed and fed the cavalry's steeds, and he picked up a wooden bucket. On the iron hoop that bound the slats, he scrawled with red chalk a series of barbaric sigils. 'Take this bucket, fill it with tarn water, the more black with leaf-rot the better. Then post yourself outside the tent of the stricken. Watch the water. When you see the vampyre reflected—' Merlin clapped the wooden top to the bucket. 'Catch the devils this way. They move among us unseen, because they come in astral guise, too wary to expose their physical forms. But we will catch their souls!'

'What am I to do with the capped bucket?' asked Bedevere.

Merlin merely smiled. That night, he equipped the steward with a dozen marked buckets, each filled with water dark with steeped leaves. By dawn, a sleepy Bedevere had capped all of them. The wizard lined them up in a clearing where the red dawnlight climbed down the trees. With the sun at her back, Morgeu came striding through the haze of the cooking fires and shoving past the horses being saddled for the day's march.

'Do not destroy them, Lailoken.' Morgeu placed a red-slippered foot on the first bucket that Merlin reached to uncover. 'They came at my behest.'

'And what ire the survivors will harbor against you, Morgeu!'

A crooked smile bent his lips. 'They will come for you –
and yours.'

Her round face squeezed a frown. 'You want to destroy
me.'

'I want you to oppose our king no more.'

Morgeu gripped Merlin's robe. 'Give me back my child's
soul.'

'Never, you incestuous harlot!'

Morgeu raised her hand to strike the wizard, her small dark
eyes flashing – but checked herself with a snarl.

Merlin's smile widened to a grin of yellow, snaggled teeth.
'If you hurry, you can carry each of these buckets to a dark
place before we break camp. But do not dare thwart me again,
Morgeu, or next time I will forget I am a Christian.'

The Beauty of Horses

Spring rains sizzled through the trees when the king's army
arrived at the River Amnis and Camelot hove into view.
Much work had been achieved in the long months that the
warriors had been away, and the bartizans, spires, belvederes, and
curtain-wall towers had all been completed. Even against the
gray sky, with the black-and-green dragon pennants of the king's
ancestors and the banners in Arthor's own colors of red and
white hanging limply, the citadel offered a spectacular vista.

While the army marched through Cold Kitchen, greeted
by the trumpeting of elephants and joined by dancing bears and
the antics of wise dogs, King Arthor rode swiftly ahead. The
fortress-city stood triumphant under the stormy cloudbanks and
the deepening green of the mountains. Waterfowl flapped up
out of the grass before his gallop, egrets, herons, and cranes that
had returned to the River Amnis with the clement season.

On the champaign around Camelot grazed a herd of slender-
legged, sleekly muscled horses shining almost blue in the rain,
silent and fluid as running ink. Arthor slowed to a stop and
sat enraptured by the beauty of horses. He watched their
ebony hooves dancing in the morning groundmist, their long,
intelligent heads bowing and lifting, swinging to regard each

other with smirking eyes of grace. Already they were well aware of him studying them, the wells of their nostrils sampling the news of his arrival.

The master masons and carpenters who greeted the king upon his entry into the slate-paved ward of the castle informed him that the sable horses had arrived at Cold Kitchen on a barge from Palaestina Salutaris as a gift of the *dux Arabiae* at Bostra. The Christian *dux* had heard of the boy-king's struggle against pagan invaders and the opposition of Severus Syrax. The redoubtable Syrax family had long been trade rivals to the *dux Arabiae,* and he was glad to do what he could to offer help to any of their foes.

'When last we stood in this citadel, sire,' Bedevere remarked to the king after they dismounted and strolled awestruck across the bailey, 'your hair yet bristled like a hedgehog's and you'd rather have worn a common tunic than a royal chemise. And now—'

Arthor did not hear his steward, so engrossed was he by the many towers and battlements of the outer ward – and then, the elegant spired archway to the central court, where a tall fountain of carnelian and green tourmaline waterspouts emptied onto interlayered basins all carven with images of dolphins, salmon, squid, conger eels, and mermaids.

'Last we were here, sire, you told me you did not feel like a king in your heart.' Bedevere admired how regal Arthor appeared with his hair grown out and his royal attire well worn to his form. 'How does your heart feel now?'

'So much blood of our own people has spilled in the slaying of our enemies,' Arthor answered quietly, almost absently, absorbed by the graven heights of the inner ward, 'if I am not a king, Bedevere, then I am a heinous murderer.'

Mother Mary, Camelot is beautiful. Evening falls on the central garden, where I kneel before you. Bats flutter about the cloister. Shadows climb the battlements. My sister still appears in my evil dreams, and she plays with my fate. But I feel safe here among these towers of cold stone. She has a suite of chambers entirely to herself within Lot's wing of the castle, and this fortress-city is so large, I could live here years and never see her. A bell rings from the chapel. Three crows scatter, and a golden cloud dissolves. What compels me to remain kneeling among the rose shrubs as darkness encloses all and the lantern-lighter on the ramparts calls out the o'clock? Merlin speaks of a dark age to come. A thousand years of forgetfulness. We in this citadel are, by God's grace, a bright encounter before the unspeakable dark descends. But the night that follows is not everlasting. A brighter age will ascend. And the call from within to serve that time yet to come scatters my sad dreams.

Dark Morning

Black smoke rose from the horizon in a titanic wall that blotted the sun. 'The pagans are burning the hamlets and their outlying fields!' Count Platorius reported to Severus Syrax.

'Not pagans – Foederatus troops.' The *magister militum* sat on his red stallion where the Belgae plains rose to gaunt rills above a river benchland. 'Our allies are destroying the farms of our enemy, the tyrant Arthor. Why does this alarm you, Platorius?'

The sullen count, wearing a beaverskin cap and white leather riding jacket collared in black sable seemed better attired for the sport of hunting than war. 'I understand the tactic, Syrax, but I question how Bors will respond. He is already displeased with our – allies.'

Severus Syrax grinned at the dark morning. 'I have already taken precautions to safeguard Bors's fidelity to our cause.' He adjusted his turbaned helmet and brushed ash from the furred shoulderguards of his red leather cuirass. 'I had the foresight to position him well east of us, in Calleva Atrebatum, where his large army will be handsomely provisioned and out of the way until we need it. Reports have already been forwarded to him indicating that the tyrant has set fire to his own farmlands to keep them from falling into our hands.'

'But surely this flagrant an act of destruction will provoke a response from the tyrant.' Count Platorius watched a squad of Wolf Warriors punting along the stream, the gunwales of their boat draped with the flayed scalps of farmers and their families.

'I suspect he will send Marcus or Urien to counter us here.' The *magister militum* turned in his saddle with a smug expression. 'But we won't be here. By that time, Bors will be where we are now, and he will crush Urien, whom he hates for his pagan faith – and if it is Marcus, then the battle will not be as bloody but it will be as equally decisive. Bors cannot accept defeat.'

Count Platorius viewed uneasily the Wolf Warriors' booty in the thwarts of their boat – pink peeled skulls. 'And where will we be when Bors is finishing the conflict that we have inspired this dark and grisly day?'

'Ah, we are bound on a bold military venture, dear count.' Severus Syrax swept one silk-sleeved arm west. 'We are destined to take Tintagel and capture the tyrant's mother, the converted pagan queen Ygrane!'

The Guest in the Tree

Dagonet's back ached unrelentingly on his two-day ride north. He cursed the heavy stone he had lugged through the forest and prayed that the next treasure he located for the king would not prove so ponderous. The second evening of his journey settled through the forest in a misty rain. No stars shone through the dense clouds, and he spent that night and the next three days hunkering in a hawthorn grove, trying to keep warm and dry. By day, he and Lord Monkey foraged early berries, dug edible cypress roots, and snared squirrels and rabbits. At night, they crouched under a hawthorn bower out of the rain and close to a twigfire whose flames fled down the wind, and they discussed the life they would have for themselves when their mission was complete and the king rewarded them for replenishing his coffers.

On the third day, the sky cleared. Among tufts of pink cloud, Dagonet watched for the second star to appear, a white arrow notched to his recurved bow. The moment he spied it, he aimed and fired. With a cold whistle, the pale arrow shot into the sky, flashed red at the top of its arc, and plummeted into the blue woods. He signed for Lord Monkey to wait, and he hurried among the trees as swiftly as his sore back allowed.

Shining with reflected light from the bloated red sun among the trees, the white arrow stabbed the trunk of a mammoth chestnut tree. Dagonet climbed the crevassed bark to reach the arrow and there found a mansized hole bored open years ago by lightning. He peered into its thick darkness and saw nothing. Only after he climbed in and braced his way down through the gnarly, cauterized chute in the pith did he realize he was not the only occupant.

With tentative and trembling fingers, he felt the smooth roundness and pitted orbits of a skull. His small cry resounded loud as a scream in the enclosed darkness, and he scrambled quickly away. But as he sat on the ledge of the hole in the cool, crepuscular dark, he realized he had to go back down. Whatever treasure there was lay with the skeleton.

Gritting his teeth, Dagonet returned to the arboreal sepulcher. He lowered himself until the skeleton's brisket pressed against him, then felt blindly for jewelry but found none. With his feet, he tapped the support beneath him and heard then the thud of a cask. Muttering an oath, he embraced the bony remains and tried heaving them out of the tree so that he could reach the cask, but, at his touch, the carcass fell apart. He spent the better part of that night rigging saddle straps from his horse and the dray cart and crawling back down into the tree, muddling among the scattered bones and trying to hoist the cask.

It was midnight when he finally gave up and began hacking at the tree with his sword. The dead wood gave way more easily than he had expected, and, groaning with the pain of his cramped muscles, he used the saddle-strap rigging to lower the cask to the ground. When he pried it open with his sword, black coins of silver caught starlight on the tarnished profiles of Emperor Trajan.

Confronting the Wizard

Morgeu's scarlet robes no longer hid her pregnancy. Yet, large as her gravid belly had swollen, no life stirred within. No matter the fortifying elixirs she drank or the enlivening spells she chanted, the unborn child floated inertly. The enchantress took to her bed in a garret of Camelot, spending ever more time out of her body, searching through the mysteries and secrets of the astral realms for ways to lure her child's soul back into her womb.

Gawain and Gareth feared for their mother. In desperation, Lot confronted Merlin in the wizard's grotto beneath the citadel. The chieftain had vowed to himself that, in deference to his wife, he would strive to avoid the demon-man who had caused her father's death, but Morgeu's increasingly remote condition spurred him to descend the winding stone steps guarded by gargoyles and arcane graven images.

The iron door, embossed with a giant coiled dragon, stood open, revealing flowstones slick and fluted, whiter than snow, some the color of fresh meat, others fiery green. Beyond, stalactites of similar lurid colors fanged from the carinated ceiling, many hung with globular oil lamps of blown glass that cast aqueous reflections upon a chamber curved and layered as a sea cave. The natural rock formations of rock scallopings, uvular alcoves, and slag platforms served as work surfaces for the wizard's intricate metal- and glass-shops. Esoteric machineries of bronze pots, copper coils, and whirling vanes stood interspersed among alchemic retorts and alembics aswirl with yolky tinctures and soupy distillates. A tarry reek hung in the air, pungently infernal, an exhalation of hell.

Merlin sat upon a malachite stump loded green with copper, contemplating vast and obscure charts of the heavens hung from the stone teeth of the high domed roof. His head tilted as though listening to the whirring machinery, percolating vats, and the timeless dripping of subterranean leakage. He seemed oblivious of Lot. Trepidatiously, the chieftain advanced among the ribbed stones. 'Wizard – I would speak with you.'

'Be gone from this place, Lot.' Merlin did not even budge his stare from the celestial charts among the hanging spires. 'You come seeking mercy for your wife, but I have none for her.'

'You have taken the soul of my child from my wife's womb.'

Merlin turned, slow as a snake, the bonepits of his long eyes agleam with barbed light. '*Your* child, Lot?'

Lot stood motionless as a tall eldritch doll. 'What?'

Merlin smiled dreamily. 'Ah, she has not told you. Then, go.'

'I will not go.' Lot advanced, eyes baleful. 'Whose child does my wife carry? Is it yours?'

'Enough!' With an annoyed grimace, Merlin stood. 'I will not answer for Morgeu. Be gone from here, pagan Lot. Be gone or you will know pain without remedy. Go – and do not ever return!'

Lot backed away, intimidated by the wizard's sudden wrath. He tripped over a glossy step, spun about on his hands and knees, and scampered out of the grotto. Fright unreeled through his limbs, and he tripped twice more on the spiral stairs, appalled to imagine Morgeu in the arms of the gruesome wizard.

Unspoken Wishes

Preoccupied with plans for countering the internecine war that Severus Syrax foisted upon him, King Arthor dispatched Cei to Tintagel to oversee the transportation of the Round Table and the Holy Graal to Camelot. Cei went reluctantly. He still cringed with dreadful memories of his tour of hell, and he wanted to serve his king on the field of battle, not on diplomatic missions – especially those of magical portent.

On the journey south through Cymru and the lands of the Dumnonii, Cei stopped at every church, chapel, and chantry he encountered and sought the blessings of the holy residents to protect him from what lay ahead. He feared the king's mother, well aware of her reputation as a powerful priestess of *wicca* beloved of the pale people. No matter to him that she presently served the Savior as an abbess of a convent devoted to charity for the impoverished, he staunchly prepared himself to meet the mother of the woman who had cast him into infernal darkness.

The afternoon he arrived at Tintagel, a storm thrashed the coast. Tintagel reared dimly against banks of green clouds and twisted cables of lightning. Lay brothers in sack habits stabled his horse, and nuns in gray linen gowns escorted him to a central hall warmed by a large hearth. A score of indigents sought shelter here from the storm, and the nuns had seated them at a long table and provided a meal of salt fish boiled in milk and butter.

Cei declined a private meal in a chamber of his own and, after drying himself by the fire, ate among the destitute. To no avail, he tried politely to decline a summons to meet with Ygrane in her private quarters on the western terrace, hoping to defer their meeting until the morning and the promise of less ominous weather. But the nuns could not disobey their abbess, and they led him by both of his brawny arms up the broad staircase to the expansive suite that opened on the western prospect above the sea-thrashed cliffs.

Ygrane stood before the Round Table, the Graal in her hands. At her back, through the colonnade arches of the terrace, wings of rain flapped. 'Cei – my son's stepbrother, I want to welcome you as a mother. Please, do not kneel before me. Rise, brother of Arthor. Why are you so pale? Here, hold the Graal. Its grace will heal your troubles and answer all your unspoken wishes.'

Cei accepted the chrome, gold-laced goblet, and at its touch, his dread did vanish. Serenity enclosed him, and as the abbess had promised, his unspoken wishes came clear: Ygrane's face opened before his gaze to the soul within her – an immense field full of wild wheat and sunlight spilling over – and he knew then he had nothing to fear from this good woman.

The Spiral Called Eternity

Cei spent a joyful week at Tintagel abbey, working with the lay brothers by day, helping to repair storm-damaged roof tiles, driving the daily wagon of prepared meals to the local hamlets to feed the sick and elderly, joking and laughing with the nuns as they toiled together in the busy spring gardens around the castle, and chatting easily and amiably in the evening with the abbess about the day's work. As though he were her own son, she visited him each night before he slept and confided in him memories of her childhood as a peasant in the hills of Cymru and of the faerïe who visited her like wasps of flame and of the druids who took her from her family to teach her the occult lore of their ancient lineage and to make her their queen.

From Ygrane, Cei heard about the spiral called eternity. 'The Celtic truths are the same as what our Savior preached,' she told him in a voice of lullaby. 'Our people have long known of the trinity, of *Abred*, God's struggle to create the world through evolution, *Gwynedd*, the triumph over evil that our Savior has attained, and *Ceugant*, the radiant rays of God's love, the Holy Spirit. Each of us is on the spiral journey to the eternity of God, guided by the Holy Spirit. Through every form that can hold life, under water, on earth, in air, we evolve, knowing every severity, every hardship, evil, and suffering until we become worthy of goodness by knowing everything. And that is why we must endure what is painful, my son, for it is not possible to know all without suffering all.'

Cei wept when he left Tintagel. Had he not been bound by fealty to his king, he would have doffed his sword and his black dragon-bossed corselet and donned a cassock to serve the abbess and her humble, industrious nuns. But he knew that he had his small but vital role to fulfill in the salvation of Britain, and as Jesus, who so inspired Mother Ygrane, had given all, he would give no less. Thus, on a luminous May morning, he and a dozen lay brothers stood the Round Table on its side and rolled it as a great wheel along the Roman highways of the Dumnonii.

Wrapped in lambskin, the Graal rode with Cei, strapped to the pommel of his horse's saddle. Its propinquity intoxicated him with a celestial joy. Each day passed through his arms like a lover to be cherished. At night, though the musk of his horse had seeped into his garments and he slept with dead leaves strewn over him, the air felt lambent and aromatic as though he were surrounded by roses. He dreamt of Tintagel, believing while he slept that he had never left, believing he still labored laughing in the garden fields, still rode the dirt traces among the hamlets delivering meals to the needy, still lay in a fragrant bed gazing through an arched window at the promiscuous stars as Mother Ygrane spoke intimately of the soul's journeys on the spiral called eternity.

Fish Drinking in the River

The ivory shaft and platinum fletch feathers stood in a brook, the golden, twilit water unfurling around it. As Dagonet approached, limping with the pain of his aching, bent back, the arrow moved deeper into the narrow stream and away from his outreached grasp. He splashed after it, and it coursed upstream, cleaving the bright current before it. His sandaled feet sloshing through the cold water, slipping on the mossy rocks, he fell and thwacked his head against a rock. Stars dazzled his vision, and through their spun light he spotted the arrow and seized it.

It stuck from the back of a large fish that thrashed in his grasp, then lay still, its mouth wagging as if drinking in the river. *I am dying!* the fish spoke. *I am entering a great light. Once I was a hazel tree. Now I am a fish. But my soul is still the shape of a hazel nut. I think I will be a tree again. And you! You, Dagonet, who killed me for what I carry in my belly – why do you trust a wizard? He loves his magic more than you.*

'You speak?'

The fish thrashed in the muscles of water, but Dagonet would not let it go. *You are surprised I speak – you who lived as Rex Mundi, who climbed the Storm Tree, who walked the horizons of time and faced Hela herself in Sleet Den, the asylum of the wicked dead? You doubt a fish can speak?*

'By what power do you speak, fish?'

By the power of the white arrow that pierces my back, Dagonet. And by the clarity conferred on you by brother rock, who kissed your head.

'What do you want of me?' Dagonet lay with his cheek on a slimy rock, staring into the agate eye of the fish. 'I cannot release you. I am on a mission for my king. You are his prize.'

I ask not to be released. You have already killed me. All I ask is that you look. Look at yourself in the water, Dagonet. Look and see the price that you must pay for your royal mission. You are becoming again what once you were.

Dagonet painfully pushed himself to his knees and peered at his reflection in a standing wave of the rushing current. Hunched over from his laborious efforts to claim for the king the bird in the stone and the treasure in the tree, he did indeed appear hump-backed – and his facial features seemed haggard and less fair.

You see, Dagonet – Merlin uses the Fire Lord's magic within you. As the angel's power is depleted to fulfill the wizard's lust for treasure to serve his king, you become more of what you were.

'What can I do? I – I must fulfill my mission.'

Must you? You are handsome and strong. Make your own way in the world. What do you care for the boy-king or for Britain?

Dagonet held the fish to his face to reply, but the finny creature had already died, its mineral eyes glazed over.

'This is our treasure, master,' Dagonet sullenly announced to Lord Monkey when he returned to the dray cart and outheld the fish by the arrow that impaled it. He cut open the fish to remove the shaft, and a large, iridescent pearl rolled out. The monkey chattered with surprise. As instructed, Dagonet placed the pearl and the arrow upon the dray cart and helped Lord Monkey face in the direction they had come. In moments, the night once again accepted the beast-driven cart, and before Dagonet turned to find kindling for his fish-roast, the sound of the creaking cart and the horse hooves vanished suddenly into the chill forest.

The End of Caprice

King Arthor remained in the war counsel room after the chieftains and commanders left. They had detailed for him the insidious cruelties that Severus Syrax and his warlords had inflicted upon the provinces loyal to the king: farms destroyed, dams broken, vineyards and orchards torched. All agreed that the king had no choice but to confront Syrax's forces before they overran any more territory. But Arthor knew that so long as Bors Bona backed the *magister militum*, the battle for dominance of Britain would be unbearably bloody. He had asked Merlin to devise a charm that would win Bors Bona's affections – a love charm for a warlord.

'This matter is no easy one,' Merlin had confessed. 'Though I have scrutinized the star houses of Bors Bona and have found his aspects of affection sufficient to craft a charm, the manner of delivery is essential. Whoever hands him the charm must embody attributes alluring enough to activate his affections. Once activated, those affections will be assigned to Britain and to you as Britain's high king. But who can evoke such feelings in this battle-hardened and embittered warlord?'

'Create the charm, Merlin,' Arthor commanded. 'I will summon the ideal messenger.'

Eufrasia found the king alone in the war room. 'I pray you have not beckoned me to renew our awkward winter friendship. I will tell you directly, Arthor, my heart is given to Dagonet.'

'Your father warned me you were a mutable lass.' He stood surrounded by map easels and tables mounted with terrain models. 'Perhaps Dagonet holds your interest because he is unavailable. He is away raising funds to finance our war against the Foederatus and their British allies – Syrax, Platorius, and Bors Bona.'

'My actions have been fickle, Arthor. You saved my life in the Spiral Castle, and though I have repaid that debt to you, I still feel great warmth for the brave young man who risked his life to rescue me from a cruel death. My behavior this past winter – I cannot excuse it. I was inebriated with war – with so many battles and such long traveling. The prospect of winning the love of a king inspired me to act foolishly. Since our arrival here in this elegant castle, I tell you honestly I am more myself. I was wrong to entice you, more wrong yet to call you a boy and dismiss you.'

'Eufrasia, I did not call you here for an apology.' Arthor opened his palm to expose a small mauve phial with a tiny scroll encased within. He explained to her the nature and purpose of the charm. 'You owe me no debt and I have no right to ask you to risk your life for me again . . .'

Eufrasia plucked the charm from the king's palm. 'I will deliver this to Bors Bona – not only for you, because you believe in me despite the graceless way I treated you – but I do this also to mark the end of caprice and the beginning of what I hope will be a future – for myself and my beloved Dagonet.'

Mother Mary, I entrust my future to a woman whom I have denied, a woman who now flaunts her new love in my face. In truth, I pray for her happiness, for she would have none with me and my polluted soul. But will she serve Britain – or spite me? I pray to you, watch over her. Though she is a pagan, guide her on safe paths to Bors, whose might we must turn to our cause.

The Maker of Snakes

They came in the night, riding by moonlight along paths white as salt. Tintagel itself shone like a craggy chunk of the moon fallen to earth. Past the lay brothers who guarded the gate that was never closed, soldiers rode into the main court and leaped from their horses while they were still moving. They wore the blue tunics and brown riding jackets of the *magister militum*'s elite cavalry and paid no heed to the gray-frocked nuns who met them in the ward. They shouldered past these gentle guardians and stormed up the broad and gracefully curving marble staircase, not pausing to remove their bronze-banded leather casques.

On the western terrace where the Round Table had once rested, they found the abbess in her white habit kneeling in prayer before the cabinet altar that had housed the Graal. They said nothing as they lifted her by her arms and dragged her from the suite.

Ygrane made no protest. She struggled to get her feet under her and allowed herself to be run quickly down the stairs. To the alarmed nuns who tried to block the soldiers who had seized her, she said only, 'Return to your prayers.' And to the lay brothers who rushed across the bailey with staves and threshing tools, she loudly admonished, 'Put aside violence! Go and pray for our king.'

At the horses, she made no struggle and was allowed to ride sitting up in the musky embrace of a cavalryman. Onto the moonpaths they rode, leaving Tintagel behind shining like a heap of bones. Silver wands hung in the forest. The empty outcry of an owl heralded their swift passage, and the soughing wind carried the chill news of rain to the north.

Severus Syrax and Count Platorius stood waiting her arrival in a glade amber with firelight. Two score men milled among the trees where they had camped, eager to see for themselves the renowned queen of the Celts, mother of Morgeu the Fey and the boy-king Arthor. They kept a respectful distance from where stood the *magister militum* in his turbaned helmet and fur-trimmed metal breastplate and the count in a beaverskin cap and long fur cloak.

Ygrane said nothing as the cavalryman eased her to the ground. In the firelight, her placid face seemed carved of amber and occupied from within by the flames' restless shadows. She gazed without ire or anxiety at the two warlords.

The count bowed before her and crossed himself. 'Mother, forgive us, but your son's stubbornness forces our hand.'

She made no reply, and Severus Syrax appraised her coolly, the thin lines of his mustache curved in a smug smile. 'Do you know why you are here?'

Her green eyes lidded knowingly. 'I assume I have been summoned by the Maker of Snakes.'

Obsessed with Red

Before life, there was sleep. Morgeu returned there between her long astral flights and the brief time she spent awake, tending the needs of her body. She felt desperate to find a way to retake Gorlois's soul from Merlin. Yet all her adult life she had been desperate for vengeance against the wizard whose magic had doomed her father. That was why she was obsessed with red. As well as her scarlet robes, the draperies of her tower chamber in Camelot hung scarlet. Rugs of crimsoned fleece covered the stone floor. The bower of her bed caught the window breeze in veils of red gauze. Even the stools, the bed table, and writing desk gleamed with vermilion lacquer. The color carried the power of blood, of life, of the eternal wound between day and night, and it conferred on her the mortal strength to avenge what a demon had taken from her. In her meditations on how to thwart the demon who had thwarted her, she often fingered her red hair and pulled it to her teeth to gnaw on it. At those times, only her hair seemed truthful, for it was already dead.

She lay among the tangled scarlet sheets of her bed, gnawing a tress of her hair when Lot entered. The crease between his storm-gray eyes warned of a grief that cleaved his brain, some conflict that he waited until he sat at the edge of her bed to voice. 'Merlin tells me that I am not the father of this child. Yet, I already know you will say he lies – he is Merlin, your foe.'

Morgeu said nothing. She gnawed her hair and watched.

'I know he has stolen the soul of the child – the soul that is your father.' Lot's mouth was not visible behind the dense gray whiskers of his drooping mustache, and his soft, nearly whispered words arrived as if telepathically rendered. 'I care not at all whose soul you carry back to this world. You are an enchantress. You have this power to summon souls. I accept this. But you are my wife. The flesh you use to garment this soul must be mine woven with yours. I am Lot, son of Lug Lamfada of the Long Arm, father by Elen of the warriors Delbaeth, Loinnbheimionach, and Cohar, father by Pryderi of the Golden Hair of the warrior twins Gwair and Galobrun, and father by you of Gawain and Gareth. I will not father a son sired by another.'

With the little strength she had left from her tedious journeys in the ether worlds, Morgeu reached out and pressed her thumb between her husband's eyes. In a chant voice, she sang quietly for him, 'You are a great warrior and the father of great warriors. Save your ire for the enemy. Save your strength to break the enemy. Or else the houses burn and the fields run wild. Until you, good and strong were twins, two different brothers. But in you, they are one soul.'

When her thumb came away, Lot felt peaceful and sure of

himself. Bird chatter filtered through the red draperies among glimpses of cloudlight. A wisp of baking bread climbed the morning from the cookhouse below. His wife smiled at him, and his heart beat proudly in his chest as he rose to go, admiring the crimson fleece underfoot, the dark grain of the door, the fine mating of archstones on the lintel – the world so full of everything that he did not notice the nothing she had given him.

Wings of Twilight

At each twilight, both at dawn and evening, motes of spectral light flitted among the tall grass, the hedges, and the tree boughs, drawn to the giant wheel of the Round Table that Cei and the lay brothers rolled toward Camelot. Cei initially paid them little heed. To his mind they were lightning bugs, fireflies, or will-o'-the-wisps. Sunrise and nightfall were busy times, preparing meals and the campsite. Not until the fifth night did he overhear one of the lay brothers' prayers nervously mention *faeries*.

'That's what those lights are,' the lay brother informed him when he inquired. He looked, but by then night had fallen.

In the morning, he paid more attention to the flitful shapes so proficient at riding the breezes down from among the trees. The size of the wheel required the men to follow the major highway east and avoid the more direct forest routes where low-lying boughs would block their progress; so, Cei moved from one roadside ditch to the other, chasing the sparks that gusted from the woods on either side. At last, a roadside peddler chanced to clap his hat over a fiery mote. When Cei peeked, he indeed saw a tiny being, vaguely human, with diamond-carat halo, mica-fleck eyes, and fog-blur raiment.

Fear glinted in Cei like a musical note spun over and over again on his taut heartstrings. He prayed fervently during the breakfast of barley bread and salt fish, pleading for angels to guide and protect them.

By nightfall, with fatigue from the long day's trek weighing heavily and fog seeping across the highway from the woods,

Cei felt his prayer had gone astray. Shadowshapes of gnomes and trolls appeared to rear from the ditches, and the faeries gusted in swarms down the highway like fiery balls of swamp gas. Cei turned to mouth encouragement to the lay brothers, but the milky fog had enclosed them entirely. What silhouettes he saw stood immobilized, like statuary in a foggy garden.

'Cei, son of Kyner, what a handsome and practical table you have there.' The darkly gleaming voice came from a tall man in yellow boots and red vest, his pixie-slanted emerald eyes shining with an enigmatic light. Behind him, the fog sheared away to reveal a burning sunset among the trees to the west, a fiery horizon streaked with purple clouds. 'Will you let me pull the Round Table along with wings of twilight? I could lead you to a place in the Happy Woods where the Piper plays tirelessly and the celebration never ends. Or, if your Christian soul prefers, I'll just stroll beside you, a faerie escort back to your king. What say you, Cei? Will you dance merrily – or risk the road ahead?'

Whimpering fearfully, Cei flung himself at his horse and hurriedly began unwrapping the lambskin from the Graal. By the time his trembling hands revealed the chrome, gold-filigreed goblet and he turned about, the elfen stranger had vanished. A lay brother slouched out of the fog carrying kindling. 'Brother Cei, lay away the Graal – please. There's no priest about to recite the Mass, and we're all too weary for long prayer.'

The Ghosts of Lovers

The king's escort accompanied Eufrasia from Camelot through the forests of the realm, across streams swollen by spring rains, four days' ride to the wooded fringe of the plain where Bors Bona's army had encamped. They arrived after moonset in the midst of a starblown night, and, as they had been ordered, the escort went no farther with the chieftain's pale-haired daughter. Eufrasia rode alone out from among the trees, fingering the small phial that Arthor had given her and that she had loop-knotted with a fine gold chain and hung about her neck.

Before she had departed Camelot, the hollow-cheeked

wizard had held her with his odd viper eyes in their dark wells and said, 'There's much magic upon that phial. Your beauty carries it. All who look upon you at night, from scouts and sentinels to company commanders and the warlord Bors Bona himself will see for themselves the ghosts of lovers they've lost. Every man has lost one whom they have loved, whether that be his mother, grandmother, sister, wife, or carnal friend. You will be that shape for them. But beware women. They will see you for who you are.'

She went past a ploughed field where early barleycorn stood in uneven rows upon the rocky ground. A horseman on patrol stood in his shadow at the sight of her. With a tentative voice, he hailed her, but she rode on and made no reply. Ahead, a sulfurous light ignited and waved. Dimly, she discerned a bowman among the dark alcoves of the wood, his underlit face ajar with surprise.

Campfires twinkled in the meadow beyond the turned fields. She rode slowly, giving ample opportunity for the watchful eyes in the tenanted dark of the forest to observe and see what their hearts told them. A few quavery voices called to the ghosts they saw, but most watched silently as she trespassed their watch slow and solemn as the specter they discerned her to be.

Out of the black solitude of the night, she rode into the camp and paced upon the dancing shadows from the fires toward the central pavilion tent, where Bors Bona's eagle standard stood beneath a snapping banner with a boar's head emblazoned upon it. Dogs shied from her, horses whinnied, and ranks of soldiers lifted themselves from their elbows where they lay, eyes agog.

At the pavilion tent, she dismounted. The standing guard backed away from her, lance slipping from his fingers. Bors was on his feet when she entered, roused by the sound of the falling lance, hand on his sheathed sword hung from the tent pole. In his gray wool nightshirt and stocking feet, he sat down on his trestle cot and gazed at her, eyes white in the dark tent. 'Mother?'

Star House of the Gods

Dagonet rode four days north and, at dusk, fired a white arrow at the fourth star that quivered in the blue heavens. 'Wish me luck, master,' he said to Lord Monkey, who sat patiently on the riding board of the dray cart. Into the twilight he hobbled, his back throbbing from days of hard riding – and the curse the talking fish had inflicted on him. As he limped under the cold starlight, beneath Arcturus and the Ploughman, he could not accept that Merlin, who had lived and adventured with him as Rex Mundi, would exploit the magic that the Fire Lord had used to grant him stature over his prior dwarfhood. The dying fish had said that to spite him, to cause him doubt. But he would allow no uncertainty to taint his purpose. He would win worthy station in the king's court and make something more of himself than the vagabond he had been before.

The arrow was nowhere to be found. He searched through the gloaming, growing more desperate as night fell. Darkness encompassed him. Then, the moon rose, and the nocturnal forest accrued silvered and dusty blue shapes. A polychrome glint of motion caught his eye, and he saw the platinum fletch feathers of the arrow wink in and out of sight among the wicker of a hedgerow. He bolted after it, his cramped back muscles punishing him.

A hare had been struck by the arrow and darted across the moonlit terrain. Dagonet followed it doggedly, ignoring the ache of his back, running bent over, arms outstretched. Into a cleft in a tussock the hare slipped, pulling the arrow shaft after it. The bowman fell to his knees before the opening and thrust his arm in. He felt root cables or what he thought to be thick tendrils until he pulled one through and saw in the silky light a root-braided cylinder. Pulling away the woven roots, he uncovered a tarnished bronze scroll-case, its central tube engraved with the coils of a snake-bird, its caps winged with sphinxes. The tangled roots twined umbilically into the crevice, connecting to other scroll-cases.

As the moon climbed to the cope of heaven, he withdrew a mound of these bronze-encased parchments, over two hundred and thirty ancient documents, a library buried in a former century. He lugged them several at a time back through the woods to the dray cart. After he finished and Lord Monkey's cart trundled away with the moon in the treetops, Dagonet collapsed exhausted.

Birds yammered all about and the sun lay as a warm blanket atop him when he woke to find Lord Monkey nibbling gooseberries from a wicker basket with a small note attached. *Brave Dagonet – You have unearthed the library of Hipparchus, the Greek astronomer who drafted the blueprints for the Star House of the Gods, a copy of which later served Ptolemy. They were carried off to Hyperborea by Greek navigators to hide them from Roman barbarians. I doubt I will sell these. They are a treasure worth more than money. Go five days north now – and be wary, for you enter upon the Pictish realms. Trust in God and keep faith with our king. – M.*

Guardians of Dusk
At each twilight, Cei made certain to unsheath the Graal, stand upon his horse to place the chalice atop the upended Round Table, and kneel with the lay brothers in prayer. After that, the faeries stopped intruding, but just to make certain there were no further visitations from the pale people, he convinced a priest from the church at Isca Dumnoniorum to accompany them to Camelot. Dawn and dusk, he conducted the synagogal service of scripture reading, psalm singing, and homiletic sermonizing that, at this time in the history of the Church, comprised the Mass: In turn, under the priest's supervision, each of the lay brothers and Cei had the opportunity to lead the ceremony and to serve as Christ's surrogate by administering the Eucharist.

The giant wheel rolled easily enough on the old Roman highways with the dozen and more men of the company to bend their backs to it. When potholes and rifts in the road blocked their way, sturdy planks were laid down to bridge the gaps. During the frequent rains, the men sang to keep their spirits up, and the wheel rolled on. At streams where the slat bridges were not sturdy enough for the Round Table, the men gathered flat rocks and devised ripraps.

The greatest obstacle was not the ill-repaired roads, the weather, or the terrain, but the cities. On the journey north, the Round Table rolled through the port of Isca, where the priest joined them, then the tree-lined boulevards of Lindinae, Aquae Sulis with its famous baths, magisterial Corinium, where in the autumn Cei had gambled away his horse and sword, Letocetum with its many vintners and cellars of every blush of wine, the equestrian town of Uxacona and its boisterous race courses, and busy Viroconium of the ample markets. All greeted the Round Table with jubilant celebration – for all had been terrorized by the roving war parties of the *magister militum*'s army.

In each city, the elders and council members sought to entertain and laud the bearers of the Graal and the Round Table. They believed that these ambassadors of the king, if properly propitiated, would summon the royal forces: Arthor had cleared out the brigands from the surrounding farmlands in the prior season and each municipality wanted him to defend them from Syrax. They knew the king's might was limited, and each made a strenuous case for why their city was most deserving of regal intervention.

Time and again, the Round Table had to be wheeled out the city gates in the middle of the night to elude the supplicating crowds who wanted to hold the king's men until he sent defenders. In the outlying fields, cruel evidence of Syrax's army everywhere abounded – torched orchards, trampled fields, shattered mills.

The labor of pushing and pulling the great wheel with hawsers proved utterly exhausting on the hilly north road that followed the River Amnis to Cold Kitchen and Camelot. In the evening, none had strength for more than a cursory prayer of thanks to God. During one such meager prayer under a fiery sky, Cei noticed that the man kneeling beside him wore yellow boots and a red vest and smiled mischievously, green eyes aslant. 'When the king inquires how you managed to roll the Round Table through the countryside unmolested by the enemy, tell him the Guardians of Dusk, the Daoine Síd, provided protection and kept you hidden from malicious eyes.

Tell him that, for he is the son of our former queen and we do him honor.'

Cei jumped to his feet, fell backward over the lay brother behind him – and when he looked again, the elfen man was gone.

The Magister Militum*'s Ambition*

Severus Syrax provided a lavish feast for Ygrane. In his pavilion tent on the Belgae plain, an ebony table carved with foliate patterns stood mounded with lemons, oranges, figs. 'Imported from my family holdings in Canaan,' the *magister militum* proudly announced. 'These are the goods we could bring regularly to Britain – and more. Silks from Cathay. Ivory from Ethiopia. Saffron from the Indus Valley. Rare woods and the finest incense out of Kashmir. Persian tapestries. Oils of sesame and olive from Libya. My family has trade facilities in all these remote places, and they are eager to do business with us. They want our fine wool, our cattle and hunting dogs, our tin, copper, gold and silver, our salted mackerel and our delectable oysters, our pewter ware unrivaled in the world. With ports on every side and the Roman roads already in place, trade will be brisk, the profits high. Think of it, Ygrane – an island of affluence and abundance!'

'Affluence for the Celts and the Britons, Syrax?' Ygrane inquired skeptically, refusing to sit on the cushioned chair he offered. 'Or are they to serve merely as another resource – cheap labor, while our Foederatus masters reap the profits of our abundant island?'

'There is plenty for all to share.' From a silver decanter, Syrax poured into a crystal goblet an amber wine and offered it to the abbess. 'An alliance with the north tribes will benefit all.'

'This is our island, Syrax, built by the toil of Celts and Britons.' Ygrane waved away the goblet of wine. 'The north tribes have no love of industry. They are plunderers. That is their faith.'

'Faiths change.' The *magister militum* saluted her with the goblet and sipped the wine. 'Look at yourself. Now you are a fanatic Christian, yet in earlier years you were a pagan queen. Let us share this island with the Foederatus and in a generation they will have acquired a taste for linen over animal hide. Trust me.'

'I do not trust you, Syrax. If you yourself believed what you say, you would have given pledge to Arthor as your king and persuaded him of the merit of trade. But you and I well know that your alliance with the Foederatus requires rulership of Britain to pass to them – not a British nor a Celtic king.'

'What does it matter who wears the crown?' Syrax asked with a dismissive wave of his hand. 'Wesc or Arthor, what difference really? It is trade that is important. Commerce is the lifeblood of the nation. If we do not share this island with the Foederatus, they will take it whole from us. Let Wesc be king. For Arthor there will be other titles, any of them he wishes – and all profitable.'

Levels of Dream
Eufrasia approached Bors Bona in the dark of his tent, Merlin's charm outheld in her hand. He sat on the edge of his cot, arms dangling between his legs, integral with the darkness but for the whites of his staring eyes. 'Mother – is this really you?'

The tent interior flared brightly as the flap behind Eufrasia lifted and the matron of the army's tailors burst in, a broad blade flashing with the camp's firelight. She seized Eufrasia by a hank of hair and twisted her to the ground, blade thrust to her throat. But before the knife could bite, Bors seized the matron's beefy arm and yanked her aside.

'What are you doing?' he shouted. Immediately, guards rushed in with lanterns and fell back against the canvas walls, each amazed to see the ghost of their lost love sprawled before them.

The matron broke the gold chain from about Eufrasia's throat and thrust the mauve phial into the lantern light. 'A heathen charm on a pagan wench! I saw her ensorcel her way to your tent, lord. I saw the guards agog. It is witchcraft! I saw it!'

Bors glowered in astonishment at the beautiful pagan woman lying before him and felt as though he were still asleep and drifting between levels of dream. 'Who sent you?'

'The king's wizard – Merlin.' She stood and passed an angry look to the matron, who glared back at her. 'I am Eufrasia, daughter of Aidan, who is chief under Lot of the North Isles.'

'Of what evil did you hope to possess our lord?' one of the guards growled, angry to see the ghost he loved gone.

'No evil at all!' She raised her chin indignantly. 'That charm will win your lord's affection for our king – Arthor.'

Taking a lantern from one of the guards, Bors dismissed the onlookers. 'Destroy that charm and leave us undisturbed.' He hung the lantern beside his sword on a hook of the tent pole and motioned wearily for the young woman to sit on the cushioned bench opposite his cot. 'Merlin is not so wise as I had once thought.'

'Wise enough to deliver me unseen past all your army,' Eufrasia said defiantly from where she remained standing.

'Oh, his magic is beyond my ken, I'll grant you that.' Bors wrapped himself in a brown mantle and sat on his cot, running his blunt fingers through his gray, brush-cut hair, still amazed and wondering if he were truly awake. 'But to think, he believes he needs magic to win my affection for the king! That diminishes my opinion of him.'

Eufrasia sat on the edge of the cushioned bench. 'You have affection for the king?'

'As I did for his father, Uther Pendragon.'

'But why – why are you serving the enemy?'

'Syrax lured me to Londinium with the threat of his alliance to the Foederatus. I intended to dissuade him of that. But he used magic – Merlin himself – to entrance me. I don't know how he did that, how he won the wizard to the Foederatus cause. But he did. Or he seemed to. And when I came to my senses, my army was in the enemy's control. If I had openly defied the *magister militum* then, I would be dead now and my realm in the Parisi lands destroyed by the Picts. The north tribes restrained their destruction of my lands only because of my alliance with their masters. But now you tell me that the wizard who baffled me in Londinium strives to win my loyalty to a king I already admire!'

'Why did you not give your pledge to Arthor at Camelot?'

Bors shrugged. 'He was untried. A boy. But I'll tell you this – he won my loyalty by his victories against the invaders across the land.' He rubbed his eyes with the heels of his hands. 'Now, if I can be certain I am not dreaming, we will decide what we must do to save our king.'

The Making of Warriors

After Cei arrived at Camelot with the Graal and the Round Table, regal ceremonies and Christian rituals greeted him. He retreated to his quarters to sleep for a day and a night while the festivities accelerated to an almost carnival delirium. At their peak, when the elephant parades and Bacchanalian flower dances spilled from the bailey out of the fortress-city and onto the fields, Arthor called a halt to them. He painfully remembered his drunken carousing of the previous summer and understood far better now the grim responsibilities of his regal station.

With his brother and seneschal, Cei, seated to his left, and his aide Bedevere to his right, King Arthor called to order his first meeting of the Warriors of the Round Table. Discussions, arguments, and strategies ranged for a full day and well into the night about the best course of action to take against the *magister militum*'s army arrayed to the south and the east and Bors Bona poised in the north. News of Ygrane's capture had reached Arthor days before, and that fact, as well as the widespread destruction that Syrax had wreaked upon the royal provinces, hampered any hope of a peaceful settlement.

Arthor did not sleep that night. At dawn, he left the castle on foot and waved away his entourage so that he could stroll alone on the flower-strewn bluffs above the Amnis. Below him, the thick dark current ran, impersonal as timeflow itself, talking up from its depths in ceaseless and myriad murmurs the voices of history, profoundly impermanent, swirling along the yellow surface for an instant before fading back into the lazy alertness of the moment.

Laughter distracted the king from his brooding, and he spied Gawain and Gareth frolicking on the river banks, dueling with swords improvised from river canes. He observed the making of warriors intently, noting their already accomplished stances, feints, and parries. They eyed him a moment later and silently fell to their knees. Compelled by the recollection of his own youth when he and Cei had similarly mock-dueled, he strode down the bank to the boys and hailed them, 'Nephews, rise and stay your weapons.'

He removed his chaplet and placed it upon the head of the youngest. 'It's heavier than it feels, Gareth.' To the eldest, he handed Excalibur drawn from its sheath. 'And this, Gawain, is sharper than you know, so mind where you swing it.'

'Will you take us with you to war, Uncle?' Gawain asked, lopping off the tufted head of a river weed.

'There may not be a war. Not if I can negotiate peace.'

Gawain and Gareth shared a perplexed look. 'Peace?' the eldest asked, expression startled. 'With the men who abducted grandmother? The men who burned the fruit trees and vineyards?'

'These men are under my protection too.' Arthor sat down on a rock shelf and tossed into the river a pebble that skipped thrice before plunking out of sight. 'How can I kill those I protect?'

Gareth placed the chaplet back on Arthor's head. 'Because you are king – and the king serves God first.'

'God—?' The word pierced him. For a long minute, he was stunned into a shameful silence. 'Mary, mother of Christ, I've been so concerned about doing right – I'd forgotten about God.'

Mother Mary, today a child has led me, even as Isaiah portends. How can I hope to serve Britain if I do not first serve God? And has not our Father put Excalibur into my hand that I may protect our island from all her enemies? What before was uncertain is now suddenly clear. My disquietude over slaying the people I must protect is allayed, for now God shall strike through me those who oppose His righteous kingdom. My arm shall be strong, my hand steady. I only pray that my hesitancy has not jeopardized the faith of those who follow me – for fear knows no friend.

To the Edge of the World

Dagonet had ridden so far north by the time he loosed his fifth arrow that the world had changed. He rode through high vast country of fir and dark spruce, where cranes flew above lines of lakes and heather shimmered like blue fur on the slopes. The wind in the high forests sang down from heaven with resinous scents, carrying silver storms across long horizons, and at night blustered green auroras through the black of space. Rain fell slantwise coming from over the curve of the Earth, sometimes from clouds he never saw. A faerïe dust of snow sprinkled the higher rock ledges and the purple gorse, and cold gray mist swirled in the rocky gorges. Under a mauve-brown sunset, he fired his white arrow, and it flew in a red arc as if to the edge of the world.

Lord Monkey waited in his dray cart under a rack of twilight clouds troweled orange while Dagonet climbed down the shale shelves, across small, pebbly creeks and stone pools. The arrow had struck a large, black wolf between the shoulder blades, and it fled from him across the sunset land toward a serrate horizon. There, the wind sucked fire from the sky. He ran doubled over, with a back pain so severe he felt permanently warped by his past efforts. He had drafted Merlin a letter, inquiring if the talking fish spoke the truth, that he was becoming again a dwarf through the gradual loss of the Fire Lord's magic. When he found this night's treasure, he would send the letter along with it.

For the moment, he cared not how Merlin replied. He was the king's man and noble station was not won lightly. He scrambled over the gray stones and heather slopes with all his might. The wolf loped on, the arrow wagging from its back. It vanished among a clutter of tall, frost-veined rocks. As in a maze, he wandered between the monoliths until he found the white arrow. It had fallen from the wolf's back and lay upon the flint-littered ground. When he looked up, he nearly sat down with surprise. The arrow pointed to a statue graven from a rock his own height.

Through the long twilight, Dagonet returned to Lord Monkey and guided the dray cart over the gorse slopes and rocky terrain to the rough-hewn statue. Its primitive shape seemed no treasure to him – a stocky woman with a swollen belly and pendulous breasts. Her simple face bore only the vaguest semblance of features. Her quiet eyes and a dim smile weathered to shadows in the rock by millennia of erosive wind and rain gave off stillness in the red air.

The effort to dig the statue loose from the rocky grasp of the earth and then lower it onto the dray cart cost him all his strength. The cart groaned as if about to split asunder, and Lord Monkey shrieked and set the horse going before Dagonet's bruised hands could extract the parchment letter he had drafted for Merlin.

Night in the north was short. Lightning from a clear sky lit the sky pools where he had crawled to sleep upon the moss ledges. Raindrops whispered in the clear water briefly and woke him to a dawn bright as a huge orchid in the south. The dray cart had returned, and Lord Monkey sat placidly on the riding board eating from a sack of cherries. No note accompanied the cart. No note of gratitude or direction from the wizard. Two white arrows remained, and the way north opened onto taiga, a treeless distance wide as the Earth.

Immortal Silver

Ygrane rode between Severus Syrax and Count Platorius as their army advanced across the Belgae lands and into Cymru. The destruction of hamlets, the burning of forests, the slaughter of herds and their drovers appalled her. 'How can you murder your own people, lay waste to your own lands and yet hope to rule this island?' she queried angrily when they brought her to their command tent the evening before the march toward Camelot.

'Abbess, your priorities are skewed,' Severus Syrax assured her. 'We are not destroying for the sake of rule. I care not who rules this dismal island. We are destroying to break the rule of your tyrant son so that we may take what has always been the true prize of war – wealth.'

Ygrane stood with her arms open in appeal before the elegant *magister militum* and the dark-eyed count, who both sat on ornate, lacquered chairs. 'Do you truly believe silver will sate your souls? Immortal silver should be your prize. Seek the welfare of the people and wealth beyond measure will be yours. The love of the people is the favor of God. Count Platorius – you are a Christian nobleman of venerable lineage, surely you do not condone this brutal campaign that lays waste our lands?'

The count tugged at his earlobe. 'For all my venerable lineage, never has the favor of God been negotiable for goods. You yourself, my dear abbess, agreed that you were summoned to our presence by the Maker of Snakes. God who fashions birds assigns the snake to stalk their nests. This is the argument of our general, and I certainly believe he speaks the truth.'

Severus Syrax clapped his hands, and into the lamp-lit tent strode a scar-faced man with thick shoulders and black hair pulled back and braided to a long rat's tail. '"I the Lord create good and I create evil." Isaiah forty-five, seven.'

'Our field commander, King Gorthyn Belgae,' the *magister militum* introduced. 'King Wesc accepted him into the Foederatus after your son exiled him from Britain.'

'You destroy your own realm?' Ygrane asked, outraged.

Gorthyn snarled at her indignant tone and struck out with his fist. His blow smote her in the face and sent her flying backward in a flurry of robes and a spray of blood.

Count Platorius leaped to his feet, while Severus Syrax snickered from behind his beringed fingers. 'My God, Gorthyn – you may have killed her! No ransom in a corpse!'

'And no ransom from a corpse,' Gorthyn growled. 'We march on Camelot tomorrow. We have blocked all roads to the south. Bors Bona holds the north and east. There will be no escape for the tyrant or his people. And there will be no prisoners.'

Ether Worlds

In her trance wanderings outside her physical body, Morgeu the Fey peered upon the hilly landscape of Cymru. From the ether worlds, she saw the arterial tributaries of the Amnis and her sister rivers shining like spilled quicksilver. The forests shimmered in silks of thermal colors, a geography of feverish hues. Shadows breathed. The moon in the day sky gleamed like a cool lake. And the sun in its savage feathers danced.

Since arriving in Camelot, the enchantress had searched the ether worlds for the magic she needed to take back from Merlin the soul he had stolen from her womb. She had come full term corporeally and the birth of her child was already late by several weeks. Yet she well knew that, if she gave birth without first securing the child's soul, she would deliver a stillborn.

Enraged and bitterly frustrated by Merlin's power over her, she soared drunkenly through the ether worlds. The blue sky appeared like blocks of ice, transparent blue auras lumped together randomly and rayed with tracks of trapped air – pathways that led to the afterlife. She did not want to go there. Nor did she wish to rise above the sky into the eternal night where stars flared like silver hollyhocks. She wanted vengeance in this world.

All that mattered to Merlin was his precious hope of a united kingdom, and she searched for a spiteful way to thwart that. She saw the armies below, among the billowy vapors of heat swirling through the forests. Their banners were recognizable to her: the blue pennants of Londinium that her father had died defending – they ranged among the hills south of the handsome spires of Camelot. To the east, she saw the numerous boar's-head banners of the mighty warlord of the Parisi, Bors Bona.

Trained by her father in military strategy, Morgeu noted from her ethereal eyrie that Bors Bona's army had abandoned its offensive positions against Camelot and had shifted south, moving threateningly against the *magister militum*'s forces. In her pique, she determined that Arthor would not have the help of this warlord's superior army. Merlin and his puppet king would taste defeat, even if that meant risking the life of her own husband.

Into clouds that flourished like opulent blossoms above Bors Bona's army, she fixed her attention. Her voice cried out to the Furor, 'Storm-maker, hear me! Let me be your eyes. See the enemy of your ambitions as I see them. Bors Bona moves to attack the forces gathered against the demon Lailoken. Strike now! Gather your might, Father of the North Tribes, and release your power!'

Acres of cloud the color of pearls swelled, gathering heat from the sun-warmed earth. Energy suddenly convulsed. Lightning flared with blinding intensity, and Morgeu rocked with the force of it. 'Wake up! You are dreaming!'

Morgeu snapped alert, once again inside her physical body, lying among the scarlet satins of the bed in her red room atop a tower of Camelot. Lot sat beside her, straps of battle leather across his naked shoulders, a shield braced against his back. 'I must go to war to fight for your brother,' he said and stroked the sweaty hair from her gleaming brow. 'No more fitful dreams until I return.' He placed a hand on her swollen belly. 'Fear not. Even Merlin's hard heart will soften after our victory.'

The Heart of Fire

'I will lead the attack against Syrax,' King Arthor determined. He sat at the Round Table flanked by Cei and Bedevere. Facing across the varnished expanse of the table and the Graal at the center were his warriors, Marcus, Urien, Kyner, and Lot. 'After the archery assault, I will bring our cavalry to bear against the *magister militum*. If God favors me, I will take his head.'

'Sire, I must object,' Kyner spoke first even as the others moved to voice their concerns. 'Your place is at the command station outside Cold Kitchen.'

'If this were a battle against invaders, I would agree,' the king replied wearily. 'But we will be fighting Britons. They must see that they are opposing their king – and it is the king's wrath that they have provoked by their brutal destruction of our farmlands.'

'Your banner will announce your presence,' Marcus spoke. 'All who see the Red Eagle will know they are fighting you.'

'The Red Eagle is the king's fire,' Urien added.

'But I am the heart of fire.' Arthor spoke adamantly. 'It is my heart that suffers for the many hundreds of people under my protection who were betrayed by Syrax and his cohorts. Those traitors must die. And if Britons must die against the king, then they will die under Excalibur. I will have it no other way.'

'You put yourself at great risk, sire,' said Cei, both of his fists on the table. 'And that will weaken us. Don't you see? To protect you will distract us from our battle assignments.'

'No one is to protect me.' The king moved his stare slowly around the table. 'Understand that. No one is to protect me. In this battle, I am one of you, a warrior among warriors.'

'And if you fall?' Bedevere inquired. 'If you are killed? Our kingdom will never be united. Britain will revert to the battlefield of warlords that it was before you drew Excalibur. Is that wise, sire?'

'No, this is not wise what I do.' Arthor spoke solemnly. 'Philosophers are wise. Counselors are wise. But kings have only one duty. To be strong. We are for our people God's strength. A child reminded me of that – your child, Lot. Gareth. He made me remember that the king serves God. Not wisdom, which is more noble than kings. Not truth, which wears a different face for every king. But God. His sanctity anoints us in blood. As His servant, I serve at His whim. There is no truer form of validation for a king than war and victory by his own hand. If I fail, all of history henceforth is changed – and that is God's will. And if I succeed, my authority remains absolute and irrevocable by God's strength.'

At these words, Lot, who had remained silent, forgot his disgruntlement at the king and the king's wizard for thwarting his wife, and rose to his feet, chanting, 'To battle – for king and Britain!' And the other warriors rose and joined him, lifting their swords, proud to stake everything on the king's faith.

In the Dark Dream

'That was a noble speech,' Merlin whispered to King Arthor as the warriors departed the Round Table to prepare their troops. The wizard emerged from the alcove where he had sat in shadows listening and, with a glance from his strange eyes, dismissed the king's aide before leading Arthor by the wrist to the balcony overlooking the battlements and tiered rooftops of Camelot's inner ward. 'A noble speech indeed. The nature of war forces the unity of chance and existence. And by that unity, fate is revealed. And is this what you believe is God? Fate?'

'Fate is God's expression in the world,' Arthor answered forthrightly.

Merlin nodded thoughtfully and gazed out across the fortress skyline and the tapers of the forest beyond. 'What if God, too, is subject to fate?'

Arthor gave a look of disgust. 'That is not God. The gods may be so subject. But the Uncreated One, the Formless, Nameless God of Whom no image may be made in His likeness, of Whom no name may be fashioned or assigned, the God of my faith, the father of our Savior, of Him all fate is handiwork. He is the Holy of Holies, the Creator of the Universe.'

'I see.' Merlin stroked his forked beard. 'Well, then, consider that all that we perceive, all that we take to be real, the universe entire – including our conception of God as the Creator – all this is in the dark dream of God.'

'I don't understand.' Arthor turned away with annoyance. 'I have a battle to prepare for, Merlin. I have no time for your casuistry. My people need my full attention.'

'Of course, sire.' Merlin took the king's arm in a grip cold and severe as iron. 'I will take but one moment more of your time. The value of all you put at hazard, you place upon God. In my experience, it is God who looks to us for value. We define the stakes. We determine the validity of a man's worth. Kings and paupers, they are the same to God. History is a fabrication, of no consequence whatsoever in the dark dream. If you are going to put your life at risk, you risk everything – even God's hopes.'

'You speak like a madman, Merlin.' Arthor twisted his arm free. 'Where were you when my fate lay within the Spiral Castle? Where were you when I had to prove myself to Marcus and Urien? What counsel did I get from you when Nynyve won my heart with her mystic wiles? I needed you then. Where were you, Merlin?'

'Sire, I will not leave your side again.' Merlin removed his tall hat, and his hoary head bowed gravely. 'It is God's hope that I serve you. In my absence, I learned another lesson in humility.'

'Will you prove that by riding with me into battle?' Arthor put his hands on the wizard's bony shoulders. 'This is a battle I must win, and I intend to use every weapon I have – even magic.'

The Bear Spoke Next

The dray cart with Lord Monkey harnessed to the reins creaked and rattled behind Dagonet as he rode north. The sixth arrow had flown to the sixth star of twilight eight days earlier and had struck a bear. Since then, the bear had led them wandering over the tundra. The sun rolled on the horizon, finding its way through long sunsets to brief nights of hissing auroras.

Hunchbacked by perpetual pain along his spine, shrunken by fog-chilled nights, scorched by wind and sun, Dagonet had come to believe that the talking fish had been right and that he was reverting to his former self. Stopping to drink at rain pools where mosquitoes hazed like shadows, he saw his swollen face reflected as ugly as he had ever looked. Fevers racked him on his journey, and when they passed, they left his tongue swollen, his palate warped so that his voice once again lisped, 'Oh mathter, thith ith tewible. The magic fith wath wight! I have lotht the Fire Lord'th stwength.'

Mountains of ice floated upon the gray sea beyond the black fingers of the rocky coast. The bear sat on the shore, the stub of a white arrow stuck at the back of its hackled neck. The fletch arrows had been lost somewhere on its long meanderings, rubbed off against a glacial rock or broken on the hard ground of the tundra. The large beast sat beside a beached ship, an ancient sea vessel, its broken hull preserved by the cold and the salt winds. A Phoenician eye stared from the prow of the blackened timbers, and mummified sailors lay toppled against the gunwales and thwarts. Even from a distance in the pellucid arctic air, Dagonet could see their leathered skin wrinkled tight against their bones, their withered bodies hung with the gray rags of old hides.

'I am twuly thorry I hurt you,' Dagonet called to the bear. 'I obey a demon withard – and I will thuffer for thith, even ath you.'

The bear spoke next, in a warm, velvety voice, 'Come closer, Dagonet. I would have words with you.'

'I am afwaid, bear. You are tho vewy big, and I am thmall.'

'I am dying, Dagonet. You need not fear me. I have not the strength to strike you. Come closer, for I am too weak to raise my voice anymore. Come closer.'

Dagonet dismounted and warily approached the sitting bear.

'Sit down and listen to me.' The bear's small, close-set eyes glistened with tears. 'Your arrow has told me all about you. I know about your vagabond days after you left your home in Armorica, ashamed of your dwarfish stature. I know of your adventure as Rex Mundi with Merlin, Azael, and the Fire Lord. I am even aware of your doubts about your quest for the king. With my last breath, I want to tell you – have no doubts. Throw away the whole pile of vanity in your heart. Empty yourself. The fish lied to you. It could not help itself. A fish lives its whole life by deception and vanity. That is the way of survival in the waters, where life is perpetual struggle for food and procreation. No wonder it yearned to become again a hazel tree.'

'Gweat bear, ith thith the tweathure I theek – your withdom?'

'No, Dagonet.' The bear lay forward and rested its dismayed face on its paws. 'The king's treasure is in the hold of this ship.

Reliquary gold from foregone dynasties of Ægypt – ancient gold of sarcophagi and statues plundered by grave robbers millennia ago. The curse upon them has been paid in full by the doomed mariners who lost their way to this arctic shore. Leave their carcasses untouched and take only the treasure for your king, and no part of the curse will follow you.'

'Gweat bear, thank you! But tell me, why are you tho kind to me? I have thlain you – I have taken your life.'

'You have given me a meaningful death with your magic arrow, Dagonet.' The bear's voice dimmed, and its wet eyes closed. 'Now, I leave behind this noble form that lived long and proud upon the bounty of the earth. I go where there are no forms, no boundaries. Illusions carried through many lives disappear. Something beyond happiness awaits me. Look! I see it now! You already stand in the midst of this deep truth. Only your eyes deceive you.'

Mother Mary, everyone knows except me! Cei has told my warriors, the priests, even the stable grooms about his journey to hell, where he learned that Merlin has stolen the soul of Morgeu's child. That is why the wizard was away from me for so long: he had hopes of returning the child's soul to the hollow hills, to be abandoned there so that Morgeu would miscarry. When I confronted Cei, he claimed he did not tell me for he was certain that Merlin already had. But Merlin has told me nothing of this. From Cei, I learned that the soul that Merlin has taken is the soul of Morgeu's father, duke Gorlois! Can this be? Mother Mary, are our immortal souls destined to transit from one life to the next? I know that Mother Ygrane has told me that my own soul is that of an ancient Celt warrior, but I thought – or I wanted to think – that she spoke in poetry, not actuality. Cei informs me that Merlin holds the soul of the unholy child in a gem. If I say nothing, then the wizard will say nothing of it. He intends for Morgeu to deliver a stillborn. That will end the evil that the enchantress worked on me. And yet, this solution – it does not feel just and good to me. Mother Mary, what should I do? Now that I know, I cannot ignore what is happening. Always you have taught me, 'Love is first.' But can I love Morgeu? Dare I love her? She intends my destruction. And yet, your Son, our Savior . . . if I am to live what he has taught, I must act – at once.

Friend of Innocence

Arthor went alone to Morgeu's chamber and bade her maid announce him. She lay in bed, covered in scarlet satin sheets, her belly large, her orange hair in disarray, the small, black eyes in her round face hard with suspicion. Arthor accepted the stool that the maid offered him and sat beside the prone enchantress. 'I leave for battle soon, and I have come to forgive you for the unholy deed that you provoked from me.'

'Your Christian conscience is tweaking you, brother?' A smear of disdain wrung her fatigued face. 'I seek not your forgiveness.'

'I offer it nonetheless, Morgeu.' Arthor placed his hand upon hers, and she withdrew it quickly. 'We come from the same womb, you and I. Sister, what you did with me was wrong – evil. I abhor it.'

'As I abhor you, brother, sired on my mother by the man responsible for my father's death.'

'Is that true?' Arthor asked with genuine anguish. 'Did Uther Pendragon murder Gorlois?'

Morgeu's tight eyes grew tighter. 'My father followed yours onto the battle plain outside Londinium – and Merlin cursed Gorlois so that he fell beneath the knives of the enemy.'

Arthor bowed his head. 'I see now why you hate me. You believe I am Merlin's creature.'

'Are you not?'

The king looked up sharply. 'No! I serve God and the people of Britain.'

'Do you think you would wear that lovely gold chaplet now had not Merlin arranged for you to draw the sword from the stone?' Morgeu turned her face away in disgust. 'You are Lailoken's foil – nothing more, Arthor. You do not serve God. You serve a demon.'

'Sister—' Arthor sagged where he sat, shoulders slumped, arms dangling between his knees. 'I did not come here to win your affection. I came to forgive you, to assure you that I have forsaken all anger toward you for what you have done to me. I seek no retribution for your cruel deed. I understand better now your rage against Merlin – and against me. I cannot undo that. But I will not further it. I will not be your enemy, Morgeu. You are my sister, and I love you no matter what you do.'

Morgeu made no reply. Her mind circled upon itself, seeking the king's motives while searching for methods of enchantment that could bind him to her will. But before she could act, his hand reached out and lay upon her taut womb.

'The child does not move.' His touch caressed her gently, with caring. 'I have just this morning discovered why. Merlin holds the child's soul.' He removed his hand and stood. 'I will go to him now and command the release of Gorlois's soul. This child will live. Not by my will shall life, which can only be granted by God, be denied any soul – even one hostile to me.'

Morgeu felt as though enchantment had turned upon her and enraptured her with words she could hardly believe. Her mind could fathom no motive for Arthor's succor – unless he lied. Yet, her keen senses had read no lie in his voice nor in his touch. He spoke the truth. And when she turned her head to query of him 'why' – he was gone. She sat up, surprised, beginning to accept that he had meant every word, and that his motive was simple: being a friend to innocence, he could not kill the child within her, unholy or not.

I Turn Death Toward Me

Arthor found Merlin in his grotto below Camelot. Shadows cognate with dragon's teeth descended from the cavern ceiling, slick in the blue glow of rock shelves where hellish pharmacopoeia cluttered: glass flaskets boiling squalid infusions that suffused chemical luminescence, flaring kilns, steam-seeping vats, and hissing bronze boilers. The bare-headed wizard stood up from where he had sat with his face warped to homuncular proportions by a crystal sphere. Before him, metal-cased scrolls lay strewn upon a stone table and behind him, a crude, man-sized statue of a pregnant woman flickered with fire-shadows from the alcoves of alchemic apparatus. An acrid, infernal pall tainted the air.

'Merlin, I know about Gorlois's soul.' The king strode agilely over the glossy, mineral steps of the cave. 'I've come to command you to release that life to Morgeu.'

In the red atmosphere of the grotto, Merlin's face shone with a demonic cast, the owlish tufts over the dark sockets like little horns, the straggly beard grumous, the long, bald head misshapen. 'Sire, I cannot obey you.'

Arthor stopped in midstep. 'What do you say?'

'My lord – I *dare* not obey you.' Merlin sighed profoundly and stepped from behind the stob of rock that served as a table. 'I have put my own soul in jeopardy to spare you the evil of this incest child.'

The king cocked his head, trying to keep the shapes before him ordered and discrete in the blurry light. 'How is your soul in jeopardy, wizard?'

'The Nine Queens have ordered me to return Gorlois's soul to Morgeu's womb – and I have disobeyed.' Merlin's chrome eyes caught the burning colors from the colossal horde of retorts and alembics and shone by turn red and blue. 'If I do as they command – as my king commands – I doom you. This evil child will grow up to slay you. Of this, I am certain.'

'Then, I turn death toward me.' Arthor stepped forward, his yellow eyes afire. 'I am not some king of ancient Greece who seeks to flee his mortality and thus only inspire a greater tragedy. My doom was assured when I was born.'

'Of a certainty, sire. But not *this* doom.' Merlin reached out with his large, waxen hands. 'I can protect you from Morgeu and the incest she provoked from you. That is in my power.'

'Merlin!' Arthor took the wizard's hands, cold, hard hands. 'You abrogate God's will! That is wrong. It is luciferian. I will not have it. You are *my* wizard. I am your king. You must obey me.'

'In this, my young, my innocent king, I dare not.'

'You must!' Arthor held Merlin's doomful chromatic eyes with a stern gaze. 'I am a Christian king. I need your demon powers, but if you are to stay at my side, you must put aside forever your demon will. You will further my will before God – or you must depart from me.'

Merlin withdrew his hands from Arthor's grip and stepped back. From under his robe, he produced a diamond big as his thumb. He held it up in the mercurial light, and a moth of fire seemed to flutter within it. Then, he dropped it to the ground, and it clinked across the varnished rock floor to the toe of the king's boot. 'Crush it, and the soul will be released and return at once to the body Morgeu has prepared for it. But do so and you bring into the world the very enemy who will take you from this world.'

Arthor hesitated one cold moment, the will in him suddenly drowsy as a snake at the thought of his doom. 'God help me!' he cried from the depths of his fear and shame and brought his heel down upon the Dragon's gem, shattering it underfoot like powdered ice.

Animal Souls

Ygrane stood upon a wagon, her body strapped with leather thews to a cedar post. The rags of her habit, stained brown with dried blood, fluttered in the cool wind that rummaged through the trees on the hillsides. Lancers rode to either side of the wagon, and foot soldiers led the battle-dressed horse that pulled the witch before the main phalanx of the *magister militum*'s army.

Gorthyn came riding from ahead, a shark's grin shooting straight back from a mouth of missing and yellowed teeth. 'Cold Kitchen is ten leagues distant. We'll take that hamlet at noon. Our scouts say that your boy remains walled in at Camelot. Syrax will have an opportunity now to employ his mighty siege engines.'

Ygrane ignored the warlord and lifted her bruised face to the pollen wind. Since she was a child, she had seen invisible things. She saw them still, the faerïe glints among the blooming linden, animal souls browsing in the creekbeds, and the pale people loitering in the darkest corners of the forest, watching her solemnly. Once, she was their queen. They would have come to her aid then, at twilight, when the smiting rays of the sun had cooled. The lancers, the foot soldiers, and the leering warlord would have fallen feverish, pierced by the poison arrows of the Daoine Síd.

But she was the Celtic queen no more. She had put her faith in the Nameless God's only-begotten. The pale people had braved the hurtful daylight to see for themselves if the Deity would save her. But she knew their risk was pointless. Her God did not dwell in the ragged clouds of spring or in the running rivers or in any created thing. God originated in the unexpected geometries far smaller than Democritus's atoms. During her long, tranceful prayers before the Graal, the Fire Lords had informed her that God had created the entire universe from a point of light smaller than an atom, smaller than the very grain of space. Existence lost half its oneness when that happened.

God would not intervene. Because whatever happened in this world happened to only one half of what was, and God had concern only for the whole. The animal souls she espied among the narrow lightshafts of the woods seemed to know this. They drifted calmly between the trees, mindless of their bodies lost to winter, slowly fading into the incandescence of spring.

She would die that way, she decided. When Gorthyn came to cut her throat, she would not flinch. Her soul would flow with her spilled blood, and she would float away across the earth, mindless to the mocking queries and jeering taunts of the pale people, who would wonder aloud why her God had not saved her. Like the animal souls, she would explain nothing to them.

'No word from your boy,' Gorthyn shouted. 'No ransom. No reply at all.' He drew his horse closer, and the lancers pulled aside to make way for him. 'You abandoned him as an infant. And now he abandons you.'

She lowered her swollen face to meet her tormentor's merry

eyes. 'I forgive you for what you have done to me.' Her raspy voice broke in her parched throat. 'But Arthor – he cannot forgive you – for what you have done to Britain. Fear him.'

'Haw!' Gorthyn yanked his horse away from the wobbly wagon. 'I fear no man and certainly not your gentle Arthor. I took the measure of him at Cunetio. He had not the stomach to kill me then, and so he sealed his doom. On a pike, his head will ride south beside yours to King Wesc's realm. There, your skulls will serve as goblets for the true masters of this island.'

Gorthyn rode off to report to Syrax and Platorius, and Ygrane returned her attention to the pale people hidden from the yellow heat of the day in the deeper shadows of the forest. Around them, animal souls came and went, like a happiness that never grew old.

Mother Mary, if only I could hear your voice. If only I could know that I have chosen wisely. Syrax demands ransom for my mother's life. Merlin has provided a large cask of ancient silver to buy her freedom. But I will not send a penny to the traitor who has burned our farmlands and doomed so many to famine. Not a penny! Am I wrong? Mother Ygrane is your Son's devoted servant. I know in my heart that the only salvation she seeks is from Him. And yet, she is my mother. Merlin believes I should do all I can to spare her. Once, he was her servant, when she was queen. He has become so sentimental since I took the soul of Morgeu's child from him. With teary eyes, he tells me stories of his mother, blessed Saint Optima, and he weeps for the evil he did as a demon. I believe he feels remorse for what he did – for a grim future he sees as clearly as memory.

Sickness of Moonlight

Bors Bona squatted under the bellied canopy at the entry of his pavilion tent, watching the rain seething in the forest, the gray shape of trees gathering out of the fog. The clearing where his army hunkered in their tents had flooded, and many of the soldiers had withdrawn into the forest, to build shelters among the higher boughs. 'Eight days now,' he mumbled. 'Rain and more rain. Not even our messenger birds can escape this storm to inform the king that we are with him. If I weren't a Christian, I'd say the gods have cursed us.'

With malefic tendrils, the fog infiltrated the tents, moving with menace out of the forest and across the clearing. It glowed like phosphorus in the vague daylight as it slouched into ditches and root furrows. Scouts returned to announce that clear weather lay a day's march south, but each day that they slogged through the mud, the spring thunderheads followed.

'Syrax works magic against us,' Eufrasia spoke from inside the tent, where she stirred a pot of whitebeans. 'This storm has every trait of magic. The unnatural fog. The following clouds.'

'Syrax is a Christian for all his foppish pagan garb.' Bors picked up a pebble and tossed it into the dimpled water. 'Money is the only magic he knows. And money doesn't buy rain.' He stood up with a weary groan and stretched his thick body. 'Besides, he has no notion we've turned against him. He would need Daedalus's wings to fly over our position and see that we have shifted from an offensive stance against Camelot to an attack posture against him.'

'Witches fly.' Eufrasia ladled the whitebeans into a clay bowl. 'In Caledonia, there are witches who fly with the cranes. They track the herds for the hunters. And they are never wrong.'

'Morgeu the Fey,' Bors whispered and stepped into the fragrant tent. 'She is a witch as her mother was before her. Perhaps this is her curse.'

'Your priests' prayers seem ineffective.' Eufrasia handed him the bowl with a wooden spoon and a rusk of barley bread. 'My father, Aidan, has become intrigued by your religion. But I tell him it is better to keep our trust in *wicca* and the old ways.'

Bors accepted the food with a grateful nod. 'I've heard enough of the glories of Caledonia from you these many wet days. Do not dun me now with the wonders of *wicca*. Do you think your true love – what's his name? Dagomere?'

'Dagonet.'

'Do you think Dagonet is going to give up his good British

comforts to return with you to cold Caledonia where witches fly and the herds run?' he asked around a mouthful of hot beans. 'I think not, fair lady. Ah, this is good. You are accomplished with the kettle. That more than makes up for your incessant blathering.'

'As if you haven't given me your share of chatter during our damp confinement. If I didn't . . .'

'Hush!' Bors held his wooden spoon aloft, eyes raised toward the sagging ceiling. 'Listen. The rain has stopped!'

Outside, the sky had abruptly cleared. Blue heavens, streaked with mares' tails, let down broad slants of sunlight among retreating towers of stormclouds. And on the ground, the fog crawled off like a thing alive, like a sickness of moonlight.

The Goal Without a Journey

Seven days north from where he killed the bear, Dagonet released his last arrow at the seventh star of twilight. He stood at the northern limit of land, upon a cold jade sea far from everything familiar. White bears watched him off an island of blue snow. In the distance, other icebergs herded in drifting euphoria like ghosts frozen to corporeality. Schools of silver fish veered through the green water at his feet and vanished into the nightworld of the ocean's depths.

Long ago, by some faerïe path, he had left Britain far behind. This was an alien shore. His arrow flew through a sky hung with seven stars and draperies of windy, plutonic light and fell into a sea that closed around it in viscous ripples.

By chilled starlight he found her a short while later, washed up on the gravel shore. The arrow had pierced her breast, near her heart. He carried her to the driftwood fire upon the rocky strand, where Lord Monkey danced excitedly at the sight of another human being. But Dagonet wondered if she was human.

Her cinnamon hair carried tiny lights within it that rhymed with the fire. Her gray eyes watched him sleepily, peepholes to a winter day. He gawked at her, a man made lonely by her beauty.

'I'm thorry! My arrow fell into the thea. How could it hit you? Are you a mermaid?'

'I am the Lady of the Lake.' Her eyes rolled in pain, and she gazed silently at the pelt of stars.

'I'm thorry! I'm thorry!' His hands flustered in his matted hair, and he looked despairingly at Lord Monkey. 'What can we do?'

Lord Monkey leaped from the riding board onto the bed of the dray cart and chittered excitedly.

'Yeth! We mutht take her to the withard!'

He lifted the beautiful woman onto the cart and strapped Lord Monkey into his leather harness before snapping the reins. Even as he turned to hop out of the cart and go to his horse, the darkness closed like a tunnel. He saw his horse far away, watching him cat-eyed on the shore of the cold sea. It dwindled to a star and was gone.

Blood hammered through his head in a fright of abrupt darkness. Sunlight splashed over the cart, and he and the monkey winced against the brightness of a spring day at the seashore. The beach could have been Armorica, where he had frolicked as a child. But it was not. It was a rocky coastline of unfamiliar contour, but natural. Crescent dunes climbed toward hills of dense trees, and overhead gulls wheeled and shrieked.

'Where are we?' he asked, crouching over the wounded woman.

'The goal without a journey.'

'I don't underthtand.'

'Poor Dagonet. You have served your master Merlin well, though unwittingly.' Nynyve closed her eyes and breathed shallowly and with much pain. 'He used you to strike me with a magic arrow, so that I am forced to leave this world – until I return to this shore in Cymru for your king.'

'Why? Why would Merlin do thith?'

'To protect his king. If Arthor loved me too well, he would leave this world, to live with me on Avalon.'

'The Apple Island . . .' Dagonet began to understand. 'That ith the goal without a journey – the plathe outthide of time.'

'Yes, Dagonet. Avalon lies across the sea from here.' Her lovely face contorted as she tried to sit up. 'Take me to the water.'

Dagonet obeyed. He carried her over the shell-strewn sand and kelp mounds to a placid cove, where the water lapped gently. As soon as he lowered her into the sea, she dissolved away, a mirage, a reflection that dimmed into the smooth water. The white arrow drifted on the surface, and when he reached to pluck it, he saw himself in the sea's dark mirror. All magic had drained from him, a hunchbacked dwarf with a large, freckled face.

Going Invisible

Fog silvered the grass. Like a nightbeast, it came crawling through the trees. Initially timid of the daylight, it slinked along the root ledges and into the shadowed gullies. Ygrane, strapped to the cedar post, her blackened, swollen eyelids painfully squinting in the sunshine, watched the animal souls flee from the slitherous fog. And by that, she knew these mists were not natural. Magic thickened this haze, and it moved through the woods with a lyrical obscenity. Feverish shapes rose up from the tuffets, quivering tendrils stroking the hillsides and hedges with long and lingering caresses.

The foot soldiers and lancers looked up with perplexity at the blue sky and muttered disconcertedly about the fog rolling up from the creekbeds and flaring through the forest. A scout galloped out of the fallen cloudbank on the road ahead, pebbles clattering behind the horse's heels, its mane streaming, the rider flapping his leather hat in one hand and clutching the reins in the other. 'The tyrant's coming!' he shouted as he slashed past.

'Merlin . . .' Ygrane whispered and closed her eyes.

A whistle of winter wind jolted her to a wide-eyed stare, and the footmen leading her wagon fell under a volley of arrows. The lancers lowered their weapons, crouched behind their shields, and formed a defensive ring. Like moonsmoke, the fog billowed over them, and the landscape went lunar, white and sterile. Even shouted voices sounded mute. The boreal wind whistled again. Wounded groans and shrieks surrounded her, and the clatter of lances and shields on the road bricks followed.

Out of the swirling mists, a figure of shadowy robes wobbled, far shorter than Merlin and more stout. A woman with frizzled hair and a swollen belly strenuously pulled herself up and into the wagon. 'Mother! What have these whoresons done to you?'

'Morgeu—' Ygrane's mind jarred as the leather thews loosened from her limbs and she fell forward into her daughter's strong arms. 'This – this is your magic?'

'We must not dawdle here.' Morgeu hoisted Ygrane upright. 'Arthor comes now like the whirlwind, and we are in the midst of it. You must listen to me. Your pain is a dream – and now you are awake. Your legs are strong. Your body is light. Together, we fly!'

Morgeu's enchantment erased all suffering in the older woman's flesh, and indeed she felt airy as they descended from the wagon and clambered over the fallen bodies of the lancers. 'Where are we going?'

Morgeu's arm tightened about her mother's waist. 'We are going where these clashing armies will not crush us. And to get there, we are going invisible.'

'Morgeu – you put the child you carry in jeopardy!' Ygrane glanced about wildly at the rushing shadows in the fog. 'We are in a battlefield.'

'Have no fear.' The enchantress guided Ygrane down into a weed-choked ditch. 'My child moves now and is ready to be born. There is no better place for this warrior to enter our world than here among the furious battling of men. Help me, mother.'

'Morgeu!' Ygrane knelt in the bracken beside her daughter under the shouts of soldiers and the thunder of hooves. 'You are giving birth *now* – in this dangerous place?'

'Danger is the fate of this child, mother,' she spoke through gnashed teeth and braced her legs apart against the sides of the ditch. 'Danger is this child's path – to the throne of Britain!'

Blood Brotherhood

'Merlin's magic has spun a fog upon the highway to Cold Kitchen,' Severus Syrax said to Count Platorius as they rode upon the high trail above the River Amnis. Below them, they could see the red pantile roofs of the hamlet hot with sunlight, and on the highway to the south, a cloud had fallen to earth. 'No matter. Our siege engines are stopped, but Gorthyn has fanned our army into the forests, and we will outflank the wizard's pitiful fog.'

Platorius unscrolled a message-ribbon handed him by an attendant. 'Merlin has rescued the abbess Ygrane. That was the intent of his magical haze. She offers no protection as a shield now. I told you we should have listened to Gorthyn and sent her head to Camelot. We lost a chance to inflict terror on our enemy.'

'Let them have the tyrant's mother.' The *magister militum* adjusted his turbaned helmet as he peered down the river gorge at the streams of soldiers hurrying along the banks. 'King Wesc has bolstered our numbers with three legions of Wolf Warriors. Three legions, Platorius! Eighteen thousand blood-crazed fighters! The tyrant is doomed. I have no concern that our ally Bors slogs through mud in the north, tied down by rain. We don't need him. All we ever needed was to remove him as a rival. And now that he is not a true contender, there will be less that we must share with him when we achieve victory. A victory that is as certain as the sunrise that follows nightfall. Our forces are overwhelming – too strong even for Arthor's fanatical blood brotherhood.'

'We fight for peace and alliance, Severus.' Platorius pointed across the steep gorge at the distant bastion walls and garret towers of Camelot. 'They fight for dominance. Victory is not always assured the noble of cause. Base as their motives are, the tyrant's blood brothers are desperate and will fight without hope of quarter. You may withdraw to your family's estates in Gaul, Canaan, Ægypt. The Foederatus have sanctuary in Saxony, Juteland, and Frisia. But for Arthor, there is only Britain.'

'Do you fear for your holdings, my dear count?' Severus

Syrax smiled thinly. 'The Atrebates territory is secure. And as I promised you, once the tyrant is overthrown, you will reign as high king of Britain. I am content as *magister militum* of Londinium, managing my family's affairs of trade in Britain. But your lineage is among the most venerable on the island, and so you shall be king.'

'The way that brigand Gorthyn struts about, calling himself king of the Belgae, I believe he will covet the title of monarch.' Platorius looked nervously at Syrax, and the dark pouches under the count's eyes trembled with a frightened tic. 'King Wesc has placed him in command of the storm troops. When this war is over, he may well use them to take what he covets.'

Severus Syrax's smile widened. 'My niece yet owes me a favor for her recent failure in Londinium. Perhaps when these troubles are over, King Gorthyn will enjoy a visit from our alluring Selwa.'

The Bag of Dreams

Upon a sturdy black mare, Merlin rode beside King Arthor into battle. He had intended to wear no armor but to trust in his magic to protect him, but the king had insisted the wizard don a chain-mail vest and a bronze legionary helmet with neck- and cheek-guards and white crest feathers. He felt glad that he had complied, for as soon as they departed the fortress, the enemy rushed from the forests onto the very slopes of Camelot. Arrows darkened the sky, and slingshot rocks clanged off his helmet and the face mask of his horse.

Arthor wore a shiny bronze eagle vizard and rode with his famous Madonna-painted shield raised over his helmeted head to protect himself from falling projectiles. Bedevere gazed out from behind the mask of a woeful Greek fury. Looking at them, Merlin felt as though he kept company again with demons. At his side, slung from his shoulder, he carried a cowhide sack rattling with amulets and talismans, a bag of dreams by which he planned to bedevil their foes.

The war cries of the king's men emboldened the wizard, and he rode faster. As a demon, he had presided over numerous battles and was familiar with every hostility among men. But as a mortal he had directly partaken in only one armed conflict. During his first days away from his mother in the kingdom of Cos near Greta Bridge, he had dared take a stand with farmers against a Pictish warband. The Furor had driven him mad after that slaughter – and echoes of that madness resounded in his long skull with the sound of the arrows' cold wind and the first clang of metal clashing on metal. Merlin gritted his teeth against the jarring sounds and reached into his bag for a weapon of magic.

The king's assignment had been simple. Merlin was charged to help Arthor drive a wedge into the advancing line. Kyner and Cei would rush in behind and establish defensive positions well away from Camelot. Once the fields were cleared, Lot and his northmen would descend into the river gorge to drive the invaders south, into the marshes. Urien would hold and protect the hamlet of Cold Kitchen. And Marcus carried the responsibility of defending Camelot and advancing as summoned.

But in the midst of the fray, Merlin became disoriented. The screaming of horses, the jostling of their big bodies with scurrying foot soldiers scattering among them, stabbing and slashing, heightened his sense of madness. He chanted calming spells, and they worked as he bounded among the jammed warriors. From the bag of dreams, he withdrew a terror-amulet and tossed it at a company of ferocious berserkers, a squad of horribles clad in human skin, shriveled faces staring eyeless from their thighs, scalps hanging from their belts.

The amulet exploded panic among the barbarous warriors, and they fell over themselves in sudden retreat. Merlin hollered victoriously and reached for another magical weapon. But at that moment, a flung ax struck his helmet and split it wide, sending him careening off his horse and into the thriving melee.

Arthor shoved his steed through a throng of frenzied foot soldiers swarming about the fallen wizard, Excalibur hacking furiously. He pranced a circle about Merlin, driving the enemy off and allowing defenders and a surgeon to reach the bloodied wizard. 'He's alive!' the surgeon called – and the king waved them off to Camelot and swung his horse back toward the fury of the battle.

That Thing You Dread

The loss of Merlin signaled a drastic turn in the battle. Word that the tyrant's wizard had been slain spread swiftly through the ranks of the storm troops, and the berserkers that Merlin had sent fleeing in terror regrouped and attacked with a vicious frenzy. The forces of the *magister militum*'s army took heart from the fury of their Foederatus comrades and charged through the forests onto the plains of Camelot.

Arthor had no choice but to summon Kyner and Cei before he broke the enemy's line. Above the pounding of shod hooves, their drums and pipes sounded, declaring their entry into the battle. But to little effect. Out of the hill forests to the north, Gorthyn arrived leading a full legion of Wolf Warriors – pagans bedecked in the skins of animals and pieces of uniforms ripped from the corpses of fallen Britons.

To prevent a rout, the king had the trumpeters call for Marcus, and he emerged from Camelot with mounted lancers and archers. Soon a vast confusion ranged across the open fields. Intent on breaking the wave of assailants, Arthor drove his company to the forest line with Kyner and Cei flailing at the enemy to either side, desperate to keep the Wolf Warriors from outflanking their king.

Marcus prevailed in turning Gorthyn's attack. From the battlements of Camelot, Lot and Urien waved banners, urging the duke to turn back. But Marcus would take no orders except from the king, and he plunged into the forest after Gorthyn. And there, another legion of Wolf Warriors lurked. Immediately, he was surrounded, and Lot and Urien had no choice but to quickly lead their forces onto the field, to extricate him.

The screams of horses and men melled in the air under the scything hiss of arrows and slinged missiles. Everywhere, horses trampled the fallen or collapsed and lay fallen themselves and men scrambled over them. Lanced bodies stood erect in death. Berserkers tore away helmets and scalped their victims as they thrashed beneath them. Arrows pinned soldiers to trees.

Arthor fought ruthlessly through this horror and had vehemently pushed his company into the forest, desperate to break through the line. But there was no end to the enemy's depth. A third legion of Wolf Warriors whelmed through the underbrush. Raptor-mask uplifted exposing a grim face, Cei surged to the king's side. 'We have forced ourselves to that thing you dread!'

Arthor knew what he meant. The thing he most dreaded in battle was finding himself surrounded. His aggressive fighting style had frequently placed him in that position during his tenure as Kyner's warrior, and burdened with this reputation few warriors followed him into battle. But then, he himself had only been a warrior and those few fanatics who had dared joined him then he had felt no qualms about leaving to fight their own way out. Now, as king, the realization that he had led his entire company into an indefensible position chilled him to the marrow.

'Call for Urien and Lot!' he shouted above the screaming.

Cei shook his head and signaled the trumpeter for a retreat. 'They are with Marcus! He is caught as we are in the north forest!'

Only then, as he, Bedevere, and Cei fought their way back toward Kyner's stance at the edge of the forest, did the king realize he had terribly miscalculated the strength of his opponent. Only then, among a wild frenzy of headlong horses and the death cries of his ruined ranks leaping around him, did he understand the battle was lost.

Fields of Darkness

Nightfall did not stall the fighting. Gorthyn torched the forest, and by the raging firelight his Wolf Warriors battered Camelot's defenders on the plains. A shift in the wind alone saved the king's men from immediate defeat. The churning smoke of the burning woods poured over the fields, and the flames ate into Gorthyn's lines, forcing him to pull away from the plains.

'Fall back to Camelot!' Kyner bawled. 'Fall back and negotiate with Syrax!'

Arthor lifted his eagle-mask, his young face buckling with
rage and tears. 'No! No negotiations! They will tear down
Camelot. We must fight them here – through the night.'

The king ordered Marcus and Kyner to hold the plains
with the remnants of their troops. And he dispatched Urien
and Lot to protect the highway to Cold Kitchen while he
and what remained of Cei's men pursued Gorthyn through
the fiery wall of toppling trees and blazing brush into the
smoldering forest. Unreal directions of smoke, haze, and spurts
of flame baffled both Gorthyn and Arthor, and they circled each
other blindly.

Pale and dismembered bodies lay in the red shadows. Among
the turbulent darkness of sifting smoke, corpses feathered with
arrows mimed the reed grass and canes. The king's men stalked
their enemy in small groups – and the enemy hunted them. The
incessant crackle of the simmering woods, the gibbered calls of the
dying, and the intermittent screaming of horses obscured hearing as
deftly as the thick vapors and nocturnal shadows dimmed sight.

Whenever opponents stumbled upon each other, the fighting convulsed with brutal brevity. Combatants lunged in and
out of the dark. Weapons flashed and cries whisked away on
the flying fumes. Occasionally, the wind brisked, and the forest
flames flared, silhouetting a dark riot of assailants entangled in
smoke. Then, the wind slimmed away, and blackness swept in,
concocting anonymity once more. With frightful incongruence,
the king's men confronted themselves, swords raised, deflected
before the fatal instant by common cries.

After midnight, the last of the flames faded entirely, and
Gorthyn commanded his warriors to seek coveys and lurk in
waiting. Shouts reeled out of the night where the king's men
stumbled upon them. At last, Arthor was obliged to call his soldiers
together and return with them to the fields of darkness.

'If we negotiate now,' Kyner pleaded with his stepson as
Arthor approached the chief's bonfire, 'we may yet save what
remains.'

Arthor removed his helmet and glowered at Kyner. 'Syrax will not negotiate. He believes he is winning.'

'Believes?' Cei queried sarcastically. 'At dawn, his legions of Wolf Warriors will sweep over us and his regulars will march in to occupy Camelot.'

'You want to negotiate, too?' Arthor glared in surprise at his brawny stepbrother. 'What hope is there in surrender?'

'Much hope for the living,' Kyner replied. 'Must everyone die? We are defeated on the field but not yet before God or the Holy Father in Ravenna. The pope may yet intercede, for you are indisputably the rightful heir to Uther Pendragon.'

'No!' Arthor exploded. 'I *am* king! God has made me king! God! And God can destroy me if He so wills. But I will not surrender!'

Kyner and Cei cringed and lowered their heads, sharing doomful looks.

Seeing that, Arthor shook off his rage and frustration and reached out a gentle hand toward them. 'Father – brother—' He spoke in a more quiet voice but no less firmly. 'Your optimism blinds you, Kyner.' He accepted a flagon of water from Bedevere. 'Think for a moment like our enemy. We will be put to death and those loyal to us will be enslaved. That is the Saxon way. And do not doubt for an instant that it is the Foederatus we fight here.'

'What do you propose?' Cei asked in a near-whisper, exhausted and frightened.

'Rest.' The king drank deeply, then spoke through his teeth. 'Tomorrow we fight – we fight to the death.'

Mother Mary! Mother Mary! Mother Mary! Mother Mary! Mother Mary – Mother – Mother – Mother – Mother – Mother . . .

Locked in Nightmares
Merlin lay comatose in the king's bed. Nothing the surgeons did to revive him worked, for his soul had lofted free of his physical form. Into the ether worlds, he drifted.

He recognized warped space from his prior life as a demon:

the day sky with its transparent blue auras like jumbled blocks of ice, the night with its cubes of onyx riddled with wormfires. He knew every path to all the possible heavens and hells. And yet, hard as he looked, he could not find the pathway back into his mortal body.

The vastness of space ranged in every direction. Earth itself was but a mote, a sandgrain caught in a slow whirlpool of gravity, spinning inward toward the naked flame of the sun. And the sun, too, whirled in a vortex of suns, hundreds of billions of suns spinning in an incandescent pinwheel about a black core that swallowed all light. Into that blackness, angels and demons had fallen and never returned. Some claimed it was the way back to the origin, to the paradise of infinite energy where everything had begun. But no one had ever returned to confirm that.

He did not want to go that way. He wanted to go back to Earth, to his human body, to his mortal destiny as the king's wizard. But he could not find Earth among the vastness of black emptiness and the scattering of stars. He was adrift again, as he had been during most of his existence as a demon. After the fiery explosion that had begun space-time, that had flung him and the others free of the blissful unity that they had shared with Her, he had desponded of ever finding Her again. He had felt then as he felt now, tiny and adrift in an enormity of cold, dark emptiness. The light of the origin that he had clung to only burned sharper in the frigid vacuum, and he had let it go. Like so many of the others, he had let the light go and become dark and cold as the void itself.

Now he sought the light. He sought the one particular light that was the sun and the infinitesimal particle that was the Earth. But there was no direction in space that he could discern. It all looked the same, the slow-curving blackness strewn with dark matter, gouts of dust and gas, smoldering here and there to starfields. He drifted. A long time he drifted alone, locked in nightmares of memory and fear.

He remembered the long, long aeons of wandering through the void. At least then he had enjoyed the company of his fellow demons. When at last they had found worlds that the angels had built, they had enjoyed the opportunity to exert their despair, and they had raged exuberantly against the fragile things that the angels had fashioned. How many worlds had he destroyed? These memories of fury haunted him, and he wailed into the emptiness.

All that soothed him was his memory that at last, on Earth, he had betrayed his fellow demons to become Saint Optima's son, to become one of the very fragile gutsacks they had despised. He had given himself to the angels, to the Fire Lords. And though that memory soothed him, it also inspired the fear that he had lost that one, frail connection with the light, the original fire of creation. And he prayed, 'Forgive me, forgive me! I had become arrogant again. I had stolen Gorlois's soul as if I were God Herself. I had tried to shape lives as though I had the light of the Fire Lords. I had forgotten that I had become a man and like all men can only reflect light. And my punishment – my torment – is that I have become again a demon, who has forsaken the light!'

The World Asunder

Out of the warsmoke rolling across the night fields of strewn dead, mired in blood and battlefield dirt, Ygrane and Morgeu made their way to the gates of Camelot. Morgeu carried in her arms an infant gummed with birth-chrism. The guards admitted them at once, and a surgeon and attendants hurried them on litters to Morgeu's suite, where they were cleansed and their wounds dressed.

Revived by steaming broths from the king's kitchen and root brews from the surgeon, Morgeu nursed her baby. Ygrane examined the infant and was pleased to find it whole and unmarked by its frightful entry into the world or its unholy lineage. 'What will you name him?' she asked, sitting at her daughter's bedside.

'Mordred,' Morgeu whispered and kissed the child's brow.

'Such a fiercesome name, daughter.' Ygrane suppressed a shiver. 'That is the Brythonic appellation for Mardoc, warlord of the Other World. Do you hope for him such a bloody destiny?'

'Does his brutal birth not already bespeak the terror he will inspire?' Morgeu offered a grim smile. 'In truth, mother, I drew his name from the Latin *moror credere* – slow of belief, for his soul was kept from him by those who had no faith of his worthiness to live. Yet, he is beautiful, isn't he, mother? He is worthy of all that Merlin strove so hard to keep from him – life and power.'

Ygrane knew that her daughter would not condone a baptism, even though the soul within Mordred had been a Christian soul when it had lived as Morgeu's father, Gorlois. To assuage her own sense of responsibility for the child's spiritual identity, she went to the war counsel chamber to find the Graal, by which she would bless the child. But the Round Table stood empty. At the center, where the Graal had been placed by the king, no sign of it remained.

Immediately, Ygrane sought Merlin, and found him unconscious in the king's bed. She laid a hand upon his bony breast and felt great distances, the expanding shells of space, where light dissolved like smoking candles into black reefs of sooty clouds. The surgeon at her side shook his head and began mumbling about the liver's flux.

Ygrane returned to Morgeu's tower suite and stood at the slot window, looking out upon the world asunder. Forests burned, turning the night scarlet. Armies clashed, and screams rose on the black wind into the starless night. The Graal was gone, and though inquiries had not yet begun, she already sensed that the sacred vessel had been removed by no thieves but a wider agency than mortals. She thought back across the many forewinters to that Christmas when the mysterious Sisters of Arimathea – the Nine Queens – had delivered the Graal to her and Uther. And she felt old in her bones.

Night Wearing a Helmet

Severus Syrax recognized victory in the confident, broad stride of Gorthyn as the scar-faced man entered the commanders' pavilion tent, helmet under his arm, bloodied hand clutching the sheathed sword at his thigh. 'The tyrant is crushed,' the *magister militum* greeted him. 'That is what you've come to report, yes, Gorthyn? We've seen it already.' His broadly smiling face looked beyond the brigand king, out the lifted awning to the red night. Flames flickered in the black silver of the River Amnis far below. 'From up here, we saw it all. The tyrant's foolish charge into the forest. The entrapment and destruction of his company. His warlords' armies shattered by your legions. Behold our glory!'

Cold Kitchen burned, and on the river bluffs above it Camelot's pale walls reflected the flames like the bloody face of night wearing a helmet crested with stars and smoke. 'By morning, I will have Arthor's head on a pike – and his royal chaplet upon my head.'

'Your head?' Count Platorius queried from the fleece-draped chair where he sat watching the warsmoke caress the stars. He looked meaningfully to Syrax. 'Did I not foretell this avarice?'

'Avarice?' Gorthyn slung his head forward, black-whiskered jaw tight as he glared at the *magister militum*. 'I've won this title for myself. You have your wealth. This weasel has his noble lineage. I want mine. As of this night, I am high king.'

'Of course, Gorthyn.' The radiance of Severus Syrax did not dim before the dark, hostile countenance. 'I am pleased to call you sire. Under your protection, my trade affiliations will make you a wealthy king and this island a kingdom of abundance.'

'Syrax!' The count rose with an inflamed expression and a rebuke upon his tense lips that was never spoken.

In a blurred motion, Gorthyn drew his sword and passed the grimy blade through Platorius's neck and between his vertebrae, lifting the head from his shoulders. Arterial blood splashed against the tent canvas, and the body crashed onto the chair, the lopped head fallen upside down in its lap, the eyes in their dark pouches staring with dismay.

Syrax's smile curdled with horror.

'Fear not, *magister militum*.' Gorthyn sheathed his gory sword. 'This king finds favor with you. Together we will make Britain a paradise.'

'Yes, yes – of a certainty.' Syrax nodded vigorously. 'Of course, we shall need to reward our Foederatus allies.'

Gorthyn stepped over to the map easels and smiled at their scribbled topographies. 'There is plenty of land for all of them – the Jutes, Angles, Saxons – even the Picts and Scotii. Alas, these pagans have no love of the farm, the vineyard, or the orchard. They won't tend cattle or crawl into holes in the earth to extract ores. But then, we have the Britons and the Celts to do that now, don't we? I believe King Wesc will be delighted with this peace.'

Severus Syrax found his smile again. 'Britain will be a most peaceable kingdom when you wear the gold chaplet – sire.'

Walk the Distance

Blood-slaked, Arthor and Bedevere stalked on foot through the cinderous waste of the burned forest. Smoky rays of dawn illuminated sprawled, legstiff horses and drifts of tangled corpses. The king had lost his helmet sometime during the dark predawn hours when the storm troops charged Camelot. He and his warriors had beaten them back into the smoldering forest and down the gorge slopes of the Amnis, only to be set upon by the combined forces of Syrax and Platorius.

Arthor leaned on his shield and gawked about at the new-slain dead. He saw no sign of his other warriors. They had careened in wild combat into the darkness, and with the coming of day found themselves far from their king, engaged in strenuous battles for their own survival. The armed figures that slouched out of the steaming haze were a mixed squadron of hostile warriors – Britons in chain-mail tunics on raw-looking horses with wild eyes, accompanied by invaders in breeks fashioned out of human skin and belts woven from human hair and decorated with human jawbones.

'This way, sire!' Bedevere grabbed the king's arm and pulled him toward a charred grove. 'We'll elude them there.'

'I'll not elude them!' Arthor rasped and shook free of Bedevere's grasp. 'I'll not flee in my own kingdom!'

He lunged and brought Excalibur down on the skull of the

nearest horse, felling it with one blow and goring the rider as he spilled forward. With a hoarse cry, Arthor spun among the barbarous company that charged him. Bearded and with teeth bared like feral dogs, the Wolf Warriors swung their axes, and the helmeted Britons thrust with their heavy swords, all eager for the prize of the tyrant's head and the glory that went with it.

Bedevere slashed with his crimson scimitar, his back pressed to the king's. Together, they held the filthy, brutal lot at bay. Through the golden haze, more warriors assembled, drawn by the excited shouts and whistles of the warband that had found the king. Soon a crowd milled among the burnt trunks and trampled shrubs of ash, yelling for blood.

Boldly, Wolf Warriors leaped in for the kill, their scapulars of human teeth and shriveled human ears jumping about their throats as they swung strenuously with their axes. Excalibur and the scimitar flashed and glinted, and the brave ones fell, choking on their own blood. It was a craven one, an archer on a scorched knoll, who shot the arrow that pierced the king's thigh.

As Arthor fell, the grisly warriors surged forward. Bedevere's scimitar dropped two in one stroke and repelled the others. 'Lean on me, sire!' He wedged his armless shoulder under the king's arm and tried to bolster him upright. 'Lean on me and we will walk the distance to the grove.'

'I will not retreat!' Arthor gnashed, lurching upright, tears of pain and anguish running down his smudged cheeks. Another arrow clanged off his shield, and he raised Excalibur and shouted, 'For God and Britain!'

The Terrible Victory

The king's cry lost itself among the rabid yells and war-shouts of his assailants, and he heard nothing of Bors Bona's army until they crashed through the scalded trees and trampled the furious wall of men around him. Bedevere held Arthor down, protecting him with his shield from the stray arrows of the warlord's bowmen. 'God has truly heard your cry, sire!' Bedevere's blood-freckled face grinned. 'We are saved!'

The mounted archers at first did not recognize Arthor,

and Bedevere stood up and cried, 'Stand fast! Your king is wounded!'

Plastered in mud, Bedevere and the arrow-struck man at his feet appeared to be two more of the enemy, and the chargers stampeded toward them, crushing Saxons and rebel Britons under hoof. Bedevere waved his arms to no avail. Then Arthor lurched to one knee and lifted Excalibur over his head. The sudden arrival of these soldiers come to crush his enemies lifted him above his pain, and he staggered upright, rocking to his feet, Excalibur pointing to heaven.

'Britain!' he shouted. 'Britain!' His body filled with joy so fully at God's answer to his prayers that he would have been glad to be struck by these men, glad even to be struck dead. He stood tall before the onslaught of heaving horses, pouring all his strength into his cry, 'Britain!'

'The king!' a mounted archer yelled and seized the reins of the rushing steed beside him. The muddy forehooves churned in the air a hand's breadth from Bedevere's proud face.

Warhorses reared backward as their riders caught sight of Excalibur and the shout rose louder with more strong voices joining, 'The king! The king!'

The nearest horsemen leaped from their steeds and knelt before Arthor. He lowered Excalibur, and Bedevere eased him to the ground, to the very bottom of the cliff of mercy. And there the king lay, smiling up at the clouds that carried away the souls of the dead, his heart jumping inside him. He had lived to see Britain saved. The words that the soldiers spoke excitedly to him cleansed all the last stains of fear from him: Bors Bona had arrived. The fierce warlord of the north had declared his allegiance to Arthor before all his men and had won their fealty to the king, to the last man.

Britain was saved, and suddenly Arthor lay in the mud outside the house of his life. He could have died happily then. All that he wanted as king, he now possessed: the allegiance of every powerful British warlord and every Celtic chieftain – all united to repel the invaders and to preserve for Britain the sanctity of peace and the hope of prosperity for her own people.

A surgeon was summoned, and the king laughed tearfully through the pain as they cut the shaft from his thigh, laughed with joy for the dead from his ranks, who had sacrificed everything and won victory for the living ones they loved. He laughed for his native land. And as his laughter spun out to tears of relief, pain swarmed in and jolted him unconscious. Bedevere laid Excalibur along his side, and he was carried on a litter to the surgeon's wagon and escorted out of the scorched forest to Camelot.

When he woke, Ygrane and Bedevere sat beside him where he lay upon a ticking of swansdown in the sunlight of the citadel's central garden. Ygrane had ordered him brought there so that he would not wake beside the Round Table to find the Graal gone or come around in his own bedchamber and learn that Merlin lingered in a coma. She had dressed her son's wounds herself and cleansed him with her own bruised hands.

Reports from the field, scratched hurriedly onto parchment, lay upon the garden sundial in a heap of small scrolls. Bedevere had read them all as they came in and, before the king could speak, happily announced, 'Bors Bona offers his pledge to Arthor, high king of Britain. He regrets not offering his fealty sooner, but apparently sorcery bedeviled him in Londinium and the weather stalled him south of Greta Bridge.'

'The commanders . . .'

'All are alive, sire.' Bedevere held up parchments from each of them. 'Kyner, Cei, and Lot are in the field with Bors. Marcus patrols the Amnis, blocking the enemy's escape by river. And Urien scours the hills north of Camelot, routing the adversaries who have fled there.'

'The Foederatus legions – the Wolf Warriors – there are so many . . .'

'We have learned that there were three legions – and not enough have survived our battle with them to pose a threat to Bors,' Bedevere replied and then calmly related the details of their terrible victory.

Bors Bona's army had crossed the River Amnis at Cold Kitchen and swept into the burned forest. His mounted archers had sent the battle-weary foot soldiers of Syrax and Platorius fleeing, and his lancers had broken the already damaged Foederatus legions into smaller units that his troopers swarmed over. Bors Bona himself, knowing his enemy, had crossed farther downriver and, at midmorning, had met Severus Syrax and Gorthyn Belgae on the highway hurrying south. With the *magister militum* weeping and pleading profusely and Gorthyn snarling and cursing, the warlord had them hanged at the roadside, both from the same bough, and gave strict orders for their corpses to be left untouched save by ravens.

Down Near the World

Merlin plunged whimpering through the black abyss of infinite space, through eternal night. Where among the endless aisles of stars, among the empty vectors of the void – *where* was the hidden sun that warmed the one tiny world where he had known mercy? Where were the blue and silver weathers of the Earth? *Wrap me again in the wind – bless me with the murmurmous rain – warm the black and dreamstrewn deeps of my brain with sunlight – return me, oh please, return me to the wide Earth's keeping—*

The lives of the dark that he had lived in his prehuman existence haunted him – the hatred he had felt for these cold meridians of outer space, the evil he had embodied out of rage for the good of heaven that he had lost, the phantasmagoria of terrors he had carried from world to world through this very vacuum returned on him with vivid clarity. And he concluded that he was a loss to God. She had embodied him in mortal form on Her little planet, had given him a purpose in Her creation, a destiny that would have redeemed his murderous past, and he had betrayed Her. He had arrogated to himself Her powers, as if he were Her unique agent instead of what he really was – a simple tool She had reclaimed from the lightless warehouses of Hades.

The Nine Queens had tried to warn him. He had stolen a soul. They had tried to warn him to return it. He would have killed that incest child if he had not been stopped by the boy – halted not even by a full-formed man, but by a *child*, and his charge, the boy he was supposed to guide to Her purpose and in whom he was responsible for instilling faith in a justice greater than the ken of mortals. He had failed. He understood that now as he hurtled through the blind depths. He had failed miserably, for he had behaved again as a demon, had used his powers to assert his will, to fulfill his animosities. He had failed, because he had met evil with evil.

Merlin accepted his infamy and stopped whimpering. He knew he deserved his calamitous fate, and he gave himself to his suffering and to the fullness of time.

At that moment, a star glinted brighter. He saw then, it was not a star. It was a chalice of chrome laced with gold. The Holy Graal floated before him in space. It retreated ahead of him as he plunged through darkness toward a brightening star, an orb of yellow refulgence among the tarnished stars – and there! – the blue crescent of the Earth!

The Graal fell toward the blue planet, and he followed, swollen with relief and joy, swearing aloud in his mind, again and again, that he would never forget the lesson in humility and devotion that he had learned on his dark journey. Down near the world, the Graal vanished. Understanding flexed in him. The Fire Lords had removed the sacred chalice from the king's citadel, for this vessel belonged in the company of those joined by the sharing of bread, not the sharing of enemies.

Merlin grasped the import of this and the certainty of how to quickly retrieve the Graal. He fell to earth laughing with joy, eager to share this bright knowledge with his king.

Mother Mary, all is well. All is well at last! The kingdom is secure for now. Our enemies are broken. And those many who have died to defend our land, both pagan and Christian alike, are surely beloved of our Father. What they have won with their blood I will safeguard with my life and my watchful soul. Now, in this enormous flowering of hope, we cherish the chance to create an order of law and mercy, whose memory will endure the thousand years of darkness that Merlin predicts. And what we do this day and in the days to come, that is a fable yet to be told, legends ours to shape, to be remembered when our children shall wake from their millennial sleep.

Lips of the Moon

At the massive open gate to Camelot, guardsmen halted the wagon with the strange dwarf bedecked in tatterdemalion parody of a king's soldier, a frisky monkey at his humped shoulder. As he began to explain himself, loud cheers resounded from the bailey, and the guards lifted their lances in salute. The dwarf stood on tiptoe atop the riding board and saw the bent top of Merlin's conical hat moving among the jubilant crowd of the castle's outer ward.

The wizard had revived from his coma. In the company of King Arthor, who supported his wounded leg with a crutch, and the king's seven commanders, Merlin marched out of the castle onto the battle plains. The beautiful sable horses from the *dux Arabiae* waited for them. Too delicate for battle, these proud horses were ideal for the swift journey Merlin had in mind. The victorious party would mount these fleet stallions and the wizard would guide them toward the secret place where the Fire Lords had delivered the Holy Graal for safe keeping.

Dagonet leaped up and down, waving his arms, until Merlin noticed him and budged through the crowd to the dray cart. 'Welcome, Dagonet!' The wizard clapped a congratulatory hand upon the dwarf's shoulder, and Lord Monkey startled and clung to Dagonet's head. 'You did well in the service of the king – very well indeed – and you shall be rewarded. The position of royal exchequer is yours. With that title of high station comes a generous remuneration and land holdings. Henceforth, you shall be Lord Dagonet!'

'But look at me, Merlin!' Dagonet smacked his open hands against his chest. 'I am ath I wath. I've awived where I began!'

'What does that matter, Lord Dagonet?' Merlin gripped both of his shoulders. 'You are a man of station, as I promised you would be. That will surely impress Aidan.'

'But not hith daughter!' Dagonet seized Merlin's robe.

'Pleath, Merlin! I therved you well – in Wecth Mundi and on the quetht for the king'th wealth. Don't leave me like thith! Give me back my phythical beauty before Eufrathia seeth me.'

A dark shadow clouded the wizard's long face. 'Dagonet, you know not what you ask of me.' He glanced over his shoulder and saw that the king and his men were still engaged in greeting the happy crowd of soldiers and their families. 'I have just returned from a great journey myself to find that our Holy Graal is missing. Without it, our kingdom is just a military confederacy with no spiritual center. I am on my way now to guide the king and his men to where the angels have hidden the Graal.' He squeezed the dwarf's shoulders urgently. 'You must understand. My powers are limited. If I use this magic to restore you to the physical stature that the Fire Lord imparted to you, I will lose my reckoning of the Graal's location forever. You understand, Dagonet.'

The dwarf nodded slowly. 'Of courth. The good of the kingdom ith at thtake – and that *ith* gweater than my dethire for mythelf.'

'Good!' Merlin smiled benevolently. 'I knew you would understand, for you are a virtuous man. Beauty, after all, is within.' He turned to go – and stopped abruptly. The air had gone utterly still and silent. The sun above gazed down like a large friend, the fleecy clouds around it motionless and birds on the wing unmoving in midair.

The wizard spun about. No one was moving. In the gateway, the large crowd around the king stood locked in their various attitudes of joy and admiration, their gesticulations paralyzed, their faces flawlessly immobile, mouths open, eyes unblinking. Merlin walked around Dagonet and touched Lord Monkey. They felt cold as sculptured ice. Not even a hair of the monkey's fur would budge. Time had stopped.

Sick fear enclosed him. He was certain that if he looked straight upward he would see a diadem of night bejeweled with stars and the limitless depths of black space. A coldness in his heart instructed him: Into darkness he had been delivered for using his magical power with the arrogance of a demon. They were coming for him again, the Fire Lords who had helped Saint Optima fit him into a human body. They were coming because humanity did not properly fit him. He was a demon, doomed to peregrinate in darkness.

'No!' he shouted, and his cry echoed like a clumsy spirit, tripping over everything as it fled from him, unable to get away: *no – no – no – no . . .*

'I'm doing it again, aren't I?' He looked with stricken alarm at the dwarf, who had lifted a perplexed frown toward him. Time erupted around him, loud with laughter and boisterous voices from the crowd in the wide gateway. Birds flashed, clouds raveled.

Merlin shrunk visibly under the shadow of his wide-brimmed hat and spoke with a voice blasted almost to silence. 'I'm using my power like a godling instead of like a man.' He put both bony hands to his face and shook his head, stunned by the enormity of the task that God had set for him. '*How*? How can we possibly succeed if I am to tend to every one of Your mortal creatures that comes to me?' He turned his clasped face to the heavens, a howl in his wild eyes. '*How*?' Then, with a huge sigh, relieved to see the infinite heavens blue and lively with birds, he accepted his fate. His hands fell away from his hollow cheeks, and he smiled wearily at Dagonet. 'Ah, how, how, how – that is not for me to know, is it, my precious friend?'

'I don't underthtand.'

'Nor do I, dear Dagonet. Nor do I.' Merlin pointed beyond the gate of the citadel to where the five-day-old moon smiled above the scorched timbers of the forest. 'Go wait for me there, faithful servant, beneath the lips of the moon. I will meet you shortly after I have gathered the implements I need, and you shall be made beautiful once again.'

How Old the World Is

When King Arthor and his commanders finally emerged from Camelot, a star burned in the charred depths of the forest. Moments later, Merlin and a tall, strikingly handsome man emerged from the cinderland, a monkey prancing wildly around them. Bors whispered to the king, and Arthor summoned Chief Aidan from the crowd in the bailey.

'Here is the man your daughter loves,' the king announced as Dagonet, in rags like clotted cobwebs, knelt before him. 'Merlin has informed me of the arduous quest he completed to fund our treasury. Thanks to him, we have the resources now to rebuild Cold Kitchen and to help to pay for the damages wreaked by Severus Syrax. He is a noble man, our Dagonet, and I decree him our new exchequer. Will you have him for your son-in-law?'

Merlin stepped away from the giddy crowd, exhausted by the magical effort that had transformed Dagonet. He wandered off toward where the corpse wagons sorted the dead. Priests and druids and the families of the missing combed the open fields and the incinerated forest searching for the remains of the king's fallen. Ravens and dogs searched as well, less discriminately.

Sitting on a seared stump, the wizard contemplated what he had done. He felt disengaged from himself. A feverish chill occupied the vacant place in him where but minutes before he had possessed the knowledge of the Graal. The holy vessel was lost now, secure in some secret sanctuary, he knew not where.

The intelligence of the wind brought him news of the cooking fires of the living and of the journey of the dead into the mineral kingdoms. The day was waning and soon he should have to inform the king that he had been mistaken about his certainty of the Graal's location. He watched an old woman cutting the long golden hair from the head of a dead Saxon, hair to be sold for wigs in the market towns of the south.

An angel came walking through the fire-blackened corridors of the forest. The wizard sat up straighter. The silver face was too bright for him to discern features, yet he sensed that this was the Fire Lord who had watched over Dagonet and who had occupied Rex Mundi with them. The angel sat beside Merlin on the stump, and the wizard's feverish chill vanished.

'I am glad you have come,' Merlin whispered, filled with a

beauty delivered entirely over to him. 'Yet, I am surprised. You Fire Lords are suffering – burning. I remember how it was. And I know that your numbers are stretched thin across creation, all of you working as hard as you can to hold together your fragile assemblies – the complex organisms and societies you have fashioned to honor Her. Oh, yes, I haven't forgotten. What you do is more than just honor. You work so hard, you endure such painful burning out here in the cold, because you believe there is a way back. You believe that the light of heaven that has frozen to matter out here in space can be used to construct machines for perceiving Her. The human brain is one of those machines, yes?'

The angel rose and walked off, leaving no footprints in the burnt grass. But a scent, like a heap of flowers, cut through the corpse stench, and the feeling of beauty that he had imparted to Merlin lingered.

The wizard nodded like the doddering old man he appeared to be. 'I did right to give beauty to Dagonet after having taken so much from him. That's what you came to tell me. You are kind, but you need not have troubled. You reminded me strongly enough in the darkness why God has put me here. And I have not forgotten how old the world is – or why you built it.'

In the Garden of the Heart

Dagonet, tall and strikingly handsome as a Greek marble come to life, accepted the king's gratitude and Aidan's proud blessing, and strode toward the massive gate of Camelot, looking for Eufrasia. His entire body tingled with the remembrance of lightning, of the magical power that minutes before had transformed him. Even Lord Monkey, perched alertly upon his shoulder, his fur fluffed, eyes sparkling, smelled clean as thunder.

Amazed by what the wizard had accomplished, Dagonet paused among the ranks of yews beside the mammoth pylon of the citadel and looked back, hoping to catch Merlin's eye and salute him. But the wizard stood engaged in a somber discussion with the king and his warriors. Merlin's big hands turned palms upward, offering ignorance. The king and his men shared disconcerted looks, and those atop their sable horses began to dismount.

Dagonet determined he would find out later what troubled them. For now, he had to locate Eufrasia and discover for himself if his quest for the king offered the one treasure he desired above all others. He crossed the busy bailey, sidestepping bustling market-workers conveying barrows of vegetables and sacks of milled grain to the cookhouse for that day's feast. The outer ward thrived with soldiers from the barracks, who were airing their wounds in the morning sun, cleaning their weapons, talking, some sullenly, others excitedly, about the battle they had survived.

Aidan had directed him to the inner ward and Lot's cloistered wing of the castle, where Arthor's pagan Celts lived when in Camelot. Children frolicked about the Maypole the druids had erected in the grassy courtyard for their sun ceremonies, and women sat on settles in the cool shadows of the colonnade, chatting and stitching torn buckskins. A cypress garden opened behind the yard's chuckling marble fountain, its flower-banked rivulets fed by the run-off. Eufrasia, in a saffron gown, her flaxen hair braided intricately down her long back, sat on a mossy boulder, watching small birds splashing in a rill.

Lord Monkey leaped among the curtains of a willow to explore its shaggy depths, and its excited chitterings caught Eufrasia's attention. When she saw Dagonet, she rose, and a blush lit her cheeks. Already she knew, looking from inside her soul, she could never get close enough – there was no such thing as enough, not with this man. And as he came to her, she saw by the soft light in his eyes and his pupils widening, opening his deepest self to her, that he had already taken her into himself.

Gaze by gaze, without words, they knew that they had started on their journey together to that place beyond all other places, where even memory would remain limitlessly alive and awake and all that they would share, the whole blurred moment of their lifetime together, an entire future, lay before them like a beautiful recurrent dream.

Sky Deep as Heaven

Days later, when all the king's fallen had been identified and properly buried and when the enemy dead were burned and King Wesc's death poetry for his warriors recited over their ashes, the coronation of King Arthor jammed the wards of Camelot. In the central courtyard, a platform stood draped in the red and white banners of the king, and Arthor sat at its center upon an oaken throne carved elaborately with the devices of the dragon and the unicorn from his lineage.

The bells of Camelot rang incessantly that day and fell silent only for the spoken invocation and the recitation of the king's ascendancy. Flanked by his commanders and attended by his mother and by the wizard Merlin, Arthor received the blessing of the archbishop, who read aloud the official recognition from Pope Gelasius of Arthor's unchallenged title as high king of Britain.

After anointing the king's chaplet and placing it upon his head, the archbishop conducted Mass with Arthor, and the priests distributed the Eucharist among the crowd. The Celtic hieros and his green-robed druids also knelt to receive the sanctified bread of *Yesu*, the all-heal, and to drink of the vine that climbs to the light. Urien as well as Lot and his sons, Gawain and Gareth, knelt with them and afterward led the Celtic sundance in honor of the king. Only Morgeu was absent, refusing to abide the presence of Merlin. Yet, in honor of her brother, whose love had spared her child Mordred, she draped the king's red eagle from the windows of her suite and stood upon the open balcony of her tower with her infant in her arms when the archbishop placed the anointed chaplet upon Arthor's head.

After the king and his commanders had stepped down from the platform and mounted their steeds to parade through Camelot and lead the populace on a celebratory march around the citadel, Ygrane blessed them as she had promised she would do. But instead of holding aloft the Graal as she had intended, she spread wide her white-robed arms and said loudly to her son and his men, 'You are the hope of Britain. Your blood will be the tears of generations. Gifts of God, you have come to be given. And what you give will lead us who follow you to the thankful days. Hold fast, brave warriors, to your faith in God and to each other. Hold fast against the ancient order of might and brutality. You are protectors of the meek. Your strength champions mercy and love, and your bravery defends a perilous order. Love well, and there is no end to how loved you shall be.'

Urien, naked but for white kid-leather boots, fawnskin thong, and a sword strapped to his back led the parade with his salt-blond hair streaming free in the spring breezes. Lot and his two sons followed, dressed as sparely, in the manner of the old Celts who lived to feel again the goodness of the day after the fierce battle. Marcus, blond and bearded as a Saxon, rode proudly after them, waving the king's white banner emblazoned with the red eagle. Bors Bona, his squat frame gleaming in polished breastplate and helmet, accepted the boisterous gratitude of the throng with a raised sword. Kyner and Cei came next in their white tunics marked by red crosses, bearing a chi-rho banner between them. Bedevere pranced afterward in full battle regalia, frequently turning to keep a protective eye upon the king, who rode laughing like a boy among the adulate throng, arms upraised victoriously, happy face lifted to a blue sky deep as heaven.

A Dawn of Butterflies

Weeks later, on the anniversary of the summer day when he had drawn the sword Excalibur from the stone, King Arthor left Camelot in the dark before dawn. Alone, with Bedevere a distant shadow, he limped across the champaign, through the grassy upland fields, to the woods behind the citadel. He wanted to be alone before this day's festivities began. He needed time to reflect on what the coming day meant for him.

A full year had passed since he had known the freedom of anonymity. After the battles and the carnage, the heaviest burden for him as king was renown. No one saw him as a man anymore. He was the agency of their ambitions and the claimant of their loyalties. There was no one with whom he could speak simply as a man. And there was surely no woman who could accept him simply as a man. That was the weight of his life's truth.

The lust that, the year before, had made him vulnerable to Morgeu's seduction added its weight to this truth. He felt desire. The whole world seemed to carry that desire. Standing at last on the wooded bluff above a cataract spilling from the mountains into the river, the boulders in the dark below looking as though whitewashed with milk, he felt aghast at the desire of the stream for the sea. That was a power no one could resist, not even a king. He would have to find a woman – his woman. That was his personal quest, as urgent and necessary as the river's journey.

But there was another mission that summoned him. The Graal had not been found, though every cranny of the citadel had been searched. Merlin claimed the angels had spirited it away. The wizard wanted him to conduct a search for it across the kingdom. Shrouded by epics and sacred legends, the chalice offered his warriors a purpose other than war, Merlin claimed. It united them to an ambition greater than combat. But Arthor needed his commanders for more quotidian services – patrols against the ever-encroaching invaders, protection of the highways and outlying villas from brigands, and maintenance of municipal properties: bridges, dams, harbors, and the decaying roadways. So much work.

He sat down and counted clouds, melon-pink and apricot in the rising light. The wound in his thigh throbbed. It had not healed cleanly, despite the best ministrations of his surgeons. Merlin feared it was a supernatural wound, his kingship maimed by the deaths of the many Britons who had died opposed to him. The Graal would heal that regal injury, the wizard seemed certain. *The Graal – the Graal . . .*

Mingled bells rang upward from the lower meadows, announcing the day – chapel matins, shepherds driving their flocks to graze, goosegirls tolling for their birds. In the widening dawn, he looked down on the towers of Camelot, misty fields, the scarred forest, and the scaffolded rooftops of Cold Kitchen still under repair. The sight pressed his heart with emotion. This was the center of *his* kingdom – the glory he served. Here was the secret of himself that he knew led to a happy death: the chill in the air, the thatched roofs, plumes of smoke from hearth fires, a dog by the gate, hedgerows at the end of the lane, blackthorns and elms, and slopes of half-awakened flowers.

Arthor sat still as the lustrous sun cleared the hills and stirred the mists in the dells to move like invisible horses. A dawn of butterflies climbed down the high bluffs with the ruddy sunlight. Across the ashes and cinders of the fields, where the blood of the slain had soaked the land, acres of flowers bloomed: Lilacs lifted their pale torches, gold trumpets of daffodils shone among pink morning glories, blue gentians trembled into the unraveling wind. And everywhere over the blossoms, butterflies jostled, flitting with busy love like souls released from the night, free from pain and terror, free at last to thrive on beauty and light.